PRINCE
OF
STORMS

OTHER TITLES BY KIT ROCHA

The Beyond Series

Beyond Shame

Beyond Control

Beyond Pain

Beyond Temptation

Beyond Jealousy

Beyond Solitude

Beyond Addiction

Beyond Possession

Beyond Innocence

Beyond Ruin

Beyond Ecstasy

Beyond Surrender

Beyond Doubt

Beyond Forever

PRAISE FOR KIT ROCHA

Daughter of Tides

"A sumptuous queer romance with blush-inducing, spicy scenes . . . Romantasy fans will enjoy."

—*Booklist*

"Rocha delivers possibly even more steamy, magic-infused god-on-god lovemaking . . . Fans will be gratified by the intrigue and spice."

—*Publishers Weekly*

Queen of Dreams

Named One of *Washington Post*'s 10 Best LGBTQ+ Romance Novels and

One of Book Riot's Best Romances of 2024

"The thrilling training and battle scenes are interspersed with moments of magic-infused eroticism. Readers will be excited to see where Rocha takes the series next."

—*Publishers Weekly*

"It's satisfying to see strong women at the forefront of the story . . . Fantasy and the fight against evil take the pole position."

—*Kirkus Reviews*

Consort of Fire

"A glorious, epic, and erotic firestorm of a book! I could not put it down!"

—Nalini Singh, *New York Times* bestselling author

"By combining life-and-death stakes with off-the-charts eroticism, Rocha keeps the pages flying. The scalding sex scenes drive both plot and character development and incorporate the fantastical world-building in fascinating ways. This is an exciting start to what promises to be a thrilling new series."

—*Publishers Weekly* (starred review)

"The fiery breath of a dragon pales in comparison to the incendiary heat of this epic erotic fantasy."

—*Kirkus Reviews*

"The story layers are peeled back slowly enough to immerse readers . . . Rocha's new offering is set in a rich, erotic fantasy world, filled with lush characters and a magical landscape of secrets, power, and betrayal."

—*Library Journal*

Gideon's Riders

Ashwin

Deacon

Ivan

Mercenary Librarians

Deal with the Devil

The Devil You Know

Dance with the Devil

Bound to Fire and Steel

Consort of Fire

Queen of Dreams

Born to Sea and Storm

Daughter of Tides

PRINCE

OF

STORMS

KIT ROCHA

Published by Montlake, Seattle

www.apub.com

Amazon, the Amazon logo, and Montlake are trademarks of Amazon.com, Inc., or its affiliates.

EU product safety contact:
Amazon Media EU S. à r.l.
38, avenue John F. Kennedy, L-1855 Luxembourg
amazonpublishing-gpsr@amazon.com

ISBN-13: 9781662523649 (paperback)
ISBN-13: 9781662523632 (digital)

Cover design by Hang Le
Cover images: © Android Boss, © Qasimphotographer, © Triff / Shutterstock

Printed in the United States of America

For Alex and Kat.
You told us to write it. So we did.

THE ICE QUEEN'S STRAIT
THE GLASS SHORES
AYNALKA
TEMPLE RUINS
THE CRYSTAL PALACE
KASTHER OUTPOST
THE FROZEN HARBOR
W
S
N
E
JAMYSKAR
RAHVEKYA

Chapter One

The goddess teaches us that the world around us is alive. Rahvekya is more than the stones and sand that we walk upon, more than the trees that offer us shade or the rivers that spill into the sea. Our home may not always speak to us in words we can understand, but it still speaks—and the goddess bids us to listen with our hearts.

The lost journal of High Priestess Tona

Naia floated on the waves.

The cool water roared in her ears, a wild contrast to the affectionate way it embraced the rest of her, gliding over her bare skin with the reverence of a lover's touch. The sun shone, bright even through her closed lids, and the scent of flowers wafted on the gentle breeze, the smell rendered almost cloying by the heat of the day.

"Naia."

No. She rolled over, face down into the water, blotting out the voice. Conviction gripped her, a fist closed tight around her heart, and she knew—it was not yet time to leave this place.

But the deep, rumbling voice persisted. "Wake up, love."

She could not comply. Not because she wanted to ignore the warm, whispered request, but because she *was* awake. She was simply . . . someplace else, awash in a memory as vivid, as *real*, as the coaxing hand on her cheek.

Naia opened her eyes. The sensation of the water lapping at her skin lingered, mingled with the feel of soft furs and rumpled linens. For the span of a heartbeat, two things were true: she was floating, naked, in sun-warmed shallows, and she was lying, equally naked, in a massive bed.

The *captain's* bed. But it wasn't the commander of the Kraken who leaned over her, watching her intently.

It was the Lover.

Aleksi had dark hair and even darker eyes, rich brown depths that sparked with affection and a hint of golden heat. His features were finely wrought, rough and delicate at the same time. He defined the words *classically handsome*—literally, as only the god of love could. For millennia, songs and poems had praised his divine beauty. In fact, Naia was fairly certain she'd once read an ode devoted exclusively to celebrating the lush curve of Aleksi's lower lip.

An ode consisting of no fewer than two dozen stanzas, far too long by anyone's reckoning. Though as Aleksi held her gaze and slowly licked the corner of his mouth, Naia found it impossible to fault the author for his unbridled enthusiasm.

Especially while she lounged in Einar's bed, surrounded by their mingled scents—and the Kraken's lingering magic.

"I wasn't asleep." Naia lifted her arms and arched her back. As she stretched, the thin, finely woven sheet slipped down to bare her breasts.

Aleksi rewarded her with a sharp indrawn breath that kindled anticipation low in her belly. But he only flashed her a knowing look as he drew the sheet back up to cover her. "Distracting me won't earn you any more idle hours in the captain's bed, little nymph."

What a pity—though perhaps their lover could help her change Aleksi's mind about that. "Where *is* Einar?"

"At the helm." Aleksi's voice lost all traces of teasing humor. "We're close."

To Akeisa. Naia sat up, clutching the sheet to her breasts. "How long?"

"Within the hour."

Was she ready to go back there, to swim in that deadly mix of Imperial ambition, deception, and hidden violence? Not remotely, that was the honest answer. But she didn't exactly have a choice, did she? Someone in Grand Duchess Gwynira's court had kidnapped the three of them, planned to kill her and Einar, then spirit Aleksi away to the Empire—and an even worse fate.

They had to find out *who*, and hopefully *why*.

"I'll get dressed," she murmured.

Naia slipped out of the bed and hurried behind the screen in the corner. Einar's cabin was the largest on the Kraken, and every conceivable comfort had been provided. Still, it was oddly stark, devoid of the decor and hints of personality that filled the rest of the ship. There was a desk along the far wall, laden with maps and weapons. Shelves had been built into an alcove just beyond that, each one filled with books.

There were no little mementos of the Kraken's travels, no souvenirs from all the places they'd seen. No personal keepsakes at all, save for the books.

Their absence spoke of a loneliness that made Naia shiver.

The washstand stood ready, the water in the full jug steaming lightly as she poured it into the basin. She washed quickly, then wrapped up in the thick robe she'd left hanging on the peg set into the curving wall.

Aleksi was still in the cabin. Instead of leaving, he'd retrieved her trunk and waited patiently beside it, ready to assist her in getting dressed.

It should have been ridiculous, a member of the High Court acting as a lady's maid, buttoning her bodice, tying her sleeves, and brushing her hair in contented silence. But each tiny gesture was filled with the same care that Aleksi exhibited in everything he did, without a single indication that he resented any of it.

He simply took care of her, just as he always did.

Naia swayed toward him, dreading the inevitable moment when they had to leave this room. Being back on the Kraken since their rescue had been like a dream, intimate and safe and far, far away from the harsh reality that awaited them back at Gwynira's court.

"Worried?" Aleksi asked softly.

"Yes," she admitted, unashamed. "How could I not be? That wretched place almost *killed* you—"

"But it did not. My lovers saved me, and you will again, should the unfortunate necessity arise." He dropped a quick kiss to her lips. "Now, come. Einar is waiting for us."

Naia grabbed her heaviest cloak. This part of the North Sea was cold enough to test even a Dreamer's constitution, and she lifted her fur-lined hood into place to cover the damp, curling ends of her hair.

The captain's cabin had been dim, lit only by a single window above the bed. Outside, the day was stunning in its brilliance, and Naia blinked and slowed as she strode out onto the deck. The morning sun sparkled off the bay, nearly blinding her, and she lifted a hand to half cover her eyes as they adjusted.

The glare wasn't from the surface of the water, after all.

When they had arrived in Akeisa the first time, they had been met by a wall of ice that had been erected by Grand Duchess Gwynira, the Imperial ruler of the island. Naia still couldn't say whether the wall had been a practical defensive measure, a show of magical power, or simply a test, but in the end, it had not mattered. As proof of her own power, Naia had torn it down and cleared the way for the Kraken to sail into the harbor.

There were now several *rows* of walls, staggered like fortifications set outside a city's gates. The mammoth sheets of ice jutted toward the sky, one in front of another in front of *another*, each at least twice as high as the one they'd first encountered. They rose from the icy water like grasping hands, just waiting for an unwary ship to venture too close.

Then, just in case the warning had not been conveyed with crystal clarity, a line of armed ships extended the blockade on each side of the ice wall.

"An even warmer welcome than the last one," Aleksi observed dryly from just behind Naia. "It does make one wonder what, exactly, Gwynira thinks happened to us. Or what trouble she expects to come from it."

"I don't blame her one bit," Einar rumbled, then greeted Naia and Aleksi each with a kiss on the cheek. "A member of the High Court was poisoned on her watch and kidnapped from her palace. She probably thinks your friends are coming for her head." He shook his. "I'd be on *my* guard."

Assuming, Naia pondered silently, that Gwynira had not been responsible for those calamities in the first place.

Aleksi grasped Naia's shoulders and leaned down, close to her ear. "Well, little nymph?"

She took a deep, shuddering breath. She wasn't certain that she was capable of bringing down this much ice, and she was even less certain of the wisdom of it. The turbulent wake from that volume of sinking ice could easily pull a ship under. The Kraken would be safe—Einar and his crew were too skilled to fall victim to such a fate—but could she say the same for the Imperial ships that formed the blockade?

She opened her mouth to confess as much, but the ship suddenly heaved, and she clung to Aleksi. Einar reached for them both, steadying them as the deck pitched beneath their feet again. Water churned around the hull, and a cacophony of noise cracked through the air as the walls before them splintered. Massive sheets of ice dropped into the outer bay, rocking the other ships into dangerous lists.

Naia broke free of her lovers' clutching hands, desperate to settle the waves. She closed her eyes and reached out, communing with the turbulent depths, begging them to calm before they claimed lives just as they'd claimed the shattered ice.

Please, she whispered silently. *Do not do this. Be still.*

Her frantic efforts paid off as the Imperial ships rocked and slowly righted. But Naia's relief was short-lived, and she watched in horror as the ships' gunports swung open.

"Battle stations!" Einar barked, his deep voice booming out across the decks. "Ready for attack!"

The crew hurried to comply, manning their assigned stations with a quiet, grave efficiency that spoke of long years of bloody experience.

But no attack came. A loud bell clanged out over the bay, and the beleaguered Imperial ships closed their gunports and began to withdraw.

"Well," Aleksi said. "That was . . . terrifying. And impressive."

He clearly—and reasonably—had assumed that Naia destroyed the walls. She could breathe again, so she dragged in great lungfuls of searingly cold air as she willed her hands to stop shaking. "I don't *understand.*"

Einar exhaled sharply. "Not in the mood for subtlety, love?"

The words echoed strangely in Naia's ears, and she shook her head as she turned to him, prepared to explain that whatever force had swatted aside this ice like a child tumbling a stack of wooden blocks, it had not come from *her.* "No, I—"

But the face she saw was not Einar's. The weathered skin was the same color, but this face was thinner, the cheekbones higher. Long silver braids, tied with leather and adorned with bits of shell and volcanic glass, swung as he tilted his head.

And the eyes that stared at her with soft, teasing amusement and familiar, fond affection—

The bluest eyes Naia had ever seen, like a perfect, cloudless summer sky.

She blinked, and the image vanished, there one heartbeat and gone the next. Einar watched her, his dark brows slowly drawing into an impending frown. She opened her mouth to head off that frown, to reassure him somehow, but, to her horror, all that came out was a muffled sob.

He lifted a hand to her cheek, the frown now in full effect, fixed in an expression of concern that bordered on alarm. "Naia?"

Aleksi stepped closer. "Too much?" He wrapped his fingers around the back of her neck with firm, grounding pressure, just as he had during their first arrival, when the rush of magic from dragging down Gwynira's wall had threatened to overwhelm Naia.

He had no way of knowing that it wasn't the ocean's magic that held her this time, bound and speechless, but an inescapable *confusion*. She felt like there was something just beyond her grasp, part memory and part realization. It was like a song she had once known, but whose lyrics had abandoned her, leaving behind a melody she could barely hum.

Her heart slammed against her breastbone. Everything suddenly hurt, and she couldn't figure out *why*. "I . . . I don't—"

"We don't have to do this," Einar whispered, an offer and a vow. "Say the word, and I'll turn the ship around."

He would—and Naia absolutely could not let him. She dragged herself back under control and grasped his wrist. "And go where? We cannot escape this, Einar. We just have to get through it."

"She's right," Aleksi murmured. "I don't like it, either, but she's right."

Einar hesitated, his eyes flashing teal, and magic crackled around the three of them. The part of the ocean that Naia could still feel thrummed beneath them, churning with fierce, protective power. The *Kraken's* power.

Then he nodded, stroked his thumb over her cheek, and slid his hand down to rest lightly on the front of her throat. The gesture mirrored Aleksi's hold on the back of her neck, though not the pressure. "Then we go."

"Thank you," she breathed.

He nodded once more, dropped his hand, and stepped back. "Take us in," he ordered the crew. "Slowly."

Naia remained still, right where she stood, half expecting a renewed attack from the withdrawing Imperial ships. But the Kraken sailed uneventfully into the bay. In what seemed like moments, they had reached the palace docks. The crew bustled about, readying the gangplank, and Naia held tight to Aleksi's hand as they disembarked.

The Grand Duchess's palace sprawled before them, an imposing structure made of the same white and gray stone as the docks, its windows glazed with ice instead of glass. Beyond, in the distance, Naia could just glimpse the ancient and oddly beautiful ruined temple that sat at the peak of the highest point on the island.

The last time Naia had set foot in those ruins, she had been answering the call of an unknown magic she still did not understand. The time before *that*, she had found delicious, bewildering pleasure in Einar's arms.

She did not wonder if she would enter those ruins again, only what she would discover about herself—and the island—this time.

Gwynira waited for the three of them, flanked by her lover, Isa, and her personal guard, Arktikos. The Grand Duchess's hands were hidden under her cloak, but Naia could still see them shaking beneath the thick fabric. And though Gwynira's pale face betrayed no expression, her eyes were painfully wide.

When Aleksi had been ill, dying from a poison that should not have affected him at all, much less that gravely, Naia and Einar had asked Gwynira to send a missive to the mainland. In it, they had begged Sachi and Zanya to fetch Inga and bring her to Akeisa. If anyone could help Aleksi, they thought, it would be the Witch, the Dream, or the Void.

But Sachi and Zanya never received the message, and Naia had wondered, more than once, if it had ever been sent at all.

And now, here stood Gwynira before her. The woman radiated fear and shock, but also an achingly vulnerable *hope*, and that was what convinced Naia of the truth. Though she did not know what had happened to delay or obstruct their pleas for assistance, she knew in that instant that Gwynira had not been directly responsible for it.

She was too damn relieved to see them alive and well.

Belatedly, Gwynira dropped a shallow curtsy as Aleksi approached. She did not shift her gaze from his face, and she had to visibly unclench her jaw to speak. "It is very good to see you, my lord."

"How formal." Aleksi's warm smile melted into a laugh. "Did you miss us?"

"I . . ."

"It's true. I'm a bit of a bad boy, stealing away under cover of darkness. And without saying goodbye?" He lifted one shoulder in a smooth shrug. "What can I say? I was quite swept off my feet."

It wasn't even a *lie*.

For a moment, silence. Gwynira seemed to be weighing the reality of the situation against the casual cheer of Aleksi's words. Einar and Arktikos faced one another, each bristling with incipient protective violence. And Isa peered intently at all of them in turn, as if trying to decipher the intricacies of a heretofore unseen language.

Finally, Gwynira inclined her head in a gracious nod. "I'm most eager to hear the details of your adventure. Would the three of you care to retire to my study for some refreshment?"

"That sounds lovely." Aleksi kissed the back of Naia's hand, then released her to walk ahead with Gwynira. He bent his head to their host's, and the two of them murmured together like beloved old friends catching up on the grudging time that had separated them.

It was amazing, how Aleksi could just fall into such an intimate moment of connection, even with his very safety—and the safety of everyone around him—in peril. With anyone else, Naia would have thought it false, a desperate cover to hide his deep turmoil. But every word, every moment, came from a place of absolute sincerity. In fact, he seemed able to cover so well *because* he was unwilling to chance hurting Gwynira—either by making her look weak, or, worse, by making it seem as if she had tried to harm a diplomatic envoy.

Einar folded Naia's arm through his, and she flashed him a grateful smile. "It's so effortless for him, isn't it?" she whispered softly. "Aleksi just seems to know what to say and do."

"He always has." Einar squeezed her hand. "He's good at this sort of thing. Making friends out of strangers. Or even enemies."

Genuinely making friends, not simply going through the motions to secure someone's shallow goodwill. "He cares so much." And now she and Einar were a part of that.

Before she could make the observation aloud, a flurry of movement caught her eye. An unending line of staff—all, it seemed, island locals—had gathered at the palace entrance to welcome them. But they weren't showing deference to the Grand Duchess as she passed.

They were bowing and curtsying to Naia and Einar. Their long-lost crown-prince . . . and the woman they believed was their goddess.

The reverence on their faces made Naia's chest tighten. Just like last time, they'd seen the walls of ice fall and taken it as a show of power that confirmed all the stories they'd been told about their island's ancient benefactor.

Naia couldn't tell them that she hadn't destroyed the walls, not this time. She had only minimized the carnage out in the churning bay. Hells, she had not even had a chance to tell Aleksi and Einar the truth . . . or ask them the most important question of all.

If she had not brought down the ice blocking their way . . . what *had*?

Chapter Two

She's cold. She's cruel. She already doesn't like you—and you are dying for an invitation to her court. The Ice Queen's castle might lack modern amenities, but Grand Duchess Gwynira has been at the cutting edge of fashion for centuries. Surviving a trip to the Crystal Palace will guarantee you invitations to every exclusive table in Kasther—as long as you're willing to share the gossip.

The Illicit Lives of the Imperial Court
Anonymous
(banned in the Empire)

It was difficult to know where to begin.

The refreshments materialized, as promised, with Gwynira's staff laying out an assortment of items to sate every hunger and quench every thirst. But when the servers had departed, leaving the six of them alone, no one touched the food.

Gwynira's aura almost blinded Aleksi, not because it was bright but because it was so *unsettled*. It was a color that spoke of simmering terror, confusion, and the tiniest hint of shame.

That would not do. "First of all, none of this was your fault, Gwynira."

She scoffed in disbelief and began pacing, shaking off Isa's restraining hand when the other woman tried to soothe her. "I find that difficult to believe, my lord. But do elaborate."

"I will—if you will sit." He waited until she complied, and chose to interpret her baleful glare as an unfortunate result of thwarted nervous energy, not true ire. "Well, I suppose I was quite unconscious when this ordeal began."

Gwynira flinched.

Naia spoke up. "We were in the infirmary, keeping watch over Aleksi. And this . . . woman came in. Blonde, blue eyes. She was dressed like the other healers, but—" Her voice cracked, failed her, and her next words were hoarse. "She wasn't one."

Her pain pierced Aleksi's heart. Somehow, he knew that it was not elicited by Naia's recollection of her ordeal, but her recollection of *his*. She and Einar had spoken only in passing of those hours when they had sat vigil by Aleksi's bedside, slowly watching him die. Torn between acting or waiting, when either option could easily spell his end.

"She had magic," Einar said, his jaw tight. His gaze was fixed straight ahead, seeing not what was in front of him, but his own horrifying memories. "Like nothing I've encountered before. It was as if her mind took hold of ours. I could not move or fight, only obey her orders. She forced me to pick up Aleksi, then led us out through the servants' hallways."

"No one saw you?" Arktikos rumbled. "No one *stopped* you?"

"It was well-timed," Naia explained. "Coordinated, perhaps. But even if someone had seen us, I'm not sure they would have realized anything was wrong. Her control was absolute."

Gwynira inhaled sharply. "And so she marched you, unimpeded, right to her vessel."

What had happened next, Aleksi remembered well. "I regained my senses on the ship," he confirmed. "Already well underway. I was tied to a mast and surrounded by mercenaries."

Arktikos dropped his hand almost absently to the hilt of his sword. "And the magic user?"

A cold chill crawled up Aleksi's spine. He steadfastly refused to blink, because the last things he wanted to see painted across the backs of his eyelids were those dead eyes, set in a serenely pretty face.

She had been newly awakened. The crackling light of the Dream still surrounded her like shards of glass whose edges had not yet worn smooth. He did not know if she had been insane before the sudden, violent manifestation of her magic, but she had certainly been a dark soul. She had wielded her control over others with an ease that spoke of practice, and a glee that had whispered of bad intentions and worse outcomes.

She had been far too good at inflicting pain not to love it.

"She tried to suffocate Naia and Einar." Aleksi marveled at how even his voice sounded. How calm. "She simply reached inside them and . . . squeezed. They could not breathe. I had to do something."

"You said you were bound." Arktikos had gone very, very still. "What *could* you do?"

Aleksi met the man's guarded gaze without hesitation. "I held up a mirror, and I showed their attacker what all that pain felt like."

Gwynira's excruciatingly competent guard—a god in his own right—nearly recoiled. Aleksi could see the bunching of muscle in the trembling effort it took Arktikos not to give in.

"It broke her hold on Naia and Einar. Frankly, it broke more than that. She would have done anything to escape me," Aleksi admitted. "But there is nowhere to run, not on a ship at sea."

Gwynira rubbed her chin. "So she stood and fought."

"Hardly," Naia countered. "She jumped overboard."

Arktikos cursed under his breath.

She went on. "*That* terrified the mercenaries into trying to kill us as quickly as possible. We managed to free Aleksi, and then Einar—" Naia abruptly snapped her mouth shut.

Gwynira froze. After all her frenzied pacing, the surcease of movement was jarring. "And then Einar *what*?"

"No, I meant—"

"It's all right, love." Einar caressed Naia's cheek before turning to Gwynira. He studied her for a moment that seemed to stretch on forever, then tilted his head. "The parents of the Empire have been telling stories about me to frighten their children into good behavior for generations. Most are exaggerations, at best, or outright fabrications. But one is not." A vicious smile curved his lips. "The Kraken is not a title of vanity. When the need arises, it can be *very* literal."

Gwynira's eyes narrowed. "Surely not."

Einar seemed to enjoy her confusion. "Arktikos changes into a bear. My kraken form is significantly larger. Large enough to tear apart a ship when motivated, and after what happened to us, I was *very* motivated."

"You turn into a squid," she said flatly. "A giant *squid*."

Einar grimaced. "It sounds less terrifying when you say it like that."

"It shouldn't." Naia stepped in front of him. "Because Einar smashed that ship to pieces."

"With the two of you still on it?"

"I am *of the sea*, Grand Duchess." Naia somehow made the statement sound like a rebuke. "I kept Aleksi alive in the water while Einar carried us to safety."

"We took refuge on a small island," Aleksi explained, "and waited for Einar's crew to rescue us."

Isa made a soft noise of rueful amusement. "We did wonder about his ship's hasty departure."

"The Kraken will always find its captain." Aleksi clapped his hands together. "Anyway, that is the entirety of the tale. It happened, but we are all fine, and it is in the past. Now is the time to look ahead."

"Yes, it is." Gwynira's countenance had turned stormy once again, and she resumed her pacing, radiating fury like a frigid gale. "Arktikos, get the details on that ship from the harbormaster. I want everything—passenger and crew manifests, under which flag did it sail, where and under whose authority did it dock." She paused and squared her shoulders. "And find out why those messages to the mainland were never received."

"Or if they were ever sent at all," Isa muttered.

He bowed, already backing toward the door, his hand still resting on his sword. "At once, Your Grace."

Gwynira turned to Isa, who tilted her head, nodded, and spoke once more. "The impostor healer. We'll need to find out who brought her here."

Aleksi could only wish the task before them could be so easy. "I doubt we'll have any luck with that line of investigation."

"If they're clever at all, they won't be easily connected to her presence," Einar agreed. "And if they *weren't* clever, then Arktikos would likely have found and killed them already."

Isa acknowledged his point with an upraised brow, only to immediately counter it. "While I'm sure Arktikos would appreciate the vote of confidence, there is something more dangerous than *clever*. There is *reckless*. And reckless people are impossible to predict."

"But they are occasionally sloppy," Gwynira added. "Especially when they believe there will be no one left alive to testify to their misdeeds."

Aleksi could hardly argue with that.

She turned to him then, an achingly vulnerable expression clouding her features. "I apologize," she murmured haltingly, "for the blockade. You must understand, I thought you had been *murdered*, and that the rest of the High Court—"

"And that the rest of the High Court was about to descend on your home in full, violent, vengeful force," he finished. A fair assumption, since Aleksi had feared the same outcome when he had so recently lain dying.

What a strange thought. He certainly didn't feel like he was hovering on the brink of death now. His senses were still erratic, with everything a bit brighter and louder than usual, but nothing that felt dangerous, much less fatal.

"Your friends would have been right to attack Akeisa." Gwynira's jaw clenched. "This should not have happened at my court, because of me."

On that count, at least, he could set her mind at ease. "Oh, but it didn't."

"What do you mean?"

"That whoever orchestrated this abduction was targeting me, and with specific purpose. We learned that from our kidnapper before she died."

Gwynira froze, her gaze darting back and forth without lighting on anything as she processed his words. Isa started, and, for a moment, Aleksi thought she might move to comfort her lover. But she stayed where she was, her hands clenched into fists, as if betraying any concern would only endanger them both.

So he laid a careful but reassuring hand on Gwynira's shoulder. "It wasn't your fault, my lady. Not in the slightest."

It seemed to release some of her tension, and she sagged for just a moment before straightening. Then a cold, terrifying smile curved her lips. "Still. You'll forgive me if I'm determined to find out who violated the diplomatic sanctity of my palace."

So this was why they called her the Ice Queen. "Grand Duchess, you are *terrifying*. I approve."

"I owe you this much, my lord, and so much more." She bowed her head, then turned to Naia. "I am pleased that the blockade posed no particular challenge for you. Though I should have realized, after last time, that it would not."

Naia returned the woman's tentative smile with equal hesitation but said nothing. She merely dropped into a curtsy so deep that her hair swung down to obscure her face, almost as if to hide her reaction.

Odd.

Gwynira didn't notice, simply turned her attention to Einar next. She nodded her welcome and said, "Your quarters remain as you left them."

Best to get *that* out of the way as soon as possible. "Thank you, but they won't be needing those rooms," Aleksi told her.

Her tension returned in an instant. "I beg your pardon?"

"Mmm. You can have their things moved to my suite."

Understanding dawned on Isa's face, but Gwynira did not yet catch his meaning. She drew back, then squared her shoulders and spoke with urgent gravity. "I swear upon my word as vassal of this land, my lord—I *will* keep you safe this time. That oath includes both of your companions. I—I will set a contingent of guards for each of them, ones personally and thoroughly vetted by Arktikos—"

Aleksi grasped her hands in his and hummed to stem the desperate flow of her words. "Relax, please. They won't need their rooms because they'll be sharing my bed."

"Oh." Gwynira blinked, then arched one eyebrow. "I see. That's quite a development. Perhaps *you* are the one who owes *me*."

"I would not go that far." Aleksi bowed and backed toward the door, intending to take his leave.

"Wait." Isa stepped forward. Everything, from her breath to her gait, was made unsteady by nerves. "What happened to the three of you may not have been Gwyn's fault, but guarding your safety *was* our responsibility. We will make it right."

The things Sachi had told him about Sorin's court, combined with what little Aleksi had seen for himself, painted a picture of full and abiding sadness. All Sorin's makeshift replacement family had were obligations that served only him and his whims, along with duties they were pressed into service to attend. There was no joy in any of it, only fear.

"I understand acting out of duty," he told her carefully, "but I would much rather be a friend than a responsibility."

She swallowed hard and simply stared at him for a moment, then lowered her gaze as she inclined her head. She said nothing, but Aleksi could feel her disbelief, spiky and metallic, shot through with wry, almost morbid humor.

"If you need us," Aleksi murmured, though he let the rest of the sentiment lie.

"Rest," Gwynira answered just as quietly. "We know where to find you."

Naia and Einar followed him out into the hall. By tacit agreement, none of them spoke as they made their way toward the large guest chamber that Aleksi had been assigned.

The room was relatively open, with privacy screens and alcoves rather than separate rooms for dressing and bathing. Aleksi had thought the architecture odd at first, but now he appreciated that it offered few places for an intruder to lie in wait.

The bed dominated the space, large enough for a dozen to sleep comfortably, and laden with heavy velvet and furs. A sizable sitting area completed the living space, with chairs and a sofa arranged around a low marble table. Woven rugs and embroidered tapestries broke up the unrelenting chill of the stone walls, floor, and vaulted ceilings, and a merry fire had been laid in the hearth.

Aleksi's belongings were much as he had left them. If the room had been searched in his absence, it had been done with care—either to preserve his possessions or conceal the intrusion.

None of that mattered as much as the question he now had to ask of his companions. "Are you angry with me?"

Naia had lifted a wine carafe from the elaborate shelf along one wall, and she paused now in the act of sniffing its contents. "Angry? Whatever for?"

"For unilaterally deciding the two of you would be sleeping here, with me?"

Her mild frown melted into a secret smile. "Sleeping, you say?"

"Naia . . ."

She relented. "No, Aleksi. I would rather stay here."

Einar's mood was far less teasing. "I didn't care for being separated from either of you last time. Now? I'll not even consider it."

Aleksi hesitated. What he had to say next would not be welcome. He wasn't even sure it was the right strategic move. Naia and Einar were here for reasons, very good ones that had only grown in importance. Naia's nature and power had been meant to elicit respect, but the islanders had hurtled straight past that and into fervent belief in her divinity. And Einar, while he and his ship had been meant to serve as a quick escape route, had turned out to be the local people's long-lost crown-prince. The two of them had purpose here. Use.

And Aleksi still wanted to send them back to the Sheltered Lands.

He had to try. His heart could not bear anything else. "The two of you could head back—"

"No." Naia capped the decanter and placed it back on the stone shelf with a sharp *clack* that was as firm as her denial. "I know you're thinking it—how could you not be? But don't. Please."

Einar stepped up behind Naia and embraced her as she leaned back, cradling her with a familiarity that belied the budding newness of their relationship. "You said we had to do this. And you were right, Aleksi. *We* have to do this. We won't let you go it alone."

Aleksi wanted to press the matter, for Naia was right. How could he not? Their safety meant more to him than the undeniable pleasure of being close to them. But the words dissolved on his tongue as they stared back at him, determined and a little challenging, as if they both anticipated his continued argument.

So he relented. "Fair enough, loves. Whatever we face, we will do it together."

"Together," Naia echoed with a smile, holding one hand out to him in invitation. "I like the sound of that."

Aleksi went to them, helpless to resist. He could not bear to send them away to safer shores, and he could not stand the thought of any harm coming to them, so his only path forward was to keep them close and protect them.

Even, perhaps, at the cost of his own life.

Chapter Three

The Crystal Palace is the seat of the Grand Duchess of Akeisa, and undoubtedly a destination that anyone who considers themselves well-traveled cannot afford to miss. Before you arrive, I heartily recommend you prepare yourself by reading my multiple volume history of the island, as well as my recent works exploring the flora and fauna, historical figures of note, and its fascinating religious rituals.

Akeisa: A Contemporary Guide
by Guildmaster Klement

Einar often dreamt of the sea.

Sometimes they were peaceful dreams, full of the endless horizon and star-studded skies and gentle waves caressing his ship as the wind carried them to places unknown. Sometimes the dreams were seductive fantasies, redolent with an irresistible song ready to lure him into depths from which he would never escape and didn't want to. And sometimes they were terrifying nightmares, of angry storms and vengeful tides, of everything he loved shattering under the force of a screeching gale.

The dreams that had curled around him last night had been of the sweeter variety, and he relinquished them with great reluctance. Only the warm silk of Aleksi's skin under his hand and the soft touch of Naia's fingers on his arm could possibly tempt him to leave a world of still waters and Siren song. But when he opened his eyes, that song still whispered over him, the brush of Naia's power like a joyous melody that he *felt* instead of heard.

They were curled together in Aleksi's bed, the Lover cradled between them. Several layers of thick quilts and Einar's own body heat kept them warm, even though the room had grown uncomfortably chilly. A glance at the hearth and the angle of the sun slanting through the windows held the answer—they'd slept well past breakfast, and clearly no servant had dared to disturb their rest, not even to build up the fire.

Einar certainly would not complain. Aleksi was a solid, *living* warmth against him now, but Einar could still remember the terrifying stillness in the Lover's body as he had lain dying only a scant few days ago.

Hard to believe that so much could happen in so little time. Aleksi's near-death, a kidnapping, the destruction of the mercenaries' ship. Einar's desperate flight through the water, praying Naia could keep Aleksi warm and breathing until he could find solid land.

Einar propped himself up on one elbow and stared down at his lovers. His *lovers*—that felt impossibly strange, too. Lust had swirled between them in various ways since the start of their journey, but on that rocky island, huddling together for warmth in a run-down little shack, lust had become passion. And passion had become . . .

His heart gave a funny little leap in his chest as he swept Aleksi's dark hair back from his elegant brow, then performed the same service for a long tendril of tousled brown hair that had slipped across Naia's cheek. He'd felt frozen for eons, his heart encased in the safety of icy distance. He'd lost too much, too young, to give his heart easily.

It hadn't been a choice this time. Aleksi and Naia had melted those icy walls and laid claim to every part of him—the man *and* the monster.

Now he had to keep them both safe in this strange, frozen palace surrounded by enemies, built on the ruins of his ancestral home. The former Emperor—the *Betrayer*—had escaped from his confinement and could be anywhere, with access to an endless chaotic land full of those who had awoken abruptly after the last war with wild and uncontrollable magic.

There were people out there now with powers Einar had never imagined. If one had been able to manipulate their bodies as if their limbs were tied with strings, what could others do? Einar had been to war too many times to count, but it had always been against enemies he could predict, with weapons he understood.

How did he keep them all safe when any person in this palace could have unknown power and orders to see them all dead?

No, not all of them. The last one had been ordered to kill Einar and Naia. Aleksi, their unknown commander had wanted alive—for reasons Einar could all too easily imagine and did not remotely want to consider.

Part of him wanted to rise and storm into Gwynira's court to find anyone who might do harm to those under his protection. Most of him wanted to keep Aleksi and Naia locked in this room and safe in this bed for the rest of the day.

Naia breathed out a soft noise of protest and pressed her fingernails into Einar's chest. "Shh. Not so loud."

Aleksi didn't open his eyes, merely chuckled quietly. "He didn't say anything, love."

"No, but he was thinking it." She lifted her head and peered at Einar. "Am I wrong?"

"Rarely," Einar replied dryly, covering her hand with his own. "My duty and my desire are waging war with one another."

"You are in the Lover's bed." Naia slipped one leg across Aleksi's body and nudged Einar's hip with her toes. "Is desire not your duty?"

"Don't be a bad influence, little nymph." Despite the admonition, Aleksi hauled Naia on top of him and bit her bare shoulder. "Our pirate lord speaks of our duty to our host."

Naia's smile was slow—and a little predatory. "I do not give a *damn* about Gwynira right now."

Neither did Einar. The only duty *he* cared about was the one he owed the two people in this bed: to uncover any who might wish to harm them, and to eliminate those enemies swiftly and completely.

Something ancient and ravenous stirred within Einar, a craving that so eclipsed the word *desire* that it was laughable, entwined with a protectiveness that made his human skin feel too tight. The wicked curve of Naia's lush lips and the mischief sparking in her eyes were challenges the monster could not ignore.

He skimmed his fingers up her bare arm to the slope of her shoulder. Loose curls of silky brown cascaded wildly down her back, and he took his time savoring the feel of her hair as he wrapped it slowly around his hand. Not tightly enough to pull, just enough to force a soft inhalation as he tilted her head back.

The pulse fluttering at her throat was impossible to resist. He licked her skin, reveling in the taste almost as much as in her shaky gasp. She tugged against his grip on her hair then, seeking his mouth with hers. A pleased chuckle rumbled up as he kissed his way up her neck and along her jaw, a victory in each indrawn breath he elicited.

By the time he claimed her lips, he didn't care about enemies or Gwynira or leaving this bed ever again. Judging by the eagerness with which her mouth welcomed his, neither did Naia. The song of the sea thrummed in his blood, sweet and playful in one moment, sharp and dangerous in the next. Her teeth found his lower lip, a warning not to underestimate her any more than he would underestimate the ocean itself.

Their kiss broke with a jolt as Aleksi sat up, hauling Naia along with him. "I cannot believe you two are making the *god of lust* be the responsible party here." He brushed Naia's disheveled hair back from her face with gentle care. "We've already missed breakfast. It would be unconscionably rude to miss luncheon, as well."

She relented with a groan. *"Fine."*

Einar sat up as well, but he couldn't resist the bare expanse of Aleksi's broad back. Dark hair curled at the base of his neck, tickling Einar's cheek as he brushed a kiss to the spot where neck curved into shoulder—a promise he sealed with a teasing bite.

Politics might come first today . . . but not always.

Cool air nipped at Einar's skin as soon as he was out from under the covers. It had been centuries since the cold had bothered him in any form, but Naia and Aleksi still felt it, so Einar started for the hearth to build the fire back up.

As if to lend credence to his thoughts, Naia grumbled through a shiver. "It's too cold to get up."

The air seemed to shiver around him. Some ancient instinct prompted him to jerk his hand back from the piece of wood he'd just placed in the fireplace—and just in time. Teal flames leapt from the cold embers, burning so fierce and bright that they swallowed the wood entirely. Then they faded, leaving a cheerful fire burning in the usual golds and oranges.

Einar glanced back at the bed, but Aleksi was oblivious, his gaze following Naia as she wandered toward the wardrobe, clad only in the unbound waves of her hair. "Aleksi."

"Mmm?"

He couldn't fault the Lover for his distraction, but neither could he ignore odd displays of power, no matter how benevolent they seemed. He returned to the bed and touched Aleksi's chin, tilting his face up. "Did you feel that?"

Aleksi smiled and ran his fingertips up the inside of Einar's forearm. "Feel what?"

Einar tilted his head toward the fire. "I didn't light that."

"No?" Aleksi arched an eyebrow, then frowned. "What are you thinking?"

"That Naia said she was cold, and the fire simply . . . lit."

Aleksi gazed up at him, that searching little light glinting in his eyes, and lowered his voice to a whisper. "You're starting to believe."

Einar wanted to deny the words, and he didn't even know what they meant.

Liar.

The voice echoed up from the same place as that instinctive warning had, a place that recognized that shiver of power—and the distinctive color of those flames. Long before he had manifested as the Kraken, Einar had been the goddess-touched Crown-Prince of Rahvekya. This island's magic was his birthright.

Einar tore his gaze from Aleksi's to find Naia, who was pulling a fresh linen shift over her head. He'd recognized her magic in the same way, drawn to it as if her touch in the waves held the answer to a question he'd never even known to ask. The locals thought she was their goddess, returned to them. A quaint superstition, for such a thing was not possible.

Was it?

"Naia, love?" Aleksi sought and held Einar's gaze as he stretched out a hand. "Can you come here for a moment, please?"

She was grinning as she crawled onto the bed once more and pressed her cheek to Aleksi's waiting hand. "Did you change your mind about staying in bed today?"

"Unfortunately not. I need to ask you something."

"Anything." She turned her smile to his palm.

Aleksi sat up, pulling Naia along with him until they were facing one another. "Has anything odd happened to you since our return to the island?"

Her smile melted away, and she bit her lip. "I was going to tell you."

He nodded encouragingly.

Her chest heaved, and her eyes tracked back and forth between Aleksi and Einar. "The ice walls," she said finally. "I helped control the seas in the aftermath, but I did not bring the walls down. I don't know what did."

The destruction of those towering, protective walls—held up with Gwynira's magic—had been intimidating enough when Einar had thought it to be Naia's work. To imagine someone, or some*thing*, had the power to destroy them on a whim made the trick with the fire seem like an afterthought.

Einar reached out to touch her cheek. "When you said the room was cold, the fire lit itself. With teal flames." The color of the goddess.

Naia laughed softly. "You mean when *you* went to light the fire," she corrected. "Isn't it obvious, Einar? This island is a living thing, and it is welcoming you home."

Could it be that simple? Was that why the magic felt so familiar? "Perhaps," he conceded. "Whatever the reason, we have to acknowledge that *something* is happening here. If we can understand what, perhaps it will make the rest of our task easier."

"Fair enough." Naia rolled up to her knees and kissed Einar's chin. "Do you need help getting dressed?"

He didn't, but he was hardly going to turn down the chance to linger a few more precious moments with her hands on him. "If you please."

He had long understood the pleasure to be had in the leisurely removal of a partner's clothing, but he had too little experience with the reverse. There was something profoundly sensual in the way Naia's fingers brushed his skin as she smoothed his shirt into place, and deeply adorable when her brow furrowed in concentration as she fastened the shiny bronze buttons of his vest.

Aleksi's gentle fingers coaxing Einar's hair into some semblance of order was another impossible intimacy, over far too soon as the Lover turned to help Naia lace up her simple dress. Einar took his own satisfaction in letting his hands linger on Aleksi's body as they helped him dress—in his own stylish but relaxed fashion from the Villa instead of the stiff Imperial style—and Einar could privately admit the relief of having another chance to reassure himself that Aleksi was *here* and growing stronger.

That terrifying fragility of a few short days ago felt like an aberration, like a nightmare that had shattered when Aleksi had seen Naia and Einar in peril and clawed his way back to life on a wave of protective fury. Love, in its purest form—a power that dwarfed petty hatred and vengeance.

Einar doubted he had been the first to look upon the god of love and underestimate the danger he represented, but he would never make that mistake again.

Besides, Aleksi's skills were what they needed now. "Politics is your battlefield, Aleksi," Einar said as he sorted through his tangle of jewelry. Perhaps nothing too ornate today—the pirate lord, prepared to work. He slipped on his favorite ring and glanced at Aleksi. "How do we track down our enemies? Most of my usual methods would cause a diplomatic incident."

"Simple. We don't try." Aleksi straightened his shirt in the mirror. "If we ask questions—*any* questions—then we risk alerting the wrong people. So we keep our own counsel, hold our tongues . . . and listen."

Naia frowned. "You think whoever tried to kill us is just going to admit it?"

"Of course not. But the fact that they'll also be keeping their mouths shut is something we can use."

"I don't follow."

He turned and half sat, half leaned on the edge of the dresser, the very picture of relaxed ease. "People tend to notice odd things, and they want to know if *other* people have noticed them. Especially if no ready explanation presents itself."

Understanding dawned on Naia's face, smoothing away the frown. "Our enemies' silence will create mystery."

"Mmm. And a court loves nothing more than intrigue."

"So we listen to them gossip." Definitely not Einar's favorite way to spend an afternoon, but undoubtedly Aleksi and Naia would bear the brunt of it. Even without his terrifying pirate outfit, most of Gwynira's court was still too afraid of him to make casual conversation.

"It's merely our opening gambit, darling." Aleksi crossed to Einar's side and surveyed the jewelry before lifting a hammered wrist cuff that sported a massive black diamond. Dianthe herself had given it to him on his two-thousandth birthday, claiming she'd salvaged it from deep in the ocean, from a rock that had fallen from the stars when their world was still young. Einar held out his wrist, and Aleksi fastened it in place with a smile. "Worry not. We'll be laying our traps soon enough."

Well, at least one person in the court would no doubt be eager to corner Einar. "I suppose I can let Klement rattle on at me. He does love to talk."

Naia slipped into a fur-lined overdress so reminiscent of the local fashions that the servants must have made it for her. "I can mingle with the nobles, though I'm a curiosity to them, at best. The palace staff, on the other hand . . ."

"Brilliant." Aleksi lifted her chin and kissed her lightly. "Leave the nobles to me."

With their respective battle plans in place, Einar squared his shoulders and opened the door, gesturing for Aleksi and Naia to precede him.

The corridors of Gwynira's icy palace were mostly empty at this time of day, with the bulk of those who made up her court no doubt gathered in the ballroom where they whispered and plotted and vied for Gwynira's favor—or tested her patience. But every servant they passed inclined their head to Einar before bowing deeply to Naia.

She seemed to be growing used to their deference—or at least comfortable enough with it that the smiles she offered in return held genuine warmth. There was a *rightness* to her in this place that defied explanation, a belonging that sank into Einar's bones and made him think about his first mate's words on the night they'd left on this journey.

When I look at her . . .

Petya had not finished the thought. She hadn't needed to. Petya gazed upon Naia and saw the goddess she had worshipped for endless centuries—the Mother of Rahvekya, who had once walked the shores of a tropical island and loved its people so dearly that she'd traded her own immortal life for their safety.

The servants they passed saw their goddess returned. For the first time, Einar wondered if they could be right. Or if their belief could *make* them right, for was that not the way of their world? Dreams came true, quite literally.

How many generations had dreamed that a goddess with a love for the sea would walk these shores again and protect them? Dozens? A hundred?

Enough to make it come true. Naia did not even need to be the goddess of their myths to be the fulfillment of three thousand years' worth of dreaming. And they would love her for it.

The doors to the ballroom were thrown wide, the murmur of voices audible as soon as they turned the final corner. Gwynira's court enjoyed casual midday meals, circulating between heavily laden buffet tables while the Ice Queen herself stayed safely ensconced on her throne.

She was there now, the three steps up to her dais discouraging casual conversation almost as much as the hulking presence of her personal guard at their base. Arktikos had the rare talent of looking forbidding even with a perfectly pleasant expression fixed on his handsome features—or perhaps what Einar felt was an entirely rational wariness of a man who could change into an enormous polar bear in the time it took to blink.

He wasn't the only one whose presence prickled warning down Einar's neck. A second throne had been added next to Gwynira's. Isa perched there, her odd, steel gray eyes sweeping straight to Einar and his lovers as they entered the room.

She still made Einar uneasy, even from across the room. He could recall her abrupt arrival too easily. Appearing from nowhere and tumbling to the floor naked should have been the oddest part, but what loomed large in Einar's mind was how she'd immediately lashed out, pinning him to the wall with shadows that felt like the Endless Void itself.

He'd only seen Zanya wield magic like that, and she *was* the Endless Void—or at least the manifestation of it, born into the body of a woman with shadows in her eyes and murder in her heart. There were few things that Einar feared, but weapons forged from the Void were one of them.

At least Zanya's ties to the High Court were unshakable. Einar didn't understand the allegiances of this strange woman, except that she was clearly devoted to Gwynira—and Gwynira to her.

If only Einar could be as confident as Naia and Aleksi that Gwynira was a friend to be trusted.

The crowd parted naturally before them as Aleksi led them across the hall. One or two clutches of nobles whispered behind their hands with arch looks that all-too-clearly speculated as to what had kept the three of them abed so late. Einar ignored them—for now—and kept his attention focused on the powerful women waiting for them.

Aleksi bowed before the dais when they reached it. "Good morning, Grand Duchess. Lady Isa."

"Is it?" Gwynira asked archly. "Morning, that is."

He flashed her a rakish grin followed by a wink. "I apologize for my late arrival."

"Your smile betrays your lack of remorse, my lord." Gwynira's lips twitched. "You are anything but apologetic."

Aleksi straightened. "You see me far too clearly, Your Grace. I admit it—I was enjoying the society of my companions far too much to relinquish it easily."

Gwynira's usually icy expression broke into genuine warmth as she laughed. "What a delicate way to convey that you would have much preferred to remain naked in your bed."

"I am nothing if not delicate."

"I'm going to get something to eat." Naia stretched up to kiss his cheek. "Try to behave, Aleksi."

"When I could scandalize the nobles instead? That would be a pity."

Naia drifted away with a sweet smile, pausing next to Einar long enough to twine her fingers with his. There was a promise in the quick caress, a vow that they might be forced to separate now to pursue their individual missions, but they *would* find their way back to that bed.

With a tiny smile, Einar teased his thumb suggestively over her knuckles before her hand slipped away. Aleksi had already turned to address an older woman with a tower of gray hair threaded with flowers—an extravagance more telling than jewels in this frozen kingdom—and Naia had her sights set on the end of the buffet table where several servants waited to assist the guests.

He supposed it was time for him to face his own trial.

Biting back a long-suffering sigh, he turned . . . and was utterly unsurprised to find his quarry already bearing down on him with a positive gleam in his eyes.

The man stopped in a swirl of gold-embroidered robes, his thick golden medallion thumping against his chest. The medallion apparently betokened an elite status in the former Empire, one so coveted that Klement had been among the few in his generation to receive it. His promising career had taken a sharp turn, however, when his research into the cultures the Empire had crushed in order to build their capital city made the nobles—and the Emperor—uncomfortable. The result had been his banishment to this island, where his research would languish unread and his presence would serve to annoy Gwynira.

That last part had been a wild success. Einar had seen firsthand how annoying the Grand Duchess found the loquacious scholar. "Captain Einar!" Klement exclaimed, clapping both hands together in front of him. "I'm so glad to see you."

At least someone in this court was, even if the old man's obsessive fascination with Einar could be off-putting. Over the centuries he had grown used to those who revered him as a god or feared him as a monster, but this was the first time he'd encountered someone eager to make a name for themself by writing a book about him.

Perhaps he should ask Aleksi how to deal with it. After all, the Lover had spent thousands of years with storytellers and musicians flocking to his gorgeous villa, eager to bask in his presence and make him their muse. Einar had heard the others on the High Court joke about it dozens of times—the devotion of artists and poets had kept Aleksi's allure strong, after all, even when the Mortal Lords had tried to turn the people against their gods.

For the first time, Einar understood how unsettling that must be. But he'd been given a task, so he managed something approaching a smile. "Guildmaster Klement."

His half grimace must have passed as welcome—at least to Klement—because the man beamed at him. "I was starting to fear you had taken your leave of us for good. I must say, your abrupt absence from the court's festivities was a terrible disappointment."

The words seemed earnest. Self-involved, certainly, but earnest. Fortunately, it wouldn't take much to encourage the man to elaborate. "Oh?"

"Oh yes, terrible, indeed." Klement reached into his robes and pulled out a leather-bound book with gilded pages. Shiny foil caught the light as he held it up, revealing the title: *Akeisa: A Comprehensive History (Volume One)*. "I've been carrying this with me in hopes of seeing you again."

Of course it was more of the man's obsession with the history of the island—and Einar's place within it. Einar had found a dozen of the man's dry and endless tomes in the library, interesting mostly for what they revealed about the flora and fauna of the island itself. Reading the Imperial perspective of Einar's own family story had been less amusing. Einar suspected that Klement thought himself an objective scholar, but Imperial superiority practically seethed beneath every word.

Einar reached out a hand to accept the book, only to blink when Klement pulled it back, cradling it against his chest. "Oh, my apologies, dear boy. That was misleading, wasn't it? No, this copy isn't for you, though I'd be happy to personalize one for you, as well."

He wasn't sure if he should feel affronted, or as if he'd had a narrow escape from a terrible fate. Maybe the grinding of his teeth was audible, because on the other side of the hall, Aleksi glanced his way and arched one perfect brow in a look so eloquent, Einar could practically hear the Lover's teasing words as if whispered against his ear.

You've survived terrible battles and weathered epic storms. Surely you can manage one single conversation with a self-important scholar without punching him.

No, Aleksi likely would have been far kinder. But the gentle encouragement in his gaze was a reminder to Einar. This was a game, and he had to play it out.

"Who is it for?" He thought he'd managed to sound mildly interested. "The book, I mean."

"It's for Petya, of course." Klement stroked the gold leaf on the cover with unmistakable pride. "I've signed it and inscribed it to her personally. But since she still has not left the ship, I thought it only right that I bring it to her."

Oh, no. Not a chance. The woman who had raised Einar refused to leave the ship at all. The last time she had set foot on this island had been over two thousand years ago, on the night General Akeisa had finally seized victory for the Empire in a war of conquest that had been raging for three generations.

Petya had been the head of the Queen's Guard, a renowned warrior married to Rahvekya's High Priestess. She had been fully prepared to lay down her life in defense of the land she loved, but her queen had given her a far more difficult task—to take the infant crown-prince across the mountains to the northern side of the island, and flee with him to safety.

Einar had heard the story so many times he could recite it word for word, in the reverent cadence Petya gave it that made it more than just a story. *Twelve of the Queen's Guard left the palace at dawn. Six reached the northern coast. Only two survived to see midnight. But the crown-prince lived, and with him, hope. You are our hope, Einar.*

Petya had left her wife, her queen, and the home she'd spent her life protecting. She had carried Einar to safety and had raised him to respect the history of his people—and to hate the Empire that had tried to destroy them. She would not leave the Kraken while a scion of the Empire still ruled in the land she'd once served.

The last thing Einar planned to do was send an Imperial scholar to violate the sanctity of the only home Petya still had, to poke and prod as if her very real memories of tragedy were nothing more than fascinating historical anecdotes.

"I'm afraid you can't do that," Einar said. "The ship is off limits to all but her crew. For everyone's safety."

The man's expression drooped, then rallied. "But surely if I am willing to undertake the risk—"

"I'm sorry, but no."

His shoulders sagged now, too, and Einar might have felt bad about it if he hadn't opened his mouth again, his tone almost wheedling. "I understand perhaps it is an imposition, but I assure you that I would treat Petya with the utmost respect. I should like her to see how well I have preserved her story—"

Could the man not take *no* for an answer? "It isn't possible," Einar said sharply, with the rumble of the Kraken in his voice. He could tell by the way Klement took an abrupt step back that his eyes had begun to glow their eerie teal—the warning that power stirred within him. His skin felt too tight again, and it was tempting to let his other form rip free. Not the full monstrous kraken in all its glory, but the demigod form that let no one forget that he was so much more than a simple man.

He might have done it, too, had Naia not caught his gaze from where she stood beside the table, raised her eyebrows, and tilted her head in teasing admonition.

Fine. He wouldn't spoil the afternoon—or his very nice clothing. Glaring was enough—perhaps too much, from the way Klement had to wipe at the sweat beading on his too-pale face.

For once, the scholar said nothing. Einar almost felt bad. *Almost.* Unbending somewhat, he extended his hand again. "If you would still like for her to see it, I could bring the book to her. If she wants to meet you after that, I will make an exception."

Einar imagined the chances of that were roughly equal to the chances that the sun would reverse course in the sky and turn time backward, but Klement beamed as if he already had an invitation in hand. "Wonderful!" he exclaimed, pressing the book into Einar's hand. "Oh, I absolutely cannot *wait* to meet her."

The man certainly had confidence in his literary achievements. Einar struggled for something passably polite to say, but had only gotten as far as parting his lips when a prickle of warning skittered up his spine.

Instinct swung his gaze to Naia. She was watching the large double doors with calm expectation, as if waiting for . . . *something.* Aleksi, meanwhile, sighed deeply and bowed his head.

Something brushed across the edge of Einar's senses like a whisper heard from leagues away—the crashing of angry waves. The prickling intensified, raising the fine hairs on his arm as an impossible feeling of *power* thrummed through the island. He glanced up, unsure what had prompted the instinct, until thunder cracked above them, shaking the entire palace.

Glass shattered behind him. Someone in the crowd cried out in panic. Wind whipped through the ballroom, carrying the gasps of shock through the room as it tugged at gowns and coats and perfectly coifed hair before gentling as it found Aleksi and swirled around him in teasing greeting.

Einar knew the taste of that wind.

All at once, the flames on every candle in the room surged, drawing more startled yelps from white-faced nobles who huddled away from the wildly dancing fire. The ground beneath the palace shivered—not a violent shaking, but a gleeful welcome.

Einar knew *that* feeling, too.

He turned toward the door just as a smartly dressed herald bustled in, wild-eyed and flustered. He waved a trembling hand, and the guards on either side of the door banged their staffs against the floor in three sharp raps.

Silence fell across the room. All gazes turned toward the man, who drew in a deep breath and unleashed panicked whispers with the booming announcement Einar already knew was coming.

"Your Grace, may I present the High Court of Dreamers."

Chapter Four

When time was new and the world barely formed, the Sheltered Lands cried out for a protector. So the Dragon appeared from the flames, and the Siren rose from the depths of the seas. A handful of others followed, gods who could hear the whispers of the world itself.

They were the Dreamers, and where they walked, the world thrived.

When they Dreamt, the world changed.

Then they fought, and the world broke. And, in darkness and fear, our nightmares formed the Endless Void.

The War of the Gods
Author unknown

Some of Einar's earliest memories were of being a boy without a homeland. The island of his birth, where his parents had ruled, had fallen beneath the sword of the Empire in his first week of life. If the Emperor had realized the crown-prince still lived to undermine him, he would have spared no effort in eliminating the threat. That made settlement in any of the kingdoms which made up the Empire impossible, even if they'd wanted to—which they had not.

There were distant lands in their world that most had never heard of. Several of Einar's crew hailed from those mysterious places—islands to the south that never saw winter, and a continent so far to the east that it took a full moon to sail the Sunrise Sea to its shores.

Einar had never known why Petya decided to settle in the Sheltered Lands instead, but he had his suspicions. That it was the closest safe harbor to the island that still held her heart had likely factored into the decision—straying too far from the shores of Rahvekya might have shattered her already bruised soul. But Einar had always assumed the true reason was much simpler: the Sheltered Lands were ruled over by gods who were the Emperor's sworn enemies.

The High Court of Dreamers. Seven of the most powerful people— not including Sachielle and Zanya—to walk their world. They had lived for so long that Einar's two thousand years and more seemed youthful. Their whims and moods could rattle the earth or stir the wind. Fire and water danced to please them, and the creatures of the woods and wilds spoke to them—and listened to them. They were terrifying and glorious, and the Emperor—the Betrayer, as they called him—loathed each and every one of them both deeply and personally.

Aleksi was one of them. The least outwardly intimidating, perhaps, which was one reason he had been dispatched to form an alliance with Gwynira, as few suspected treachery and violence from the god of something as gentle as love itself. But the High Court were his oldest friends, fearsome not just in their power, but in their unrelenting protectiveness.

Apparently, they had found Aleksi's assurances that he was unharmed by his ordeal insufficient, and had arrived to find out for themselves—and possibly wreak vengeance upon Gwynira's court if they were not satisfied with what they discovered.

Gwynira must have understood that, but she was too experienced at hiding her true thoughts to show it. While her court whispered and fluttered, she sat straight and unmoving on her throne, her face fixed perhaps a little *too* firmly in an expression of casual disinterest. Her too-tight grip on the arms of her throne was the only thing that betrayed her fear, but Arktikos responded to it by subtly shifting until he was in a position to lunge in front of her if necessary.

A courageous but foolish move—if the High Court decided they wanted to destroy this court, not a single stone would be left standing atop another by midday.

Gwynira understood that, as well. But she still lifted one hand in a gracious gesture. "Please present our guests to the court."

The candles were still dancing wildly, so Einar wasn't surprised when the herald's voice boomed out again in the first introduction. "Returning to the court, we welcome the Dragon, Lord of Earth and Fire, Protector of the Sheltered Lands, with his consorts, the Princess Sachielle, Guardian of Dreams, and the Lady Zanya, Mistress of Shadows."

Sachi appeared in the doorway, the usually subtle glow around her like a violent storm. From the way the court was staring at her, Einar wondered if even the mortals could see that brilliant rainbow, like the Dream itself swirled around her in colors not yet invented. Instead of her usual simple gown or traveling leathers, she wore pearlescent white dragonscale armor. Crystals embedded in the breastplate caught the light as she moved, throwing even more sparks of color.

The first time Einar had met her, she'd been a simple mortal princess fading under the weight of a curse meant to sever her from the Dream. A vile threat by a vile man who had turned out to be an agent of the Emperor, sent to soften the Sheltered Lands for an easy conquest from within. That plan had backfired on the Emperor in the end, for in endangering Sachi's life, Sorin had woken her true nature.

Not a simple mortal at all, but the manifestation of the Everlasting Dream itself. Though she had walked the earth for fewer than thirty years, her essence was *ancient.* She was a force beyond even the High Court, and her power eclipsed any Einar had ever known. As she strode into the Great Hall, that power seethed around her with an aggression Einar had never seen before.

She was flanked by Ash and Zanya, and *their* aggression was no surprise. For most of Einar's life, Ash had been the most powerful creature to walk their world—and not simply because he could turn into a dragon and raze entire armies in heartbeats. The very earth shook where he walked, and fire answered his call.

On any other man, his old-fashioned armor with its burnished gold studding would have seemed a laughable affectation. It didn't even cover most of his body, with the strips of his leather skirt barely brushing his knees and the chest plate leaving his strong arms fully bare.

No one in the abruptly silent hall seemed likely to laugh, however. Maybe it was the way his eyes danced in the color of fire, or the candle flames shuddered as he passed while the marble floors trembled in excitement with his every step.

Or maybe it was Zanya, prowling on Sachi's other side with shadows licking around her body. *Her* armor was the opposite of Sachi's, made of ebony and obsidian, and she wore it with the confidence of a born warrior. The Kraken stirred inside Einar, his skin itching with the need to slide into a stronger form as she passed him. Not that it would help—the blades she wore trapped and hoarded light. Void-steel, one of the only things that could hurt a god. Wounds taken from Void-steel healed slowly and poorly—if they healed at all.

And that wasn't even the most terrifying thing about her. The Emperor's reckless plan hadn't awoken only Sachi. Zanya had found her own power as Sachi's equal and opposite—the Endless Void born into not-so-mortal flesh.

The Dream and the Void. Creation and Destruction, opposites that always walked hand in hand, manifested into the forms of two young women because the threat Sorin and his Empire had presented had been so vast, only the primordial forces that ruled their very world had a chance of stopping him.

Einar feared few things, but he held a deep and respectful wariness of Zanya, and found no shame in acknowledging it. Only a fool would tangle willingly with the literal power of destruction.

The tense silence was broken by the herald's somewhat shaky voice. "Presenting the Siren, Mother to the Wind and Waves, Queen of the Deep."

Shocked gasps and whispers raced through the crowd as Dianthe stepped through the doors. In spite of the fact that he had already tasted her presence on the wind, Einar nearly joined them in gaping. He had served the Siren for centuries, obediently appearing at her main seat at Seahold for important feast days and celebrations . . . and he had *never* seen her dressed like this.

Wide blue skirts flowed around her with every step, giving the impossible illusion of moving like water. A split in the front revealed tight pants glistening with iridescent scales like a deep-water creature and knee-high armored boots. Her tightly fitted bodice was studded in hundreds of iridescent seashells interspersed with embroidery. Glittering beads formed a cresting wave over her shoulders, flowing into a wide collar that framed her face and brushed the waves of dark curly hair piled atop her head, hair dotted with crystals like the stars reflecting on the dark of the ocean at night.

Her power flared in her eyes as she paused next to him, their wild blue depths as dangerous as he'd ever seen. It was instinct and long habit to bend his knee to her, eliciting even more murmurs from the crowd around him. At his side, Klement muttered, "Fascinating," as if planning a new chapter in his book.

Dianthe smiled at Einar and continued on.

The staff thumped again, and Einar straightened, his head whipping toward the door. The four who had already arrived were an almost terrifying show of force, especially with Aleksi already in attendance.

But the herald drew in another breath and proclaimed, "Presenting the Phoenix, Keeper of the Sacred Flame, Ruler of Rebirth and Renewal."

Those nearest the entrance drew back in a frightened wave as Nyx entered. Not because of the elaborateness of their costume—if anything, Nyx's simple trousers and wide-sleeved shirt cinched with an embroidered vest were modest compared to those who had preceded them. But they walked surrounded by flames—not the orange and gold of the Dragon, but the Phoenix's eerie silver and blue flames that burned with a different kind of ferocity.

Long before Einar was born, it had been the Phoenix who had drawn the final line that had led to the War of the Gods. Legend held that Sorin—then known as the Builder—had fouled the land with a factory meant to speed technological advance. The Phoenix had walked into it, alight with their own fire, and razed the structure to bare earth.

But the Phoenix's fire didn't destroy. It renewed. It was rebirth. Their flames purged the corruption from streams and soil, returning ruined land to pristine condition.

How Sorin must have loathed a god with the power to destroy anything he built. No, not just destroy—*erase*, as if it had never even been.

"Presenting the Huntress, General of the East, Seeker of Knowledge and Keeper of Truth. Along with the Wolf, Lord of Beasts and King of the Wild Places."

This time the gasps were even louder. Frightened whispers wove through the crowd, but the noise was not loud enough to drown out the sharp sound of Elevia's heeled boots . . . or the click of nails on stone from the giant wolf who kept pace at her side.

The Huntress wore an even more elaborate version of her usual armor, tan leathers studded with steel that bore the distinct golden hue of metal from the Blasted Plains, where her keep of Blade's Rest stood. The lush velvet beneath the leather was the Wolf's deep forest green, a color repeated in the dyed belt that held her weapons. She moved with the easy grace of a born warrior—and with her bow already held loosely in one hand, an open challenge stripped of any artifice.

Ulric had clearly decided to be even more aggressive. In his wolf form, he was so large that his head was even with Elevia's elbow, and his eyes glowed a fierce gold as he bared his teeth and surveyed the crowd. As he drew even with Sir Balian, the man dropped a hand to his sword—and Ulric's growl of warning had him stumbling back.

Elevia reached down absentmindedly with her free hand to stroke soothing fingers through Ulric's fur. The Huntress and the Wolf were a pair Einar would not like to face across the battlefield.

But if *they* had come, too, then the only person left was . . .

"The Witch," the herald announced, his voice trembling a little. "Bringer of Life and Death, Weaver of Magic."

Einar had to bite his lip not to laugh as the overwhelmed nobles braced for someone even more terrifying, only to fall into confused silence at Inga's entrance. The Witch had always enjoyed whimsy and drama far too much for Einar's tastes. He had never visited her castle deep within the Witchwood, but even descriptions of its chaotic whimsy had given him an actual headache. In her free time, she cultivated flowers in colors no artist with good sense would have ever considered, flowers that could pulse with the mood of those around them and cause insects who fed on them to glow in the moonlight.

Apparently, she had decided to bring all that melodrama to the court of the Ice Queen. She floated through the door in a black gown that brushed the floor in front of her and swept behind her in a train that encompassed an impossible rainbow. He had no idea how the woven threads shifted color from one moment to the next, but the butterflies following in her wake matched every wild hue. The black-crystal-encrusted bodice of her dress was cut in a deep vee nearly to her waist, and the collar that flared dramatically around her neck gave way to a headpiece that radiated glittering spikes of ebony around her head like a dark sunburst.

Her kohl-rimmed eyes met his, their intense pink depths seething with mischievous power. Her black-painted lips quirked into a tiny smile of acknowledgment before she lifted one beringed hand. The butterflies swarmed into a glittering storm that swept over the heads of the assorted nobles, drawing startled gasps as several people flung up their arms as if to ward off an attack.

The entire High Court was here—and they were not in a subtle mood.

The eight new arrivals stopped before the dais. Instead of a line or semicircle, they broke into an arrangement vaguely reminiscent of a battle formation. Tension tightened through the room, the promise of violence a whisper against the back of Einar's neck.

Gwynira rose, steady even in the face of such an overt threat, and stretched both empty hands out in a gesture of greeting. "You are welcome to the Crystal Palace, though I cannot account for the honor of such a visit."

Ash turned, his gaze seeking Aleksi in the crowd. The Dragon lifted one eyebrow in obvious question. Aleksi looked as if he wanted to pinch the bridge of his nose and sigh, but instead he answered his friend's unspoken question with a gentle smile and a slight nod.

The High Court barely moved, but the tension abruptly dissipated. Stances that had screamed imminent attack softened into friendly curiosity. Fingers that had brushed weapons relaxed. Ash reached out to touch Sachi's arm, and she stepped forward with a smile that banished any lingering ill feeling.

"We have come in friendship," she said in a musical voice that carried easily over the crowd. "And to demonstrate—unequivocally, Grand Duchess, should anyone wonder—that you have the support of the entire High Court. We are at your service."

Murmurs rose from every side as the court grappled with the implications of such an announcement—and undoubtedly tried to discern if this could be leveraged in any of their own petty squabbles.

Fabric rustled at Einar's side, followed by the crinkle of paper. He glanced at Klement to find the scholar scribbling frantically in a tiny notebook with one of those odd Imperial quills that needed no ink. ". . . what an opportunity," he murmured.

Einar suppressed a sigh and returned his attention to Gwynira in time to see her shoulders relax almost imperceptibly. She stepped down from her dais and gestured for the High Court to approach. "Please, join me. We have some introductions to make."

The air swirled around Einar, tugging at him in silent summons from the Siren. Aleksi had already broken free from the crowd and was walking forward to join his friends, with Naia not far behind him. Einar left Klement to his frantic note taking and ignored the speculative looks from the assembled nobles as he strode to stand with his lovers.

Sachi glanced at Elevia, who nodded. Then the Dream raised one hand, and a shimmering veil formed around her. It slowly expanded, a glittering cloud of energy that enveloped the High Court—and Gwynira's dais.

Arktikos started forward, his hand falling to the hilt of his sword, but Gwynira halted his advance with one sharp gesture.

"For the sake of privacy," Sachi explained. "We can speak freely now. No one outside this field can hear us, though they can still see us." She cast an almost mischievous look at Zanya. "At least, they think they can."

Zanya grinned and stroked her fingers over Sachi's hair with approving fondness. "You're getting devious."

"I prefer *creative*."

"Mmm. And maybe a little wicked."

The affectionate heat in Zanya's eyes burned hot enough to singe anyone who stood too close, rivaled only by the look Sachi gave her in return. Ballads might have been written about Einar's sexual exploits, but one must give the Dragon his due. It took a man with nerves forged from the strongest steel to climb into bed between the forces of Creation and Destruction.

Uncharacteristically, Aleksi seemed oblivious to the flirtation playing out next to him as he sighed heavily. "I told you all everything was fine. You couldn't have taken me at my word?"

Dianthe's smile was gentle—and still somehow terrifying, like the inviting surface of the ocean hiding jagged rocks just beneath to trap the unwary. "We did, darling. But even you must admit that your words were . . ."

"Alarming," Ash finished gruffly.

Aleksi rubbed both hands over his face. "Some of the High Court you already know, and the rest were just announced. Everyone, this is Grand Duchess Gwynira and the Lady Isa."

Sachi froze as her smile vanished, replaced by an expression of pure shock. "Isa?"

"Yes," Gwynira whispered. "My Isa."

Sachi's stunned bewilderment seemed to last an eternity, then broke on a soft laugh. She dropped a hand to one of the daggers hanging from her belt, hesitating. Then she pulled it free slowly, while arching one questioning eyebrow at Arktikos. "If I may?"

It was Gwynira who answered. "Please."

Sachi stepped up and offered the blade, still sheathed, to Isa. If Zanya's weapons exuded the dark menace of the Void, the knife Sachi held up was a whisper of sweetness wrapped in ominous shadows. Einar knew the story of that blade all too well—it was why Aleksi was *here*.

When Sachi had been held prisoner in Sorin's court, Gwynira had been the one to show Sachi . . . Well, kindness was undoubtedly too strong a word, given the woman's frosty demeanor. But the Ice Queen had proven a willing conspirator in Sachi's plans to escape, and had provided the princess with a blade forged by her long-destroyed lover. A blade imbued with the magic of the Everlasting Dream *and* the Endless Void.

A blade that could kill a god—or an Emperor.

In the end, Sachi had defeated Sorin through her own power, but that knife remained as hopeful proof that at least one member of the Imperial Court might be sympathetic to their cause. It was on that fragile hope that they had sought to cement an alliance with Gwynira, one that could give them access to the knowledge and resources of a former member of Sorin's court.

"I believe this belongs to you, Lady Isa," Sachi said. She smiled once more, the expression bright with amazement. "It is so good to meet you."

Isa stared at the knife, eyes wide. "I—" Her trembling hand darted out, fingers curling around the hilt as if she couldn't quite believe it was real. Power rippled through the air as she cradled it against her chest, the silky shadows of the Void mixed with the bright shimmer of the Dream.

"Thank you," Isa said softly. "This was special to me. It is . . . good to see it again."

Gwynira laid a protective hand on the small of Isa's back, steadying her. Her gaze took in the glittering veil that still protected them from the avid curiosity of the court, and she actually smiled, if a little wryly. "As much as I am enjoying the respite from noble chatter, I suppose it is time we finish this official welcome. If you would be so kind, Princess?"

Sachi returned the smile and gestured, and the veil burst like a popped bubble, tiny hints of rainbow magic dissipating into the air. The excited murmur of court gossip surrounded them immediately, and Gwynira lifted her voice to be heard over the sound. "The Crystal Palace is open to you, my friends. Rooms will be arranged for your comfort, and I bid my court do everything in their power to make you welcome."

Einar let his gaze slide over the assembled nobles. Some looked frightened. Some horrified. Plenty looked eager—either at the opportunities presented by guests of power, or simply at the horror and fear displayed by their enemies in the court. Several had expressions so blank, Einar knew they were hiding their true feelings. One was Gwynira's infuriating seneschal Jaspar. Another was Sir Balian, who must surely be wondering if Aleksi's friends had heard that it was Balian's poisoned sword that had nearly claimed the Lover's life.

Klement hadn't even looked up from his notes.

Politics might not be Einar's game, but it was clear enough that the unexpected arrival of the High Court had upended the routines of Gwynira's palace. Hopefully their enemy—or enemies—would be off balance and uncertain. If Einar was very lucky, one might make a mistake.

Einar didn't care if Aleksi's oldest friends thought they took precedence when it came to avenging a threat to one of their own. If Einar found the person who had conspired to kill Naia and kidnap Aleksi, he would deal with it. Personally.

Chapter Five

Want to make a hardened warrior or a ruthless assassin hide under the bed? Tell them that the Stalker is annoyed with them. It would be bad enough if Grand Duchess Eirika was only a ruthless fighter—or a merciless killer—but she's also a genius tactician and has no fewer than two Grand Dukes under her thumb. She is also the main reason I'm staying anonymous. If I ever turn up dead, it was probably her.

The Illicit Lives of the Imperial Court
Anonymous
(banned in the Empire)

For the second time in as many days, Aleksi found himself staring down a sea of curious faces.

At least these were unquestionably friendly. The High Court's arrival had caused such a stir that night had fallen to darkness before they managed to retire to his chambers to speak privately—or, as Aleksi suspected, to corral him for intensive questioning.

But the expected interrogation did not come. Instead, they gathered around Aleksi's suite with drinks, made themselves comfortable . . . and waited for his explanation.

He gave it quickly and dispassionately—he was poisoned, then kidnapped along with his companions. They escaped their abductors, returned to the island, and Aleksi was back on his feet. "So I'm fine now," he concluded, "and nothing about any of this was remotely surprising. We all knew an Imperial Court was likely to be a treacherous place—or, at least, we should have."

"What a neat, practiced summary," Elevia observed from her spot behind the sofa. "But don't you think you might be omitting a few key details?"

"Such as?"

"What kind of poison could have done you such serious harm?" Inga demanded.

"And who kidnapped you?" Ulric added.

"And Isa," Ash cut in. "Sachi told me she *died*. The Emperor killed her centuries ago."

"All fair questions," Aleksi allowed, for it was nothing but the truth. "And I will answer as many of them as I am able. But first, we must acknowledge the reality of *why* you all shuffled me off to Akeisa in the first place—because you did not want me any closer to the fights in the Empire."

Despite the guilt that shadowed his features, Ash tried to protest. "Aleksi, that isn't—"

"But it *is*, Ash," he countered. "The truth, as beautiful and brutal as it can be. You all knew I had been wounded emotionally, and so you wanted to protect me. I understand that. Moreover, I respect it. Only . . ."

Sachi rose slowly, her brow crinkled with confusion and a growing concern. "Only that wasn't what happened, was it?"

"No, love." Aleksi did not know *how* to tell them the rest of it, so he loosed his tongue and let the words pour forth without thought as he paced the width of the room. "What Sorin's witch did harmed me more than even I suspected at first. But she severed me from the *Dream*. I have never lived a human life; that was everything I had ever known. She tore away my sense of self, ripped at me until I no longer believed in anything, much less the sanctity of what I represent."

"She wounded your *soul*," Zanya whispered.

"Yes," he admitted. "She killed my beliefs, and what *are* any of us but reflections of belief? Without them, what did I have? Nothing. No powers, and no protections—not even against the most mundane of poisons."

Sachi stepped in front of him, halting his pacing. Still frowning, she grasped his face between her hands and peered up at him, as if staring *into* him. "I thought there was *something* wrong," she murmured. "But I had only seen you in the Dream for so long, I figured it must simply be that your emotions were so unsettled. Oh, Aleksi. Can you forgive us?"

"There is nothing to forgive," he told her gently. "And I'm doing much better now."

"But are you *well?*" Inga pressed.

"I am not. But I *will* be, Inga. I promise." It was something Aleksi could not, in good conscience, have said before just this moment. Broken vows were far worse than silence, so he made it a point never to offer any he was not absolutely sure he could keep.

At least Inga knew that. She settled back into her chair, looking moderately reassured.

"As for the kidnapping," Aleksi went on, "their goal was clear—seize me, and get everyone else out of the way. So I have definitely pissed off someone powerful."

"Sorin," Nyx suggested.

Sachi looked grave. "Or one of his court."

Dianthe frowned. "I believed Sorin's cell to be secure, but his escape proves that I underestimated his resourcefulness."

Nyx frowned and rubbed their hand over their chin. "He couldn't contact anyone, but could someone have had the power to communicate with him?"

Sachi shrugged one shoulder helplessly. "I don't know. There was his witch, Varoka—the Dreamweaver. She could have done it, I'm certain, but she's dead. One of Zanya's Terrors tore her apart."

Aleksi quelled a shudder. He was never exactly happy to think of death. The sudden cessation of *growth* and *life* went against the core of who he was and what he worked every day to build.

But he did not regret Varoka's end.

"She was the only one that Sorin didn't create by pulling her from the Dream." Sachi frowned. "He found her, nurtured her worst instincts. She was a tool to him . . . but I think he loved her."

Elevia snorted, but her voice was pure steel. "Sorin isn't capable of love."

"No," Sachi allowed. "No, you're probably right."

"I *know* I am." Elevia crossed her arms over her chest and cast a quick but pointed look at Ash. "You wanted like hell on fire to think he could be saved, but—"

Ash's face was hard, his eyes dancing with a hint of flames. "I had hoped that some of our brother might still be in there somewhere. But he is not. And, after this, he is past saving." He took a breath and shook his head. "Who else?"

There was the Beast, a mindless, rapacious killer who represented all the worst things about Ash that didn't even exist, but Sorin saw them anyway. He had certainly possessed the vengeful nature required to carry a grudge, if not the delicacy for secretive operations. But a newly awakened Dreamer, one who had suffered torture at the Beast's hands, had torn him apart at that final battle.

The Shapechanger had been Sorin's version of Ulric. But instead of having a nonhuman form that felt like his true self, the Shapechanger had stolen the visages of others and used their identities to his own ends. He had successfully infiltrated the Mortal Queen's court, so he was absolutely capable of stealing onto the island to plot and execute an abduction.

He would have been Aleksi's main suspect for that reason alone . . . if only he still lived. But Aleksi had run him through with a sword when the man had attempted to assassinate the young queen.

"I suppose we can discount the Beast and the Shapechanger," he noted wryly.

"The Seducer," Sachi said flatly. "He has the power to shroud his words and deeds in shadow, but I don't know if that extends to hiding his presence from someone as strong as Dianthe."

The Seducer was Aleksi's counterpart in Sorin's twisted little court. Sachi had mostly refused to tell Aleksi anything about him—likely to spare him the pain of knowing how Sorin truly saw him, bless her. But from what little Aleksi had been able to ascertain, the Seducer was the worst sort of predator, a pretty, smiling face to distract from the horrors he would happily inflict on a person.

"He escaped during the final battle," Aleksi noted. "That lends credence to his powers of obfuscation."

"The Stalker also managed to evade our grasp." Elevia smiled viciously. "*My* dark shadow. From all accounts, the nastiest, cleverest bitch you'd hope never to meet."

Nyx did not hesitate. "So it was likely her, then, who helped Sorin escape."

"Oh, almost definitely," Elevia confirmed.

Sachi drew in a sudden sharp breath. "The Shapechanger was her lover."

And Aleksi had killed him.

"Just out of curiosity," Aleksi asked dryly, "did she seem the vengeful type?"

Elevia rolled her eyes at his attempt at humor. "The Stalker is our likeliest suspect, but she could easily have had help. Maybe even help that's right under our noses."

Dianthe frowned. "You mean Gwynira?"

Elevia cut off Aleksi's attempt to protest. "The three of you were in her home, under her protection. She had the greatest opportunity."

"*No.*" Sachi was usually so soft-spoken that the sharpness of the denial made Elevia lean back a little. "Gwynira would never harm Aleksi. I feel that very strongly."

Ash laid a gentle hand on her shoulder. "But are you *sure*, darling?"

"Absolutely certain."

Elevia pursed her lips, a clear sign that she was marshaling an argument, so Aleksi stepped in. "I . . . have done Gwynira a great service."

"What the hell does that mean?" Elevia demanded.

But Zanya straightened in her chair, her gaze suddenly intent. "Is *that* what that was?"

"What?" Ulric asked.

"A few days ago, I felt a . . . *pull* through the Void. Almost like a plea?" Zanya sought Aleksi's gaze. "Someone that my heart recognized needed something, so the Void answered."

"And Isa was trapped there," Ash murmured. "So it . . . what? *Returned her* at Aleksi's request?"

"A literal hole opened up," Aleksi explained. "And she fell out of it."

For once, Elevia seemed at a loss for words. Finally, she breathed, "Well. That's a neat trick."

"Not exactly." They wouldn't like it, but they deserved to hear all of it, didn't they? "I was in terrible shape," Aleksi admitted. "My body was trying to fight off the poison, and losing the battle. In my mind, all I could see were the repercussions—of my death, and of my failure to make a firm ally of Gwynira. So . . . yes. It wasn't a conscious plea, but it was a plea, all the same."

Zanya smiled shakily, then pressed her fingers to her lips. "I didn't understand what was happening at the time, but the Void would never ignore a cry for help from my big brother."

Aleksi grasped her hand and kissed the back of it. "And now? Isa lives again."

Ulric scratched his beard, studying Zanya through narrowed eyes. "How many people do you have in there?"

"I didn't know I had *any*," Zanya retorted. "I wouldn't even know how to tell. I don't have time right now to sit around, trying to figure out how it all works." She squeezed Aleksi's hand as waves of exhaustion rolled off her. "But I'm glad I had the one you needed."

"The look on Gwynira's face when she told me what Sorin had done to Isa . . ." Sachi shivered. "Even after hundreds of years, the pain was still fresh. Isa means *everything* to her. Having Aleksi bring her back is a debt she can never, *ever* repay."

"So she wasn't involved." Ulric leaned forward to rest his elbows on his knees. "Not that the Stalker would have needed help. If she has half of Elevia's tactical skills, breaking Sorin free would have been simple. No offense, Dianthe."

"None taken," Dianthe murmured. "And I agree. Though I shudder at the thought of having to face an Elevia free of morals or compassion."

Elevia's jaw tightened. "Truly, you should."

"It's worse than that," Ash said. "Don't forget that there are hundreds—*thousands*—of people scattered across the Empire with newly awoken magic, able to access both the Dream and the Void."

It was a harsh reminder of the trials the rest of the High Court had been facing in the former Empire while Aleksi played diplomat. Sorin had spent centuries siphoning the will and imaginations of his subjects through magic. He had usurped their connections to the Dream, and stolen the power those connections typically bestowed to keep it for himself.

When Sachi had severed Sorin's hold on that magic, it had rebounded through the Empire. Anyone with the potential to bend reality, whether through the Dream *or* the Void, had awakened to that potential in a heady, sometimes maddening rush.

Just like the woman who had kidnapped Aleksi and his lovers.

Zanya slumped back in her chair. "Sachi and I have found more newly awakened people than we can possibly help. And they have powers none of us have ever imagined. It truly feels as if nothing is impossible now."

"And if we have found so many," Ash pointed out, "that means our enemies have, as well. Sorin's assistance could have come from beyond his existing court."

"We shouldn't close off any avenues of investigation." Nyx drained their goblet of wine, cleaned it with a quick flash of blue flame, and replaced it on the shelf. "Not that we ever should anyway."

"I believe that Gwynira will protect Aleksi," Dianthe said. "But what about Naia? Is she safe here? And we know the Empire bears no love for Einar."

Aleksi almost laughed. "If Gwynira does not protect them, as well, then the entire island stands ready to hold her to account."

Only blank stares greeted his jest, and Aleksi slowly realized that no one understood his words.

How could they, when they did not *know*?

Elevia started to hand her glass to Nyx, then reconsidered and topped it up again. "Care to let us in on the joke?"

"Not a joke, exactly." Aleksi ran both hands through his hair. "This island is where Einar was born. The day it fell to the Empire, he was still an infant. He was spirited away to safety by the Queen's Guard and raised in the Sheltered Lands."

"By the *Queen's Guard*?" Dianthe stared at Aleksi. Her expression was blank, but shock tinged the space around her an uncharacteristic shade of yellowish green as her hands tightened around the arms of her chair. "His parents ruled *here*?"

"Yes." The moment called for absolutes, unequivocal statements of fact. "Einar is the Crown-Prince of Rahvekya."

Silence. Then Nyx whistled, long and low, and Elevia refilled her glass yet again.

Ulric merely tilted his head. "A prince, huh?"

"Whose parents were killed by Sorin," Ash murmured. "That *does* explain a few things."

But Sachi kept staring at Aleksi, so intently that he could practically see the thoughts whirling behind her eyes, ready to coalesce into suspicions. "And Naia?"

"Also safe," he assured her. "For more complicated reasons."

Elevia almost choked on her wine. "*More* complicated than being the island's long-lost, uncrowned ruler?"

"In a way. Though we fully expected the locals to respect Naia's command of water, it's gone a little further than that. They had a goddess once, and she . . ." Aleksi hesitated. There was no way to fully explain the goddess's fate without placing blame directly on the High Court—and Ash, in particular. "She died."

It was Nyx who forced his hand. "*How*, Aleksi?"

There was no way to soften the revelation, so he did not try. "When Ash fought with Sorin, and the world threatened to split apart."

As Sorin fled the bloody fight, Ash had managed to coax the earth itself into holding together. But in its eagerness to protect the Sheltered Lands from further treachery, the earth had raised the mountain range known as the Western Wall between the two former brothers, separating them.

But entire mountain ranges could not rise in an instant without causing calamity. "The upheaval threatened to wash away Rahvekya entirely. Their goddess shielded the island until the seas calmed . . . but at the cost of her life."

Ash's face tightened as he whispered a curse. When Sachi reached for his hand, he grasped it, giving her a stricken look even as Dianthe closed her eyes and bowed her head.

And Aleksi could not alleviate their pain.

"So now they think Naia is their goddess. I suppose that having her arrive with the crown-prince did nothing to dissuade them from reaching that conclusion." Sachi sighed, seemingly torn between sympathy and relief. "She will have their protection, but at a steep cost. She will be devastated to disappoint them."

Inga watched Aleksi closely, with eyes gone bright pink with curiosity. "Do you have any other earth-shattering revelations you forgot to share with us?"

He held both hands out at his sides. "That is everything."

"Is it, now?" Elevia had drifted back toward the bathing area. She stood by a chair situated halfway behind the privacy screen, squinting down at it. Slowly, she lifted a discarded silk camisole from the chair with the tip of her finger and turned to Aleksi, one eyebrow raised in a perfect, questioning arch.

Shit. He fought to sound casual as he answered her questions, spoken and otherwise. "Naia and Einar are staying with me. In this suite."

"Naia *and* Einar. I see." Elevia smiled at him with faux innocence. "Safety in numbers?"

Aleksi groaned. "What do I have to do to make this not happen?"

"Come, now. Fair's fair," Ulric rumbled with a feral grin. "You saw what she did to poor Ash while he was busy falling in love."

Zanya covered her face. "I don't want to know."

Nyx almost managed to quell a snorting laugh. "To summarize," they said brightly, their lips trembling with mirth, "Aleksi has gone on a diplomatic mission, been poisoned and kidnapped, rescued himself, brought a god back from the dead, and taken a lover."

Elevia tossed the camisole on the bed and raised her hand, wiggling her index and middle fingers in the air. "*Two* lovers."

Sachi hid a smile behind the back of her hand. "You have been very busy."

"Don't forget," Inga added, "that he also brought the crown-prince back to this island and possibly started a religious uprising." She paused. "Are we *sure* Gwynira isn't trying to kill him?"

Ash raised both eyebrows, then shook his head. "If Gwynira wanted him dead, there are much quicker methods."

"Indeed." Elevia grabbed Aleksi's shoulders, pulled him down, and planted a smacking kiss on top of his head. "I will advise her on the best ones."

"I'm glad you're all so amused," Aleksi muttered, though he couldn't help a smile to match those around him. He had missed this so much. Recent months had separated him from the rest of the High Court in more than proximity. After the final battle against Sorin, Aleksi's friends had been so anxious not to add to his pain that they had treated him differently. *Carefully.* It had not been the same.

However.

"I would appreciate it, though," he went on, "if we could all remember that there actually *is* someone, presumably still on this island, who tried to kill me. Even worse, they tried to kill Naia and Einar—and they almost succeeded." He bared his teeth in a fierce grin. "I would very much like to *not* have that happen again."

"All right." Elevia slipped her arm around his waist and leaned into him. "Tonight, we'll all take dinner in our rooms and rest up. Tomorrow will come soon enough, and the work begins."

The others murmured their assent. When the Huntress deigned to make a suggestion—or to give an order—it was best to follow it. She did not do so lightly, or without cause.

But as they broke apart into quiet conversations, Sachi pulled Aleksi aside. "It's curious," she murmured.

"What is, love?"

"This place. It's starting to feel like them—like Naia and Einar." She tilted her head as she gazed up at him. "Haven't you noticed?"

He had not. Then again, how could he?

To Aleksi, the entire world felt like the two of them.

Chapter Six

I have read the journals of all of those who come before me, and if there is one thing the goddess has never let us forget, it is that she is not our ruler. The Mother of Rahvekya will always love us, but like any good mother she wishes to see us grow up and make our own choices—and our own mistakes.

The lost journal of High Priestess Tona

Even if Aleksi had not warned Naia that word had gotten out about the intimate nature of his relationship with her and Einar, the knowing looks from the High Court would have spoken loudly enough on their own.

Rather than gathering in the Great Hall, people milled about outside in the antechamber. Its vaulted ceilings were normally solid stone, but this morning, sunlight flooded the room. Large sections of the roof had been lifted away, leaving behind only the bare stone arches. As a result, the room felt more like an open courtyard. A line of stone tables along one wall held pastries, hand pies, and fruits, and servers moved through the slowly growing crowd, bearing trays laden with steaming drinks.

Across the way, Elevia leaned against a pillar and stared assessingly at Naia. Unable to avoid the scrutiny, Naia lifted her face and studied the sky with more dedication than was strictly required.

But such things could not deter the Huntress. She prowled over, still eyeing Naia like a newly discovered wild creature—or a battlefield map. "We haven't had many opportunities to speak, have we?"

It wasn't exactly a subtle opening, but Naia imagined that very well could be part of Elevia's strategy. Predators did not always lie in wait; sometimes they preferred to ambush their prey. "I imagine I haven't done much to merit your curiosity," Naia told her. "Until now."

Elevia arched one eyebrow in clear appreciation of the return salvo. Maybe she enjoyed playing with her food. "On the contrary. Ulric and I took great notice of you. On the battlefield, I mean."

"You protected him," rumbled a low voice from behind Naia.

Ulric. Naia had to laugh, honestly. She had forgotten that a frontal assault could be just that. But, other times, it served as a mere distraction so the real attack could begin.

She turned to face the Wolf, who was dressed in his customary simple leathers and furs. "Protected who?"

"Aleksi, of course." Elevia caught a passing server and lifted a tiny cup of coffee from the tray he carried, thanking him with a brilliant smile. "When Sorin's witch severed him from the Dream, and he was too staggered to stand and fight."

There were large swaths of the battle that Naia barely remembered. The moments had simply run together to form a desperate, bloody blur. She could not recall now if she had noticed Aleksi on his knees and gone to him, determined not to let his momentary distraction be the end of him, or if Einar had led the charge. Perhaps they had decided together, in a split second of unspoken agreement. "He needed me. *Us.*"

"He did." Ulric plucked the coffee from Elevia's hand and took a sip before handing it back. Then he tilted his head and studied Naia. "He does."

Naia bit her lip. Agreeing felt vaguely traitorous, as if she would be betraying a lingering weakness, but arguing felt like protesting too much.

So she said nothing.

Elevia's gaze sharpened, and the corner of her mouth ticked up. But before she could comment, a prickle of awareness washed over Naia. Goose bumps rose on her arms, and she turned her head just as a protective hand touched the small of her back.

Einar stepped up beside Naia, a small mug of her favorite honeyed tea in his free hand. He handed it to her, then nodded respectfully at the Huntress. "Elevia." The nod he offered her companion was briefer. "Ulric."

"Relax, Kraken." Elevia squared her shoulders. "We were just having a conversation with your clever girl."

A bustle of activity near the corridor caught Naia's eye. Sachi, Zanya, and Ash had entered the makeshift courtyard, wearing far more casual attire than they had the day before—simple, unadorned shirts and trousers, along with sturdy boots. The nobles nearest them immediately began vying for their attention, but Sachi hurried past them all, a bright smile lighting her face.

"Naia!" She threw her arms around Naia's shoulders and squeezed tightly. Then, in a low voice meant only for the two of them, Sachi whispered, "Are they giving you an immense amount of trouble?"

"I would never do such a thing," Elevia said blithely. "And good morning to you, too, Princess Sachielle."

Naia laughed, both at Elevia's mild defense of herself and the way Sachi rolled her eyes in acknowledgment of it. "The Huntress and the Wolf have been on their best behavior."

"Precisely what I'm afraid of," Sachi rejoined, eliciting a growling laugh from Ulric.

Ash stopped in front of Einar, his dark eyes unreadable. For a moment, tension and a hint of power twisted through the crisp morning air as the two men stared at one another. Then Ash pulled Einar into a fierce embrace.

At first, Einar stood stiffly, his arms held awkwardly at his sides. He cast a wild, seeking look at Naia, then gingerly folded his arms around Ash and returned the embrace.

Ash drew Naia into a hug next. "It has been too long since I saw my brother so happy."

The words made a painful lump swell in Naia's throat, and she had to swallow hard before she could answer. "I only hope you're never able to say that again."

He pulled away with a grin just as Aleksi walked into the courtyard with Gwynira. Elevia brushed past on her way toward them, suddenly intent, all teasing and humor forgotten.

She met Gwynira halfway and dropped a proper, though quick, bow. "Grand Duchess. May we speak?"

Gwynira nodded to one of the guards, who edged open one of the doors to the Great Hall, permitting only their assembled group entrance before securing it behind them.

Now that they enjoyed a measure of privacy, Elevia dropped all pretense of social politeness. "Have there been any developments in your investigation?"

Rather than answering immediately, Gwynira shifted uncomfortably. "Yes, there has been one. My harbormaster is missing."

Elevia nodded, clearly unsurprised by the news. "That's to be expected. Either he was directly involved in allowing the mercenary ship to dock, or someone bribed or threatened him to facilitate its arrival. Whether he is dead or has fled, you'll not see him again." She paused. "Has he any family? I'd like to speak with them."

"Even if he did, I doubt they would know anything," Gwynira said icily.

But Elevia was unfazed. "They might, without even realizing it."

Aleksi stepped into the brewing standoff. "Elevia means what she says, Gwynira—talk. No harm will come to them."

After several heartbeats, Gwynira relented. "He has a wife. *Had* a wife."

"Thank you." Elevia began to turn away, then stopped. "Do I remind you so much of her, then? The Stalker?"

"The physical resemblance is . . . strong," Gwynira admitted reluctantly. "You could be sisters."

Again, the Huntress did not seem shocked by the revelation. "Makes sense. Sorin always did like the way I look." She leaned closer, catching the other woman's gaze and holding it steadily. "It was everything else about me that he despised."

Gwynira's eyes widened, but then she nodded in grateful acknowledgment. "However much you might remind me of Eirika, you are *not* her. I should remember that."

Elevia smiled softly. "I won't let you forget."

Gwynira's eyes glittered with what looked like unshed tears, but she cleared her throat and blinked them away quickly. "I wish I had time to properly entertain you all this morning, but I am afraid I do not. I have a prior engagement today, in Jamyskar."

"The village we defended?" Aleksi asked.

"Yes. I will be overseeing efforts to rebuild."

The assembled members of the High Court all cast glances at one another. Some were accompanied by raised eyebrows or intrigued expressions, others by nods or shrugs, but no words passed between them.

Finally, Ash turned to Gwynira and inclined his head. "We will accompany you. It sounds like you could use the help."

Gwynira scoffed. "Nonsense. I could never ask it of you."

"Why not?" Dianthe pinned Gwynira with an assessing look—reminding Naia with a jolt that the Grand Duchess was Dianthe's counterpart in Sorin's twisted little court. "Do you believe we consider such work beneath us?"

"I know my way around a hammer," Ulric added with a feral smile. "I built my home with my own hands."

Gwynira blew out a breath that managed to sound both long-suffering *and* exasperated. "And so I learn that you are *all* like this."

Aleksi laughed and threw a loose arm around her shoulders. "Yes, we're relentless. Best just to accept it."

She groaned, though the noise trailed into something that sounded suspiciously like a laugh. "Fine."

Naia was pleased—to escape the Great Hall with its endless crush of Imperial nobles, to get outside, and to see Jamyskar again under more pleasant circumstances. "Will we be riding reindeer again?" she asked.

Sachi perked up. "Reindeer?"

"No." Gwynira's smile held a hint of apology. "It's such a lovely day. With no imminent threat requiring speed, I thought we'd just walk."

They filed out of the Great Hall. As the herald announced the morning's plans—much to the clear and obvious disgust of the gathered nobles—Aleksi made his way to Naia and Einar. "Tell me—was it absolute torture?"

"Dealing with your friends? You underestimate us," Naia admonished. "Ash hugged Einar."

"Really?"

Einar huffed. "I thought he was going to challenge me to a fight at first. And that might have been less shocking."

Naia nudged a laughing Aleksi with her hip as they walked out into the bright midmorning sunlight. "I am not intimidated by your friends."

"It would be fair to feel at least a little daunted. They *are* gods who have roamed this world for thousands of years."

"Be that as it may, I will not be cowed."

"Because you're fearless, little nymph." He nuzzled her temple. "I need to speak with Ash. I'll be back."

As Aleksi jogged away to catch up with Ash, the wind kicked up suddenly, tugging at Naia's clothing and teasing through Einar's hair. Up ahead, Dianthe crooked a finger at Einar, echoing the breezy summons.

He sighed and lifted Naia's hand to his lips. "I suppose it would not be wise to ignore her."

"Not wise at all," Naia agreed. "Attend the Siren, as is your duty, Captain. I will be here."

He hurried off, though reluctantly, and Naia walked on alone. She was thrilled to hear, perhaps for the first time, the twittering of birds overhead in the trees.

"I think I've been spoiled by the warm weather in the Witchwood."

Startled, Naia looked over to see Inga walking beside her. The Witch had not greeted her, and Naia had neither seen nor heard the woman join her on the wide path. She was simply *there*, her heavy cloak swirling around her as she walked.

"You grow accustomed to the cold, I promise." Though the sun shone brilliantly, and the day seemed warmer than any other Naia had experienced thus far on the island. The warmth felt almost *expectant*, as if someone had drawn in a breath and was about to say something unforgettable.

"I would have liked to have seen the giant reindeer. Perhaps later." Inga studied Naia for a quiet moment before lowering her voice. "Aleksi says he's better. You'll tell me if that changes, won't you? I worry about him. Mostly because he doesn't like to worry the rest of us."

It was another of those moments where answering—whether honestly or with misdirection—felt like betraying Aleksi's confidence. But Naia had been on the receiving end of Aleksi's protective silence, and she knew how scary it could be. So she understood why Inga, Aleksi's closest friend save Ash, would want to know.

But Naia also understood why Aleksi would keep them in the dark. He felt everything so deeply. If he shared with his friends a vulnerability, anything that made them see him as weaker, he would *know*. And she wasn't sure he could ignore it.

In a way, it seemed as though hiding his frailties was less about protecting himself from their judgment and more about protecting his friends' well-being. Though his friends did not realize it, they had forced his hand. Because they would never, ever survive knowing that they had, in their own misguided attempts to shelter him, made him feel *weak*.

So Naia could not, in good conscience, answer Inga's question. But she could say one thing without reservation. "I would give my life for him. Whether he wanted me to or not."

Inga reached for Naia's hand and squeezed it. "As would I."

No hesitation. "In that case," Naia managed, "I think we can contrive to keep him safe, even from himself. Even from us."

"I think we can." Inga did not release Naia's hand. "I always thought you were sweet, you know. But now I see that you are also steel. That's good."

Before Naia could respond, Guildmaster Klement hurried toward them, almost stepping between her and Inga in his eagerness. "Lady Naia," he panted. "May I speak with you?"

She hesitated, but Inga swept into a nod that was very close to a bow. "We will talk more on this matter." Naia blinked, and then Inga was gone, as quickly as she had appeared.

Klement began to offer his arm to Naia, then awkwardly pulled it back in favor of walking beside her. "It is good to see you back at court, my lady. And to see Captain Einar's ship safely returned to the harbor."

It seemed strangely probing, like a query without the question. Naia smiled vaguely. "The Grand Duchess is most liberal with her hospitality, and I am thankful for it."

"Oh yes, she seems to quite enjoy your company. A rare achievement, I must say. In all my time at her court, I'm not sure I've ever seen her enjoy *anyone's* company."

"Perhaps she hasn't, then."

Klement laughed, despite the fact that Naia had been completely serious. "Perhaps not. We are often stuck in our odd ways, those of us from the Empire. But that isn't why I wanted to speak to you."

"Oh?"

"I know much of the crown-prince's story, but I must say, yours is something of an enigma. It seems you are quite close to Princess Sachielle." He peered down at her, looking for all the world as if he was examining a new book. "I would love to hear the story of how you came to know her. And the rest of the High Court, of course."

Naia had not spent much time conversing with Klement. Since discovering Einar's true identity, Klement had focused much of his attention on learning everything he could about Rahvekya's prince.

Now, pinned in place by Klement's curiosity, Naia felt a cold chill slide up her spine. It wasn't danger, but disgust. There was a peculiar sort of ownership in Klement's questions, lurking behind his obsequious politeness, as if he believed the answers already belonged to him. Hell, half the time, he didn't actually *ask* at all. He simply told her what he wanted to know, and fully expected her to comply.

Naia did not like it.

It lent her voice a cool edge when she replied. "I met Sachi when she first traveled to Dragon's Keep as Ash's intended consort. The Siren—Dianthe—sent me along to oversee the journey upriver, from Siren's Bay."

"That is on the far eastern side of your Sheltered Lands, is it not? The bay on which the capital city sits?" He didn't even wait for her to respond. "Is that where you grew up, then? In the court of the Siren?"

"I did not *grow up* anywhere. I walked out of the sea, just under a year ago."

The scholar stared indulgently at her, as if expecting her to laugh uproariously at her joke. When she didn't, his eyebrows shot up. "You . . . But how could you—?" A frown. "I'm afraid I don't understand."

Naia revised her former thought. She did not like *him*, and it made her just petty enough to enjoy his astonishment. "I have never been human, Guildmaster. I was born of the Dream."

"*Well.*" He studied her as if seeing her for the first time. "I will confess that, as a scholar and an educated man, it seems impossible.

But I could hardly doubt your word. To imagine, you have lived but a year . . ."

The words did not come close to encompassing everything that Naia was, or all the memories she carried. She was made of joys and tragedies—of fishing victories and sailors' laments, of tears and laughter—all carried in those bits of the Dream that were bound up in the sea.

She was far more than Klement imagined, but one could not explain a miracle to someone who did not believe. "It happens sometimes."

"Fascinating. Perhaps you would allow me to interview you. At a more convenient time, of course." He smiled with a baffling mix of pride and affected modesty. "You may have heard that I am starting my next great work of research. An authoritative history of the High Court."

"You're assuming, then, that such a work does not already exist." Written by people who had witnessed that history, and would know—and understand—those events far better than Klement ever could.

He hesitated only a moment before nodding. "You are correct. The fact that I have never come across one in our Imperial libraries means little, what with the long-standing conflict between our two nations. Perhaps our new friendship with your High Court will give me access to new scholarly works."

"An excellent first step to expanding your scholarship, Guildmaster."

"Agreed, Lady Naia!" He beamed down at her. "On that note, I had hoped that I might beg you to intercede with Captain Einar on my behalf. It is a matter of some scholarly importance."

What could he possibly feel free to ask of her? "I doubt it, but I am listening."

He charged ahead, oblivious to her reticence. "I have the chance of a lifetime. To have a figure of legend like a member of the Queen's Guard here, within reach? It would mean the world to me to have a chance to speak to Petya, but I am afraid Captain Einar has proven resistant."

"No."

"No?"

"No." Naia stopped and folded her hands behind her back as she faced Klement. "The captain's crew means more to him than anything else. If he has seen fit to deny your request, then he has a reason. A good one."

"Be that as it may—"

Naia's fingertips began to tingle, and she flexed them to dispel the sensation.

"Naia! I've been looking for you." Zanya appeared at her side, throwing an arm around her shoulder. She smiled at Klement, looking for all the world like Ulric baring his teeth. "I hope your friend will forgive me for stealing you away."

The near-feral smile worked. Klement bowed quickly, already backing away. "Of course. Lady Zanya. Naia."

He scurried away, and Zanya stared after him, her brow furrowed. "That's the historian, isn't it?"

The tingling had spread to Naia's palms, and her hands had begun to tremble. She shook them. "Yes. Master Klement of the Scholar's Guild."

Zanya touched Naia's arm, her voice low. "Are you all right? You looked as if you needed only a ready escape, but I will gladly drag him back by the scruff of the neck if he deserves a slap across the mouth."

"No, it's just . . ." Most of the people she'd met on the island viewed her as someone worthy of respect, whether out of fear or adulation. Even Gwynira plainly considered Naia her equal, or close to it. But Klement saw her merely as a curiosity—or, worse, as a *tool*, a lever through which to exert pressure on Einar. And he did not even bother to hide the transactional nature of his regard beyond the tiniest efforts at superficial politeness. "I don't know how the Imperial guilds are run, but they don't seem to spend their time teaching their scholars much in the way of manners."

Zanya made a rude noise as they resumed walking. "From what Sachi has told me about Sorin, he certainly seems like the type of man to reward arrogance. Not that I'd know with Klement. Last time we were here, he seemed to go out of his way to avoid us. Even Sachi, and she usually charms everyone eventually."

He had likely disregarded them because he did not think they would be useful to him—a laughable misapprehension, to be sure, but what else could Naia expect? Klement continued to pester Einar about Petya, never seeming to grasp how close he'd often come to inciting Einar's wrath. The man obviously wasn't as smart as he thought he was.

Naia almost said as much, but there were too many eyes and ears around them. So she tucked her arm through Zanya's and murmured, "Lucky you, to have enjoyed such peace."

Zanya's laughter rang through the clear morning air, accompanying their progress down the path.

The people of Jamyskar were amazed and more than a little confused to see a line of gods filing into their village. But their confusion quickly gave way to a mix of relief and joy as the members of the High Court rolled up their sleeves—proverbial *and* literal—and got to work.

Elevia started with a quick survey of the various tasks already in progress, then directed those of her friends who were most suited to assist. The rest of the High Court, presumably accustomed to being bossed around in this manner, simply followed her orders.

Some of the structures on the beach had been completely obliterated in the attack. People were dismantling those and sorting through the debris to see what could be repurposed and what had been lost. They pulled nails out of shattered planks and beams, and set aside intact windows along with the rest of the wood that could be saved.

Other buildings were damaged but still standing. Ash crouched next to one, examining its compromised stone foundation. As a handful of villagers watched in awe, he touched the cracked stone. Dust billowed up as the stone shifted, knitting itself back together at his command.

The awe was a commonality, and it did not seem to matter to the villagers whether the gods employed magic or simply picked up a tool and began to use it. Ulric hung off the side of a building by one arm as he busily swung a hammer with his other hand. Meanwhile, Inga had gathered a group of children, and their delighted laughter joined the busy sounds of sawing as the Witch pulled an endless number of chocolates from her small reticule.

The people of Jamyskar held the efforts of both in equal regard.

Naia paused in her own work. She'd taken over the task of picking up sharp little bits of glass where heat and magic had melted the sand. It was too dangerous for the locals to do without heavy protective gloves, which not many of them had. She had been careful, of course, but had still sliced her fingers half a dozen times. Though the cuts healed quickly, blood still smudged the sack she held.

A group had clustered on the beach to set up a makeshift kitchen to feed the crowd. On one side, tables had been hastily constructed of doors and planks set across pillars of stone. On them, the fishermen had laid out the day's catch for cleaning, and Elevia had joined them. She might have been a staggeringly gifted military general, but she was also the *Huntress*. She deftly gutted a fish and tossed the refuse to a nearby dog, whose backside wiggled furiously as he snatched his prize from midair. Then Elevia waved her knife and said something that elicited a burst of uproarious laughter from the fishermen.

Just down the beach, a huge cauldron had been set over a crackling fire. Dianthe was listening intently as she helped an ancient man tend the bubbling pot. Naia watched as they added a huge mound of chopped vegetables to the stew. Though it had been made with fresh catch, it smelled very much like the salted fish stew that Petya—and Naia—favored. Maybe the recipe had even originated here, in this tiny village, and was still being shared from cook to cook as the generations passed.

The very ground beneath Naia's feet began to shake, and a moment later, Arktikos rumbled by. He was positively *huge* in his polar bear form, something she had not had the time to fully appreciate during the attack, and surprisingly fast, even as he hauled a sled piled high with shattered stones, ruined roofing, and splintered boards.

He pulled it up a small hill to a clearing that overlooked the beach. There, the Phoenix had already conjured their cleansing fire. Nyx glanced down and lifted a hand in greeting, one Naia gladly returned. She understood the Phoenix, and believed in the justice of their mission. They were dedicated to seeing wrongs righted and damage not simply repaired but *undone*, a truly noble goal.

If Naia had walked out of fire instead of the ocean near Seahold, she could easily have followed the Phoenix.

Aleksi led a small group of men and women up the hill to help unload the sled. Together, they tossed the debris into the heart of the blue and silver fire, where it burned in that fascinating way that made Naia think of renewal instead of destruction. There was nothing left behind, no ashes or scorched places where the debris once blazed.

The giggling grew into shrieks of laughter and excitement. A smiling Sachi had joined Inga in entertaining the children, and was making small toys and trinkets fall out of the sky. The children hurried about, utter joy on their chocolate-smeared faces, chasing the baubles and trying to catch them before they hit the scrubby sand.

Even Gwynira and Isa were having a good time. Isa had taken over the small forge at the heart of the village. With Gwynira's help, she had been hammering hot iron into nails and hinges and latches all morning. Their lighthearted chatter and laughter drifted out of the smithy, punctuated by the sharp rings of Isa's hammer. A thin, shimmering veil of protective magic surrounded them both, an aura that looked like the combined midnight starshine sparkle of both Sachi and Zanya.

It all seemed painfully familiar—the bustle of activity, the smell of the stew, the hints of magic mixed with very practical sweat and labor. Even the *sounds* felt like echoes, the hammer blows and shouts and laughter all bouncing around in Naia's head, making it swim dizzily.

Then there were the people. Mostly, they had curtsied and bowed as they walked past, but left her to her own devices, as if they had been instructed not to bother her. But a few had approached her anyway, to ask if she needed anything or to deliver small gifts of woven bracelets and carved seashells.

Every query and offering—for that was what they were, Naia realized—had been accompanied by a fervently whispered prayer.

"It's uncanny," a low voice murmured from just behind her. She turned to find Einar, stripped to the waist and wiping sweat from his brow with his discarded shirt.

He had said something, Naia knew that much, but she could not recall what it had been. For a moment, all her brain agreed to register was miles of bare, sweat-slicked skin, along with the fact that all she had to do to touch it was reach out.

Finally, she managed to clear her throat as she tossed another bit of glass into her rough-woven sack. "What?"

"How familiar this village is."

Had he also been experiencing the same dizzying sense of having been here before? No, surely it was different for him, a secondhand but decidedly real knowledge of the place. After all, this was his heritage, whether he had lived it or not. "Petya must have taken so much of this with her."

"She did." His gaze drifted over the busy activity that blanketed the village. "We settled down for the first time when I was . . . oh, maybe fourteen or fifteen? It was a little village on the coast north of the Blasted Plains. Mostly fishermen and others who made their living from the sea. Our little cottage could have been one of these."

Naia could easily picture it in her mind, and she wondered if that was what she had been experiencing—a million tiny bits of memory, all blended together and snagging on the sharper edges of this moment.

"I've been feeling the same way." She bent, uncovered another wicked bit of glass, and carefully pried it up out of the sand. "There must be so many little places just like this, dotted all along the coasts. I think I even remember some of them."

Einar crouched down and stirred his fingers idly through the sand. "I've seen dozens over the years. Hundreds. But this island . . ." He paused as his fingers found a bit of glass and worked it free before lifting it up to her. "I suppose you understand better than anyone how odd it feels to remember a place you've never been."

She had to smile at that. "Yes, I do." Then, though she did not decide to do it, she found herself asking, "Do you think you could be happy, Einar? Staying here and being their king?"

He didn't answer right away. His fingers returned to the sand, but instead of sifting through it to search for more glass, he traced an absent-minded spiral into its surface. "I don't know," he said finally. "When we're in the palace, surrounded by the court? The idea seems absurd. I'm no kind of ruler. But out here, working with the villagers?"

Naia's gaze locked on the rough spiral. A buzzing sound filled her ears, broken only by the thumping of her heart.

"It feels good to help the people."

The words echoed, piercing sharply through the hum in her ears. Naia shook her head to clear it, but the action blurred Einar's face. When her eyes focused once more, he was no longer himself but the man she'd seen on the ship—older, lankier. He knelt on the beach in front of her, silver braids woven with shells hanging down around his weathered face as he traced a nautilus shell in the sand.

Her heart convulsed, splintering an ache through her chest so strong that it stole her breath. Her vision blurred again, this time from the unshed tears that welled in her eyes. She blinked, and the tears flowed down her cheeks.

Einar stared up at her, concern shadowing his features, but it was *him* once more as he rose and touched her wet cheek. "Naia?"

Across the way, Zanya called Einar's name.

Naia covered his hand with hers and smiled, though the effort felt shaky and unconvincing. "They need you."

"They can bloody well wait," he rumbled, his brow creased with worry. "Are you all right?"

"I'm *fine*." It was only a small lie. The buzzing sound in her ears had begun to fade, and she could now clearly see only what was before her and nothing else. She dried her cheeks and pushed lightly at his shoulder. "Go."

He stroked her cheek, but when Ash shouted his name this time, he sighed and dropped a kiss to her forehead. "Call if you need me."

He jogged over to where Ash and Zanya had been working on replacing the damaged roof of a dwelling large enough to house several families. They had removed the broken beams and rafters, and now needed to place new ones. They conferred briefly, then Zanya vanished in a swirl of shadows. Gasps and a few scattered cheers accompanied her reappearance on the home's roof.

Ash and Einar gripped the center beam and began to heave it up. The muscles in Einar's arms and back bunched with the strain, and Naia's cheeks began to heat.

"You're blushing, little nymph."

Aleksi's whisper shivered up Naia's spine. "So are you."

"Guilty." He made the word sound positively delicious—though not as delicious as what he said next. "But I sincerely hope he does not tire himself out. I have plans for the two of you tonight."

She looked over at him, grateful that no traces of tears remained on her face. "Oh? Please, do elaborate."

But of course Aleksi saw. He always did. His suggestive smile vanished, the heat replaced by warmth as he cradled her face between his hands. "What has happened? Are you hurt?"

"No, I—"

A crash and a commotion nearby commanded their attention. An older woman had dropped a heavy bucket near Sir Jaspar, and dirty water had splashed onto his polished boots. Jaspar, who had very obviously loathed every moment of the day and accomplished absolutely nothing, lost control of his temper.

"You useless waste!" he shouted at the cowering woman. "These are Rehesian leather! They cost more coin than you'll ever touch in your lifetime, but I'll see to it—"

So many things happened, all at once. Indignant protests rose in a cacophony of sound that still could not drown out the woman's sobs, and Naia and Aleksi started toward the ugly scene just as others did the same. But before anyone could draw near, Jaspar raised one hand above and behind his head.

Preparing to strike.

No.

Blood thundered in Naia's ears, an angry sound like howling winds and crashing waves. The entire world seemed to slow as she dragged in ragged breaths and willed the burning rage in her breast not to explode.

It did not work. A volcano erupted inside her, burning her alive as it flowed outward in a very real, very tangible burst of heat. Jaspar flew off his feet, yanked into the air by an unseen force, and slammed against the side of a rebuilt hut. He hung there, expensive boots kicking helplessly as his reddened face contorted with fear.

Everyone froze. Only Naia continued to advance. Hot wind stirred her hair as it lifted her off the ground and carried her forward, toward the old woman, who had crumpled to the ground in a silent, staring heap.

Naia pulled her back to her feet, the action effortless in a way that she did not understand and had no time to ponder. All she could feel was a steadying warmth that flowed from her hands and into the woman's frail arms.

"You will be fine," Naia assured her. "No one will hurt you."

Especially not Jaspar. Naia turned on him, and the soothing warmth flared and fled, melting once more into incandescent fury. The horrible man stared at Naia, his eyes just as wide as the old woman's, but with fear instead of awe.

"You already do every other cruel and dismissive thing you want," Naia told him. "One thing you will not do is *touch my people.*"

"I don't—"

Naia squeezed, her entire body trembling as she cut off his air.

She only planned to do it for a moment, because she could not bear to hear his justifications or excuses. But that moment stretched into several, and he deserved this *so much*. For his terrible attitudes toward the locals, for his fervent belief that an accident of birth had made him worthy of *anything*, much less *everything*—

"Naia, love." The voice surrounded her. Suffused her. "Either release him or end it."

End it. The words made no sense until she realized that Jaspar's face had gone purple, and his tongue protruded from his mouth. She relaxed her grip with a startled cry, and he dropped to the ground, gasping and choking.

"It's all right," the ethereal voice murmured. "I'm here."

Aleksi. She turned toward him, and all she could see was *light*. Every color that had ever or *would ever* exist, dazzling and unformed and wrapping all around her. It gentled the rage, made her think of fond, easy laughter and the quiet, intimate hours before dawn when everything was still and peaceful.

Perfume filled the air, and petals floated down around them—soft pink and red and yellow—as she clung to him.

"Naia!"

This voice wasn't ethereal; it was *visceral*, crashing thunder and the silence of the deep. Storm and sea, as familiar to her as her own name. It was a part of her very soul, the reason she had torn free of the Dream in the cool dark of the ocean. The place that belonged to him.

Bronzed skin. Silver braids. And the bluest eyes Naia had ever seen, like a perfect, cloudless summer sky.

Theron.

The memories crashed over Naia, and she floated where they carried her, unable to do anything else lest she drown. She drifted through the haze of the very beginning, when the seamounts had boiled up, parting the ocean to make way for her island. Hot and green, teeming with wildlife and later with people. Her children, whom she had grown to love with a ferocity matched only by those final days of turmoil, when the quaking earth and roiling seas had threatened to wash away everything she had ever cherished.

Then, the end.

She stumbled into Theron's arms, a thousand questions tearing at her—and only one that truly mattered. It tumbled out of her, over and over, until the words barely made sense. "Where have you been?"

He stared down at her in agonized confusion, blue eyes one heartbeat and brown the next. Of course he did not know. He could not, because this was *Einar*. He had never followed her across leagues of water or chased her through the verdant jungle or stolen a kiss under the summer stars.

He did not remember her.

He did not remember her.

Pain pulsed from her in a wave that stirred the petals blanketing the ground. Instantly, Naia pulled it back, ashamed of herself—for her loss of control, and for letting herself be swept away by sadness. What did it matter if Einar did not remember, if he was *here*, safe and whole?

She took a calming breath and let her power wash outward again, this time redolent with the essence of Rahvekya. This was not a place of pain, but of hope. She remembered that now, and eventually so would he.

Until then, all the memories, the joys and regrets, were hers to bear.

A low rumble of voices rose all around them, and Naia looked to see the villagers kneeling. Even the oldest among them clutched at others and struggled to take one knee. The rumble resolved into voices—"by Her grace" and "through Her blessed intercession." They had been murmuring these prayers of thanks to Naia since her initial arrival to the island, but now she recognized them for what they truly were.

Pleas.

For a moment, Einar stared at her in utter shock, then he hit the ground on both knees as understanding washed over him. His expression changed, all the affection he carried for her subsumed by sheer *awe*. He gazed up at her reverently, the way a sobbing sailor would eye his first piece of solid land after being adrift at sea for months.

She wanted to lift him to his feet, to urge him never to kneel, not for her. To somehow convince him that she was the same person he'd lain in bed with only hours before.

The words died on her tongue.

Aleksi knelt beside Einar, one arm around his shoulders and a few whispered words in his ear. Naia heard them, though she should not have been able to, just as she saw them take form on Aleksi's lips.

Your goddess.

Someone clutched at Naia's elbow, and she turned to find that one man had risen and approached her. Tears streamed down his pale cheeks, tracking clean paths through the soot that smudged his face.

The blacksmith, whose forge Isa had borrowed for the day.

"I'm sorry," he sobbed. "I'm so sorry, my lady. I did not believe—"

"It's all right, Larus." She grasped his hands, which quaked in hers from the sheer force of his tears, and smiled up at him. "Neither did I."

Others had followed his lead, taking to their feet and crowding around her. Naia tried her best to connect with them all—to touch their hands or catch their gazes, to repeat their names or answer their desperate questions.

To soothe their pain.

They had been awaiting her return for thousands of years. Hoping beyond hope, telling stories of her in secret. Risking their safety and freedom to keep the memory of her alive so they could pass on that hope to their children.

This was the least she could do.

Chapter Seven

I sometimes wish I had lived during the years when the storm god first came to our shores. How thrilling it must have been to watch their courtship, to watch as our goddess tamed the storm itself. But the priestess of that time will never know the joy that I do, of watching a love that has bloomed across years beyond counting. It is beautiful.

The lost journal of High Priestess Tona

To Aleksi, the story of the goddess's demise had always sounded like a legend.

Everyone knew that she had raised a wall of water to protect her people and held it for three days and three nights, until the mortal danger had passed, sacrificing her own life in the process. The tale had a certain inescapable poetry to it, the kind that spoke of generations of storytellers gently nudging events to fit a beautiful narrative.

Reality was rarely so accommodating.

He had not doubted, not for a moment, that their goddess had died while trying to save the people of Rahvekya. But he had imagined it to be a far more sudden and violent, even humble end, one that would not make such a pretty ballad to be sung in the taverns. The idea of anyone, even a god, standing for that long—bleeding power, slowly dying—was unfathomable.

Or perhaps Aleksi simply had not *wanted* to fathom such a painful thing.

And so the goddess had perished, and her people had not. Aleksi had assumed that, in their quest to glean some meaning from such unthinkable tragedy, they had turned her end into *myth*.

Now, watching Naia smile and offer reassurances in the midst of an unending crush of ecstatic villagers, he finally understood. She pulsed with power, but also with exhaustion and a raw vulnerability that made his chest ache. But she would not leave a single soul unacknowledged.

The story of her slow-moving death could very well be true, because she would give and give and *give* until she had nothing left.

The others—Gwynira, Isa, even the rest of the High Court—hovered, strangely reluctant to interfere in this reunion. In an instant, Naia had claimed the ultimate authority over this place, a long-standing stewardship that no one else, even another god, could hope to match. They would not stop her, even for her own good.

Fuck that.

Aleksi grasped Einar's arm. The other man still looked dazed, but Aleksi turned him until their gazes clashed. "After what's happened, she needs to rest, Einar."

His expression cleared, and he nodded firmly. "Of course."

Einar waded into the throng of devotees, anxious to dispel the crowd. It was clear that only his status as Crown-Prince of Rahvekya kept them from shoving him aside and continuing their pursuit of Naia's attention.

Then she swayed on her feet and nearly fell, eliciting horrified gasps from the crowd, and Einar's voice rose enough to carry clearly. "That's enough for now."

He wrapped her arm around his shoulders, his around her waist, and half carried her toward Aleksi, who met them midway.

Where can we go, and quickly? He was opening his mouth to ask Einar when Naia's free hand seized his.

"I know a place," she murmured, her voice all vine-covered cliffs and dry seashells and sand-smoothed stone.

The world fell away.

Aleksi braced himself for the inky blackness and the disorientation and the sick lurch in the pit of his stomach, all the things that knocked him flat when Zanya carried him through the Void.

But this was not the Void. It was dark, yes, but more like a warm, moonless night. It felt *close*, as if he dwelled for the moment not in empty nothingness but in a careful, protective embrace.

As if he was being spirited away to safety.

They came back to the world in a secluded glade, beside a deep-blue pool that bubbled and steamed lightly. Despite the chilly air, lush trees in full leaf bent all around them to shade the mossy bank.

Naia knelt beside the pool and trailed her fingers through the water. "That was abrupt. I'm sorry."

"Don't be," Einar hurried to tell her, despite his breathlessness. "What is this place?"

Naia stared up at him, and her hand trembled in the water. She quickly rested it on her lap and took a deep breath. "The island created it for us. A long, long time ago."

Then she could not mean for the three of them. "Who is *us*?" Aleksi asked softly.

"Me and Theron. The storm god," she clarified.

"The Kraken," Einar breathed.

A light that looked almost like hope lit Naia's eyes. "Yes."

But Einar's eyes were clouded with confusion. "This is on no map of Rahvekya that I've ever seen."

"It wouldn't be. There are no paths that lead here. It can only be reached through the aether."

The word was unfamiliar to Aleksi. Perhaps she meant through the Dream, only that wasn't quite right. The darkness that had surrounded him had not felt like Zanya or the Void, but neither had it felt like Sachi. It had felt . . .

Like Naia.

The truth struck him, hard, and he hit his knees before her, heedless of the unyielding stone beneath the moss. "You *are* the island."

"I do not know which of us came first." She drew her knees up to her chest and folded her arms around her legs. "I would tell you if I did. Maybe . . . we have always existed together, as one."

Einar rubbed a hand absently over his chest, as if soothing an ache. "Petya always said that when the first people came to these shores, the goddess welcomed them. They settled here because they knew she would keep them safe. As for what came before . . ." He shook his head. "There are so many stories, each one different."

"I see," Naia whispered.

"But one thing never changes: the goddess is the Mother of Rahvekya." He stared down at Naia, soft wonder dawning once more on his face. "*You* are the Mother of Rahvekya."

She smiled. "It was a word, a dynamic, that the people understood." Her expression dimmed. "And it was better than some of the other things they wanted to call me."

Aleksi took her hand. "Such as?"

"Creator. Savior." Her voice lowered to a grim whisper. "Ruler."

No, Naia would not have wanted that. She was too circumspect, too thoughtful, and she cared too much about independence and the freedom to choose one's path.

And now Aleksi understood. Someone as young and new as Naia should have required time to learn the wisdom and necessity of such things. But she had simply arrived with those beliefs etched firmly on her heart.

Just as she had arrived with all that *power*. By all rights, it should have been raw strength, coarse and clumsy. But she had exercised a delicate and precise command over her abilities that Aleksi had rarely seen. Gods of a thousand years or more could not wield their powers the way she had. And she had stood fast during the battle against Sorin and his Empire, holding the line with fierce determination when even a seasoned soldier might have fled.

Her wide-eyed appreciation for and curiosity about the world, he had chalked up to eager inquisitiveness. Now, he could instead see in her the sheer joy of rediscovery. She behaved as though she was visiting a place she remembered, but only vaguely, so that seeing once more the exact shapes and colors of stone and earth was a wonder too glorious to bear.

Even the memories she'd brought with her from the Dream marked her as an ancient soul. She had so many, more than Aleksi ever had, and he had always remembered feelings and sensations more than events and places and skills. Did she bring more of the material details with her because she had lived before, and as such possessed the context required to understand and remember them in a way that he never had?

He lifted her hand, and a warm breeze caressed his skin as he pressed his lips to her palm. "You make so much more sense to me now, little nymph."

She laughed softly and curved her fingers to cup his cheek. "Did I mystify you before?"

"More than a little," he admitted readily. "Not that I minded, not one bit."

Einar sank down beside them, still looking stunned. "Does this mean . . . Do you remember? The truths behind all the myths?"

"They're not myths. Not to me." Sadness wreathed Naia, and at first Aleksi thought it was the ache of memory. But the pain intensified somehow when she looked at Einar, even as she offered him an encouraging smile. "What do you want to know?"

Einar did not answer. He seemed lost in all the endless possibilities, struggling to decide where to even start. The silence stretched on for so long that Aleksi almost stepped in, but then Einar squared his shoulders. "They called my mother goddess-touched. Petya said that was why she was so much stronger than a mortal man. But I've never understood what it *meant*."

"The title started out as a blessing," Naia told him. "A physical ward, rather like when Aleksi bestowed his protection on young Queen Anikke. It allowed the recipients to access the power of the island in a very small way." She paused and laughed softly, as if to herself. "The island must have continued to honor those blessings, even after I was gone."

"It did." Einar touched her hand, folding his fingers around hers with the reverence of a man touching a sacred relic. "If it hadn't, I would not be here. Petya only escaped with me because my mother had the strength to stop an army on her own."

No wonder Einar could not seem to find his footing in the face of Naia's awakening. In an instant, she had become not only his future, but the entirety of his past, as well.

Naia opened her mouth, then closed it again and rose. Once on her feet, she kicked off her shoes and began to slowly unbutton the bodice of her dress. She let the garment fall across Einar's knees, then shed the rest of her clothes.

For a long moment, she simply stood there, naked, with dappled sunlight and shadow caressing her curves. Then she slipped into the rock-lined spring, submerging herself completely.

When she broke the surface of the pool once more, her hair and skin steamed in the frigid air. Wordlessly, she held out her hand to Einar.

Just as quietly, he rose and tugged off his boots. His shirt had been left behind, abandoned on the village beach, but he stripped off his pants without taking his eyes off of Naia. The same intriguing juxtaposition of light and shadow played across his skin as his muscles flexed with anticipation, then followed him into the water, where Einar reclaimed Naia's hand and pulled it to his lips for a soft kiss.

Then they both turned expectantly toward Aleksi.

Though the water looked warm enough, the air around it was as frigid as the rest of the island. He was feeling better than he had since before having his connection to the Dream wrenched from him, but he could not tell how *much* better.

Finding out that he was still physically weak by dying of hypothermia while naked with his lovers after exiting a bubbling pool would just be sad.

So he gently shook his head. "I'm not sure I'm up to it."

Naia tilted her head in silent challenge. "Do you trust me, my lord Lover?"

"You know I do, love."

"Then join us."

Aleksi felt oddly self-conscious as he undressed. Not about being naked, but about shivering under their gazes while goose bumps pebbled his skin and his lips turned blue.

Except . . . that did not happen. The chill air seemed strangely distant as he dropped the last of his clothes to the rocky ledge and slipped into the water. Even his now-wet skin, above the waterline and exposed to the cold air, felt warm.

Naia smiled and stroked his jaw with her thumb. "Goddess-touched, remember?" she murmured. "Who in this world now can carry that mantle more truly and faithfully than you and Einar?"

Startled, Aleksi met her eyes. "Surely you don't mean—"

"Yes, I do." The air stirred around them, hot and redolent with the scent of tropical flowers. "The island protects me, and the two of you are my heart. It will shelter you."

Einar brushed her wet hair back from her forehead. "It always has."

The words served as a stark reminder. They had all known that Einar belonged here, on this island. His parents had lived and died to protect it. Rahvekya was his legacy.

Now, with the morning's revelations, it seemed that it was Naia's, as well.

The two of them shared a destiny, and there was no room for Aleksi in it. Even the warm, steaming pool was small, as if the island had created it for only two. Which, of course, it had.

For the goddess and the Kraken.

Einar nuzzled Naia's jaw and cheek before resting his forehead against hers. As affectionate physical contact went, it was almost chaste. Yet it somehow managed to be more intimate than a kiss.

When Aleksi had considered leaving them before, it had been out of sad necessity, because he had been anticipating his own death. His absence could still wind up being no less necessary . . . and no less tragic.

Because Aleksi loved them both too much to stand in the way of their shared destiny.

Naia's hand brushed his hip beneath the water, driving away his melancholy thoughts in a rush of liquid heat. Aleksi moved closer and wrapped his arms around them both.

The time for difficult decisions *would* come, but it was not here, and it was not now.

So he sought Naia's ear with his lips and whispered, "Welcome back to the world, goddess."

Chapter Eight

The final person to hold the prestigious position as head of the Queen's Guard was Petya of Stenyar. Official Imperial history tells us that Petya perished with the rest of the castle defenders in foolhardy defiance of General Akeisa's offer of amnesty to those who threw down their swords. Local legends, however, attest that she escaped with the infant prince. Perhaps that is why Petya and its derivations remain one of the most popular names among locals even now, more than two thousand years later.

Akeisa: An Overview of Prominent
Historical Figures
by Guildmaster Klement

Though Einar was loath to give the Empire credit for anything, even he had to admit that the deep-water harbor that sat beneath Gwynira's palace was a marvel of innovative construction. Even Dianthe's harbor at Seahold—the most sophisticated in the Sheltered Lands, with ramps leading to floating docks that rose and fell as the moons tugged at the tides—could not compare. The village that served the harbor had still been built on solid ground, after all.

Here, they had built on the ocean itself.

The steps were the most fascinating part. They connected the main stone landing to the massive floating platforms. At the highest tide, it was only a few steps down to the first dock. Now, nearing low tide, the platforms had dropped with the water to reveal several dozen wide steps. Einar wasn't entirely sure how they worked, but he suspected Dianthe would find out before she returned home.

The first platform held the office of the harbormaster, and a guard who bowed deeply to Einar as he passed. Ramps branched off in all directions, leading to floating warehouses, berths for smaller boats, shops, and even inns. He crossed over onto the next platform, and music from the tavern reached him. There were three such establishments, apparently, in the massive sprawl that made up the harbor—his crew had sampled them all and found their personal favorites. Other vendors sold food from little stalls, cooked fresh from the haul brought in that morning.

The deeper into the labyrinth he went, the larger the ships got. Fishermen, traders, merchants . . . even a few that seemed to ferry folks across the Ice Queen's Strait to the Port of Kasther on the other side—though the captains of those ships had clearly seen a stark drop in interest. Einar imagined the chaos in the Empire had disrupted many businesses.

The Kraken had delivered them to the main landing in full ceremony upon their arrival, but now it floated in a place of honor at the end of a long, narrow dock reserved for Gwynira's personal, long-term guests. His burly third mate was the only one on the deck, lounging with his feet up on a crate and a book open on his lap. He looked up when Einar stepped onto the deck, and tossed him a jaunty salute. "Captain."

"Brynjar. Everything quiet?"

"More than usual." Brynjar grinned. "They're over at the Anchor Ale House again. Silvio has struck up a friendship with the owner, and the whole lot of them drink for free on tales of the Kraken's greatest sea battles."

Einar tried not to wince. He trusted his crew to protect his personal privacy with their lives, but he did *not* trust them not to encourage the locals in their awe of their lost crown-prince. And those who had been with him for centuries—like Silvio—had plenty of stories of Einar's private war against the Empire. Einar imagined that the crowds who would flock to hear those legends would fill the tavern coffers and more than make up for the fact that his crew had hearty appetites for ale.

Then again, once news of Naia's display this morning spread, Einar suspected the locals would be far more interested in tales of their goddess. The crew had plenty of *those*, too, after watching her fight against Sorin in the final battle of the last war. The tavern owner would be beside himself once he found out—and Einar suspected the only reason the harbor wasn't buzzing with the news already was thanks to Naia's new and unorthodox methods of travel.

He'd still do well to hurry if he wanted to be the one to tell Petya. News this momentous would move as swiftly as those reindeer. "Is Petya in her cabin?"

"Last I heard, she was."

"Good." He clapped his third mate on the shoulder as he passed him. "Make sure you take a chance to enjoy free drinks, too. The youngsters can keep watch."

"I don't mind it." Brynjar picked up his book with a satisfied smile. "It has been far too long since I had a chance to enjoy a book."

True enough. Life had been hectic for the crew of the Kraken in the long moons leading up to that final, desperate battle in the heart of the Empire—and equally busy in its aftermath. Trouble would come again soon enough, which Brynjar knew well. So Einar left him to his story and made his way to the narrow hallway where his officers enjoyed more comfortable quarters.

Petya's cabin was at the end, the door slightly ajar to indicate the crew could come to her with questions. Einar still knocked, and waited for her clear "Come in!" before pushing it wide.

His first mate's home on the ship was surprisingly spacious, with a generous bed, a comfortable chair, a tidy desk, a screen hiding a hip bath, and a table large enough for several people to share a meal with her. Two large portholes above the bed were thrown open to let in light and the fresh sea breeze. Between them hung a framed painting of a much younger Petya standing on the cliffs of this very island, gazing down in adoration upon a woman in the distinctive robes of a Rahvekyan priestess, with flowers wound in her curly red hair.

The Kraken's cartographer had the rare gift of being able to pull memories from the people she touched and coax ink to render them on paper. The original painting of Petya on her wedding day had been lost when the island fell, but Nusaiba had recreated it as a gift that had become Petya's most prized possession.

It wasn't the only memory of this island that adorned Petya's cabin. Shelves held seashells and brass tokens. One wall had a weaving of a still ocean night made of what Einar now recognized as Rahvekyan tundra cotton—its deep-teal hues as vibrant as the day she'd found it a thousand years past. One shelf had a miniature that Bexi had carved from driftwood—Petya had told him once that it was his parents' castle. Clean stone, strong lines—a fortress more than the fantastical palace Gwynira had raised in its place, but Einar imagined he would have preferred its unpretentious simplicity.

This entire cabin was practically a shrine to a world that waited only steps from this ship. But Einar knew better than to invite her onto the island. Petya would not set foot upon its shores while an interloper still ruled. Her grief was simply too vast.

Not for the first time, Einar tried to imagine what it had been like that night—Petya's last on her beloved island. The castle aflame. The queen she served fallen. Chaos had reigned as the priests tried to organize the people to flee, overseen by the High Priestess—Petya's wife.

Had there even been time for a hasty goodbye, or had duty torn them apart without even that simple closure?

What had come next must have been even worse. A fast gallop into the mountains on the giant reindeer native to the island. Realizing that Imperial soldiers had given chase. Twelve of the fiercest members of the Queen's Guard had been tasked with carrying the infant crown-prince to safety, but when the midnight moons rose over the newly conquered island, only Petya and Jinevra had survived to steer the tiny, fragile sailboat into the deadly tangle of icebergs known as the Storm God's Maze.

Einar, barely a week old, had made the journey strapped to Petya's chest, a prince who would never be crowned king.

Petya's voice broke into his thoughts. "I can't imagine you came here just to stare at my bookshelf."

He turned to where she sat in her comfortable chair, one leg hooked over the arm. Her cat was curled up in her lap, its too-knowing eyes glaring at him as if she *knew* already that he brought news that would shatter their peaceful afternoon.

The cat was not wrong.

Petya herself was eternal—wiry and strong even with wrinkles creasing her face and silver streaking her hair. A book rested on her knee with her finger marking her place—Klement's book, which Einar had asked one of the servants to deliver to her. He bought time by nodding to it. "Are you enjoying the book?"

The withering noise Petya made certainly did *not* sound like enjoyment. "That's one word for it."

So much for Guildmaster Klement's literary aspirations. "Is it that bad?"

"Oh, he got enough details correct, I suppose." She opened the book and paged through it, then adopted a haughty tone that dripped condescension. *"Many wonder why Akeisa lacks the comforts of civilized life seen throughout the rest of the Empire. The truth is that the common folk of the island prefer the rustic traditions of their ancestors . . ."* She made a disgusted noise. "The man certainly thinks highly of the Empire. And not so highly of us."

And that must be why the man scratched so relentlessly at Einar's nerves. He had no doubt that Klement's fascination with the island and its history was real enough, but his reverence held an uncomfortable proprietary edge. Paternalistic, even, as if even Einar's ancestors' greatest achievements had been little more than the tricks of a clever child, for which Klement offered only backhanded praise.

There was no denying that condescension seethed from the passage Petya had just read. Then again, a man who wore a giant gold medallion around his neck in token of his position was unlikely to be humble. "I suppose someone who grew up around whatever modern monstrosities the Empire was built upon would find the way the rest of us live . . . rustic."

"It's not just that." Her lips pursed. "He trained in the Empire, did he not? In the very shadow of the Emperor's own castle. It's clear that he's met many members of the Imperial Court. And he wrote this book while dining at Gwynira's table. He *must* know that the power of gods is real. But he speaks with such disdain of the goddess, as if she could not have been just as real."

Well, that was an opening if he had ever heard of one. He rubbed a hand over the too-long strands of his hair. Usually he'd have cut it by now, but he liked the way Naia ran her fingers through it. "That's actually why I'm here. Something happened today while we were helping rebuild Jamyskar."

Petya sat up at once, swinging her leg over the chair so that both boots were on the cabin floor. The cat yowled in surprised outrage, twisting to hit the worn carpet on all four paws. Einar was given another baleful look before the cat stalked past him, clearly tired of human follies.

Petya hardly seemed to notice. "Has Sorin attacked again?" she demanded.

"No, nothing like that," Einar reassured her. "It's just . . ."

His words trailed off. Petya stared at him, waiting, but Einar couldn't think of any way to say something so momentous. Perhaps if he worked up to it . . . "Gwynira's slimy bottom feeder of a seneschal tried to strike a villager, and Naia threw him against a wall."

Petya relaxed with a snort. "Good for her."

"She did it without using her hands."

"So she used water?" Petya studied him, her wrinkled brow furrowing. "No, that wouldn't have you so shaken. We all saw her fight against Sorin. What *happened*, Einar?"

"She almost choked him to death. I think she would have, if Aleksi hadn't stopped her. And she . . ." His mouth felt dry. He wished he had some of Brynjar's mead. Even one of the terrifying experiments. "She told Jaspar that he would not touch *her people*."

Petya went utterly still. Her unblinking gaze caught his, demanding silently that Einar just say the words.

So he did. "She remembers. She remembers all of it. This island, her life before. She's—"

"The goddess," Petya whispered.

"Yes," Einar agreed just as softly.

Einar wasn't sure what he had expected. A gasp of shock, perhaps. A cry of revelation. Tears, or laughter, or *something*, certainly—something momentous enough to mark a moment so huge it hardly seemed real.

But Petya simply stared past him and tilted her head to one side. He measured the endless silence in five slow breaths before she finally said, "Well, then."

All of his tension escaped in a disbelieving laugh. "The goddess you've worshipped your entire life appears before us, and that's all you have to say?"

"I *did* tell you, didn't I?" She reached for the leather cord around her neck and drew out her necklace—the ancient symbol of the goddess. What had once been a seashell cast in bronze had worn almost smooth from centuries of Petya's thumb rubbing over it like she did now. "That she reminded me of home. And I warned you not to trifle with her."

"I didn't," he protested.

Her faint smile melted away, replaced with *the look*—the one that she'd pinned him with after every teenage misadventure or childish rebellion, when he'd inevitably tried to cover his misdeeds with denials or justifications. It was still strong enough to heat his face, and make him grateful that no one else was here to find out that the terror of the seas, the Western Wall, the immortal Kraken himself, could be brought so easily to heel by one eyebrow quirked in disbelief.

But he *wasn't* a misbehaving youth anymore, and of all people in this world, Petya should know exactly where things stood. "I might have trifled with her to start," he acknowledged. "But what we're doing together now is *not* trifling, Petya. I'm not playing a game with Naia *or* with Aleksi. What we have—whatever else it is—it is real."

Her expression softened. "I know, my boy. And it is good. It is *right*. The Kraken—" Her voice hitched, the swell of emotion he'd expected finally rolling through her. "The Kraken is the goddess's lover again."

Einar was unprepared for the sudden yearning that rose from depths unknown to tangle around his heart. Fear came with it, tiny pinpricks that tried to seed doubt. Now that she remembered, *would* she find him lacking? She'd known the storm god in his prime. She'd loved a legend who was so much more than Einar had ever been. "A pale shadow of the Kraken, maybe," he corrected softly. "I hope I can live up to him."

"You will," Petya whispered, closing her fist around the bronze pendant. Her eyes had gone liquid, as if she was fighting back tears. Einar knelt before her, resting his hands on her knees. She was old but strong, like stone weathered by the tide. She'd looked the same for as long as he could remember, all lean muscle and weathered skin, and short hair that was a combination of silver and sun-bleached.

She'd spent most of her life away from it, but her bones were made of the bedrock of this island, the salt in her blood from its shores. "Do you want to come and see her?" Einar asked softly. "I know you didn't want to leave the ship, but maybe now—"

She pressed her fingers to his lips, cutting him off. "I'm not ready," she replied. "This island . . . *her* palace."

Gwynira's icy home had been constructed on the bluff where his parents' castle had once stood—the place where Petya had lost everything. Einar was unsurprised she still couldn't face setting foot inside. "I understand. I can bring Naia to the Kraken. I know she'd like to speak to you."

"When there's time." Sudden steel filled her eyes, and she cupped Einar's cheek. "It is even more important to find out who at court meant her harm. Power is dangerous, and if she has reclaimed her memories . . ."

Then she would be dangerous, indeed. The goddess had been ancient before the High Court took their first steps as Dreamers. A primordial force, like Sachi or Zanya. But Sachi and Zanya had been born as mortals who had to feel their way into their new powers. Naia now walked the world with unknown centuries of knowledge.

Eliminating her would be essential to their enemies now.

Abruptly, Einar was uncomfortable being away from the palace. Petya sensed it in his sudden stiffness, and nodded before urging him to his feet. "Protect her," she commanded. "That has always been the Kraken's duty. You've been preparing for this since the first time you took us to war against the Empire's armies."

Perhaps he had, at that. Petya had raised him on stories of the storm god and his fearsome alter-ego, the Kraken. Those had combined with his rage at the Empire and his grief at everything he'd lost.

In this world where they walked, dreams could come true. His dream had always been to be a strong protector for those in his care. Strong enough to shelter the people he loved from the Empire, as he could not have done as a mortal. That dream had made him what he was—fierce, dangerous. A monster hiding in the body of a man.

After nearly two thousand years, Einar was finally strong enough. And anyone at this court who meant his lovers harm would learn that truth swiftly enough.

He'd let them live just long enough to realize it. And then he'd do what monsters did.

Protect what was his.

Chapter Nine

It is simple enough to trace the Imperial concept of the Dream as a source of power to Emperor Sorin's roots in the Sheltered Lands. There are strong threads in common, including the idea of power as a defined duality. Creation and Destruction. The Dream and the Void. It is fascinating to compare this to ancient Akeisa, whose traditions evolved entirely independent of such influence. Their goddess embodied both creation and destruction.

Untitled manuscript in progress
by Guildmaster Klement

To welcome the High Court to her palace, Gwynira had decided to host a ball in their collective honor. The announcements had gone out early that morning, before their visit to the village, though a revised version appeared in the afternoon, clarifying that the ball was also meant to thank them for their generous help with the restoration efforts in Jamyskar.

Naia had anticipated the clarification. What she had not anticipated was being added to the list of honorees. But there it was, in sloping script, on thick, bleached cotton paper.

The Goddess Naia, Mother of Rahvekya.

She also had not expected the revised announcement to arrive with an endless string of servants, though she probably should have. They filed into the room, led by a stern-looking older woman wearing an apron. Naia was fairly certain the woman worked in the kitchens—the head cook, perhaps?

Naia greeted them as they watched her with fervent anticipation. "Hello."

The head cook squared her already broad shoulders and spoke with a formality that made Naia's chest ache. "My lady goddess. We have come to help you prepare for the ball." She gestured sharply, and a younger girl stepped forward with a large flat box cradled in her arms.

The head cook opened the lid, and Naia drew in a startled gasp. Inside, nestled on a bed of fur, was a bundle of gauzy teal fabric. A mere dress in name only, the featherlight confection had been embroidered with flowers in a multitude of colors. Instead of lying flat against the fabric, the edges of each flower curled up like actual petals. "This is *exquisite.*"

The pride that filled the older woman's eyes was too personal to attribute to delivery or even acquisition. "Thank you."

"You made this?"

"I did. My grandmother taught me."

"Your work honors her memory." Naia reached for the box, only to have it drawn just out of reach. She sighed. "Hilja—that is your name, yes?"

The pride bloomed. "It is, my lady."

"Very good." Naia waved a hand to the room. Though large, it was now rather full. "I thought that Lord Aleksi and Crown-Prince Einar might appreciate having the space to themselves, so I planned on getting ready with a couple of friends. Princess Sachielle and Lady Zanya?"

"At once." Another sharp gesture, and the entire contingent of servants filed back into the corridor. Hilja bowed her head to Naia. "Shall we?"

The servants followed as Naia headed toward the room that had been assigned to the Dragon and his consorts. She imagined she looked like a mother duck with an unending line of ducklings, and had to bite her tongue to quell a giggle.

The urge to laugh faded a bit when they reached the door. Hilja intercepted Naia's outstretched hand and hurried to knock. The woman seemed determined to spare Naia even the slightest effort, and she couldn't help but wonder if Hilja would insist on doing *everything* for her.

The door swung open. Zanya's lips twitched when she spotted Naia's entourage, but she did not comment, merely stepped back. "Naia. Come in and join us."

"Thank you," Naia murmured gratefully. "I thought it might be fun to get ready for the ball together, like old times."

Sachi leaned around the edge of a screen at the corner of the room, her wet hair swinging heavily. "Naia!"

Naia walked into the room, still somehow expecting the group of servants to hand over her dress and take their leave. Instead, they also entered the chamber, one by one. Since they had crowded Aleksi's much larger suite, the sight of them trying to squeeze into a far smaller space was almost laughable.

Naia had to do something. She pulled Hilja aside and lowered her voice. "Sachi and Zanya are particular friends of mine," she explained. "There are things I would like very much to discuss with them. Private things."

The older woman's stern expression softened. "Yes, of course you would, my lady." Then she frowned. "But who will see to your hair?"

"I'll manage, and Zanya will help me. She's quite adept."

Hilja nodded, then bit her lip. It was a surprising bit of vulnerability that suddenly made Naia see her the way she had once been—a young woman, skilled with a needle and eager to practice the beloved art she'd learned at her grandmother's knee.

But the harried Imperial clerk who had been in charge of assigning her a job had only asked if she knew her way around a kitchen. When she'd replied that she did, of course she did, her future had been determined. The Grand Duchess had need of a kitchen maid, and that was that.

So Hilja had worked, boiling kettles and scrubbing pots and chopping vegetables until her fingers had been raw and sore. She had worked so hard and learned so much that they'd had no choice but to advance her position until she was in charge of it all—the kitchens, the food shipments, the greenhouses.

And the first thing she did when the new maids arrived was always, *always*, to ask if they wanted to be there.

The vision, the *knowledge*, receded just as suddenly as it had washed over Naia, leaving her eyes stinging and a lump lodged in her throat.

Hilja stepped back, her stern mien falling back into place as she gestured silently to the other servants. They bustled out, leaving behind the box containing the dress. Then she turned to Naia. "If you've need of anything, ring the kitchens," she instructed. "I'll come at once."

The door had swung shut behind her before Naia managed to speak, but it was just as well. The woman did not need to hear her words so much as the island did. "Bless and protect you, Hilja."

"You handled that well," Zanya observed.

It didn't feel that way to Naia. "How do the two of you do it?"

"Firmly." Zanya smiled. "It's easier for me than for Sachi. I still make most people too nervous to hover."

Sachi emerged from behind the screen, wrapped in a soft white robe and rubbing a cloth over her dripping hair. "Surely this isn't new for you, Naia?"

"Yes and no." In the past, when she had belonged to this island and its people, they had been accustomed to her presence. She had been revered, but in a much more familiar way, devoid of loss and fear. In the minds of the Rahvekyan people, she had always been, and would always be.

These people knew better. They had grown up with only tales of her, tales that had been defined much more by her death than by her life. It left them strangely conflicted—overjoyed by her return, but reluctant to let her out of their sight.

And how could she blame them?

She finally confessed, "They're so happy to see me that begrudging their presence feels wrong."

Sachi made a soft noise of protest. "There's nothing wrong with wanting some time to yourself."

"You *need* that time," Zanya agreed as she pulled out a chair near the fire for Naia. "Sit and have a drink."

A tray of hammered-metal mugs was warming by the hearth. Naia lifted one, its dimpled surface hot under her fingers, and the scent of the drink inside tickled her nose as she took a sip of the familiar concoction. "Tealberry wine. It seems to be the only truly local drink they still serve."

Zanya tilted her head. "Still?"

"Oh, yes. Always hot, because it's bitter if you drink it any other way, and that can be somewhat of an acquired taste."

"So *that's* why they serve it warm." Sachi laughed. "I thought it was due to the climate."

"No." It had been served that way even when the island had been hot and muggy, with green everywhere and lazy insects bobbing all around.

For a heartbeat, sense memory threatened to overwhelm Naia, and she dragged herself back to the present. Sachi's hair still dripped onto her thin robe, and Naia set her mug aside. "Here. Let me dry your hair."

Sachi dropped onto a footstool in front of Naia's chair and draped the wet cloth across her lap. "Thank you. It's such a delicate task. One I can't quite seem to master."

Naia wasn't sure how that could be. Sachi was the essence of Creation itself. Whatever she wished could simply *become*. Reality bent to her will, not out of obedience or duty, but out of love.

Then again, perhaps she could not afford to waste precious energy on trifles like drying her hair. The firelight cast flickering shadows across Sachi's face, deepening the dark hollows under her eyes. Those were new, as was the hint of sadness that hung about her like fog over the water.

If possible, Zanya looked even worse. She nursed a mug of wine and stared into the heart of the fire, as if searching the dancing flames for answers—or respite. She did not seem sad, not exactly. Just exhausted.

"So." Working slowly and methodically, Naia began to coax heavy droplets of water from sections of Sachi's hair. The droplets gathered, hovering in the warm air beside them to await further instruction. "Tell me everything. What have you two been doing in the Empire?"

Sachi drew in a deep breath. "We've all been working very hard."

She was so careful to include the entirety of the High Court in the statement. But even before she'd regained her thousands of years of memories, Naia would have known better. The rest of the gods had been toiling day and night—of that, Naia had absolutely no doubt—but their efforts had to pale next to the burdens that Sachi and Zanya carried. Only the Dream and the Void had a hope of wrangling all the newly awakened magic that currently suffused Sorin's former empire.

At least Gwynira had spared the people of Rahvekya from sharing the same grim fate as the Imperial subjects on the mainland. She had refused to let Sorin steal their ability to the Dream for himself, saving them from generations of hopelessness and disconnection—not to mention the chaos that currently gripped the rest of the Empire.

For that alone, Naia owed her a great deal.

Sachi continued speaking, her voice subdued. "We've been traveling to places where newly awakened Dreamers and Voidlings are showing up. Sometimes, all we can do is control the damage after the fact. But when we can reach them in time . . ."

Zanya finished her wine. "I thought we knew the extent of it," she said softly. "We were making progress in Kasther. Sachi founded a sanctuary for the new Dreamers there, and watching them learn to Dream was *beautiful.* But I don't think I understood how massive the Empire is."

"There are so many," Sachi agreed. "How often have we crossed the Empire now, following the reports Elevia has managed to gather? I've lost count."

"So have I," Zanya admitted.

Naia finished drawing the last bit of water from Sachi's hair and dropped the sparkling mass of droplets into a basin by the hearth. Sachi thanked her with a squeeze of her hand before turning on the stool to face her.

She met Naia's gaze. "The good days are the ones where we can reach them in time and get through to them. When we can't . . ." Her voice cracked. "Those are the bad days."

Even speaking of their work had made them sadder, wearier. They were both bending beneath this weight, and that was the real danger here, wasn't it? There was no one to truly help them. Only Zanya could safely deal with those who had awakened to the Void. And even though the other members of the High Court stood a better chance of assisting Sachi with the new Dreamers, she felt every loss so keenly—and they could not prevent the emotional toll those losses were taking on her.

"It's an impossible task," Naia whispered.

"We know." There was no denial in the acknowledgment, only aching truth. But Sachi's lips turned up in a smile as she looked over at Zanya. "But we're good at those. Impossible tasks."

Zanya's soft smile matched her lover's, and *connection* pulsed between the two of them, filling the room more completely than the crush of servants who had accompanied Naia.

She knew that the nature of Sachi and Zanya's relationship still puzzled some in the Sheltered Lands. They weren't accustomed to the idea that creation and destruction walked hand in hand. To them, one was the essence of life, and the other an enemy. The notion that their beloved Dream could also be beloved of the Void was so foreign to them that it was simply unthinkable.

This, at least, was a comfort that Naia could give them.

"You know," she murmured, "the two of you have always made so much *sense* to me, and now I understand why. The people here have different beliefs than the ones common in the Sheltered Lands. The division between creation and destruction, the Dream and the Void—it isn't a division at all. They go together. You cannot have one without the other." She gestured between Sachi and Zanya. "Just like you. Two halves of the same whole."

Sachi closed her eyes only to have an errant tear escape and slide down her cheek. Zanya smoothed it away, a grateful smile curving her lips.

After a moment, Sachi inhaled on a ragged sigh. "Tell us more," she urged. "Are you Rahvekya's answer to the idea of Creation?"

"You mean, am I you?"

Sachi laughed. "Yes, I suppose I do."

"No," Naia told her, then grimaced apologetically. "The two of you don't exactly . . . exist."

Sachi's eyes went wide, and Zanya barked out a delighted laugh.

Naia hurried to explain. "Rahvekyans don't consider creation and destruction to be entities of their own. They're more like ubiquitous aspects of being. The inevitability of both life and death exist in—and are reflected by—everything."

"I see." Sachi wrinkled her nose. "But they *do* believe in gods."

"Of course. Though they tend to offer greater respect to the ones who command the elements versus representations of more . . . abstract concepts."

Zanya huffed out another low laugh. "No wonder the locals don't seem very impressed by us, Sachi."

But Sachi leaned forward, her eyes alight with interest. "So someone like Ash or Dianthe would take precedence over, say, Elevia or Aleksi?"

"On the face of it? Yes," Naia admitted. "The Rahvekyan people's lives are so greatly affected by the earth and sea that anyone with the ability to gentle either would be of great importance."

Sachi rested her chin on her hands. *"Fascinating."*

It felt so at odds with the customs of the Sheltered Lands that Naia almost apologized reflexively. "Someone like Elevia is recognized as a god, of course, but their respect would be for her knowledge and skills. She would be viewed much like a very experienced elder. The same applies to Aleksi and his diplomatic talents."

Sachi cocked one eyebrow. "And if they knew that one facet of Aleksi's power involved enabling new life to flourish in barren soil?"

"That would instantly elevate him in their estimation, possibly above Ash *and* Dianthe." Naia retrieved her wine from where it had sat, warming by the hearth. "Surviving the harsh physical elements means little if you're only going to starve instead."

"Fair enough," Zanya observed as she began to braid Sachi's hair.

Sachi seemed so eager to learn more that Naia offered another bit of Rahvekyan doctrine. "In addition to the Dream and the Void both existing in equal measure in all things, we also believe that everything has a soul—man, beast, plant, rock. That is how the island and I coexist. There is no concept of the inanimate here."

"The differences are so intriguing, are they not?" Sachi's brow furrowed. "They obviously believe in the rebirth of souls, as well."

"Actually, they don't." There, at least, Rahvekyan beliefs aligned very closely with those of the Sheltered Lands. The prevailing thought in both lands was that death was not simply an ending, but *the* ending. Your soul would be returned—in the Sheltered Lands, back to the Dream. And in Rahvekya . . . "Here, you are conveyed back into the essence of the world, of magic, of being. And you no longer exist as a discrete entity, separate from the whole."

"Very similar to the Sheltered Lands, then." Sachi sighed. "I don't know that I agree with it. I mean, I *know* that souls return to the Dream, but the notion that they stop existing as such? I cannot accept that, for I have *seen* otherwise." Her face brightened with a smile. "So why could they not come back? You did."

"Perhaps our Naia is a special case," Zanya suggested.

Naia very much doubted that, since Theron—*Einar*—had returned, as well.

"Or," Zanya continued, "maybe everyone got it just a little bit wrong."

"Does it really matter?" Sachi asked. "How and why you came back, that is? Or does it only truly matter that you did?"

It was a question Naia could not answer, not without spilling the truth of Einar's rebirth, as well. She was happy to be back, glad to have a second chance not only to live, but to love again. She desperately needed it, considering how she and Theron had left things between them.

But the *why* was even more complicated—and elusive. Had she been returned for a chance to address all the things left unfinished in her previous life? Or did the universe need something from her now?

It was a heavy thing to consider. "Everything is so different now," she murmured, and she wasn't even sure what she meant. That circumstances had changed since this morning? Or since her last existence?

Sachi leaned forward, suddenly intense. "The things you didn't know weren't less true just because you didn't know them. They were always there. By that same token, they are not *more* true now that you remember. You are who you have always been, Naia."

Naia inhaled a shaky breath that felt almost like a sob. "Yes, but I didn't *feel* it, Sachi. Certainly not the way I do now. Ignorance truly was bliss, in a way."

"It always is. Bliss, that is." The Dream nearly vibrated with power. "Right up until the moment it isn't, because the only way to survive— and protect those around you—is to know the whole truth."

"So it changes nothing?"

"No." Sachi slowly shook her head. "I think it changes everything. But it doesn't have to change *you*."

Naia could feel herself spiraling under the weight of all the *questions*. And, as much as she appreciated the chance to talk through them with the only people in the world who might understand, none of this belonged in an evening meant for diversion and celebration. They needed to rest, and to remind themselves of their reasons for fighting so hard.

Sachi and Zanya both needed that, and badly.

So Naia finished off her wine, set down her mug, and held out her hands. "You've both been very helpful *and* very polite, so I give you full leave to ask."

Sachi frowned as Zanya slipped the final pin into her elaborate hairstyle. "To ask what?"

Zanya nudged Sachi's shoulder as she gathered her brushes and combs and pins. "For the salacious details of her affair with Aleksi and Einar, obviously."

Sachi gasped in mock outrage. "We would never be so crass!"

Zanya laughed as she laid down her tools and positioned herself behind Naia's chair. "*I* might. We already know Aleksi is capable of turning a lover's world upside down, but Einar . . ." She leaned over Naia's shoulder and pinned her with an assessing look. "Have you *heard* the songs they sing about him in dockside taverns? His passions are legendary."

Naia's cheeks grew hot, and she covered them with her hands.

Now it was Sachi's turn to laugh. "Darling, you are—officially, now—far too old to blush."

Naia had no witty rejoinder. She *was* too old to blush, ages too old. But she didn't have a lot of experience with sex, even before she died and was reborn. She'd had exactly one lover in all her thousands of years on Rahvekya . . . and he just happened to be the current subject of conversation.

So she simply said, "Einar does everything with the same amount of focus and dedication."

Zanya made a noise that was half snort, half laugh—and *all* speculation. "Then I'm honestly surprised your knees still work."

"Zanya."

"What! He's impressive on the battlefield." She snorted again. "Though I'm fairly sure I could win a fight against him on land. I would not try it near the sea."

"I wouldn't fight him at all, not if I could help it." Sachi shook her head as she rose and headed for the wardrobe. "He has hidden depths, that one."

Startled, Naia froze. Did Sachi know? Could she see or sense it? Or had she plucked the truth about Einar straight from Naia's mind? She watched Sachi closely, but the other woman only winked at her in the mirror over the vanity.

Then Sachi spoke again, still watching Naia in the mirror. "And Aleksi?"

"Aleksi is . . ." Naia could not say more past the sudden lump in her throat. Everyone from the Sheltered Lands that associated with the High Court knew what it was like to have Aleksi focus on them like no one else existed in the entire world. But when he *really* did it, not out of simple, sincere interest but out of affection—out of *love*—

The feeling was impossible to articulate, and tears sprang to Naia's eyes.

Zanya squeezed her shoulder and leaned down to whisper, "You don't have to say anything."

Naia grasped her hand gratefully. By the time she blinked away the tears, Sachi was standing in front of her, smiling.

"Your hair looks wonderful," she said.

Naia lifted a hand to the locks that still cascaded around her shoulders. "It's only half done."

"No, it's perfect," Sachi countered, then pulled Naia to her feet. "Come. We still need to do Zanya's hair and finish getting ready, and you cannot be late for the ball. Aleksi and Einar have to see you in that *dress.*"

Naia clung to Sachi, gratitude tightening her throat. "Thank you," she whispered. "For being here. For listening. For *everything*."

Sachi's soft smile reflected the light that dwelled within her. "That's what friends are for."

Naia still did not know how to navigate the path forward. Nothing was settled . . . but perhaps it did not have to be. She would make it, as would Einar.

Because they weren't alone this time.

Chapter Ten

No lad, no lass, no lover fair

can hold him past the dawn.

There's nothing in this world he loves

for the Kraken's heart is gone.

Popular sea shanty

Aleksi's suite was empty when he went to dress for the ball. He suspected that Einar had dressed early and escaped to his ship; he'd had precious little time to spend with his crew of late. Naia, meanwhile, had likely gone to prepare for the evening with her treasured friends, Sachi and Zanya. The day had been rife with upheaval, and it would no doubt comfort Naia greatly to see some familiar faces.

It left Aleksi alone, with not even an errant servant for company, a situation that, frankly, delighted him. Back in the Sheltered Lands— and especially at his villa—there were always people milling about, seeking out his attention and approval. Here, when the locals milled about, they did so around Naia and Einar.

Here, he might be a god, but he was no one of consequence.

It was shockingly restful.

At least one of the palace staff *had* been here, though, because the huge hammered-metal tub had been filled with fresh water. Aleksi tested it with one finger and found that it had cooled past the point of comfort. His sigh of resignation turned into a groan, and he stared down at the shimmering, tepid surface in consternation.

He had spent too long in Elevia's quarters, discussing the messy situation in the fallen former Empire, and now he would pay the price with a cold bath. Oh, well. Far worse things had happened to him, so he turned and undressed, dropping his discarded clothing on the bench opposite the tub.

But when he turned back to the bath, the water was gently, insistently *steaming*.

Aleksi glanced around the empty room, then smiled to himself. Naia had said that the island would protect him and Einar, but he had not realized that care extended to creature comforts. But the room felt . . . *expectant*. Heavy with anticipation.

"Thank you," he whispered aloud.

He lingered in the hot bath, just as his thoughts lingered on Naia and Einar. Though the three of them had slept together in his massive bed, they had not been physically intimate since their return to Rahvekya. They had not planned it to be so, had simply been relishing other intimacies—tender embraces and soft whispers and laughter in the quiet dark.

Would it be different now? Would *she* be different? Somehow, Aleksi did not think so. The core of who she was had always shone through the newness, the sparkle of the Dream that surrounded her. In a way, she had always been shallow, welcoming waters and warm sand.

No, if anything, any*one*, had changed now, it would be Einar. He had already worshipped Naia as a supplicant would a saint. How much more intensely would he feel that reverence now?

Aleksi shivered. Anticipation was a delicious thing, one that was not appreciated—or practiced—nearly enough. Too many people treated it as a preamble, a mere obstacle to overcome in pursuit of pleasure. He, on the other hand, had always rather enjoyed allowing the sensation to slowly unfurl until it bloomed like a flower.

But tonight? He had a feeling about tonight.

He climbed from the tub and wrapped up in one of the tundra cotton robes. The fiber seemed to vary in shade, from celadon to cerulean. This particular garment had been woven of fibers that were a cool teal, more green than blue, the exact shade of the sea glass trinkets the locals had been gifting to Naia.

Aleksi passed over the Imperial finery that had been left for him. With so many other members of the High Court in attendance, he felt more comfortable in his usual fashions. He pulled on tight black pants, knee-high boots, and a loose linen shirt.

He was just fastening the buttons on his wine-colored velvet jerkin when the knocker sounded, reverberating through the room.

"Enter," he called out in invitation, expecting a palace staff member, Einar returning from his ship, or even Elevia, with more questions about the island or Gwynira's security measures.

It was Ash who walked in, decked out in enough finery to do his beloved steward back at Dragon's Keep, Camlia, proud. He was dressed much as Aleksi was, only instead of a jerkin, he wore an exquisitely embroidered tunic shot through with orange and red threads.

It was a far cry from what he had worn when he arrived. The breastplate and bracers and bare feet were the quintessence of the Dragon at war. This, on the other hand, was Ash, heading into a different, subtler sort of fight.

Aleksi whistled as he straightened his shirt cuffs. "Very nice. The last time I saw you this dressed up, you were getting ready to greet your intended bride."

Ash's gaze lost a little of its focus as he drifted into memory. Aleksi remembered that day, as well—the curiosity, the hope tempered by pain. Longing and dread in equal measure. The very air around Ash had shimmered, his pale-blue wishes breaking through the darker emotions like light piercing a heavy fog.

Aleksi was so, so glad it had all worked out.

"And you look ready for a night of entertainment at your villa." Ash studied him, not with sartorial admiration but with . . . concern. "Are you well?"

"What, was Inga's questioning not comprehensive enough for you? As near as I can tell, I am fine. Beyond that, I have no reassurances to offer." He held up an empty glass. "Would you like a drink?"

"Very much." As Aleksi turned to fulfill the request, Ash spoke again. "Inga is worried about your body. I'm worried about your heart."

Aleksi glanced back at him, unsure exactly where his friend was going with this line of inquiry. "Is that so?"

"I know better than anyone that falling in love in the midst of a war means having your emotions held hostage," Ash said softly.

"Yes." Out of an abundance of caution, Aleksi opened a sealed bottle of wine and poured two glasses. "But life is like that sometimes. Such things are rarely scheduled for our convenience."

"And Einar . . . He's never shown much interest in anything besides his personal war against the Empire. And now I understand why."

"Mmm." He handed off one of the drinks and sank to the sofa. "Why don't you tell me what's really on your mind, Ash?"

He cradled the glass in one hand without drinking. "Even I've heard the songs they sing about Einar in the taverns. He's spent nearly two thousand years breaking hearts in every port in the Sheltered Lands."

"Ahh." It seemed that Ash believed all the lies Einar had told—even to himself—about the Kraken's lack of heart. "And so we come to the real issue."

Sighing, Ash shook his head. "It's all one issue, Aleksi. You would know his intentions better than anyone. I believe he cares about you, and I can see that he makes you happy. I'm grateful to him for that. It's just . . ." He struggled for a moment, as if he had the right words but did not want to give them voice.

"Say it, Ash," Aleksi whispered.

He finally did, his dark eyes troubled. Tormented. "Last time nearly broke you."

Of course. There was no one else in the world who knew just how much losing Alysaia had hurt Aleksi. After all, Ash had loved her as much as Aleksi had, in his own way. He had been the one to come to Aleksi's villa and sit with him, in the darkness of their shared grief, as the moons passed into years.

Aleksi remembered that grief well. It had been all-encompassing, a feral beast that had clawed at him—and everyone around him. Naturally, Ash still bore the scars of watching him go through that. Of going through it *with* him.

Only the absolute truth could assuage Ash's fear. "Alysaia was arguably an even worse idea than Einar. My best friend's wife. So many ways that could have exploded in *all* our faces."

"But it worked."

Only because Ash had . . . allowed it? Wanted it? Alysaia had been fond of Ash, and they would have been happy enough. She might even have fallen in love with him in time. She never would have been unfaithful to him, and Aleksi never would have seduced the Dragon's consort.

Ash could have kept them apart, but he had not. Instead, he encouraged their attachment, though it had cost him the closeness he might have shared with his rightful consort. In his wisdom, he had known that keeping them apart would have been tantamount to stealing something from Alysaia—and from Aleksi, as well. And he cared too much about both of them to do that.

He had let her go so that he would not lose her completely. Aleksi understood that. Wasn't it exactly what he'd been thinking about Naia and Einar all this time? He knew, in all modesty, that he could have prevented their attachment from deepening by charming and wooing one of them for his own.

But every one of them would have lost something precious.

Ash remembered those dark days after Alysaia's death, but perhaps it was time to remind him that pain was not all that Aleksi carried with him from his years with her.

"Loving Alys was a terrible idea," he reiterated softly. "And do you know what I regret about it?"

"What?"

"Absolutely nothing." Aleksi finished his wine, then stole Ash's glass and drained half of it. It was a sweet wine, with a bit of a rough edge. He liked it. "Do you remember when she decided to develop her own cultivar of grape? She wanted her very own wine—the Consort's Vintage."

Ash winced. "I don't think anyone could forget having tasted that. I've fought wars that were easier to stomach than that wine."

"And it showed." Aleksi laughed at the memory of Ash's face, screwed up in frantic disgust, as he passed the glass back to him. "I finished every bottle of that cursed swill. I refused to throw it out, even when she begged me." His laughter died. "That's what I remember most. Not the end, but everything that came before it."

Ash finished what remained of his wine and set the glass aside. "You made her happy. I had few enough consorts over the years who truly were, so I was grateful to you for that gift. But when you give your heart, you give it completely. For the first decade after her death, I was afraid she'd taken it with her."

"She did," he said simply. "Because there *is* no other way to give your heart. Alys could not help leaving me. Perhaps Einar won't, either, or Naia. Or maybe they will walk away, with their souls light and their eyes clear, to live without me. None of what might be changes what is now."

Ash reached out to grasp Aleksi's hands. "Then I hope they bring you as much joy as possible, my old friend. You deserve to be loved."

"Thank you." Then, just as sincerely, he added, "You're a raving hypocrite, you know that?"

"It has been said," Ash replied without hesitation. "But if you want to say it again, I probably deserve it."

"Of course you do, coming here to warn me about the dangers of giving my heart too recklessly. *You*, of all people."

A hint of a smile tugged at the corner of Ash's mouth. "Are you saying it was reckless for me to fall in love with two women who were sent to kill me?"

"Tragically so. And yet, who can argue with the results? That love saved your life." In so many ways—immediately, and from the far slower death of being alone and lonely. "See? Hypocrite."

"Only the kind of hypocrite we all are, brother." Ash squeezed his hands. "It is easier to suffer my own heartbreak than to watch the people I love in pain. But you're right. If you told me I would lose Sachi or Zanya tomorrow, I would only love them harder today. Every moment with them is worth a century of pain."

But would you let them go? The words echoed in Aleksi's heart but died on his tongue, because he already knew the answer. Ash would tear his own heart from his chest—literally—if that was what it took for Sachi and Zanya to be happy.

How could the god of love do any less?

But if he said that, Ash really *would* be worried. So he changed the subject instead. "How are Sachi and Zanya? They put on brave faces, but they seem *exhausted*."

Ash slumped back in his chair, rubbing a hand over his face. "Zanya is in worse shape, physically. The rest of us can help with those newly awoken to the Dream, but Zanya is the only one who can help those connected to the Void. But Sachi . . ."

She would be blaming herself for all of it—for not being able to reason with Sorin, for having to wrench away his stolen bits of the Dream without a good way to return them to their rightful owners. She had been faced with an impossible choice, and had done the only thing she felt was right.

"She takes too much on herself," Aleksi murmured. "What is happening to those poor souls in the Empire is Sorin's fault, not hers."

"So we tell her, day after day. But she can feel it in the Dream. Their pain, their terror, their confusion. And when we *can't* save someone, it's like a piece of her dies." Ash rose and retrieved the bottle of wine. He poured himself another healthy serving and swirled the liquid in the glass, staring down into it. "As I said. It is easier to shoulder your own heartbreak than to watch someone you love in pain."

Aleksi did not like any of it. "Watch out for them, Ash. And . . . take care. Aside from the obvious, we don't know what this sort of thing can do to them."

"I know." Ash sipped his wine and smiled. "We came here because we needed to be sure you were all right. But I'll admit that I was glad for an excuse to take them away from the mainland, if only for a few days. The work in the village was exactly what they needed—problems they could fix. And tonight . . ." He lifted his glass in a toast. "Tonight, we should all embrace joy. We will return to the fight soon enough."

"Agreed." Aleksi rose and straightened his clothes. "Let's go dance with our lovers."

And remember why we fight.

Chapter Eleven

One unexpected advantage to the collapse of the Empire has been the possibility of acquiring books and documents from our former enemies in the Sheltered Lands. Though my collection is still modest, it is clear that few members of the High Court have been memorialized with the devotion that the Lover enjoys. I have already acquired six books of poetry dedicated to Aleksi, as well as several pieces of artwork, three plays, and a book of collected songs.

Untitled manuscript in progress
by Guildmaster Klement

By the second step over the threshold of Gwynira's impressive ballroom, Einar knew he was going to enjoy this ball a *great* deal more than the last one.

It wasn't only his companions, though it would have taken a colder man than Einar not to feel his pulse quicken at the sight of them. Naia and Aleksi had abandoned Imperial fashion to devastating results, with Aleksi adopting his usual velvet pants and vest over flowing linen that hugged his perfect body. Naia's gown was unfamiliar, though the floaty periwinkle-teal fabric embroidered in flowers native to Rahvekya had clearly come from a local seamstress. It barely clung to her shoulders, the deep neckline plunging between her breasts and all but begging Einar to nudge it aside—with his fingers, with his lips, with his *tongue* . . .

Not yet, he chided himself, forcing his gaze from the tempting expanse of bare skin. But returning his eyes to the rest of the room underscored how very, very different tonight would be.

The assembled nobles huddled in groups, wide-eyed with nerves as they watched the High Court circulate through the crowd, somehow dressed even more elaborately than they had been at their arrival.

Gwynira's court would not have time to waste judging and gossiping about Einar, because Gwynira's court was *terrified.*

"Is it wrong to hope Jaspar irritates Zanya or Ulric?" he murmured to Naia and Aleksi.

"Yes *and* no, probably," Aleksi admitted.

Naia smiled slowly—not one of her open expressions of joy, but a cool, determined curving of her lips. "If he dares show his face—here, *tonight*—then I will handle him myself."

For a moment he felt that same urge that had overwhelmed him on the beach when she'd stood proud and glorious in her protective fury—the urge to drop to his knees and pay homage to the goddess. He settled for clasping her hand and raising it to his lips for a brief kiss. "Even better."

Aleksi chuckled. "I confess, I've never understood the allure of a dangerous lover. I've always been more partial to good-natured sweetness. But I'm beginning to see the appeal." He bent down until his lips hovered just over Naia's. "You might change my mind, little nymph."

"Nonsense." Her tongue snuck out to graze the corner of his mouth. "Why choose, when Einar and I can give you both?"

Her eyes danced with mischief, and Einar couldn't resist the urge to slide his fingers up her arm, over her shoulder, and down that tempting expanse of skin across her collarbone. "If you two keep this up," he murmured, "we'll be leaving this ball scandalously early."

Naia laughed, and for a moment he hoped they both might consider it. But then Gwynira's voice rose from the far side of the room, where she stood on the dais in a gown of pristine white sewn with so many crystals that it looked like icy armor. "We gather to celebrate our most honored guests from the east, the members of the High Court. You will make them welcome."

The chill emphasis on those final words managed to make them sound more like a threat than the opening to a joyful celebration, but at a signal from Arktikos a small group of musicians sitting on their own dais launched into their first song.

Naia smiled almost at once, as if she recognized the music. Einar felt a tug of remembrance as well—not from their recent visits, but a more primal memory. Perhaps he'd heard Jinevra whistling a tune like this on the ship over the centuries, or Petya had sung it to him as a child.

The musicians must have made the deliberate choice to feature ancient Rahvekyan folk music, undoubtedly to honor their newly returned goddess. The bright joy on her face was a suitable reward—and so irresistible he wanted to be part of it. He didn't care if he didn't know the steps to this dance—he had every intention of sharing it with her.

He started to lift his hand to Naia, only for Inga to appear in a swirl of dark skirts and clasp his hand. "Honor me with a dance, Kraken?"

Aleksi smiled his encouragement, so Einar hid his mild disappointment and accepted the Witch's hand before leading her out into the dancing. His good mood was somewhat restored by the way several of the braver couples who had taken the floor spun anxiously out of their path—and *not* because of Einar this time. The Witch terrified them.

Inga seemed oblivious to the nervous looks they shot her, turning to face Einar with a dreamy smile. She lifted one hand to his, her black-tinted nails sparkling with some iridescent sheen by the light of the massive chandeliers, and settled the other on his shoulder. "So," she mused, guiding him into the opening steps of a dance that seemed nothing like the one being performed around them. "The Kraken has found a lover."

"Two lovers," he corrected mildly, letting her lead the dance. She seemed to be moving to her own internal rhythm—but the Witch so often did.

"Two lovers," she agreed readily. Dark, kohl-lined eyes stared up at him, and there was nothing of the dreamy, amusing woman whose whimsy so often baffled those around her. The Witch studied him like a puzzle she meant to dismantle—and *might* put back together, if she liked what she found. "Aleksi is very special to me, you know."

One long nail brushed the side of his neck, and Einar remembered tales whispered over campfires or in shrouded taverns—that the Witch could heal a man with a brush of her finger, or kill him with one swipe of her poison-tipped nails.

Einar had a great deal of respect for the danger she hid beneath her fluttering gowns and glittering butterflies—but Einar had sworn his allegiance only to the Siren and the Huntress. He would back down before no other member of the High Court.

He let his lips curve in his cockiest pirate smile, wrapping the full arrogance of the Kraken around him as he took control of the dance, swinging her in a circle with enough force that her skirts flared wide to reveal flashes of brilliant pink the same color as the glow slowly suffusing her eyes. "Is this where you tell me what terrible things you'll do to me if I hurt him?"

"I considered it," she admitted, dragging her nail down his neck again with enough pressure that it would have broken mortal skin. "I would be very displeased if *anyone* hurt him."

Einar let his own power rise within him, the crash of the sea and the seductive lure of the monster. His skin prickled, his demigod form so close to the surface that Inga's eyes widened, as if she could *see* it within him. His eyes must have been glowing, too, the eerie teal of a creature of the deep to meet the inhuman pink of hers.

He leaned close, until his face was a mere fingerbreadth from hers. "Not as displeased as I would be," he rumbled, letting the rage of the sea fill his voice.

Any of the nobles in Gwynira's court would be on their knees in terror by now. Inga actually laughed, bright and joyful. Her sharp fingernails grasped his chin, holding him in place. "Good," she whispered. "Aleksi doesn't need a weakling. He needs someone who will take care of *him*."

"I can do that," Einar replied. "I *will* do that."

She leaned up and kissed him, a quick brush of lips that left behind the lingering sweetness of the prized glowing berries that grew only in the Witchwood. Then she released his chin and gave his cheek a fond pat. "You're a good boy, Einar," she said as the glow in her eyes faded, returning them to their usual warm brown. "Perhaps I will not poison you after all."

"I appreciate it," he said dryly, letting his own power dissipate. He didn't let his cocky smile slip, however. "Though it might have been interesting to see you try. Creatures of the deep survive dangers those on land could hardly dream of."

"So Dianthe always says. Though I wonder . . ." Her gaze grew distant, her lower lip disappearing briefly between her teeth as she hummed in thought—presumably lost in the fascinating intellectual puzzle of how best to murder him.

There was a reason people found Inga so unnerving.

He was spared the challenge of finding a casual way to segue away from discussion of his death when Inga abruptly shivered. "I should have packed something warmer. My wardrobe may not be suited to an ice kingdom."

No, it certainly was not. Though the endless layers of ruffled fabric that flared her skirts out might provide some protection, the neckline on her gown's bodice made Naia's look positively modest. The entire thing looked as if it was pieced together from a hundred black flower petals, narrowing to tiny winding vines at her shoulders that left her arms—and back—bare. "There's a reason the fashion in Gwynira's court tends toward many fur-lined layers," he allowed. "I'm sure she has a suitably dramatic cloak you could borrow, if you want."

"Hmmm." She pushed gently at his shoulder, taking control of the dance to turn them so that she could peer up at where Gwynira sat, talking with Isa. "I wonder if the bear is warm."

His brain stuttered for a moment, trying to follow the winding path of her thoughts. But then he saw Arktikos looming at Gwynira's shoulder, gaze watchful as it scanned the assembled crowd for any signs of potential trouble.

Oh, no.

"Ulric is always *very* warm," she pointed out, narrowing her eyes. "So is Ash."

The Wolf and the Dragon did tend to run hot. So did Einar—at least in his demigod form—but he wasn't about to make *that* offer. "He is a very impressively sized bear," he said instead, mentally apologizing to Arktikos for what was about to happen.

"He is, isn't he?" Inga worried at her lower lip for another moment, gaze distant, and then abruptly smiled. "Well, why don't we find out?"

She released his hand, offered him a smile of pure mischievous chaos, and set off across the room in a swirl of rustling skirts, not even bothering to swerve around the dancers who crossed her path. Not that she needed to; they all hastily scattered out of her way.

A sigh at his shoulder alerted him to Ulric's arrival. "Has Inga gone off to poke the bear, then?"

"Probably," Einar said.

Ulric sighed again, the long-suffering sigh of someone who had lost a battle so many times he had given up on fighting it. "A few thousand years of using me as a foot warmer and a pillow has given her a reckless disregard for the potential danger of wild creatures."

Oh, Einar suspected she had a perfect understanding of the danger of the wild creature she was currently approaching. No doubt that made it part of the fun for her. "She seems to be able to handle herself."

"Most of the time." Ulric narrowed his eyes, watching as Inga stopped at the foot of the dais and said something that made Arktikos cast a look at Gwynira. She nodded, and the big man stepped down and held out a hand to Inga. "I saw how massive he was when he changed, though."

Of course Ulric had scoped out a potential enemy during their time in the village. "He's not quite the size of Ash as a dragon," Einar said, casting Ulric a sidelong look. "I still wouldn't try to fight him, in your shoes."

No reply. Ulric's gaze stayed fixed on the pair across the room as Arktikos wrapped a careful hand around Inga's, engulfing it. The hand he settled politely on her back was so large that the span of his fingers covered much of her bared skin. Einar had never thought of Inga as a particularly small woman, but she looked tiny against Arktikos as they stepped into the flow of the dance.

A furrow appeared between Ulric's brows. He was absolutely trying to decide how to fight Arktikos. Even Einar knew *that* was a diplomatic disaster waiting to happen. "Ulric . . ."

The Wolf waved a hand at him. "Aleksi told me he is a good man." He paused, watching as Inga said something—with that thoughtful expression that meant it was likely something positively unnerving. Arktikos gave no indication of being anything but politely attentive as he responded in a way that made Inga laugh. Ulric's expression softened. "He's being kind to her, at least."

Einar imagined plenty had not been over the years. No one in the Sheltered Lands doubted the Witch's brilliance, but even at her most measured she could be unsettling to deal with. And when she had fixated that curious mind of hers on a mystery, or a project . . .

Einar remembered the first time he'd learned that Inga collected Void-forged items. Weapons, tools—even plants cultivated with the essence of the Void. Odd enough in a world that celebrated the Dream, but positively reckless when those items represented the only true threat to the High Court's lives. But even before Zanya had come into their lives, reminding them that destruction was every bit as essential to the rhythms of life as creation was, Inga had been fascinated by the Endless Void.

The discordance between her lighthearted, brightly colored whimsy and her wholehearted embrace of the inevitability of darkness had always made her a controversial figure in the Sheltered Lands. Healers celebrated the gift she had to restore life. Killers came to her to learn of poisons that could steal it.

The two did not sit comfortably together for everyone, which had always made the High Court fiercely protective of her.

A swish of skirts on Ulric's other side announced Elevia's arrival. Her gown of dark-green velvet was certainly more formal than her usual attire, with elaborate beading that swirled across the bodice and down to wind into her skirts almost like tree branches. More beads were strung across the open neckline of her dress, crisscrossing her chest all the way up to where a shimmering cape flowed from a tightly fitted collar around her throat.

Her first words, spoken with a smile over the rim of her goblet, were customarily blunt, however. "I know what you're thinking, Ulric. And I would resist the urge, if I were you."

"I wouldn't start a fight at a party," he replied mildly.

"That's very near your *favorite* place to start a fight."

He flashed her a grin that was somehow challenge and invitation in one. "Do you think I'd win?"

"Best not to risk it." She reached out and pressed her fingertips to Ulric's lips. "I like your face just as it is."

The Wolf nipped at her fingertips, his eyes glowing, and for a moment Einar wasn't sure where to rest *his* eyes. In all the centuries he'd known them, he had never been able to fully discern what the relationship between the Huntress and the Wolf was. Sometimes they bickered like siblings. Sometimes they sparred like lovers. They wore each other's colors—Ulric's midnight green in Elevia's gown, her own gold embroidered across his tight jacket—and often spoke for each other as if they knew what the other thought without asking.

And sometimes, when they'd had a bit too much to drink, standing too close to them could swiftly grow awkward.

Einar was considering ways to politely extricate himself when the current song ended. Ulric nipped at Elevia's fingers again before turning to cross the dance floor in a rolling predatory stalk that momentarily held even Einar transfixed.

His destination was Inga and Arktikos, who had just stepped apart. With another of those challenging grins, Ulric extended a hand to Gwynira's bodyguard, one brow arched in invitation.

Everyone watched as Arktikos accepted the gesture. The entire room seemed to hold its breath—including the musicians, except for one startled, off-tempo wail from a stringed instrument, which was instantly silenced. In the next moment, an almost frantically jaunty tune exploded from them in a ripple, and Arktikos and Ulric began their graceful, deadly dance.

Einar glanced at Elevia, who only sipped her drink and watched with amused eyes. "Should we be concerned?" he asked.

"That depends, Crown-Prince."

He waited for her to elaborate, but she seemed willing to wait him out as she watched as the two predators in human form circled each other, every touch of hands precise, every turn a subtle test, every step riding the tense edge between polite enjoyment and imminent violence. Finally, Einar gave in. "What does it depend on, Huntress?"

"On many things." She shrugged. "How hotheaded is Gwynira's personal guard? Are her festive events typically staid affairs, or can they get a little raucous? And—last, but certainly not least—do you give a fuck if the Wolf makes a scene?"

Einar's lips twitched. As a mortal sailor, his first allegiance had always been to the Siren, but there had been a reason he'd found himself drawn to the Huntress—and it had not merely been her superior tactical knowledge. Elevia was blunt, she cared little for the rules of decorum . . . and she loved a good fight. "Not in the least."

"Excellent. Leave the diplomacy to those better suited to the task. You and I?" She leaned toward Einar with an intent stare. "Our talents run in a different direction."

Yes, they certainly did. Aleksi and Sachi and Naia were genuinely interested in people. So was Inga, in her own unusual way. Dianthe and Ash had the dignity of visiting royalty wherever they went, and the gravity of those whose moods could stir the very elements around them. Nyx's connection to the Dream inspired an awe that was almost its own sort of diplomacy. But Einar had always been more comfortable with Ulric and Elevia—and now Zanya. Blades honed to edges so vicious, they could not hide it—and perhaps should not try to.

Ulric certainly wasn't trying to hide it now, and Elevia's lips curved into an appreciative smile. "Aww, that's nice. They decided to play."

Play seemed a gentle word for the spectacle that had now hypnotized half of Gwynira's nobles, but he supposed the Huntress played rough. "So they did."

Elevia lifted her goblet in a silent toast before turning, her sharp gaze alighting on a small cluster of older women who were watching Arktikos and Ulric's display with naked fascination. She slid into their circle smoothly, and though Einar couldn't hear her wry comment, the shocked laughter that followed it was the sound of people who had dropped their guards.

A necessary reminder that Elevia *could* play politics when she wanted—not as a diplomat but as a spy. Her friendly smiles were weapons in the hunt, and her quarry was knowledge. That had been Einar's main service to her for centuries now—information brought to her from distant shores, helping her build a picture of the world beyond the borders of the Sheltered Lands.

By the end of the night, Elevia would likely know more about Gwynira's nobles than Gwynira did herself.

Finally left to his own devices, Einar turned in search of his lovers. Naia had taken to the dance floor with Ash, who was swinging her around with more enthusiasm than grace. He caught a brief glimpse of her face as Ash twirled her, alight with giddy laughter that lightened Einar's heart.

Not too far away, Aleksi leaned down to whisper something to Zanya, who covered her mouth to hide a smile. There was an ease between them that had surprised Einar in the beginning, for there seemed to be little common ground between the manifestation of Love and the primordial force of Destruction. Now Einar understood why Zanya adored Aleksi—and why the Lover had been the Dragon's oldest and dearest friend.

Aleksi had a way of seeing straight to the raw, terrified heart of monsters—and loving them, even when they couldn't love themselves.

Then Aleksi's gaze found Einar's, and for a dizzying heartbeat the ballroom vanished as Aleksi smiled at him. Einar's heart beat faster, and heat spread through him in a languid wave. Was it possible to seduce someone across the room with just the curve of your lips?

Perhaps so, if you were the Lover. It was a reminder that Einar had only known the man's touch while his power was tenuous. What would it be like to bed Aleksi at the height of his strength?

Einar probably shouldn't be thinking about it too deeply. Not until they could escape this ball for somewhere passably private, at least.

He broke eye contact with difficulty and scanned the room again. Jaspar still had not made an appearance. Einar wished him a miserable evening, sulking in his room and nursing his bruised ego—and if there was any justice in the world, his equally bruised body.

The rest of the court seemed to be on their best behavior, even the more annoying members. Even without Aleksi and Naia to form a protective wall around him, he felt none of the claustrophobia and desperate need to leave that he had last time.

In fact, he was almost enjoying himself.

There might have been only seven members of the High Court—nine, he supposed, including Sachi and Zanya—but it was as if they had changed the entire gravity of Gwynira's court. It didn't even feel like *her* party tonight, but more as if the High Court had done Gwynira the favor of holding their own celebration in the midst of her castle and court.

The bravest—or drunkest—of the nobles had even begun to approach the less intimidating members. An older man with silver hair chatted amiably with Nyx, eyes alight with fascination at whatever story they'd decided to tell. Elevia's group of older women had doubled already, and Inga had attracted a cluster of the more rebellious younger members of the court. She was currently dazzling them by filling their empty mugs with sparkling liquid that appeared from nowhere and would undoubtedly get them delightfully drunk.

It was little surprise that Sachi had the largest group, having no doubt charmed plenty of people on her last visit. He *was* surprised to see that there seemed to be some competition for who would claim Ulric's next dance, though perhaps he shouldn't have been. He, of all people, knew that plenty of reckless souls craved the danger of a man with an inner monster.

The last member of the High Court was not faring as well. Dianthe stood in her shimmering blue gown, face fixed in the polite lines that indicated she was pondering escorting someone to the highest bluff behind her castle and letting them risk the dizzying dive into the churning surf beneath. Einar nearly groaned when he saw who had cornered her.

Guildmaster Klement. Of course.

The Siren turned as Einar bore down on them, as if she sensed his approach. Klement kept chattering on until Einar cleared his throat, causing the man to start and wheel around hard enough to send his heavy golden medallion bouncing off his chest. "Captain Einar!"

"Guildmaster," he replied mildly. "I see you have met the Siren."

"Yes, yes." Klement beamed at Dianthe, proving that he truly had no survival instincts to speak of. "I was just explaining the history of this island's goddess figure to her."

As if Dianthe couldn't ask Naia anything she wanted to know about such a thing. "I see."

"Yes. It's an interesting comparison, you must admit. My recent research into the High Court—"

"I'm sure it *is* interesting," Einar interrupted. He held out an arm to Dianthe. "However, I'm afraid I have to steal the Siren away. Urgent . . . ocean business."

Dianthe pressed her lips together as if she was struggling not to smile, and slipped her hand through Einar's arm. Klement, undeterred, kept talking even as Einar began to lead her away. "Do not worry, Lady Dianthe! I am sure we will have time later for me to tell you all about the storm god's mythology!"

The swirl of dancers and the ripple of music finally drowned out his voice. Einar lifted his free hand to his face and pinched the bridge of his nose, as if it could drive back the headache that was beginning to threaten every time he had to be polite to the man.

"Urgent ocean business?" Dianthe murmured, laughter dancing under the words.

"You sent Aleksi here to be the diplomat," he grumbled. "I'm just the muscle."

Instead of replying, Dianthe stopped walking and turned to face him, her dark eyes searching. Abruptly, he remembered that she *knew*. Aleksi had told her everything—about his parents, about their death at the hands of the Emperor. What this island truly meant to him. All things he should have told her on the day she'd tasked him with this mission . . . if not decades—*centuries*—ago.

It might have been easy to stand in his defiance if there had been anger in her ancient eyes. But there was only sadness, and compassion as vast as the sea itself. "You should have told me, Einar."

"I know."

"So why didn't you?"

"Because I didn't think it would matter."

Now she frowned, disbelief evident in her eyes. "How could it not matter?"

He groped for the words to explain, to make her *understand*. "You have seen what the Empire does. Every land they've conquered, they've destroyed. They strip away its history. They kill its myths, its stories. They destroy what came before, and build on the bones." Even now, the rage of it made his heart race. "They shouldn't have remembered me. It shouldn't have *mattered*."

"Oh, Einar." She lifted one hand to cup his cheek, and in the soft light of the chandeliers, he thought he caught the shimmer of tears in her eyes. "They could erase the memories from the people, perhaps. But that would not have erased them from your heart."

"My heart?" he echoed.

"Do you think I would so easily send you to a place that represents such grief and loss for you?" she demanded softly. "That I would care only for the success of the mission, and not what it would cost you?"

No, of course she would not have. Some mistook the dispassionate stillness of the Siren's demeanor as coldness. Sorin certainly had—it was the reason he had pulled Gwynira from the Dream when he'd made his terrifying copies of the family he had lost. This entire palace was a frozen monument to how Sorin had viewed Dianthe—a frigid ice queen, aloof and alone.

Einar knew the truth. When the turmoil in your heart roiled the sea and whipped up deadly winds, you could not afford to let the daily aggravations of life stir your temper. But Dianthe had always felt as deeply and as vastly as the ocean herself . . . and she had *always* protected those she considered hers.

"I know you wouldn't have," he allowed.

"So *why* did you not tell me?"

The truth spilled out of him in a damning rush. "Because if I'd told you, you would not have let me come."

The words sat between them in abrupt, awkward silence. Dianthe parted her lips. Closed them. Einar looked away, his gaze instinctively seeking out Aleksi and Naia. Aleksi had taken to the dance floor, leading Inga through the paces of a graceful dance. Sachi and Naia had joined Zanya, Naia's joyful laughter like the music he heard when she twined with the waves.

"You were sending them," he said, feeling his heart leap as Naia caught his gaze and smiled. "I wasn't going to let them go into danger without me. Especially *here*. To this island." He forced himself to look back to Dianthe, to face whatever judgment he found in her eyes. "I won't let the Empire take anything else from me here."

"Ahh." Finally, she smiled, her thumb sweeping out to stroke his cheek. "So the Kraken has finally found someone to hold him past the dawn."

"I simply learned the truth," he countered.

"And that was?"

"That my heart was never gone." There might have been times he would have wished it so, but not now. Not with everything he had to gain. "It was simply frozen."

"The cold feels safer, doesn't it? I admit, there are times when the demands of the world are too much for me, and I descend to the darkest depths of the ocean." Her fingers found the hair at his temple and brushed it back, a maternal gesture that reminded him of how Petya had stroked his forehead as a child. "But we can't stay there, Einar. It's good that you've come back to the world. It is good to love, and to be loved."

The warm approval in her voice eased some tension he'd barely understood was there until it vanished. Perhaps he had been braced for more of the blustering warnings that Inga had issued, dire proclamations of what she would do if he broke Naia's heart. "I thought you might be angry with me," he admitted.

She frowned her confusion. "Whatever for?"

"I thought you might be worried that I'd hurt your protégée."

"Oh, Einar. Do you think I have been so unaware of you, these centuries? That I do not know your heart?" She moved her hand to his chest, pressing it to the spot where his heart beat unsteadily. "I feel the truth of you every time you touch the sea. You care more fiercely than anyone knows. Perhaps you have even fooled yourself. But I know you. You are dangerous, yes. But you are loyal, and you are passionate, and you fight for the people you love. You came to this place of personal tragedy without a second thought, simply to see them safe."

It was as if she'd tossed a stone into water, fracturing his reflection into a thousand ripples. When the picture he held of himself reformed, it looked different. All his rough edges smoothed into strength, his obsession transmuted into passion, even the Kraken's overprotectiveness gentled into loyalty.

It was the reflection of a man who deserved Aleksi and Naia, seen through the eyes of an ancient god who loved all three of them.

He wasn't sure he could reply without his voice cracking.

Dianthe smiled in gentle understanding. "Besides, Naia is no longer the young water nymph who appeared to us from the waves. She was ancient when I first touched the sea. I have no doubts she can handle *you*, even at your most aggravating."

He was grateful for the chance to laugh, even if it came out rough. "Me? Aggravating?"

She gave his chest a fond pat. "Beyond all reason, at times. But I would never ask you to change. You are brash and you are irreverent, and you follow no rules but your own. If that makes people like the nobles of Gwynira's court nervous . . ." Her sudden smile held a dangerous edge. "Well, it is good for them to remember that the ocean and her creatures are not to be disrespected."

No, they were not. Einar clasped Dianthe's hand and bowed over it. "You honor me with your trust, Siren."

"I honor you with nothing more than you have earned." She tugged him back upright and leaned closer. "And as much as I'm enjoying your company, I think someone else has a more pressing claim."

He followed her gaze to where Zanya and Sachi stood with Naia. They were whispering about something, but Naia . . . Naia was watching *him*, luminous eyes alight with affection and longing.

Dianthe's warm laughter swirled around him, like a soft wind rustling at his hair and nudging at his back. "Go."

He didn't have much choice, with the wind playfully prodding him forward—but he didn't fight it. Not when it was guiding him in the exact direction he most wanted to go.

He reached where Naia stood with Sachi and flashed his most rakish smile. "I hate to interrupt, Princess . . . but this next dance is mine."

"I suppose your claim on Naia's time *is* stronger than mine." Sachi's deep curtsy almost hid her teasing smile. "Captain."

The look in Naia's eyes could have lured sailors to their deaths. Einar had no defense against it as she slipped her hand into his, the mere glide of her fingers against his a sweetness he could drown in.

As he led her out into the dancing, the musicians transitioned to something slower, a single clear flute winding hauntingly around the low thrum of the stringed instruments. A song of seduction, with the top melody luring you in as the soft drumbeat rose beneath it in an unmistakably charged rhythm.

Einar didn't worry about the steps this time. Not when he could follow that drumbeat. He twined the fingers of one hand with hers and settled the other on her hip, tugging her close as they began to sway. "Do you recognize this song?"

"I do." She lifted their hands and spun beneath them, her skirts flaring. "Most of what they have played tonight has been traditional Rahvekyan folk music."

Undoubtedly to honor Naia. At Gwynira's last ball, many of the servants and villagers had suspected and hoped, but now they *knew*. "I like it much better than the Imperial music."

She smiled a little wistfully. "Perhaps it is . . . familiar to you."

"It probably is." He twirled her again, because he liked the way she laughed breathlessly as she spun, but letting her go for even those scant moments was almost intolerable. He enjoyed it much more when he tugged her back against him, far too close for the polite confines of a dance. He didn't care—he liked how her body fit against his. "Petya doesn't sing much, but Jinevra has a flute. She used to play it on night watches."

Her smile faltered for just a moment before returning, and he cursed himself. It must be hard for her to think about all the things that had happened to her people and the island after her death. She had saved them all, but their lives had been hard.

No. Tonight wasn't a night for grieving the past or for worrying about the future. They had given enough of themselves to diplomacy and wars and the weight of history. He would steal tonight just for *them*.

Naia's dress was cut so low in the back that he didn't have to slide his hand up far before his fingertips found soft skin. He stroked the line of her spine as they followed the swirling path of the flute and the primal beat of the drum. She turned her face into his throat, her breath turning unsteady as he splayed his hand wide and pulled her even closer.

Their next slow turn brought Aleksi into view. There was an Imperial noble talking animatedly at him, and the Lover's expression held nothing but polite interest. But his gaze followed Einar and Naia, the banked heat smoldering there both promise and warning.

Einar lowered his lips to Naia's ear. "Look."

She lifted her head, her gaze dreamy and distant. But when she saw Aleksi, a bright smile lit her face. "Do you think he would like to dance with us?"

"I certainly hope so," Einar responded, lips brushing her temple. "How shall we lure him into our net?"

"Well . . ." She tilted her head. "We could always play coy. Dance over until we're a little closer and just . . . wait. Or we could be more proactive."

Proactive sounded *wonderful*. "Do you have a wicked plan in mind?"

"Perhaps I do." Her full lips curved into the wickedest smile he had ever seen, and she tugged away from him. Before he could mourn the loss of her body against his, she pressed her back to his chest, the lush curves of her ass grinding back against his suddenly *painfully* interested cock.

The drums grew stronger, their rhythm more explicit. Naia moved with it, rocking back as if she was riding him already, every movement languid. Across the room, the noble talking to Aleksi had fallen silent. Most of the room followed suit.

There was only the music, and Naia, primal and shameless, one hand tangling slowly in her skirts as Aleksi followed her every movement with parted lips.

Her skirt came up, revealing her ankle.

Aleksi stepped forward.

Naia smiled.

The skirts drifted higher. Her calf. Her knee. The drums pounded in Einar's ears as he gripped her hips, as deeply under her spell as Aleksi was as he approached them in a slow, gliding stalk. His eyes burned— not embers of fire, but the rare violet of his power as it thrummed between them.

Stunningly graceful. Deadly serious.

Einar hoped everyone in this damn court was gnawing on their own livers in envy that this ethereal goddess and this glorious god— both radiating sensuality and power—were *his*.

Aleksi stopped in front of them. Two elegant fingers touched Naia's chin, tilting her face up to meet his eyes. He said nothing.

Naia's laughing sigh was pure affection. "What took you so long?"

He moved his hand slowly, trailing his fingers through her loose hair and higher, to brush Einar's lips. "I was admiring the view."

Einar closed his teeth on Aleksi's fingers before soothing the bite with his tongue. "So were we."

Naia caught the edge of Aleksi's velvet vest and pulled him closer in wordless demand. He gave in, wrapping one arm around her waist. The hand that lingered on Einar's jaw slipped around to grip the back of his neck.

Trapped between them, Naia exhaled on a sigh of satisfaction and let her head fall back against Einar's shoulder. He was about to touch the soft skin of her throat when the candles flared on every chandelier, drawing gasps from the crowd as the room went painfully bright for a moment and then extinguished, one by one, starting in the center and rushing out, snuffing faster and faster until only the torches on either far wall burned.

It should have plunged the ballroom into mostly darkness, but instead—

Butterflies swarmed the ballroom, glowing in wild colors as they fluttered over the crowd. Pinks and teals, silvers and blues, the lightest violet and the most startling green—all the colors of the Witchwood dipping and twirling as their wings shifted in time with the music, as if they had become part of it.

Naia looked up with a gasp, her lips parted in wonder. Aleksi smiled and nuzzled her cheek. Past his shoulder, Einar caught sight of Inga standing on the edge of the crowd with Ash.

The Lord of Fire. So *that* was what had happened to the candles.

Inga winked at him before lifting one hand, flipping her fingers in a lazy gesture. Fireflies appeared amongst the butterflies, blinking above them like a thousand stars.

"A little of the Witchwood," Naia breathed, "here in Rahvekya."

She said the name of the island differently than Petya always had, the subtle emphasis just slightly different, as if shaped by the language that came before. Few people knew the language anymore beyond a few prayers and ancient songs. Just the priestesses.

And now, Naia.

One thing was certain—Gwynira's court was no longer looking at *them.* That suited Einar perfectly. As Aleksi kissed Naia's temple, Einar gave in to the temptation he'd been resisting all evening and traced his fingers along the neckline of her dress. And the musicians seemed to have caught the mood, because the song changed again, melting into one familiar to all three of them.

They had heard it not so many days ago on the beach, as they'd joined the villagers at a festival meant to celebrate the ancient love between the storm god and the goddess. Slow, grinding, every drumbeat an invitation to slide deeper—into joy, into lust . . . into the lover who had claimed you, even if just for a night.

Einar wanted to slide so deep that he never came back up for air.

With shadows shrouding the room, Einar slid his fingers under the neckline of Naia's dress and down, stroking the curve of her breast. She gasped, arching, which only drove her hips against Aleksi. Aleksi's fingers tightened on the back of Einar's neck, and they didn't need words. Not in this moment.

All the better. They both had things they'd rather be doing with their mouths.

Einar pressed his parted lips to Naia's right temple, as Aleksi's teeth found her left ear. Her soft gasp turned into an incoherent whisper as Einar teased his fingers lower, circling her nipple without touching it.

She arched, seeking more, but he skated his fingers away. "Not yet," he murmured against her cheek. "Don't be impatient."

Her soft moan of protest melted into a lyrical jumble of sounds that he belatedly realized must be that ancient language. Of course, he didn't need to understand the words to understand the meaning. She wanted *more*.

Chuckling lowly, he nipped at her jaw and drew his hand free of her gown. "Soon," he promised, his hand finding Aleksi's as they both stroked down her side. The Lover hummed in agreement as he turned her in their arms, until her back rested against Aleksi's chest.

Her gaze found Einar's face, and his heart kicked at the feverish yearning there, as if she wanted to memorize his face and see it every time she closed her eyes.

"There it is," Aleksi murmured. "She's been gazing at you like this all night, Einar. Your goddess."

Naia lifted a trembling hand to his face. Her fingertips traced his cheek, his nose, his lips. She stared at him as if she had never seen anything so beautiful. As if he was everything she could possibly want.

As if he was enough.

Nothing could have stopped him from kissing her. He bent down, groaning when he found her lips parted and eager. She tasted like sweet wine and tealberries and *joy*, and he couldn't get enough. His hand found Aleksi's shoulder, gripping it as if to anchor them as he sank into her, licking deeper, swallowing her eager noises.

More. He needed *more*, but not here.

As if Aleksi had heard the thought, he covered Einar's hand and squeezed. And then they were moving, somehow still swaying with the music but drifting across the room with purpose. Einar realized the destination a moment later and changed his tactics. Instead of pushing into Naia, he began to drift backward.

Her hands found his coat immediately, tangling in it as she reached for him again. Her lips reclaimed his, teeth sinking into his lower lip as punishment for denying her. The sweet pain of it only made it more pressing to lure her toward Aleksi's goal, one slow step at a time.

When Einar felt the door to the balcony against his back, he lifted his head and grinned down at Naia as he pushed it open. He lifted one eyebrow in silent invitation, but she was already moving with him, out into the sheltered darkness of the night.

The balcony was empty, thankfully. It also sported several conveniently massive columns with secluded little niches perfect for hiding from the world. Einar guided Aleksi into one, until the Lover's back hit the railing that overlooked the ocean. Then he leaned down to brush a kiss to Naia's ear. "Do you want to touch him?"

"Taru." Her answer came in that musical language again, but this word, he knew.

Yes.

Aleksi watched with smoldering patience as Einar coaxed Naia to her knees and then knelt behind her, bracketing her body. He reached past her to brush one of the buttons on Aleksi's pants. "Do you want us to touch you?"

The Lover reached back to wrap his hands around the stone railing until his knuckles turned white. But his voice remained gentle. "At this moment, I cannot remember ever wanting anything else."

Neither could Einar. He eased the first button free of the fabric, then had to catch Naia's eager hands as she reached up to help. "Patience," he chided. She moaned in protest, but he kept her hands trapped as he flicked open the next button. How thoughtful of Aleksi to wear the attire he usually wore at his own villa. It might not be as climate appropriate, but it was certainly easier to get into. Two more quick flicks of Einar's wrist, and the pants were open.

Aleksi released the railing long enough to brush a strand of Naia's hair back from her face. "Is he going to torment us both, little nymph?"

"Maybe just a little," she allowed. "But what comes after will be *beautiful.*"

Einar laughed low against her ear as he freed Aleksi's cock and stroked it, earning a shuddering sigh. "What if I have no intention of tormenting you both?" he rasped, freeing Naia's hand. "What if I want you to help me torment him?"

Naia twisted to look back at him with a depth of familiarity and fondness that heated his blood. "With you? Both things can be true, *casara.*"

He didn't understand the word, but the affection was clear enough. He kissed her softly before turning her face back to Aleksi. "Taste him, love."

For all her talk about Einar's teasing, Naia seemed determined to torment Aleksi. Her lips parted as she leaned in, but instead of taking him into her mouth, she brushed a barely there kiss to the head. Aleksi's chest heaved, and she smiled and did it again. And again. Tiny little kisses, and then quick darting strokes of her tongue, humming in appreciation as she tasted him but never gave him more than those fleeting caresses.

Einar dragged his attention from the site of her tongue to find Aleksi clinging to the railing with a strength that would likely crumble the stone if this went on much longer. His entire body was coiled as tightly as a spring, pleasure as evident in his sharp breaths as in the way his cock moved in Einar's grip.

But there was no impatience in the Lover's gaze. No frustration. If this tormenting dance gave Naia pleasure, he would endure it until the castle crumbled into the sea.

Not that he'd have to. The ballads had called Einar many things over the years. They had never called him patient.

Dropping his gaze again, he watched as his fingers stroked up Aleksi's shaft. Watched Naia's sweet little tongue sweep out, dancing across his fingertips before returning to lick Aleksi again. His own cock strained against his pants, and it was far too easy to imagine her tongue stroking *him*, the wet heat of it intoxicating.

Her loose hair cascaded around her shoulders. Einar slid his free hand into it, wrapping the strands around his fist until she made a soft noise. "That's it," he whispered, holding Aleksi's cock so that only the tip was within her reach. He guided her head forward, and she parted her lips eagerly, sliding them around the sensitive head until they met Einar's hand.

Slowly, agonizingly slowly, he slid his hand down, letting Naia's lips slide with them.

Aleksi's head fell back with a groan. The railing groaned, too, his grip so punishing that tiny cracks appeared in the stone. As if spurred on by his obvious pleasure, Naia drew her head back and sank down again, fighting against Einar's grip in her hair when he tried to slow her.

So eager. He let her take more, transfixed by the erotic sight of her lips stretched wide around Aleksi's cock. "She's so hungry for you," he rasped, watching her struggle to take more. "She'd take all of you if I let her."

Naia moaned helplessly, kicking pleasure up his spine. No, something more. A bliss that slid along his skin and yet didn't feel like his own. Aleksi drew in a sharp breath as if he felt it, too, but another sound rose, drowning out the Lover's panting breaths and Naia's eager little whimpers.

The waves, crashing against the cliffs below. Einar reached out instinctively, and the pleasure slid over him again—Naia's pleasure. Her power, that song that wound beneath the waves when she touched them, but fuller somehow, deeper. Glorious, as if the island welcomed her pleasure—and welcomed those who stirred it in her.

With that heat throbbing through his veins, his patience snapped. He tugged at Naia's hair, guiding her back, and her noise of protest turned to one of approval as he took her place, wrapping his lips around the head of Aleksi's cock. No sweet teasing for him, either. He let that silk-covered steel fill his mouth, reveling in the taste of Aleksi and the hint of Naia left behind.

Aleksi's hand fell to Einar's head, and if there was one thing that could stroke a man's ego, it was making the god of love and desire make noises like *that* as his fingers clutched helplessly at his hair.

"Always so eager." Naia's breath feathered over Einar's ear as she stroked his back. "So ready to swallow your lover's pleasure."

The words made his head swim almost as much as the feel of Aleksi's cock in his mouth and the trembling of Aleksi's body. Einar slid back just far enough to seize Naia's mouth in a kiss, mingling the taste of them on his tongue. Then he nipped her bottom lip. "If you ask sweetly, I'll share."

Naia gripped his chin. "Would you deny me, Kraken?"

In this moment, he doubted he could deny her anything. "No, goddess."

Without releasing his gaze, she nudged him forward, until the crown of Aleksi's cock brushed his mouth. Then she leaned in with parted lips, dragging a groan from Aleksi as their tongues met against his skin.

There was nothing elegant in it, nothing sweet. A feverish need had seized them both, and they dueled over their prize, one dragging their tongue along the shaft while the other swallowed the head, then meeting to kiss again. Aleksi's hand twisted tight in Einar's hair as the other found Naia's, but even when his body trembled and the sounds they dragged from him were tortured, he let them play, murmuring encouragement and praise as the sea crashed behind him and pleasure wrapped around and around them . . .

Einar was the one who broke first, unable to take the song pounding in his blood. Centuries of assignations had taught him how to take even a cock as generous as the Lover's as deep as he wanted to. He swallowed it to the root, shuddering as Naia panted against his cheek and Aleksi's hips jerked. Einar did it again, and then a third time, and Aleksi broke, spilling his release hot over Einar's tongue as Naia moaned in envy.

The waves still churned in his blood, and pleasure made him drunk. He wondered vaguely if this was Aleksi's doing. Some trick of the Lover that let them feel each other, perhaps? It hardly mattered—all that mattered was the throbbing need that still burned within him—and the way Naia trembled at his side.

Easing back, Einar lifted his thumb to swipe at the corner of his mouth, catching the evidence of Aleksi's release. Naia's kiss-reddened mouth was so close, and he dragged his thumb over her lips. "I was greedy with his pleasure, wasn't I?"

"You were *you*." She licked the taste of Aleksi from her lips before grasping Einar's face, staring at him as if she saw past his skin and into his soul. "And I would not have you any other way."

She meant it. There was no part of him he could reveal that would push her away—not the hardened face of the pirate captain at war, not the inhuman face of his demigod form, not even the enormous, terrifying Kraken itself, wrapping around her and pulling her into the deep.

And not the man who rose and pulled her to her feet, dragging her back so that there could be no mistake of how aroused he was. The perfect curve of her ass taunted him as she rocked back, grinding against him until he had to catch her hips and still her. Einar waited until Aleksi had refastened his pants, then smiled. "I think it is her turn, is it not?"

Aleksi answered by dragging Einar in for a kiss—deep, hot, and relentless, the kind of kiss that melted knees and set hearts racing. Einar was breathing hard when Aleksi released him, only to claim Naia's lips for an equally thorough kissing.

It was beautiful to watch, but Einar had other plans for Aleksi's lips. He plunged his fingers into Aleksi's hair and urged him back. "Kneel for our goddess, Lover."

Glazed brown eyes stared at him for just a moment before Aleksi obeyed. He started with a line of open-mouthed kisses to Naia's cheek, and then her jaw. The hollow of her throat. Her collarbone. Naia gasped, her head falling back against Einar's shoulder, as Aleksi's lips dislodged the neckline of her dress, baring first one breast and then the other to the cool night air.

When Aleksi's mouth closed around the tight point of one nipple, Einar had to cover Naia's lips with his fingers to muffle the desperate moan. "Shh," he murmured against her ear. "You have to be quiet, love. So quiet."

She trembled against him as Aleksi moved to the other breast, her quiet little noises somehow even hotter. Einar slid his fingers down over her chin and her throat, stroking between her breasts as Aleksi finally folded his knees and sank to the floor.

Naia swallowed. Hard.

So aroused already it would not take much to push her over the edge, then. Einar began to gather her skirts in his fingers as he brushed his mouth to her ear. "Put your hands on the railing."

Slowly, so slowly, she obeyed. Her fingers curled over the stone, and she looked down, breath shuddering when she found Aleksi gazing back up at her with that beautifully terrifying intensity—the look that said the Lover was about to unleash his considerable skills with a singular focus: her pleasure and joy.

She deserved both tonight. And when Einar had her skirts gathered up to her waist, she got them as Aleksi leaned in to taste her.

Naia gasped with the first touch, pleasure shivering through her body—and somehow into Einar's. It was that *song* again, the one that twined with the waves. If he closed his eyes he could hear them, rising and breaking against the hull of his ship, as if he stood on the deck instead of on stone and earth. He turned his mouth to her ear again and whispered, "I can feel your bliss in the waves."

"I—" Whatever she might have said broke on a helpless cry, and it was a pity her skirts were hiding whatever Aleksi was doing with his tongue. Judging from the way she panted and the helpless movement of her hips, it was impressive.

Well, Einar could help with that. He freed one hand from the tangle of fabric and traced it up the center of her body. Kind of Aleksi to dislodge that wicked neckline, because Einar's fingers met no obstacles on their path to gently—so, so gently—stroking one nipple. He kept his touch soft, mostly for the pleasure of hearing her beg.

"Please." It fell from her as a breathless whisper. When he kept his touch light and teasing, she said it again—a pleading word that came out as a demand. *"Please."*

No, his goddess didn't like it soft. He gave her what she wanted, a firm touch, and then his thumb and forefinger together, tugging with just enough pressure to make her head slam back against his shoulder. "Like that," he murmured.

She moaned and turned her face toward his. Hot breath fell against his cheek in an unsteady rhythm. There was nothing unsteady about the rhythm of her hips, though—her ass pressed back against him, driving him wild as she grasped Aleksi's head and rode his tongue.

Not being able to see what was happening had grown intolerable. He abandoned her breast and reached for her leg, dragging his fingernails up the soft skin of her inner thigh as he bit her earlobe. "Can you hear the waves?"

Her chest heaved. "The—the what?"

He slid his hand higher, until his fingers brushed Aleksi's cheek. "The ocean, Naia. Can you hear it?"

She shook her head, her teeth buried in her lower lip. "All I hear is the island's heart pounding."

He swore he could hear it, too, then—pounding inside him like the beat of wild drums. It joined with the song of the sea, becoming something primal—something like the song they played to honor the love between the storm god and the goddess. A song of carnal abandon, of opening yourself to another.

A breeze swept across the balcony—not cold, like it should have been, but unnaturally warm. Perhaps he should have wondered why. But Aleksi's tongue swept across his fingertips, and then *she* was beneath him—hot, slick, trembling.

Needy.

He stroked her, and her fingers tangled in his jacket so hard he feared she'd rip it from his back. Aleksi hummed his approval, his tongue thrusting deeper into her as Einar teased his fingers in slow, relentless circles. "How far do you want to go, goddess?"

"Don't stop." Her fingernails dug into his arm so fiercely, he could feel it through his coat. "Don't—"

Aleksi did *something*, and Naia's entire body jerked. Her hand slammed back down onto the railing, as if it was the only thing keeping her from total collapse, and that *wind* was back, whipping across them hard enough to rustle her unbound hair. Einar pressed his lips to the back of her neck, groaning as her bliss pulsed within him in a way that was definitely not natural, but oh, so good.

The words spilled free, riding on that wave of reckless heat. "Would you let me take you right here? Like this? Do you want me to see how hard I can fuck you before your knees give out?"

She whimpered.

He eased his hands from beneath her skirts and groaned as he licked the taste of her from his fingers. "You have to say yes, goddess."

The word spilled from her again, the one he knew meant *yes* in their ancient language. She panted it again and again, a plea and a demand and a prayer.

He needed to be inside her more than he needed his next breath. "Aleksi." His voice was a barely human rumble. "Make sure she's ready for me."

The Lover needed no more prompting. He guided one of Naia's legs up onto his shoulder, turning to kiss her inner thigh. "For you, or for the Kraken?"

If only he could give in to that temptation. Tear free of these clothes, be *himself* in the way he had for those precious hours when they'd all been stranded on the island together. But that could come later, when they were safely behind locked doors—and not running the risk of discovery. "For me. This time."

Aleksi looked up, locking eyes with Einar as he gently bit the inside of Naia's thigh. Her soft gasp melted into an unsteady moan as his hand moved beneath her skirts. Her entire body lurched, and only Einar's arm around her waist kept her from collapsing.

Beneath them, the waves sounded louder. Was she stirring them with her pleasure? Were there ships in the harbor even now, swaying with the rhythm of her wild gasps? It was almost too easy to imagine *them* on the ship, the roll of the sea a perfect counterpart to the roll of his hips, as he sank into her again and again and again—

Heat exploded over him, in time with Naia's helpless cry. Her body shook in his arms as the warm wind swirled around them, carrying the scent of salt and sand and heavy tropical flowers under the hot sun, and for a moment Einar thought *he* was coming, too—

No, his cock was still hot and hard behind the cage of his pants, and that was intolerable. He fumbled for the fastening, already anticipating the tight, glorious heat of her as he drove deep—

On the other side of the pillar, someone cleared their throat loudly. Ash's familiar voice drifted to them on the breeze. "I am not looking. I promise I am not looking. But something odd is happening, and we thought it best to warn you."

Einar stiffened for one startled moment, then he straightened in the same moment Naia slid her leg from Aleksi's shoulder. He rose, adjusting his pants, and Naia spun to hide her half-bare torso against Einar's chest.

"What is it?" Aleksi panted.

"We can all . . . feel something." Ash cleared his throat again, clearly uncomfortable.

Aleksi touched Naia's head and Einar's cheek, then disappeared around the column to speak to Ash. Their words were hushed, nothing more than the soft rise and fall of low voices reaching them.

Naia clung to Einar. "Do you think . . . ?"

He ran a soothing hand over her hair before helping her adjust the top of her dress so that she was fully covered again. "It doesn't sound dangerous." An attack would have had Ash striding out here to summon them to battle, no matter how indelicate their position. Even an orgy would not have stopped the Dragon when a fight was in the offing.

After a few moments, Aleksi strode back onto the balcony alone, smiling gently. "Not to worry," he assured them. "It seems we may have been a bit too enthusiastic."

Naia frowned. "Too loud, you mean?"

"No, love." Aleksi lifted his hands to Naia's hair and took over where Einar had left off, smoothing the tousled curls. "It seems that your island reflects what you feel. Sometimes very strongly."

It took a moment for Naia to grasp the meaning of his words. When she did, she covered her mouth with a gasp. *No.*

"It's fine. Just fine." Aleksi pulled her hand to his lips. "No one beyond the High Court even noticed. Sachi made sure of it."

So the pleasure Einar had felt had not been her power reaching him through the sea, but the island itself, celebrating her joy.

Poor Naia. Her cheeks flamed red, and Einar wanted to wrap himself around her again to shield her from the world—and perhaps thank Sachi for her quick work in protecting Naia's privacy.

Not for the first time, Einar wished he had Aleksi's easy way with soothing words. But his tension eased when a comforting hand on her back and a kiss to the top of her head seemed to relax her. After a few moments, she gave an unsteady laugh. "That never happened to us—I mean, to *me* before."

Us. She must mean her and the storm god. Einar felt torn between that same impossible, foolish stab of jealousy, and an even more base feeling—smugness. The storm god might have been some ancient terrifying force of magic that Einar might never live up to, but *he* had never made his goddess come so hard she rocked the entire island with her.

Of course, he hadn't had the Lover's help. But Einar had never cared much about fighting fair. He smoothed Naia's hair down with a smile. "I doubt anything we did could have shocked the High Court," he said lightly. "Not after centuries of Joining Day celebrations at Aleksi's villa."

Naia groaned and buried her face against Einar's chest. Einar stared at Aleksi over her shoulder, raising one eyebrow in silent question. *You're the diplomat, what do we do now?*

Aleksi wrapped his arms around them both, and warmth stole through Einar that had nothing to do with passion. Love could burn bright and hot, but it could soothe and protect, too. The Lover always knew which was needed. "Come," Aleksi urged softly. "It is late, and the day has been long. Let's get some sleep."

Chapter Twelve

The world beyond our island is restless. The wind brings grief and rage. The seas churn. I have watched the goddess walk the shores, her eyes fixed on the eastern horizon. Something vast and terrible is coming, and I admit, I am afraid.

The lost journal of High Priestess Tona

The relatively small library near Aleksi's chamber had been a refuge for Naia. On the nights when borrowed dreams and memories had torn her from sleep, she had made her way here. Of all the rooms in Gwynira's palace, it was her favorite—close and cozy and *safe*.

This time, as she left Aleksi and Einar sleeping in their giant bed and crept out of the bedroom and toward the library, she was not in need of solace.

Tonight, she wanted *information*.

She had idly perused the shelves before, noting that most of the collected volumes seemed to have been brought over from the Empire's mainland. But, here and there, scattered amongst the rest, Naia had found books that were different. They had unique bindings, and their delicate pages were filled with an indecipherable language that had elicited curiosity and longing.

She reached for those books first. Written Rahvekyan was very formal, almost stilted in comparison to the far more relaxed verbal syntax of everyday speech. It had been reserved mainly for religious texts, official diplomatic missives, and royal decrees, with most people preferring a simpler syllabary, one that represented sounds and more closely matched the patterns of the spoken language.

Was Naia the only person left in the world who could read this?

She tore through the volumes, scanning the pages for any mentions of Theron. It was the one thing no one in the palace seemed to know, not even in the vaguest terms—what had become of the storm god after Naia's death? The servants she'd questioned had all had different stories, legends passed down from their grandparents' grandparents. He had stayed on as she had asked, remaining in Rahvekya to help her people. He had fled, unable to bear the grinding pain of living on the island in her absence.

It was the last story that made her want to fold in on herself in despair: that he had died that day along with her.

Naia's stomach lurched. She set aside the useless book in her hand and reached for another, then another, then *another*. But not a single volume possessed the answers she so desperately sought.

The door swung open, admitting a stream of palace staff. Two men headed for the hearth to stoke the fire, while others placed serving trays on the tables situated near the chairs. There was a jug of warmed wine, its spicy-sweet scent filling the room, and small bowls of nuts, dried meats, and cheeses.

Another woman draped soft-looking woven blankets across the back of each chair, while another, a short brunette with wide eyes, began to pick up the books that Naia had left scattered about.

"Thank you," Naia murmured. "I did not take careful notice of where the books were shelved, and then I did not want to put them in the wrong place."

The young woman paused in her task and turned to pin Naia with a look of shock. "You need not tidy the room, my lady."

"But I'm the one who dragged out all the books," she countered. "So I am grateful that you know where they belong."

The girl blushed. "The categorization system is distinctive, but simple enough once you've learned it."

"Are you an archivist?"

"Goddess, no." She seemed to realize what she'd said, and stammered, "I—I mean—"

Naia *had* to rescue her from herself. "What is your name?"

"Tilly, ma'am."

"Well, Tilly." Naia passed her the last book, the one she still held in her hands. "You seem like an archivist to me."

She responded with a shy smile, one that lingered as she placed the book into a void on the shelf. Then she turned and joined the rest of the staff as they clustered near the door.

Waiting for her blessing.

"Thank you all," she murmured. "The island will not forget what you've done for me."

The words elicited such joy, and that joy no longer confused Naia. These people had been waiting many generations—*thousands* of years—for some sign that their beliefs were true. That their goddess had not died and left them completely alone. That she would, one day, return to them.

Naia was fiercely glad she could give them this comfort for the cost of only a few words.

They filed out, silently closing the door behind them. Naia bypassed the chairs, sinking instead to the plush rug in front of the fire. She stared into the flames, and tears tracked down her cheeks as she gave in and finally let herself truly feel the frustrations of the night.

"See? I told you," Aleksi murmured from the doorway. "Here she is."

Einar edged past him. His brow smoothed at the sight of her, then furrowed again when she hastily dried her cheeks. "Naia?"

She managed a smile and patted the rug next to her. "Would you like some wine?"

Aleksi rubbed Einar's shoulder, urging him forward. "Sit. I'll serve it."

Einar joined her, settling so near that she could feel the warmth of his body. He'd pulled on a shirt but left it unlaced, and she toyed with one of the laces as he pulled her closer. "Were you having trouble sleeping again?"

She reclined against him, resting her elbow on his hard thigh. "Yes."

"More dreams?" Aleksi asked as he filled one of the metal mugs.

Naia hesitated. Attributing her restlessness to the usual causes would be simple, and they would not question it. But it would be a lie, and she did not *want* that clouding the warm quiet of the night.

But neither did she want to admit the truth. Confessing that she'd left their bed to frantically search for even a slip of information about a lover she knew to be long dead? How could that not feel like a slight, even if they thought they understood?

In the end, she gave them a different truth. "So much has happened."

Einar ran a gentle hand over her shoulder and down to her back, rubbing in soothing circles. "It must be overwhelming."

Naia swallowed the taste of guilt and offered them another half truth. "I'm the only one left. It shouldn't matter, should it? I was alone for so long in the beginning, just me and the island. But now it seems . . . tragic that there's no one left who remembers. Even Petya and Jinevra weren't born until hundreds of years after . . ." She trailed off, unable to say it.

Aleksi lowered himself to the rug with preternatural grace, not spilling a drop of wine on the rich cream-colored fur. "You feel alone," he whispered.

"I *am* alone."

"Naia—"

"In *this*, Aleksi." She took the mug he offered, but caught his hand before he could pull away. "I know that you are here."

He pulled her hand to his mouth and kissed the back of it. "And we're not going anywhere."

Einar cradled his own mug and watched her carefully. "Does it hurt to talk about it, or would it help? I think Petya liked to tell me the stories so there would be someone else who remembered, even if I could never truly *know* them the way she did."

He had asked before, in the little glade, and here he was, asking again. There was little chance that talking about the past could cheer Naia, but Einar was so *hungry* for details . . .

And it might help him remember. "What would you like to hear?"

His lips tugged into a self-conscious, almost bashful smile. "Honestly? Everything. Anything you want to share. I've heard the stories for so long . . ."

She opened her mouth to tell him something lighthearted and meaningless, something no one else could ever have told him. Something that would light the joy and wonder in his beautiful eyes.

What came out was "I knew I was going to die."

Einar stilled. "You knew about the war between Sorin and the High Court?"

She shook her head as she placed her mug of wine on the stone floor beyond the perimeter of the rug. "I wasn't privy to those events happening across the seas. I just . . . knew. Someday, there would be a great calamity, and I would give my life to save my people." A memory washed over her, dragging a laugh from her aching throat. "I told one of my priestesses once, and she cried for a solid week. I never made that mistake again."

Aleksi's fingers tightened around hers. "That is a terrible knowledge to bear."

"Is it?" she questioned. "I always considered it a blessing of a sort. Death comes for everyone. At least I had the comfort of knowing my end would serve a *purpose*."

Einar set his wine aside untouched and claimed her other hand. "What happened?" he asked softly.

She owed him an answer, even if he later regretted asking. "It started with the rumbling. The earth shook—which was nothing new, of course. This *is* a volcanic island. But these quakes just kept happening, and they grew more intense every time. Then the seas began to rise."

If she closed her eyes, she would see it—the confusion on the people's faces. Not fear, never fear. Even with the world crumbling around them, they had not been afraid. They had trusted her too much for that.

"We evacuated the coasts." Her voice broke, and she cleared her throat. "But by the time the worst of the earthquakes began, I knew it wouldn't be enough."

Aleksi shifted, pulling Naia against his chest. It positioned his mouth close to her ear, and he murmured, "You don't have to say it."

"Yes, I do." She met Einar's gaze. "Theron tried to stop me. He said we could leave until the waves had subsided. Take everyone to the mainland, then come back to rebuild. But there was no time left for a logistical undertaking that massive. Do you understand?"

He stared back at her, and she could practically see Theron's thoughts, his rationalizations, tumbling through Einar's head. He and the storm god had lived vastly different lives, but some things would always be immutably true.

He thought Theron had been right, that he should have *dragged* her away. But Einar merely answered her question. "You wouldn't have been able to bring everyone."

"No, and I couldn't abandon them. So I went to the temple, and I raised a wall of water around the island. At first, just high enough to stave off the flooding. But I had to keep building it higher and higher. And I had to hold it."

Aleksi trembled behind her, but his voice was low, even. Soothing. "For three days."

Three *agonizing* days. Naia could have borne the effort of raising the wall, the pain of holding out the crushing seas beyond it. She did not even begrudge the vast amount of power she'd had to burn through in order to keep the barrier whole, though by the last day, only the island's magic had kept her standing.

No, the true torment had been in watching Theron break down.

The first day, he'd begged her to reconsider. By the second, he'd moved on to threats, insisting that he would physically remove her from danger if necessary.

On the third day, he had a different threat entirely. He'd warned her through angry tears and lightning strikes that if she died protecting this island, he would sink it into the ocean in retaliation.

But she could not say that aloud—especially not to Einar. "I held the wall until the earth calmed and the seas receded. And then . . . I let go."

He rubbed a thumb over her fingers in a slow, soothing rhythm, his gaze never leaving hers. "Is that the last thing you remember?"

"I suppose it is." There were other images and impressions, flashes of something that might have been memory or just fancy. Screams, tears. A wordless song of gratitude and grief. But nothing she *knew*. Einar probably had a better idea of what had happened in the aftermath, simply by virtue of growing up with stories about the goddess's sacrifice. "It must have worked, at least to spare some of them. Because the people are still here."

"They survived. They thrived." Einar touched her temple, smoothing back a lock of disheveled hair before stroking her cheek. "And they taught their children to stand strong and wait for your return. Generation after generation. Even after the Empire came. So many people who Sorin conquered lost their history, but your island was too damn stubborn to be conquered. You gave them that."

How could she have done all of that when the thought of returning had never occurred to her? "I only wanted them to *live*, Einar. Not to grieve me for thousands of years."

"Maybe there was grief in it," he said softly. "But there was also joy. That was what Petya taught me, more than anything. To love the sea, to protect my people . . ." He smiled. "To believe that impossible things can happen if we fight hard enough to make them real."

Was that why Einar could not remember, because she had not tried to make him? Did she have to push him, as everyone had pushed her, however inadvertently, since her arrival?

She took Einar's hand. There was only one thing she could think of that Theron would have to understand. The thing that had brought memories of him rushing back to *her*.

She traced a small spiral on Einar's palm. It was a tiny gesture that she and Theron had shared, a way to silently say, *I am here. I see you, and I know you.*

A tiny furrow appeared between his brows as he stared down at their hands. Then the confusion gave way to affection, and Naia's heart leapt. But Einar only lifted her hand and kissed the back of it without a hint of recognition.

Her heart splintered in her chest.

She could not let Einar see her pain, so she turned in Aleksi's arms and hid her face against his chest. "I'm so tired," she whispered thickly.

"Then come." His arms tightened, and he lifted her as he rose from the rug. "Let's get you back to bed."

Before Naia could respond, a shock jolted through her. Her entire body felt like a struck bell, vibrating and jittery. She gasped sharply and clenched her hands in Aleksi's open shirt in an attempt to ground herself.

Instantly, Aleksi went tense. "What is it? What's wrong?"

"I don't—"

A voice cut through her words, echoing not in Naia's ears, but through everything—the room, the aether, even her very soul.

hurry

Einar's fear, loud and metallic, clashed with the strange sensation still ringing through her. "Naia?"

HURRY

Naia's mind went blank as she pushed against Aleksi's chest and slid out of his arms. But the moment her feet hit the cold stone, the struck-bell sensation intensified until it nearly rattled her teeth.

One word spilled from her lips, unbidden. "Sachi."

Aleksi was first through the door. Before the three of them reached the end of the corridor that led to the room assigned to the Dragon and his consorts, they heard it.

Screaming.

Naia burst through the already open door. The rest of the High Court had already stumbled in, the sleep driven from their eyes by the pained shrieks.

Sachi was slumped on the floor in her nightdress, clawing at the rug as she gasped in sobbing breaths between screams. "I can't feel—feel them—"

Zanya and Ash knelt on either side of her, their arms around her, as if they could protect her from the agony that was shredding her. Their frantic, devastated expressions showed that they knew their attempts were futile.

Naia rushed to them, hitting the floor on her knees in front of Sachi. She cupped her friend's face, lifted it to the light. "What's happening?"

"It's the new Dreamers," Zanya replied grimly.

"They're *dying*." Sachi shoulders shook with the force of her sobs. "I can see them. Lights in the dark. And then they're *gone* . . ."

"The Voidlings?" Naia asked.

"The same." Zanya swallowed hard, as if she could swallow her grief, as well. "But nowhere near this many."

Sachi threw back her head and screamed, a visceral sound of anguish that slowly turned into *rage*. The fire flared out of the hearth, and the icy windows fractured. Even the furniture began to rattle as Sachi heaved in another breath, her eyes burning now with frozen blue fire.

"They're killing them." Sachi's voice thundered through the room, even louder than her unrelenting screams.

A nearby table shattered, the pieces crashing to the floor.

Naia laid her hand flat on the floor. Power flowed from the stone, and she sent it back, along with a plea. *Settle, I beg you.*

The furniture stilled. Sachi fell quiet but continued to seethe.

"We have to go." Ash's words were subdued. Stricken. "Whatever this is—"

"Of course you'll go," Aleksi cut in firmly. "Whatever you have to do. Naia and Einar and I will handle things here."

"No." Inga stepped out of the shadows on the other side of the hearth, her expression just as resolute. "I'm not leaving Aleksi again." She sought Naia's gaze as magic flared pink in her dark eyes. "And you're going to need me here."

Naia did not want to believe it. But Inga's voice echoed deep in the stone and soil beneath her, ringing with truth . . . and a warning.

Whatever was happening, they could only see a tiny part of it. There were machinations that none of them could understand yet, plans that might only become clear when their enemies stood before them.

And the danger was just beginning.

Chapter Thirteen

The goddess has fallen. My heart breaks for those left behind. Especially him.

The lost journal of High Priestess Tona

It was so quiet in his suite without the rest of the High Court in attendance.

Aleksi poured himself another steaming cup of tea. The pots always seemed to be full and hot and prepared to his exact preference—an advantage he enjoyed, no doubt, because of his intimacy with the people's goddess and their long-lost prince.

He had just retrieved the book he'd set aside when the door swung open and Naia walked in. He gestured her closer with a wry smile. "Come. Save me from my solitary reveries."

Naia chuckled. "I thought surely Einar would be entertaining you."

"He has business with his crew," Aleksi told her. "I am afraid I am the only one here."

"Good." Naia's amusement faded as she sank into the chair nearest the sofa. "I actually wanted to talk to you. Alone."

Ominous words, perhaps, considering how nervous she seemed. Naia was still sweet and caring and optimistic, but since she'd recovered her memories of her past life, she'd been more considered, more serious. As if whatever she had remembered weighed heavy on her soul.

And how could it not? It weighed on Aleksi, and he had nothing like her excuse. He had not just recovered many centuries of memories. He had only this horrible new knowledge that while his brothers had been fighting, across the seas, Naia's world had been crumbling. She had been *dying* in order to protect her people.

It broke Aleksi's heart. Surely it did hers, as well.

Naia toyed with the music player in the corner, nudging its mechanical switch without pushing it far enough to power on the machine. "Have you heard from Elevia or any of the others?"

"Not as yet," Aleksi answered. "But they only just left last night."

Naia's expression tightened into a troubled frown. "Should we have gone with them?"

"If they need us, they will let us know."

"As you say."

His sweet little nymph was stalling.

He set aside his book, for good this time, and moved to the end of the sofa, close to her. "Tell me what's wrong, love."

Naia folded her hands in her lap and sat with the kind of stillness that spoke of careful, rigid control. "Aleksi . . . I remember."

"Yes, of course you do." He touched her arm and waited for her to continue.

"No, not . . . being her. The goddess." She caught his hand and held it tightly. "I remember Einar."

The words made little sense, but Naia spoke them with an urgent sincerity that left Aleksi in no doubt of the gravity of the situation. "I don't understand."

"He was my lover, Theron," she whispered. "The god of storms. The *Kraken*."

It was rude to stare, Aleksi knew. But he could do nothing else.

"There were bits and pieces before," she went on, the words coming fast and hard. "Times when he would look at me or say something, and I could swear we'd been there before, just like that."

They probably had. Odd, how this revelation managed to be unthinkable . . . and also make absolute, perfect sense. Einar had always been drawn to Naia, hungry to know her in ways that went far beyond the physical desires he'd claimed. And Naia had trusted him, wholly and without reserve, even when she'd known better. It was as if her very soul had always been open to Einar, and his to her.

It was discomfiting to think of, in a way. Not their connection—Aleksi treasured love in all its forms, and watching them rediscover one another had brought him a joy that he was, only now, able to recognize as the sweet triumph of reunion.

No, it was difficult to think of them as they were now, and also as they had been before. Naia and Einar. The goddess and the Kraken. Here were two people that Aleksi had come to love dearly, and he wanted desperately to know who they had been *then*, as well. But he could not.

It was a kind of grief, this impossible longing.

"Have you told Einar?" he asked, though he already knew the answer. If she had, she wouldn't be this nervous. Relieved or shattered, yes, but not nervous.

"How?" She shot off the chair and paced across the rug, wringing her hands. "He doesn't remember, Aleksi. Even if he thought me sincere, even if he *wanted* to believe me—how could he? It's unfathomable."

And she had some experience with that, didn't she? The island locals treating her as their long-dead goddess returned had not made the idea seem *more* likely to Naia, but far *less*. She had been so consumed with not inadvertently strengthening their beliefs that she had not stopped, for even one moment, to consider it as possible.

And this was even more complicated. If Naia whispered this truth to Einar, he would want more than anything to believe it.

He would want it so badly that he might discard it out of hand.

But Aleksi could not bring himself to admit as much, not with Naia this agitated. Instead, he held out his arms. "Come here."

Naia hesitated, then slid into his lap and wrapped her arms around his neck.

"Now, listen to me, love." He nudged her chin to turn her head until her gaze locked with his. "Einar has never doubted you, and he never will. It might take him some time to really come around to the truth of it, but that won't be because of you, or how he feels about you. It will be because of how he feels about *himself*."

"I know." The words were barely audible. "I just don't want to hurt him, Aleksi."

"Nor do I."

Except that he might do it anyway, just by being there.

He had often thought that Naia and Einar seemed destined to be together—wasn't that why he had resolved to set them up as one of his last acts on earth? Why he had vowed not to come between them?

It appeared his instincts about that had been quite good, after all. They were not only destined to love one another, they had already done so. And, down in Aleksi's soul, he could feel that their love was as fierce as a storm, as inexorable as the tides. Deeper than the darkest trench in the far recesses of the ocean.

He did not want to do this. But he needed to, because nothing mattered more to him than what was best for them.

"Naia, you and Einar . . ." He cleared his throat. "You loved each other before, but you were torn apart. Perhaps it would be better if you had fewer complications as you navigate this second chance."

Naia's dark eyes sparked with displeasure. *"Aleksi."*

"I mean it, little nymph. You just found one another again. Maybe I'm in the way, after all." Pain rendered his voice hoarse, hard as he tried to quell it. "I could step aside, as I'd planned to do all along. Leave you to it."

She pulled back a little and stared at Aleksi with eyes that were fathomless. Ancient. She gazed at him with almost preternatural awareness, as if she knew everything in his heart, all that he said and all that could never be articulated.

And, more, as if she *understood.*

Finally, she smiled and cupped his face between her hands. "No. There might have been a time we could have let you go, but if it ever existed—and that is a very questionable *if*—it is long past."

"But—"

"I did not come all this way to live a smaller life." She brushed her thumbs over his lips. "Look, and tell me that you see the truth of my words."

Aleksi hesitated, then closed his eyes. When he opened them once more, he opened his heart along with them.

Color. Not static, like the hazy auras that surrounded most people. Every shade imaginable shifted in blazing currents that encompassed not only Naia, but the entire room. There were darker shades woven in, echoes of the Void tangled up in all that light. But there was no deception.

"I see," he whispered. "All of you, love."

"Good." She kissed him slowly, softly, flooding him with all that color. Then she pulled away, and the rainbow settled into soft red, both troubled and protective. "But I need a favor, Aleksi."

"Anything." If she asked him for both of the moons, he would find a way to drag them from the sky and place them in her hands.

"*Please* don't say that to Einar," she begged. "Don't offer to walk away. I know what it means, and what it would cost you. But I'm afraid that Einar would only hear that you *could* leave. Not that you would do it for us, even if it broke your heart."

She was right, of course. "Very well. As you said—we've no wish to hurt him."

"Thank you."

"Don't thank me yet, for I have something to ask of you, as well."

"What is it?"

"Do not wait too long to tell Einar the truth about his past with you," he cautioned. "After a while, silence can begin to look like doubt, or even condemnation."

She seemed to consider that, then nodded. "I promise."

He tucked her face against his neck. She was a warm, soft weight against him, her silent presence reassuring him in a way that words never could.

But he had more questions. "Naia? What happened to Einar—I mean, Theron? You know . . ." He could not bring himself to say *when you died*. "After."

"I don't know." Tears glittered on her lashes. "That's what I had been doing when you found me in Gwynira's library last night. Looking for answers. But I found nothing."

"What about the locals?"

She shook her head. "No one could help me."

She didn't know, and that hurt her. Aleksi found himself desperate to banish her pain. "We will find out."

"How? If Einar never remembers—"

"We will find out," he repeated. "That is a promise, little nymph. And I do not make promises I cannot keep."

"I know." She laid her head on his shoulder again.

Aleksi wrapped his arms more tightly around her. "Would you like to tell me about him?"

"Theron?" Her sigh blew against the side of his neck. "He was a mess of contradictions. So set in his ways, he was practically calcified. But if he had good reason to change, he would do it like it was nothing. And he was so *funny*. But if you think Einar can be grumpy . . ."

"*Heavens*. Surely Theron could not have been worse?"

"Oh, yes." Her breathing hitched. "He used to tell me that we had to trust the tides, that they would take us where we needed to be. Unite us with the people we were meant to love."

Naia spoke with such longing and affection that it was impossible not to think of his own love affair with Alysaia. Though they'd enjoyed only a fleeting time together, Aleksi still cherished every moment. "How long did you have with him?"

"Many, *many* years. Thousands?"

It did not seem possible, since the stories had painted her as ancient even before the storm god came into her life. "How old *are* you?"

"I don't know." She rubbed his upper arm rhythmically, a slow glide down to his elbow followed by a quick stroke back up to his shoulder. "I never concerned myself with that. I marked time only by the generations that were born, grew, and died in my care. There are probably documents somewhere—the priestesses were always obsessed with recording things—but I never worried about it. The sun and moons rose and set, and every day was new and precious."

"That's a lovely way to look at living."

He felt her smile against the side of his neck. "Perhaps *I* can teach *you* a few new things then, Lover."

"Never doubted that, my sweet goddess. Not for a single heartbeat."

Chapter Fourteen

There are many legends of the goddess that have been passed down—or, frankly, fabricated—by the natives of Akeisa. Most seem to center around standard themes of preservation and restoration.

For instance, their goddess's primary temple is often lauded as a sacred place of healing. According to the locals, it houses the goddess's heart, and therefore cannot be destroyed.

As said temple now lies in ruins, I do not concur.

Fallen Goddess: An Analysis of Primitive Belief
by Guildmaster Klement

The moment Einar opened the door to their rooms, he knew something was *very* wrong in Gwynira's court.

For one thing, no servants lingered in their hallway, hoping for a chance to be of service to the goddess. There were no new little tokens on the floor outside the suite, either. No one was to be found when they stepped into the wide corridor that led to the main castle—except a single frazzled-looking noble who took one look at them and almost tripped in her haste to retreat back into her own quarters.

Aleksi and Naia met his wary look with expressions of equal uncertainty. As one, they hurried their steps, their goal the Great Hall, where the court usually broke their fast. They found Inga hovering outside the room, looking perplexed. "No one is eating, and everyone is whispering, but no one wants to talk about what is *happening*," she said by way of greeting.

"Because they don't understand what is happening," Gwynira said, sweeping out of the hall with Arktikos and Isa flanking her.

The tightness of her eyes shot dread up Einar's spine. "Has there been another attack?"

"No, nothing like that." Gwynira turned to Naia. "You are familiar with the ruins of your former temple, I assume? The ones that sit on the cliff above the palace?"

Instead of answering, Naia pivoted on her heel and rushed toward the exit that led out into the gardens. Biting off a curse, Einar hurried after her. Even with his longer legs, she was out the door before he caught up, as if something was drawing her with a force she could not resist.

He pushed the heavy door open and stepped into the garden, only to stop so abruptly that someone crashed into his back. He barely heard Inga's muffled curse, and it was not conscious thought that carried him forward, one unsteady step at a time.

No, thought had fled. Yesterday, the ruins had been barely visible on the cliffs above, just hints of shattered stone overgrown with vines. Today . . .

Today, there was a temple. *Whole*, the magnificent pillars shining in the sun as if it had been hewn from bright-white stone that morning, its very existence an impossibility. He parted his lips, and simply could not form words.

Thankfully, Aleksi still could. He stepped forward and touched Naia's shoulder. "We should go and see—"

That was as far as he got before disorientation seized Einar. The ground beneath him went soft, sliding like sand being washed away by the tides. Wind roared around them, hot and out of place, carrying the heavy scent of tropical flowers and the joyful song of birds that he had only heard far, far to the south.

His heartbeat pounded so loudly it was all he could hear. Or maybe it was the heartbeat of the island, because he could feel it all around him, frantic and strong and *alive*—just like he had on the beach, when Naia had wrapped them in her power and carried them to the secret cave deep in the heart of the island.

His boots hit solid ground abruptly. A breeze tugged at his hair, the sharp kind that immediately made Einar think of climbing the crow's nest on his ship, and a bronze lantern stood a few paces in front of him. As soon as they arrived, the wick shivered, and a bright teal flame leapt to life, dancing inside and casting light through the sections of the lantern that had been cut out.

Cut out. These were the lanterns that lined the way up to the temple ruins. He forced his gaze past it, and saw a dizzying drop off the side of the cliff. They were nearly at the top, with Gwynira's palace far below, its garden buzzing with activity as the onlookers who had surrounded them only moments before spilled toward the base of the path.

"That was unexpected," came Gwynira's voice, and even her customary chill couldn't hide the wild edge to the otherwise casual words. Einar turned to see that Naia had brought Arktikos and Gwynira with them this time, and while the burly guard's face showed little reaction, there was a hint of wildness in the Ice Queen's eyes, too. She watched Naia with a new wariness—and a new respect.

Naia barely seemed to notice. She strode up the path, each footstep confident, *eager* even. Einar followed her, only to stagger to a halt for the second time when the temple came into view.

It was magnificent.

The last time they'd come up here, it had been nothing but a tangle of collapsed stone pillars and rubble. Weeds had been lovingly cut away by faithful hands, but there had been no hiding the destruction that time and war had wrought on the place that had once been the goddess's sanctuary.

On their first visit, Einar had pinned Naia to one of those broken pillars, savoring her sounds of pleasure as she rode his tongue until the winds whipping through the toppled stones had stolen her cries.

They were toppled no longer.

Massive columns formed a wide circle at the top of the cliff, carved from a pristine white stone shot through with veins that sparkled in the sunlight. The roof was made of hammered brass shiny enough to become a beacon when the sun hit it. The vines that twined around the columns sported impossible blossoms in teal and gold, the scent of them carried on a soft wind.

Only the massive tree at the temple's entrance remained unrestored, its tired branches twisting empty and lifeless toward the sky.

And here were the servants that had been missing from their hallway, interspersed with villagers and sailors from the harbor. Their whispering stilled as Naia approached, and a path opened up before her. One sailor jerked off his hat and dropped to his knee as she passed, and then another, until there was a wave of movement that followed her footsteps.

Einar glanced at Aleksi, who nodded. They took the first step at the same moment, following her through the crowd of kneeling islanders and up three broad steps that led to the sheltered heart of the temple.

The floor was a breathtaking mosaic of the brass spiral of the goddess's emblem against the light blues and teals of a tropical sea. Einar was almost loath to set his heavy boots on its pristine surface, but Naia showed no such hesitation. She walked toward the altar at the center of the temple, and extended her hand. Her fingers hovered just above a small hammered-metal censer that sat at its center.

Joyful teal flames leapt toward her fingertips, burning even though the censer was empty.

Einar glanced back, but no one else had followed them into the temple. Even Gwynira and Inga had halted at the base of the steps, as if this place was too sacred to enter without an invitation.

And it felt sacred. Einar barely dared speak above a whisper. "Is this how you remember it?"

"No," she said just as softly. "This is how it *was*, down to the last stone."

Sudden whispers rose behind them. Naia, who was still facing the altar, turned her head, just a little. "Tell them to let her pass."

Her words must have carried. Einar turned in time to see Inga and Gwynira step aside. A tall woman with her hair braided with bits of sea glass moved through the crowd, her flowing robes marking her for what she was—a priestess of this island. But not the one who served in the local village.

She climbed the steps, and Einar felt unsteady for a moment, as if he *knew* this woman. Her hair was reddish copper and sun gold going silver, and her ancient eyes seemed caught between green and blue, almost the same color of her robes.

Then her gaze found Naia's. The woman smiled, and the shock of recognition tore through Einar. He had seen that smile thousands of times. He'd seen it barely more than a day ago, on the painting that hung in Petya's cabin. This woman—but younger, standing on a cliff above the sea with flowers braided into her hair . . .

The priestess stopped just short of the altar and bowed her head to Naia. "My lady, I am Agata, High Priestess of Rahvekya, the keeper of the island's memory and guardian of the eternal flame."

Agata. Petya's wife.

Alive.

Einar frantically gestured to Inga, who finally left the doorway and floated to his side, her face alight with curiosity. "I need you to go to my ship and ask Petya to come here," he whispered. When her eyebrows went up, he continued. "She won't want to leave, but I know she will if you tell her . . ."

"What?"

Would she believe? After all of the miracles of the past few days, how could she doubt? Faith was the bedrock of Petya's world. "Tell her that her wife is alive."

Shock widened Inga's eyes, and their deep brown melted into the first hints of pink. Then she inclined her head and hurried away.

The exchange had only taken a few moments, but in that time Naia had rushed forward to seize Agata's hands. She said something in a liquid language that Einar only recognized from the oldest prayers Petya had taught him in his youth. Most of it went too quickly for him to hope to guess at what she was saying, but he understood one word.

Theron.

The god of storms.

Agata listened with fierce attention and narrowed eyes, then nodded. "Forgive me, goddess, if I answer in the common tongue. I have little practice with the ancient language of the island. Few speak it now."

"I'm sorry. I didn't realize . . ." Distraught, Naia held out her hands in apology. "Please, tell me—what became of him?"

The storm god. She was asking about the storm god. The back of Einar's neck prickled, and he realized Aleksi was watching him with an odd intensity. Could the Lover see the uncertainty that lurched through Einar's heart every time he compared himself to that ancient figure of legend? Perhaps, judging by the sympathy that softened Aleksi's gaze.

It was sympathy better saved for Naia. Her face was stricken, her hands trembling as she released Agata only to twine her fingers together. And for the first time, Einar truly understood.

Naia didn't simply have the memories of the goddess. To her, those memories must be as fresh as if she'd simply awoken from a long dream. How many days did it feel like to her? A handful of weeks? A few short moons? Did it feel like only yesterday that she'd walked this island and stood in this temple?

Since the storm god had stood at her side?

It was madness to feel this odd jealousy of a man who had to be thousands of years gone, but how could he not when she looked as if her heart was breaking?

Agata bowed her head again. "I can only tell you what Tona wrote of the Kraken. After you fell—"

Naia flinched and closed her eyes.

"—he stayed on the island to help the people rebuild, and to teach them how to live in the new world."

Naia released a shuddering breath and reached behind her, bracing herself by grasping the edge of the altar. "He lived."

"Yes, my lady," Agata replied.

For a moment, she sagged with a relief Einar could feel in his bones. Then the words Agata had spoken seemed to penetrate. "You said *new* world," she said, her face draining of all color. She seemed terrified to ask the question. "But the people . . . Surely I did not fail?"

"No!" The glass in Agata's hair clinked as she shook her head in forceful denial. "Oh, no. On this, there is no doubt. Her journals say clearly that not a single life was lost to the maelstrom. But after . . ." She shook her head again, this time in regret. "No one knows why, but the currents changed. The island grew colder. Within a few generations, it was as you find it now. A land of mostly winter."

"And Theron taught them how to survive." *That* had not been a question.

"Yes, my lady. How to fish these waters, how to build homes sturdy enough to survive blizzards. There are even legends that he brought plants and animals from his home to this island, when the crops and beasts that only thrived in warmth began to falter."

Naia's soft, gentle smile was wistful enough to make Einar's chest ache. "That sounds like him," she said.

Agata smiled in return, a smile laced with sorrow. "I wish I could tell you more, my lady. But no one knows his ultimate fate. The stories simply say that one day he was gone."

"The stories?" Naia asked, bewildered. "What about the records?"

"There are few records from those centuries. After Tona died, no one had the heart to continue. The journals were meant to be a history of the teachings of the goddess. Those who came after . . . We dedicated ourselves to keeping the memory of your teachings alive."

Naia went pale and swayed on her feet. "Then no one knows."

Tears shimmered in Agata's eyes. "I am so sorry, my lady."

The sound that escaped Naia was that of a wounded creature. Einar swayed, every instinct screaming at him to go to her. Fear held his feet frozen in place. Should he step forward to comfort her? Would she even want it, while she was grieving another man? A man whose sigil and legend Einar had stolen for his own?

Aleksi had no such compunctions. The Lover strode forward to catch her before she could crumple to the colorful tile. "Come, little nymph. Don't lose hope. I made you a promise, didn't I?"

"But how?" she whispered, distraught. "There's no one left."

The words made no sense, leaving Einar adrift, shut out of whatever private moment they were sharing. His heart was racing, and he didn't know why. Only that something was building inside him, a tension, a *pressure*, as if something vast and unfathomable was rising.

He dreaded feeling it break free.

He *longed* for it to break free.

"Aggie!"

The cry shattered the moment, and Einar swayed as the tension unspooled in time with the sound of running footsteps.

Agata's eyes went wide. She turned in time to watch the crowd part as Petya raced up the steps. "Pet—"

It was as far as she got before Petya wrapped her arms around her, all but lifting her off the ground. A laughing sob shattered the breathless silence of the temple, and Einar didn't know which of them it belonged to. Agata grasped Petya's face, and their lips met in a tearstained kiss so intense, Einar almost felt he should look away to give them privacy.

But he couldn't. Petya's joy was incandescent, so powerful Einar wondered how Aleksi hadn't toppled over from the force of it.

Finally, Petya pulled back, framing Agata's face with shaking hands. "I don't understand," she said. "How are you still alive?"

"I could ask you the same thing," Agata replied, wiping a tear from Petya's cheek. "After you left that night, I never thought to see you again."

Petya laughed. "It's Einar's ship. After he manifested his powers . . . Well, those who sail with him don't age."

"Of course." Agata turned the full weight of her gaze on him for the first time. "I should have known."

At the doorway, Gwynira cleared her throat. "While I appreciate more than anyone the joy of being reunited with the one you loved and lost, I admit I am also curious to hear the story of how you survived."

Einar imagined she was. Here was the answer to the question that had plagued him since he had arrived on the island—and that had likely perplexed Gwynira for far longer. Spite for Sorin might have led to her studied obliviousness to the way the local island's culture thrived, but she must have wondered how it persisted with such fervor.

Still clasping Petya's hand, Agata turned to face Gwynira—and the crowd of islanders beyond her, who watched with hushed reverence. Her voice lifted, her first words falling into a rhythm Einar recognized in his bones—the cadence of a priestess telling one of the traditional stories. "On the night the island fell, I kissed my wife goodbye and led the people into the mountains, where we hid from the invaders. That night, I had a dream. A dream where the heart of our island spoke to me."

Murmurs from the crowd. But no one interrupted her. "The dream whispered to me that the years to come would be hard, the hardest we had ever known. But it also said that hope was not lost."

She released Petya's hands and walked toward the entryway. She descended the three steps to place her hand against the trunk of the tree that towered over the path to the temple. Einar imagined that once it must have given shade to all who sat on the benches beneath it, but its branches were bare and twisted now. Dead.

Agata still stroked that dry, cracking bark with reverence before glancing back at Einar. "This tree bloomed for the first time since the death of the goddess on the day you were born. We took it as a sign of good fortune to come—perhaps even a sign that you would be the one to finally drive the Empire from our shores for good."

But he hadn't. A scant week after his birth, the island that had resisted Sorin's attacks for generations had been crushed beneath Imperial boots.

"The night the island fell, I awoke from my dream with a single truth burned into my heart. I knew that you *would* be the one to deliver this island from Imperial rule. Our goddess-touched prince would return, and the goddess with him. It was my job to be the memory of the island, to keep the old ways alive no matter what the Empire did to try to extinguish them. To prepare the people for the day you both walked among us again."

No wonder the islanders remembered what they should not. Agata had sat at the heart of Rahvekya for century after lonely century, sending out acolytes to remind each generation of the goddess who had once walked their shores, the prince who had been spirited away, and the promise that both would return.

Agata turned her back on the tree, the weight of her gaze falling squarely on Einar. "At first, I expected you to return as a mortal man. But as twenty years passed, and then thirty . . . It shames me to admit that doubt crept into my heart. The only thing that sustained me was the fact that I was not growing older." A small, wry smile curved her lips. "Rahvekya was clearly not finished with me, so who was I to doubt the task set before me? I retired to the temple at the heart of the island to guard the eternal flame, and to wait."

Einar had not realized it was possible for so many people to be so silent. He wondered if the assembled crowd was even breathing. Or if they could hear the racing of his heart.

"It was the summer of my one-hundredth year when the first whispers came from the shores of the Empire." Agata smiled again, but this time there was a vicious edge of glee to it. "Whispers of a ship that made war against the Emperor under the banner of the Kraken. A ship captained by a man who had become more than a man. A man named Einar."

Einar could remember those first decades all too well. The Kraken had been a fishing vessel at the start, crewed with those hard and reckless enough to follow him into Dead Man Shoals to hunt the giant swordfish who made their home there. One trip could earn a brave soul more than a year on the ships that trawled the warm waters of the South Sea, and his crew had been *very* brave.

Then word had come of a fleet in Kasther Harbor, sleek ships outfitted to carry soldiers to the shores of the Sheltered Lands. Einar had not been able to stop the Empire as an infant, or throw back their might from Rahvekya as a man.

But he would *not* let them take his new home, too.

So the crew of the Kraken had traded in fishing gear for weapons, and Einar had gone to war for the first time.

Agata walked up the three steps to the temple in silence and crossed the mosaic tile to where Einar stood. She lifted a hand to touch his cheek. "And now our goddess-touched prince has returned to our shores under the banner of the storm god. And he has brought the goddess with him."

Unknowingly. Unwittingly. But he *had*.

Agata smiled and stepped away, coming to face Naia again. She sank gracefully to one knee, and tears shone in her eyes as she lifted her gaze. "The island stirs. I felt it awaken, and I knew it was time for my seclusion to end. I am here to swear my service to you."

"No, not to me." Naia caught both of Agata's hands and drew her to her feet. "You were right before—to the island."

"To the island," Agata agreed, smiling through her tears.

Naia's face was serene, but Einar could tell it was only a fragile mask. She would hold her own feelings tightly in check for the peace of her priestess and her people, but she must be staggering under the weight of all that she had learned.

Well, he was the Kraken, wasn't he? And the Kraken's traditional role had been to protect the goddess. He didn't know how to be the crown-prince, but he knew how to be a captain. He knew how to project his voice through storms and over the fire of cannons—reaching the gathered crowd outside was no hardship. "I think we all can understand that the High Priestess and her wife need some time together now," he said. "And the goddess would like to spend some time in quiet reflection in her temple. There will be time to speak to them later, but for now . . ."

Gwynira was more blunt. She gathered up Inga and Arktikos with a single look and issued a command in her chilly voice. "It is time to leave them in peace. Return to your homes and duties."

The crowd outside seemed willing enough to obey, their chatter audible even as they began to spill down the twisting path. Agata looked more torn, her heart pulling her toward Petya and her duty toward her goddess.

Naia solved her dilemma with a gentle smile. "Soon. Now is the time to be with your wife."

Finally they were alone, the hilltop empty, the temple silent except from the breeze that stirred the trees and carried the scent of those impossible tropical flowers with it. Naia seemed to wilt, wrapping her arms around herself as her gaze flitted restlessly around the temple.

She looked small and lost and wounded, and Einar's heart broke as he wrapped his own arms around her and said the only thing he could. "I'm sorry."

"It's not your fault." Her tone was unnaturally serious. "None of this is your fault."

"It doesn't matter whose fault it is." He stroked her hair and looked down at her. "I hate to see you hurting."

She searched his face as if looking for something—and she must not have found it, because she sank slowly to the temple floor. Aleksi joined her, and after a moment Einar did as well. For a long time, she was silent. Then she shook her head. "I didn't think it would be like this."

Aleksi leaned closer. "Like what, love?"

"That I could know so much and so little, all at once," she explained. "Before I remembered who I was, I had already seen that the people here still knew the old ways. The generations that I had watched come and go, their children survive to this day. So I did not have to worry about that, not for a moment.

"But there were so many things I didn't know," she went on. "What happened the day I died. And Theron—" Her voice broke. "I was prepared for whatever I might learn, good or ill. But I never thought the answers would remain beyond my reach."

She had been handed the good *and* the ill. To know that the storm god had survived her . . . but to have to suffer not knowing what had become of him. Einar understood the terrible pain of uncertainty, the way your imagination could provide horrifying possibilities in the absence of knowledge.

He reached for her hand, twining their fingers together. "Not knowing can be the hardest part. I know that it haunted Petya for centuries."

"It shouldn't matter this much," Naia insisted. "Not when—" The words cut off abruptly, and she squeezed Einar's hand tight.

The vague guilt in her eyes made him wonder if his own inner turmoil had been so obvious to her. Did she think him jealous of her former lover? Would she be so wrong if she did? A terrible thought, when Naia had never given him any reason to doubt her love. He stroked his thumb gently over the back of her hand. "If it matters to you, it matters. I'm sorry, love."

"No." She gripped his hands as she rolled to her knees. "What's important is here, now. You and Aleksi."

"Naia." Aleksi's voice was gentle but implacable. "This means too much to you. I'll not let you abandon it, not for my sake."

Her lips trembled, but she nodded and touched his face. "Understood."

Einar opened his arms, relieved when she slid into them without hesitation. Aleksi moved closer, until she rested safely between them, sheltered for this moment from painful memories of the past.

Three thousand years ago, she had stood on this spot and sacrificed everything to protect the people of Rahvekya. Einar had known since he met Naia that it was in her nature to risk herself for others. She'd been fresh from the Dream, so new to this world that she still glowed with it, when she'd flung herself into the war against the Emperor. She'd been fierce and fearless in defense, and for all of her gentle nature, she had been unflinching when it came time to attack.

Now Einar knew that it was not just courage and passion. It was an ancient instinct to protect those she loved at the cost of her own life. She would give everything. Every time.

It was his job—and Aleksi's—not to let her.

Einar stroked her hair, and words rose up from somewhere inside him. He didn't know from where, but he knew they were the right ones. "All we can do is trust the tides, love. Trust them to bring us back to the people we love and the place we need to be."

Naia's hand tightened on his arm, her fingernails digging through his sleeve. She raised her head slowly, eyes wide. "What did you say?"

"I don't know. It's something I must have heard once. But it's always proven true for me." He stroked one disheveled strand of brown hair back from her forehead. "The tides brought me to you, didn't they?"

"Yes." Tears filled her eyes, but she was smiling, a bright and joyful smile that comforted something within him. "They did."

Einar wiped away the single tear that had slipped free before looking at Aleksi. The Lover's dark gaze held a riot of emotions, too—compassion, and love, and surprise, and maybe even speculation. But when Einar extended his hand, Aleksi took it without thought, weaving their fingers together before lifting Einar's hand to his lips. "To the tides, then," the Lover murmured.

A too-warm breeze stirred in the temple, carrying with it the cry of birds and the scent of the blossoms on the vines, and a *peace* that settled within Einar as he held his lovers and closed his eyes.

Maybe this was what home felt like.

Chapter Fifteen

While you might admire the sea glass pendants common amongst the locals, it is a terrible insult to ask to purchase one. They believe this unique aqua glass to be goddess-touched. Children scour the beaches in hopes of finding a piece, and when one appears it becomes a cherished family heirloom.

Akeisa: Customs and Culture
by *Guildmaster Klement*

The island was thawing.

Every day dawned a little brighter, a little warmer. The differences were slight, almost imperceptible. But Aleksi was the god of all things that grew; part of his power was tied to the land, to the ebb and flow of the seasons, and to the changes that those passing days brought.

He could feel those changes, within him *and* without. So, when Naia asked him and Einar to join her on an adventure, a mischievous smile playing on her lips, Aleksi left his coat behind and rolled up his shirtsleeves before they left the shadowed confines of Gwynira's palace of melting ice.

Naia, likewise, wore no cloak today, and her light, almost gauzy dress rippled in the gentle breeze as she led them away from the palace and down a slightly overgrown path. The trees bent overhead, bare branches stark against the clear blue sky. Here and there, Aleksi could just glimpse little flashes of green—tiny buds emerging on the frozen limbs.

Not so dead, after all.

Curiosity overtook Aleksi, and he grabbed Naia's hand. "Where are you taking us?"

She glanced back at him over her shoulder, the mischievous smile now coy and inviting. "To my favorite beach."

"I see. And it was your favorite because . . . ?"

Her cheeks turned pink as her gaze flitted to Einar, and Aleksi hummed his understanding. This had been a place special to her because of its association with the storm god, and she hoped that seeing it would spark some hidden memories for Einar.

Dread tinged the pleasure of the moment for Aleksi. Naia had been so *happy* since that quiet moment in the restored temple, as if simply being there with him and Einar had lifted some terrible burden from her shoulders. Joy radiated from her, and Aleksi did not wish to see it dimmed.

Especially by something that Einar could not help.

"Actually, come to think of it, I'm not sure if the beach is even still there." That seemed to give her pause. "Though it doesn't feel it to me, it *has* been thousands of years."

"The tides change the shorelines," Einar agreed. "And sometimes they change it back. I've seen the same beach vanish and reappear a hundred times over the years."

Aleksi slid his arm around Naia's waist and drew her close. "I have a good feeling about this one," he murmured against her temple.

She looked up at him. "Do you *really?*"

"I do. Your island would never let your favorite place be lost to you." He kissed her softly. "You'll see."

Naia stopped and hauled him back down for a longer, sweeter kiss, one she finally broke with an apologetic sigh. She was still self-conscious about what had happened the night of the ball, when her emotions and sensations had spilled over, and she had been carefully avoiding intense physical contact ever since.

But all she said was "Come on," and pulled them farther down the path.

They broke out of the trees and brush at the rocky edge of the beach, and the sight of it stopped Aleksi dead in his tracks.

People milled about, chattering excitedly, but that wasn't what held Aleksi's attention. The shoreline was strewn with hundreds—*thousands*—of bits of glass. Sea glass, Einar had called it, little water-polished pieces that were all varying shades of teal, just like the one in the necklace Naia wore.

She clutched at the pendant now, her eyes welling with tears. Einar crouched, wordlessly gathered a handful of the glass, and stared at it in wonder.

One by one, the islanders began to notice their presence. A few of them approached, then more, with bits of sea glass clutched in their hands and spilling from their pockets.

"My lady. Please." One woman carried dozens piled in her outstretched apron. "A blessing?"

"Of course." Naia's voice was thick with tears, but she ran her hand over the glass, sifting it through her fingers as she murmured soft words of benediction.

Others followed suit, their voices overlapping as they begged for Naia's favor. She complied, even as tears slipped down her cheeks.

Before long, the throng of people threatened to overwhelm her, and Einar intervened, placing a protective hand on the small of Naia's back. "It would mean a great deal if we could have this place to ourselves for a little while." His voice was kind but unyielding. "It has been many, many years since the goddess was able to walk her favorite beach."

Not even the lure of having the goddess bless their treasures could make these people defy their prince. They subsided with murmured thanks and apologies, drifting away to disappear over the dunes.

When they had gone, Aleksi bent and retrieved a piece of the glass. He rubbed his thumb over the smooth, rounded surface, then pressed it into Naia's hand.

"This obviously means very much to them, and also to you." For once, he could not decipher whether the source of her tears was happiness or agony. "What is this glass, Naia?"

"It's garbage," she replied with a sobbing laugh.

"It's *what*?" Einar asked, stunned.

Naia clutched the piece of glass to her heart. "Theron and I were walking here one day, and I found a piece of sea glass. I was so excited, because it was my very favorite color. And he was just *confused*. Said they were only pieces of broken bottles, washed smooth by sand and water. And that there were millions of them scattered all across the ocean floor."

When Einar shared stories about Rahvekya's past, they were just that: stories. His tales had a certain distant quality about them, a sense of recitation, as if he had learned every detail by hearing it hundreds of times.

Naia's story was more immediate. *Closer*. Her words were more about emotions than events, and relating them to Aleksi and Einar made her tremble even as she smiled. She had lived these moments. She had been there.

This was her *life*.

Naia laughed again. "I told him that I didn't care if the glass was just refuse. It was beautiful to me." The laughter faded as she gazed out across the rocky sand. "The next day, my beach looked just like this. He never understood why I liked it. But he wanted me to be happy."

Though tears still coursed down her cheeks, Naia beamed at the memory. She shone so brightly that it almost hurt to look at her, so Aleksi did not take his gaze from her face. Did not even blink.

He wanted to bear witness to this love.

Einar rubbed his thumb over a piece of glass. "Jinevra has kept hers since the day she and Petya left the island. It's sacred to her." He smiled tentatively. "This story would probably make her love it even more."

"It should," Aleksi told him. "Because that's what love is. Giving someone what they need, even if we don't understand it."

Einar's smile gave way to a yearning so sharp it felt like biting on metal. Jealousy swelled in the space between the three of them, because Einar wanted so desperately to be the one to give this sort of gift to Naia, and he did not yet understand that he *had*, in his former life and in every day of this one.

That secret was not Aleksi's to share. Still, truth found its way to his tongue. "Theron sounds very special."

"Yes," Naia whispered. "He is."

A strange shimmer cut through the slanting sunlight off to their right. Aleksi turned his head just in time to see the shimmer solidify into two figures—a slight, unassuming woman with reddish-brown hair, and a huge, glowering hulk of a man.

The woman met Aleksi's gaze, tilted her head, and vanished in another strange ripple of nothing. She was there one moment and gone the next, as if she had simply winked out of existence.

Or stepped into the Dream.

The man remained, and a wave of pure rage nearly knocked Aleksi over. Most people with ill intentions tried to hide them; this man *seethed* with his, anger and violence lashing from him in dark, whipping tendrils.

The last locus of villainous magic they had encountered—the woman who had kidnapped them—had been dark but scrupulously self-controlled.

This man was chaos and death made flesh.

Then he roared and flung out his hands. The skin of his palms *split*, and wicked shards of metal erupted from him. The projectiles spun as they whistled through the air, some unholy cross between spikes and spearheads.

"Naia!" Einar tackled her, and the spikes barely missed the two of them as he bore her to the rocky ground. She screamed, not in fear or pain but in protest and righteous, indignant fury.

The sound of their goddess in distress began to draw people back down the beach. If they crossed the dunes once more, the carnage would be unthinkable. Incalculable.

No. Aleksi ran toward them, waving his arms. "Stay back! Don't come any—"

A shouted warning supplanted his, and a spike shot past Aleksi's head, so close that he felt its wake like a glancing blow. He looked back to find the hulking man closing the distance between them, bearing down on him with heavy, lumbering strides.

"My lord!" One of the villagers had braved the dunes to toss a staff to Aleksi.

He caught it and spun just in time to knock another projectile off its course. The staff had been exquisitely carved, expertly weighted, and Aleksi realized that this was more than craftsmanship. It was ingenuity driven by necessity.

Colonized people were rarely allowed to keep weapons. So they turned their tools to that purpose instead.

Naia and Einar had both climbed to their feet, and she gestured toward the villagers who had returned. "Get them back!"

Einar turned immediately to herd the crowd back to safety as Naia planted her feet and raised her hands. The very ground beneath them began to rumble, and even taller dunes of sand began to rise behind her, cutting off the fight from the rest of the beach.

Some of their attacker's wickedly sharp spikes buried themselves harmlessly in the sand. Others would have hit either Naia or Aleksi, only solid crags of stone erupted from the rocky beach in front of them, shielding them from the impacts before seeming to melt back into the ground.

The moment the rock shield in front of Aleksi dropped, he closed in, already swinging the staff. The hit connected with the side of the man's head, and he staggered as blood began to drip from his hair and down his face. Blindly, he threw out his hands to release more spikes, and Aleksi used both ends of the staff to knock the man's hands down so the shots would find only the sand at his feet.

With a bellow of rage, the man slammed his forehead against Aleksi's, driving him back. Aleksi blinked the pain from his vision just in time to see Einar charge back over the now massive dunes.

A rock the size of a small cauldron flew past Aleksi and hit the enraged man in the head. Naia glared at him as she launched another rock, this time at his gut. A flurry followed, and though the man managed to dodge a few, the majority found their mark.

The look on Naia's face was one that Aleksi had never seen before, not even when they had stood and fought against Sorin's armies. It was more than righteous fury. It was sheer protective determination, so intense that Aleksi could *see* it, a halo of red and gold hanging over the small battlefield.

Their attacker was bleeding profusely now, whipping the spikes from his palms with little accuracy but even greater numbers. Einar snatched up a piece of driftwood and dove in front of Naia, and half a dozen spikes sank into the wood with a chorus of dull thuds. Quick as lightning, Einar pried three of the spikes free with one hand and hurled them back at the man. One spike hit, lodging itself in his side.

Aleksi's frisson of triumph turned into horror as the shard of metal slowly sank deeper, and deeper still, until it had disappeared into the man's flesh.

A primal, throaty scream rent the air, and a huge blur darted out of the tree line and leapt at the bleeding man. It was a cat, easily the size of a small horse. It dug its claws into flesh, and its giant, curving teeth raked the man's face. He screamed and flung the cat away. He pressed his hands to his eyes, desperately trying to clear them of blood.

Aleksi and Einar both moved in to press their advantage and end the fight. But Aleksi stopped short, his gut roiling with dread. The man's aura was changing. Brightening. Each sickly color now blazed, incandescent.

Then he threw back his head and screamed again. Only this time, it didn't sound like pain or rage. It didn't even sound *human*, but rather like a closed, steaming pot about to explode.

"Run!" Aleksi was already turning, frantic to get Naia and Einar away before it was too late.

Except it already *was*. The man's scream reached an ear-splitting crescendo, and Einar spun both Aleksi and Naia away and wrapped his arms around them, shielding them. As he did, his arms grew larger, the bare skin tough but soft. Familiar.

An explosion shook the beach, and a strange whistling filled the sudden, concussed silence. Einar grunted just as searing pain raked across Aleksi's side. He tucked Naia closer as he spied hundreds of wicked little shards of metal zinging through the air.

Then it was over.

Einar released them and straightened. He had taken on his other form, the one that seemed a cross between a human and a creature of the deep. His skin was a metallic, silvered-purple hue, its texture ridged with something almost like scales, and his hair was much longer. He was bigger, as well, taller and wider, enough so that his shirt and pants were nearly shredded.

Naia gasped Einar's name and tugged at the torn fabric. "Are you hurt? Why did you *do* that?"

"Because I could." He rubbed her arms. "It's all right, Naia. My skin in this form is tough enough to withstand the pressures of the deepest oceans. It is not easily violated."

The spot where the man had been standing was empty now, save for an unspeakable amount of carnage. He had exploded, propelling bits of metal shrapnel from his body along with the gore.

"Who was he?" Naia asked, stunned. "*What* was he?"

"If I had to guess?" Aleksi sighed heavily. "Another newly awakened guest from the mainland."

The giant cat crested a dune. It moved with absolute grace, despite its large, stocky body and relatively short legs. Its fur was patterned with a strange mixture of spots and stripes, and it had a shock of black fur around its face, making its cheeks look almost comically full and round.

Then it yawned, baring sharp, curved teeth that were larger and longer than Aleksi's fingers, and any amusement he might have briefly entertained vanished like smoke.

It walked over to Naia and rubbed against her legs, like a house cat seeking attention. She reached down—not far, as the cat's shoulders were even with her hip—and petted it. A sound that could only be described as a purr rumbled out of its wide chest.

Einar stared, his mouth working soundlessly. Finally, he breathed, "Is that . . . ?"

"A lowland wild cat." Naia beamed as she knelt in front of it, her eyes shining.

Aleksi had to quell the urge to snatch her up and away from those massive teeth. The inclination intensified when Naia grasped the cat's face, her fingers sinking into its thick black fur. But the damn thing tilted its head into her touch as she rubbed the top of its head between its ears.

"I've heard of them," Einar whispered. "But I've obviously never seen one. They've been extinct forever."

Naia cooed a soft denial, her attention still focused on the cat. "But you're here now, aren't you?"

The cat dropped and rolled over, baring its belly for a few moments. Then it finished the roll, curled up, and eyed Naia expectantly.

"I know," she murmured. Then, instead of rising, she sank her fingers into the stony sand beneath her, just as she had with the cat's fur.

Power flowed out from her as she soothed the land like a mother quieting an upset child. She stroked her fingers through the sand, and the landscape shifted, gliding back into place. The dunes subsided like a traveler shrugging off a heavy burden, and soon even the blood and metal shards on the beach had been swallowed.

In a handful of heartbeats, no evidence of the violence remained, and the cat chuffed in approval.

Aleksi touched his side and just managed to suppress a wince. He was grateful, at least, that the dark-black velvet of his vest obscured the fact that he was bleeding. "Come. We need to let Gwynira know what happened."

And that whoever wanted them dead—or worse—had not given up.

◆ ◆ ◆

Inga was an undeniably skilled healer. But she tended to save her best bedside manner for those who truly needed gentle words and a tender touch—the badly wounded, the incredibly sick. The young and the old.

As she probed at the wound on his side, Aleksi very nearly reminded her that he *did* fall into that last category.

Technically.

Instead, he hissed in a breath and held his tongue.

"The wound is already showing signs of infection," she muttered, her eyebrows drawn down in a frown.

It was the least shocking thing she could have told him. Aleksi glanced down at his bare side, where Inga was still prodding the inflamed edges of the cut. It had been a glancing blow, one that might have already healed on its own . . . had the spike not been covered in bloody remnants of their attacker's insides.

Of course, it could just as easily have been magic. The hungry rage that had filled that man, given tangible form at the moment of his death. Aleksi had seen that man's *soul*; any way he could destroy even after he was gone would have pleased him greatly.

Still, there was one thing he could say in all honesty. "I've had worse. Quite recently, in fact."

That earned him a dark look before she returned her attention to the wound. "How is the pain?"

"Bearable."

"Hardly a comfort, knowing how much you can bear." She sighed and sat back. "I want to heal it."

The process she used to heal another was abhorrent to Aleksi. It involved her pulling the injury—both the pain *and* the physical damage—into herself, taking it on as one would shoulder a burden. Some wounds healed quickly, while others lingered until her body could purify itself from the inside out.

He did not like it on the best of days, and this was far from the best of days. Whether Aleksi's laceration had been fouled by evil magic or plain old viscera, it was nasty business. He would not visit that on anyone, much less a friend.

"While I appreciate the offer," he told her firmly, "I'm afraid I must decline."

"Oh, you must, must you?" She flashed him a pointed, unimpressed look and laid a hand on his arm. "It already looks as if it has been festering for a week. If you told me you'd been poisoned by one of my apprentices, I would believe you. I don't want to see how much worse this can get. Please, Aleksi."

"Just give me a poultice." He shrugged one shoulder. "It will heal eventually, and I won't even mind the scar."

"I will," she replied softly. "Don't make me watch you hurt. Nothing this wound could do to me would be worse than that."

It was the one and only thing that could possibly change his mind—and she knew that, damn her. "Fine. But only because arguing with you is even worse than watching you hurt yourself on my account."

She laughed, generous in her victory. "You sound just like Ash. Are you ready?"

"Not remotely."

She waited patiently until he inclined his head, then laid one hand just below the injury. Her fingers rested lightly on the skin stretched taut over his ribs, but something almost like pain flared as her touch grew . . . electric.

He caught a single glimpse of her eyes, glowing pink, just before her lashes fluttered and the lids drifted down. The air around her deepened, gradually spinning up into the usual colors of Inga's aura—purples and greens, reds and pinks, blues and yellows.

All the colors of the Witchwood. But at the moment, all Aleksi could think was, *All the colors of a bruise.* Then the colors shifted until no one shade stood out, and iridescent light danced in their place.

Inga always glowed brightest when she was helping someone she loved.

A tugging sensation overwhelmed him, and Aleksi clenched his fingers on the wooden arm of his chair. For a fraction of a heartbeat, his mind rioted, because he'd felt this before—magic that meant to draw, to *take.* In that moment, it did not matter that this was Inga, and all she wanted was to help him by taking on his pain as her own.

In that moment, he saw Sorin's witch, grinning madly as she ripped away his connection to the Dream.

No. Aleksi forced his eyes open and focused his swimming gaze on Inga's face. A hint of sweat had begun to sheen on her forehead and upper lip, and her brow furrowed lightly—the only outward indications that she had claimed his injury for herself.

He shuddered, and it was over.

Inga swallowed hard, and she released a shaky breath before finally opening her eyes once again. "I've never felt anything so . . . hateful. It didn't touch Einar or Naia, did it?"

He nearly shuddered again. "No. Einar shielded her, and the spikes could not penetrate the skin of his . . ." Aleksi paused. "He calls it his demigod form."

Fascination seemed to distract her from whatever lingering pain she had stolen from him. "I always heard the rumors that he could become a giant sea creature, but I've never even heard whispers of any other form. He's always kept his secrets close, hasn't he?"

"Yes, and for good reason." Aleksi offered her a rueful smile. "What is it Elevia says? If you can, always maintain the ability to surprise your enemies?"

"A lesson you learned better than any of us." She pushed herself to her feet and dropped into the chair across from him. "Sorin always underestimated you."

"And I don't think he'll ever stop." An experimental stretch resulted in only a mild twinge in his side, a sensation very much like the vague soreness that lingered after a long recovery. "Inga? May I ask you something?"

"Of course."

He studied her for several long moments. She did not fidget the way most people would, and his silent, prolonged gaze did not make her uncomfortable. She merely stared back at him, waiting.

"Back on the mainland," he said finally. "Has it been like that? With all the new Dreamers and Voidlings?"

She frowned, tilting her head slightly. "What do you mean?"

He wasn't even *sure*. He just knew that the man on the beach, for all his power, had seemed . . . small somehow. Narrow and violent.

The violence, Aleksi understood. Inga's own awakening had been horrific, as many were. It seemed part of the process, almost a requisite. Life-threatening danger—or pain—seemed to trigger the metamorphosis. But their attacker on the beach—

narrow and violent

All the Dreamers that Aleksi had ever known had awakened to something he could only describe as expansive. Possibilities that were both beyond and precisely of the realm of mortals. But that man had taken in the power of the Dream, and, although it had transformed him, he'd become *lesser*, somehow.

He had turned himself from a person, a being with all imaginable glories and flaws, into a mere weapon.

He didn't realize he'd said the words aloud until Inga hummed in agreement. "Yes, I see what you're saying. They haven't all been so violent, but . . ." Her gaze drifted past him, eyes focusing on something that wasn't there. "There's a reason Sachi's heart has been breaking. In some ways, those who awakened to the Void are easier to deal with. So many of them are furious at what has been done to them. Their cravings for destruction are righteous. But the others . . . Sorin stole their dreams. They never had the chance to understand all the glories of the world, or to imagine the things that do not yet exist in it."

The thought saddened Aleksi. It had never occurred to him that someone could awaken, either to the Dream or the Void, and immediately relinquish everything that made being a person so beautiful.

Though perhaps it should have, the very moment he'd faced their kidnapper's lovely, empty eyes on that ship.

Then again, he knew from Sachi and Zanya that not everyone on the mainland had been like this. So Inga must be correct, and these were the people who'd never known the beauty of life in the first place, not even in the smallest of ways. They had been lost long before they were ever found.

"One more thing that Sorin has to answer for," Aleksi murmured.

"The list is depressingly long at this point." She rested her elbow on the arm of the chair and propped her chin up on her hand. "Do you still think that Elevia's evil twin is the one behind all of this?"

"Eirika," he supplied. "They call her the Stalker. And yes, I do. I'm not absolutely certain, but I'd wager my vineyards on it."

"This was a little subtle for Sorin, I suppose." Inga's lips pursed. "She was testing you. Taking your measure."

"Yes." Aleksi wished that he knew what Eirika had learned from the altercation. "Which means the worst is yet to come."

Inga let out a gusty sigh. "We should tell the others."

Though he was reluctant to agree, Aleksi nodded. "But we must be careful what we say. If they think we're in danger, even for a moment, they'll come back. For all we know, that's exactly what Eirika wants. No, we'll have to be circumspect. Perhaps just . . . Say that we're handling things here on the island."

She studied him for so long that he thought she might be mounting an argument. But, in the end, she only nodded. "I'll tell them we have it under control. There is power enough here—power that might surprise Eirika." Her lips curved in a sudden smile. "I suspect your Naia has secrets, too. And that Eirika has gravely underestimated her."

Aleksi sincerely hoped that she had.

Chapter Sixteen

Spring came late again this year, and summer ends far too early. I have sent word via the priestesses to every village to prepare. The island's bounty has always been more than we needed, but I fear that may not always be true. We will preserve more than we need this autumn, and hope that we feel foolish when spring comes again.

The lost journal of High Priestess Tona

Einar's skin felt too tight.

He stood on their suite's private balcony, feet bare against the chilly stone in spite of the frigid night air. Naia had insisted on making time to speak with some of the frightened villagers, and Aleksi had shut himself up with Gwynira for another of their diplomatic conversations about the attack at the beach.

Einar didn't want to be alone. But he couldn't tolerate the idea of facing the naked need of the islanders, or Gwynira's icy assessment. Not right now, when even the slide of his clothing against human skin was an unbearable irritation. Battle-readiness still surged in his blood, but there was no outlet for it. Nothing to attack, no one to fight.

Just the wind, and the waves, and the night sky lit by silver moons and an endless expanse of bright stars.

A plaintive yowl cut through the silence, and he smiled as his gaze fell to the rocky shore far below. Perhaps he wasn't entirely alone. The large cat who had come to Naia's aid paced the beach below, its restless energy a match for his own. Just two wild creatures, waiting for the return of the goddess whose touch could soothe them.

Einar rolled his shoulders, trying to shift the fabric so it didn't irritate him so much. It didn't help. There had been times in the past when he'd felt regret upon regaining his human form, but this was the first time it had taken effort to maintain. It didn't feel like his own skin anymore, but a cage trapping the parts of him that wanted to break free.

Danger stalked the people he loved. Newly awoken Dreamers could be snatched up from the Empire by their enemies and sent against them at any time. Einar was stronger in his demigod form. Harder to hurt. Harder to kill. He could protect Aleksi and Naia more easily if he shed this mortal skin and embraced the parts of himself that felt real.

The ocean crashed against the rocks beneath him, as if churning in sympathy. Einar closed his eyes and reached out, but it was harder to feel its rhythms when he wasn't standing on the deck of the Kraken. He had considered going out to the ship to feel the smooth wood beneath his feet and sink his power into the depths of the sea, but he didn't trust his temper.

And he didn't really want the sea, anyway. He wanted Naia.

"Einar."

Her voice brushed over him, and for a moment he thought he'd conjured it from pure yearning. But the feel of her wrapped around him, soothing one ache while stirring another.

He turned, and nearly caught his breath. She was stunning by the moonlight, ethereal and not quite of this world. The moons should have been the same everywhere, but he swore their light caressed her differently tonight, painting her in silver light and stunning shadows that only existed on this island.

Her island.

"Are the villagers feeling better?" he asked, his voice rasping.

"They were mostly worried about me. About *us*." She stepped closer and raised her hand, fingertips hovering over his skin without quite touching. "You changed."

Back into his human skin, she meant. "I didn't want to make people uncomfortable."

The wry quirk of her eyebrow practically demanded *since when?* but she only murmured, "That's a shame. I rather like when you look like *you*."

Like you. The words crashed over him like a rogue wave, and his control over his human form faltered. To be not just accepted as he was, but to be desired *because* of who he was . . .

He didn't consciously decide to change. The demigod form tore free, the discomfort of the transition lost on a wave of euphoria as he stopped struggling against his instincts, stopped trying to hold back, stopped *fighting*.

Fabric ripped loudly. He glanced down, wincing. At least he hadn't been wearing his finest leather pants, or his lovingly embroidered vest. But the loose pants had not been loose enough to accommodate his larger size, and his shirt had fared even worse, the ragged tears revealing the fine silvery purple-and-blue hide that had taken the place of his human skin. "I'm going to run out of clothing if I keep doing that."

"We'll find you a robe." Her fingers finally made contact with his cheek, warm and soft. No one had ever stroked him in this form before Aleksi and Naia, so he had never realized how *sensitive* this flesh was, how the slightest touch could spark through him like lightning.

"There you are," she whispered, stroking him again. Then her smile fell away. "Are you certain you weren't injured during the attack?"

"Not a scratch." But the doubt didn't fade from her eyes, so he turned so she could see the bare, unmarred expanse of his back. "Like I said, it's hard to pierce my skin in this form."

"Good." Now those teasing fingertips were sliding across his back, tracing dizzying patterns across his shoulders that stoked the hunger burning within. "Aleksi was hurt, though he did not let us see."

"What?" That dashed cold water on his ardor as he glanced back. "How badly? Is he all right?"

"Yes. Inga already healed him."

Damn it all. He should have checked on the Lover himself. He knew too well how prone the man was to hiding his own hurts—even from Naia and Einar. "You're sure he has been healed? How do you know?"

Her gaze dropped, as if she could no longer meet his eyes. "I just do."

Einar put one finger beneath her chin and tilted her face back up. Her expression was self-conscious, uncertain, which could only mean that this knowledge had not come by normal means. And given her connection to the island—and the island's connection to her—he could guess what had happened. "You know because you're the goddess, and this is your island."

It hadn't quite been a question, but she answered anyway. "Yes."

How much was she aware of, now that the island had fully claimed her? If her pleasure could sink into the land and spiral out to touch those around her, was the opposite happening as well? Could she feel the stirring of power? Sparks of magic? Enemy feet treading on the sands? Or was it subtler, not a thing of senses, but of simply *knowing*?

He might have asked, but she'd gone back to touching him, tracing an aimless path up his arm as if she was savoring the way it felt beneath her fingertips. So a different question emerged. "You truly don't mind when I wear this form?"

"You are not a *form*," she protested. "And I do not care what you look like. I only care who and what you *are*." She met his gaze, eyes soft and yearning. "And that you're mine."

He caught her hand and held it to his chest, where his heart pounded beneath their joined fingers. "If I wore it all the time, others might care. They would fear me, and that fear might reflect back on you and Aleksi."

"Honestly?" Her fingernails dug into his chest with delicious pressure. "I'd rather they feared us on our own merits, not yours."

Einar couldn't help his low laugh. "You were incredibly fierce today. Anyone who means harm to your people *should* fear you."

He expected her to laugh as well, but her smile dropped away, and she swallowed hard. "I have something to tell you, and I don't know how, so I think I just have to do it."

"All right." He stroked a soothing hand over hers. "There is nothing you can't tell me."

Instead of speaking, she turned, tugging his hand until he followed her inside. She stopped to sweep up a robe—just large enough that he could shrug into it after he kicked free of his damaged pants—and then sat on the love seat with her hands folded neatly in her lap, waiting for him to join her.

As ominous as her sudden seriousness was, Einar tied the belt around his waist before joining her on the plush seat, which felt a great deal smaller now than it had last time he'd sat on it. "Tell me, Naia. Just tell me."

She seemed to struggle for how to start. "You are the Kraken," she finally said, the words halting and hesitant. "You always have been, Einar."

It felt like that, some days. It had been almost two thousand years since he'd walked this world as a mortal man. But she wouldn't look so distressed if she was simply commenting upon the length of his life. "You mean I was born with this potential in me? Because of my connection to the island?"

A shake of her head. "No, I mean that your birth was a *return* to the island. Because you lived here before, with me, when you were Theron. The god of storms."

The words didn't make sense. He repeated them in his mind a second time, and a third, trying to push them into coherence as his heart began to pound. If this was anyone else, he'd think they were trying to trick or manipulate him. Perhaps she was teasing him? But the look in her eyes—

"It was you who gave me the sea glass," she whispered. "You who stayed here and helped the people of Rahvekya survive after I was gone. It was always you."

Impossible. *Ridiculous.* But Naia was deadly serious. And the only way she could be, the only way she could know . . .

"You . . ." His voice cracked. He swallowed, and tried again. "You . . . remember me?"

"Yes." Tears filled her voice, and her eyes. One escaped, tracking down her cheek. "I remember everything."

He wanted more than anything to reach out and wipe that tear from her cheek, but he was afraid his hands would shake. What did you even say to something like this? To someone telling you the fondest, most impossible dreams of your childish heart had been true the whole time?

"This is impossible to comprehend, much less believe, coming from someone else. And if I had a better way to tell you, I would, I swear it. But it *is* true." Her voice faltered, and she swiped at her cheeks before trying again. "I had hoped you might . . ."

She had hoped he might remember on his own.

That had been the oddness seething beneath every interaction, every look. The inexplicable tension every time she said something and looked at him, hope and dread battling in her eyes. That impossible grief she struggled with? The grief that had stirred unwanted jealousy in his heart?

That hadn't been grief for the love she had lost. It had been grief because her lost love stood before her, and didn't remember her.

And those times he'd said something that startled her? Like his words in the temple, the ones that had felt so *right*. Had those come from some spark of memory he could not access? Had they been not his words at all, but the words of the storm god?

Naia's distress was so wrenching, his protectiveness overrode caution. He reached out and found another tear with his thumb, gently swiping it away. "There was no better way," he said softly. "And I know you would never lie to me. I want so much to tell you that I can remember this, but . . ."

"I know," Naia assured him. "It's impossible."

Einar didn't know what else to say. Aleksi's coaching in manners and thoughtfulness could prepare him for a dinner or a dance, but what prepared a man for being told that the legend he'd grown up idolizing was actually . . .

No. It was too much to believe. Even Aleksi could not have navigated *this* situation gracefully. But the thought of the Lover made his stomach flip in a different manner. "Does Aleksi . . ." No. It wasn't a question. So many things made sense now. Those moments, when the two of them had shared a look or cryptic words that left him feeling lost and adrift. "Aleksi knows."

"Yes." She twisted her fingers together, betraying her nervousness and guilt. "I needed to say it to someone, to know if it sounded as unbelievable aloud as it did in my head."

Maybe Aleksi had handled it gracefully after all, then. Einar envied him that, even as he was grateful *someone* had been able to help Naia through this moment. He certainly didn't know how. "I understand."

"I'm sorry that I didn't tell you sooner, truly, I am." Her pinched face all but pleaded with him to understand, to forgive. "But I thought it might be easier if you remembered on your own. I mean, it's one thing to reconcile conflicting memories, but how do you hear something like this when you have none?"

And he didn't. There were places on the island that had stirred echoes, but they had always felt secondhand. Petya's stories, living so vividly in his imagination that he had already dreamed of walking these shores before he'd ever set foot on them.

Naia's big eyes shimmered with worry. Einar tried to find a question. Any question. "Did he—I mean did I . . . ?" He gestured to his body, to the silvery skin that belonged more to a creature of the sea than one that walked the land. "Petya's stories never said what the storm god looked like. I'm not sure anyone knew."

"You—" She stopped. Seemed to correct herself. "Theron . . . looked like a man. Just different. Tall, like you, but thinner. Older, with long, silver hair, and the bluest eyes . . ."

So nothing like him at all, in any of his forms. "How do you know it was me? Not that I'm doubting you, I just mean . . ."

"I caught glimpses, even before I remembered everything. You would do or say certain things, and it felt like something that had happened before. But, mostly? I just feel it. Feel *you*." She stopped and took a deep breath, as if trying to recenter herself. "Whatever questions you have, if they're within my power to answer, I will."

Maybe this was the path through the awkwardness. As a young boy, he would have given anything for the chance to hear the authoritative tales of the island's powerful guardian and the woman he had protected. And maybe he would feel an echo in her words. Maybe *he* could remember, too.

"Are they true?" he asked. "The stories they tell at the Flame of Life Festival? The storm, and the ships, and the storm god following the goddess home?"

She laughed softly. "Yes and no. I did not defy the storm god to ensure my people's safety. I tricked him. And when he realized it, he *did* follow me back. But not because he was hopelessly in love. He was *angry*, and a little intrigued—though he never would confess to that last part."

That sounded exactly like the Naia *he* knew. Clever, and more than willing to use the fact that others underestimated her against them. "Is that how he came to stay on the island? He was . . . intrigued?"

"At first." Her voice dropped to a whisper. "But truly? I think he was lonely."

Einar could relate to that, at least. He knew the bitter taste of lone-liness. "Do you know where he was from?"

"From a place so distant, it wasn't on any of our maps." She gazed past him, as if seeing something far away—or from long ago. "It was a cold place, with rocky shallows and dangerous fog. Ships steered clear because it was so treacherous."

A place nothing like what Rahvekya had been in those times. The storm god had come from a frozen world to the shores of a tropical paradise . . . and he'd stayed. Out of love.

Einar could relate to that, too. "And when the war between the High Court sundered the continents. You said before that he wanted you to leave?"

Naia stiffened and looked away. After a moment, she spoke in an agonized whisper. "He begged me not to do it. Said that raising that wall to protect the island would kill me. And he was right."

The words hit him hard enough to knock the breath from him. If she hadn't raised that wall of water, his family, his life, Petya . . . This *island* wouldn't exist anymore. The selfishness of the storm god should disgust him.

But Einar could remember sailing into this harbor for the first time. The panic that had gripped him when he'd felt Naia sinking her strength into the ocean, spending it recklessly to bring down the wall of ice blocking their path.

Was that where that overwhelming sense of dread had come from? Was that why he'd snapped at her? Some ancient memory of watching her give too much, give everything . . .

Sorin had escaped his cage. A confrontation was coming, one way or another. Naia would hardly sit on the sidelines of the coming storm. Asking her to would be betraying who she was.

If he found himself in that same spot, watching her take a risk that would surely kill her, could he step aside? To save his crew, to save her people, to save this island? To save the world from what Sorin would do to it if he could?

He didn't know. And he didn't like not knowing.

"As you've seen, I do not know what became of him—of you—after that." She heaved a shaking breath. "It seems that no one does."

No wonder she had been so inconsolable in the temple. Almost eight hundred years passed between her fall and Einar's birth as a mortal. Eight hundred years when anything could have happened. He wished he could tell her *what*. "I'm sorry."

"Einar, *no*," she said firmly. "It hurts, yes, but it is no one's fault, least of all yours. And if we never find out what happened, then that is what must be." She reached up and slid her fingers through his hair, and in this form it was long enough for her to tangle around her fist. "Perhaps it is best to let it go, and to focus on what we have now. You and me and Aleksi."

He gathered her into his arms, savoring how easily they fit together. He'd been drawn to her from the start, from the first taste of her power in the waves. Drawn so strongly it had bordered on obsession at times. Was this why? Did some part of that ancient god linger inside him, desperate to find the love that he'd lost?

And what if he did? Did that make the way he felt about Naia mean less? Or so much more?

"You don't have to believe me," she whispered against his shoulder.

"Naia—"

She lifted her fingers and pressed them to his lips to silence him. "This journey is yours, and you'll make it in your own time." Her hand slid to his cheek, and she gazed up at him. "But I hope you know how much I want you. Whether you're a man or the Kraken or a pirate or a god. I love you here, now, in this life."

Aleksi would likely say that was all that mattered, in the end—and he would be right. Einar turned his face into her hand, brushing his lips across her palm. "You have never let me doubt it."

"And I never will." Not just a promise, but a vow.

Chapter Seventeen

Excerpt from Beloved,
a poetry collection dedicated to the Lover

Aleksi had always found preparing for bed to be very meditative. There were soothing rhythms in the routines—undressing, washing up. Even the dedicated clothing and space spoke of calming ritual.

But bedtime became decidedly less relaxing when your lovers chose to wander around the room naked.

The night was warm, so they had let the fire burn low. The dwindling light burnished Naia's bare skin as she pulled on one of Einar's discarded shirts. The rumpled linen immediately slipped off her shoulder, and without the ties at the neck secured, it bared her nearly to the navel.

It was good to see—for more reasons than the obvious. *Someone* should get some use out of Einar's clothes. He certainly wasn't likely to, since he'd apparently decided to remain in his larger, more robust form. For the moment, he wore only a pair of loose, belted trousers that Aleksi had never seen before.

Probably the only things that fit him.

Aleksi shifted against the headboard as he stretched his legs out before him. "Don't get me wrong, Einar, because I very much appreciate the way you look right now . . ."

Einar arched an eyebrow. "But?"

"But whatever are you going to *wear*?"

"Oh, I wouldn't worry about that." Naia stepped up in front of Einar and ran her hands over the breadth of his shoulders, as if taking his measure. "Hilja is taking care of it."

"Hilja," Aleksi echoed. "The battle-axe who runs the kitchens?"

"She's a very skilled seamstress, you know. Made my outfit for the ball." Naia winked at Einar. "And she is *thrilled* to be dressing the Kraken."

Einar caught both of Naia's hands and drew them to his lips, never once looking away from her face. They had been very intent on one another all evening, often locking eyes and lingering when they touched.

Only one explanation made sense. "No more secrets, then?" Aleksi murmured.

Naia smiled dreamily. "No more secrets."

"Good. Because we need to talk about what we're doing."

That got their attention. They both turned to Aleksi, wearing expressions of confusion mixed with concern.

"Not because we need to define it," he clarified. "But because I need you to know where I stand." Even thinking the words should have been terrifying, but they slipped free with the ease of inevitability. "Whatever you need from me, and for however long, you have it."

Naia climbed onto the bed, facing Aleksi, and settled beside his outstretched legs. "Careful," she warned. "What if we need everything, and we need it forever?"

"Then that's what you'll have, little nymph, you and Einar. You deserve it." But that wasn't powerful enough to encompass the truth. "You deserve the *world*."

"I don't want the world." Naia's hand was warm on Aleksi's thigh through the thin fabric of his sleep pants. "Just this."

Einar walked over to stand by the bed, close enough to reach both of them. He ran his fingers over Naia's hair, then touched Aleksi's chin, tilting his head up. "I don't remember my past, and I don't know what our futures hold. But my present belongs to you. Both of you."

Naia pulled him down, into a fierce kiss full of soft moans and flashing tongues. Einar's longer hair swung loose, nearly eclipsing the sight from Aleksi's view, and he had to smooth it back.

But Naia abruptly broke the kiss with a gasp. "Sorry, I'm sorry—I can't—"

Of course. She would not risk having everyone else in the palace, perhaps even on the entire island, bear witness to such a personal moment. Aleksi gripped the back of her neck and soothed her with a shake of his head. "Tell me true—would this broadcast of your pleasure bother you if only Einar and I could feel it?"

"No." There was no dishonesty in her expression, nothing hidden. "It only troubles me that there is no *consent* in it. People have not agreed to feel what I feel."

"And if Einar and I did?"

She drew in a sharp breath, and her cheeks turned pink as she lowered her gaze to Aleksi's mouth. "If it were just the two of you, and you *wanted* it . . . I would like that very much."

"Then I have a proposition for you." Aleksi dropped his hand to her knee and rubbed his thumb over the neatly hemmed edge of the linen that covered her thigh. "I did not suggest it before because it isn't something with room for privacy or halfways. And I would not offer it now, except that I trust you completely, Naia. And I believe that Einar does, as well."

Einar silently indicated his agreement with a squeeze of Naia's bare shoulder.

She licked her lips nervously. "What is it?"

"I can pull you both close," Aleksi explained softly, "and wrap you in a bit of the Dream. It would be a whole little world with only the three of us in it. It's intimate, love. Painfully so, with every feeling open to the others. But *only* to us."

"No one else?" She was made of eager hope tempered by fear, and it almost hurt to look at. "No nobles or palace staff or islanders?"

"Just us."

She nearly sagged against Aleksi with relief. "I've wanted to be with you," she confessed. "But I was so *scared*."

He gathered her closer. "Scared is something you never have to be, Naia. Not with us."

"I want it," she murmured. "But that's so simple for me to say. I'm the one whose emotions will be laid bare anyway. You and Einar are the ones who'll be taking a risk. So it has to be up to you."

"Easy as breathing," Aleksi assured her. "I would not have brought it up if I wasn't ready to do it."

"But . . . Einar?" She looked up at him, her features carefully schooled into a neutral mask that did nothing to conceal her longing.

"Aleksi has already seen inside my heart," Einar answered. "It isn't always a pretty place, but I have no secrets left from either of you."

Aleksi wanted no room for doubt. "Yes or no, Einar."

For half a heartbeat, his eyes blazed teal—the goddess's favorite color. "*Yes.*"

Everything in the room became more vivid as the rush of their acceptance flooded Aleksi. This was a gift, but it was also a responsibility, one that he took very seriously. *This* was what it meant to be the Lover. Not the sex, or the debauchery, or even the wit and charm.

The care.

He placed one hand on Naia's cheek, the other on Einar's, and pulled them close, until their heads were touching. Einar's lips grazed his jaw, and Aleksi could feel Naia's breath on his lips.

He reached for the magic inside him. He twined it with how he felt about them, then infused it with all the protectiveness and, yes, possessiveness, that burned within him. The magic expanded, slipping around Naia and then Einar.

He could tell the moment that it enveloped them both. They went rigid and then relaxed in turn, almost as if they were melting not just into the Dream, but into him, and into each other.

Naia opened her eyes, placed her hand on Aleksi's bare chest, and curled her fingers until her nails bit into his skin. Einar hissed in response, turning his mouth to Aleksi's ear. "I can feel how much she likes touching you."

Both things sizzled through Aleksi's veins. He covered Naia's hand and held it to his skin, pressing harder. When Einar groaned and bit his earlobe, Aleksi finally released her hand and shuddered as the pressure slowly eased.

Naia was breathing faster now, her gaze locked on Aleksi's. "Einar? Until I say so, you don't touch." At the other man's growl—and Naia's soft gasp—he continued. "You watch, and you *feel*."

Einar blazed with challenge, a hot mix of colors that reminded Aleksi of dancing flames. The moment stretched out, tense and fraught, until Einar's teeth grazed Aleksi's jaw in one last, quiet challenge.

Then he slipped from the bed and stalked to the vanity. He grabbed the heavy wooden chair in one hand, lifting it as if it weighed nothing, and dropped it with a clatter a few paces from the foot of the bed.

With his eyes burning that dangerous teal, he sank into the chair . . . and watched.

Aleksi pulled Naia onto his lap, settling her with her back pressed to his chest. She arched, rubbing the soft fabric that still smelled like Einar against Aleksi's naked skin. The shirt had ridden up, baring her parted thighs—and more. The low collar gaped open, nearly sliding off her nipple as she reached back and gripped Aleksi's hip.

This was what Einar saw, the rucked fabric and clutching hands and skin. His hands clenched into fists, every visible muscle tensed at the effort it took not to lunge for them.

Aleksi licked Naia's shoulder, then rumbled in her ear. "Do you feel it yet?"

She shifted her hips, grinding against his erection with a husky laugh. "I believe I do."

He swatted her thigh. "Not that, naughty little nymph." This time, he sank his teeth into the spot where her shoulder curved up into her neck. "Do you feel Einar's *hunger*?"

"He . . ." The word trailed off into a shiver that tightened her nipples beneath the gauzy white fabric. "He wants to touch us. But not as much as he wants to see what you do next."

Einar's chest heaved. His eyes glowed. He sank lower into the chair, and his borrowed pants strained over the muscles of his strong thighs. "Perhaps I do. But my patience will not last forever."

"Promises, promises," Aleksi murmured, sliding his hand up the inside of Naia's thigh. Instead of touching her, he slipped his hand beneath the oversized shirt, skimmed over her hip, and traced a path up her spine. When his hand emerged from the loosened collar, he grasped her hair and pulled her head back.

It was rougher than he usually was with her, but Aleksi did not have to worry about hurting her, not when he could feel her pleasure sliding over him like an encouraging caress. He pulled harder, just for a moment, then released her. Naia instantly turned her face to his and caught his mouth in a hungry kiss.

Aleksi teased his tongue over hers and dipped his hand beneath the shirt she wore once more, this time slipping around to cup her breast. Naia gasped at the contact, a sound that Einar echoed, and Aleksi smiled against her lips.

This was the moment Aleksi always cherished. When all the walls fell, and a lover's ardor left no room for self-conscious doubt. They were simply bodies in eager orbit, tumbling around, moving closer and closer until they crashed together in an explosion of intimacy and pleasure.

Einar ground out a curse, and Aleksi broke the kiss and looked over to find his gaze fixed to the shirt that now barely covered Naia's breast. Einar's fingers flexed on his legs, as if he was imagining shredding the fabric into pieces, and the dwindling firelight cast shadows across the hard, intriguing planes of his chest and arms.

Aleksi turned Naia's head until she was looking at Einar, as well. "How did you convince him to do it?"

"Do what?" Her voice was breathless. Dreamy.

"Keep this delicious form."

"I just told him the truth—that this is what looks like *him* to me." She rocked her hips a little. "Don't you think he's beautiful?"

"Always." Aleksi pinched her nipple, and she rocked harder. He let her for just a moment before stilling her hips with his other hand. "Easy, goddess. He isn't even naked yet."

Her low moan made Aleksi's abdomen clench.

Einar surged to his feet with animal grace, his gaze never leaving them. "Anything you want," he promised.

The light reflected off his chest as he moved, and his muscles flexed beneath the textured, silvered lines of his purple skin as he opened his pants. The fabric fell to the floor, revealing his cock. It was longer and thicker than usual, with curved ridges encircling the shaft. It was dusky purple, darker than the rest of him, rigid and pulsing and glistening at the tip.

When Naia made an eager noise, Einar curled his fingers around his cock. The caress highlighted the fact that the shaft actually widened a bit in the middle. Einar stroked himself, lingering over the swollen area, and the sound he made had Naia leaning forward, ready.

Aleksi hauled her back. "Not yet, love. Before you can taste his desire, you have to show him yours."

For a moment, she kept straining against his grip. Then a hungry curiosity bloomed throughout the room, and she gave in, relaxing against him. He rewarded her for it by easing his hand down between her open thighs to cup her.

"Thank you for your trust, Naia. That's the sweetest thing there is." He slid his hand lower. "Sweeter than the headiest wine or the most succulent fruit." Curled his fingers into her. "Even sweeter than your cunt when you're coming on our tongues."

She whimpered, but she'd caught on to the game. She did not move—except for her heaving breaths and her body clenching around his fingers.

The three of them remained there, a frozen tableau, until Einar swayed, as if fighting the urge to close the distance between him. His muscles tensed, and a low sound rumbled up from his chest.

With the standstill broken, Aleksi began to earnestly fuck Naia with his fingers.

"Aleksi," Einar growled.

Aleksi went still again, though Naia grabbed his wrist and growled in protest. "Yes?" he inquired mildly.

"Let me touch her." The words seemed torn from him, half command, half plea.

"Already?"

Einar's chest heaved. The teal fire in his eyes danced. "I want to taste her."

Naia squirmed. She was already meltingly hot, but Einar's words made her tighten around Aleksi's fingers. So he picked up the motion again, very slowly this time, and raised a questioning eyebrow at Einar. "What else?"

Einar's gaze locked on the slow movement of Aleksi's hand before fixing on Naia's face. "I want her to ride my tongue until she comes, screaming."

The words were like a physical touch, another featherlight caress sliding over Naia's skin.

"I want to know how she tastes when she comes, riding your cock."

Another tongue finding the sensitive area just behind her ear.

Einar stroked his erection again, this time with a tight, hungry pressure. "I want her to take me again. All of me. I want to fuck her so deep she's all I can feel."

Three more questing fingers fucking into her, searching for the spot that would make her fly.

Naia's gasp ricocheted through the room like a scream. Hard on its heels was a wave of pleasure that stole Aleksi's breath with its intensity. Einar threw his head back, groaning loudly enough to drown out Naia's cries, and Aleksi had to grit his teeth as molten heat enveloped his cock.

Did he move Naia, or did she seek him out, desperate for something deeper? He did not know, nor did he recall exactly how it happened. And now, he knew only her chest heaving, her skin growing hotter under his hands, and her body clenching around his.

He tore away the rumpled linen she wore, so that there would be nothing between them . . . and nothing to impede the view. Naia fell back against Aleksi's chest, shifting her hips as she did so, displaying their joined bodies more openly to Einar's avid stare.

The sight and the sound and the *sensations* shuddered through all three of them.

With one hand on her hip and the other resting lightly at the base of her throat, Aleksi brushed his lips over Naia's earlobe. "When you've had enough of waiting, reach out to Einar, and he will come to you, no matter what I say. He won't be able to resist you—he never has, and he never will."

Something hotter than desire surged through the room, a yearning beyond the physical. It echoed the hungry affection that dwelled in Aleksi's breast, making his heart thump painfully as Naia braced her hands against him and *moved*.

It was hard, almost rough, but Aleksi sank his teeth into her shoulder, urging her to fuck him harder. All while Einar watched in coiled anticipation, waiting for the moment she would set him free.

Her pleasure mounted, along with Aleksi's, a neverending circle of hunger and tension, tightening around all three of them. Shared, but heightened instead of diminished by it.

Naia ran her hand through Aleksi's hair, across his cheek and over his parted lips. She continued the caress down her own body, pausing to stroke her nipple before moving lower. Her fingers brushed the base of Aleksi's cock, and he groaned, a sound he had to echo a moment later as Naia touched her clit.

Then she reached that same trembling hand out to Einar.

In the sliver of time between heartbeats, he crossed the space between them and was on his knees, his hands sliding up her legs. His thumbs traced up her inner thighs, coaxing them wider, wide enough for his impossibly broad shoulders. The movement drove her back against Aleksi's chest, and she clung to him as Einar lowered his head and stroked his tongue over them.

They reached for Einar in tandem, clutching his head as he licked and sucked. The scent of flowers filled the air, and all Aleksi could hear was the rush of blood—or was that the ocean?—in his ears. He could not tell, and it did not matter. His entire world was this tiny corner of the Dream, filled with Naia's pleasure and Einar's hunger and Aleksi wrapped around them both.

One of them came, and so they all did. A single shared orgasm crashed through them, picking up speed and force, like a gale out at sea.

When the storm abated, light filled the room, tiny sparkles that drifted down and lingered on bare skin before finally winking out. Naia was draped over Aleksi's chest, and Einar was draped over *her*, his head pillowed against her hip.

Then Naia raised her head, and it was no longer Aleksi's little nymph who stared down at him. Not anymore.

This was the *goddess*, Mother of Rahvekya. A being who had been old eons before the High Court had ever even thought of existing.

And it was *her* turn.

She licked the corner of his mouth and lightly touched her tongue to his when he sought a kiss. "Yes or no, Aleksi?" she murmured liltingly, echoing the precise words he had demanded from Einar.

There was only one answer to give. "Yes."

An unseen force pushed his arms wide and pinned them to the headboard. "*Cintah*," she whispered. "It means stop. Now you know what to say if you need to."

He wouldn't need to say it, but he still appreciated the gesture. It was just good manners. "I'll remember."

Her eyes glowed. Not teal, like Einar's, or even the sunlight or starshine of the Dream or Void. This light was *everything*, all at once, and it swirled dangerously as Naia looked at him. "Good."

Yes, she was an ancient force.

And she was going to eat him alive.

Chapter Eighteen

Do you remember every kiss? Every touch? Every scream?

If you do, then you have not been bedded by the Lover.

Not truly.

Excerpt from Beloved,
a poetry collection dedicated to the Lover

Einar thought he had experienced the full range of emotions it was possible to feel for another person. Lust had been simple and easily come by over the years. Love might be more precious, but he had known it in many incarnations—a son's love for the woman who had raised him, a man's love for the people who earned his loyalty, even a captain's love for the crew who trusted him with their lives. He'd known respect, too—for the Siren, the first time he had knelt before her and felt her power. For the rest of the High Court.

Aleksi and Naia had taught him new shades of all three—love twined with yearning, respect married to lust, all three so tangled together they became something more than their parts. They'd taught him how it felt to be *in love*.

But no one in his life had ever inspired true awe. Not even Zanya and Sachi, whose power was so vast and unfathomable only a fool would not bend before it, because even in their strength, they were still so untested. New to the world, in the way Naia had been when she first walked out of waves with the memories of a thousand sailors and none of her own.

Naia was not untested anymore. When she glanced back at him, her eyes alight with power so ancient it made him feel like a trembling youth, there was no other word for the feeling that flooded him, riding hard alongside love and lust and respect, twisting them up tight in its grip.

Awe. She inspired naked, undiluted *awe* in him, a feeling so strong he forgot for a moment that lust had made fire of his blood, that all he wanted was to make her sob with pleasure until her body was slick enough to take him.

She was a primordial being, ancient long before the High Court first walked the land, and everything in him screamed at him to yield. If he had been on his feet, he would have fallen to his knees.

Instead he eased closer to her, reveling in the soft press of her back against his chest, shuddering as her ass brushed teasingly against his straining cock. He sank his face into the unbound masses of her hair and breathed in her scent—salt and sand and the heady scent of flowers stirred by a tropical breeze. "Tell me what to do."

"The Lover is at our mercy right now." Even her soft voice seemed to resonate, vibrating through the warm air around the three of them. "Let's not squander this moment."

She took Einar's hand and reached out, guiding his fingers to brush only lightly over the crown of Aleksi's cock before pulling them away, despite the sudden, eager arch of the man's hips. Then she leaned forward, smoothing Aleksi's hair and running her hands out along his pinned arms. The position left one of her nipples hovering a few inches from his face, though she jerked back when Aleksi tried to capture the taut peak between his lips.

"The insolence," she murmured. "And this, after he's teased you so, Einar."

There was a dark satisfaction in having their positions reversed. Not that Einar would ever object to watching Naia squirm, but Aleksi did seem to take an almost dangerous glee in ordering Einar to watch. Smiling slowly, Einar spread his fingers wide on Aleksi's hip, knowing that the rough texture of his skin in this form would rasp tauntingly. "He does like to make me wait."

The Lover seemed unbothered by his relative vulnerability. He simply tilted his head with a slow, devastating smile. "Are you planning to torment me?"

His voice was a growl, and a purr. It was everything seductive that had ever existed, somehow rolled into this moment.

It was a lure.

Naia almost fell into it. She leaned in again, and her mouth was a scant inch from Aleksi's when she caught herself—and chuckled softly. "The answer *was* no. Now? It's a definite *yes*."

She finally touched her lips to Aleksi's skin, but not to his mouth. She started at his jaw, where stubble darkened the clean lines. First a tiny kiss, then the glancing brush of tongue. She moved on to his ear, then down to the side of his neck, and beyond.

They were beautiful to watch, but Einar had no patience left for being a mere spectator. He dragged his fingers slowly up Aleksi's chest until his fingertips found Naia's seeking mouth. A teasing swipe of her tongue left just enough wetness behind to turn his rasping caress of Aleksi's nipple into a taunting glide. "I wonder if he likes teeth as much as you do. Should we find out?"

Naia turned her head and closed her teeth on the inside of Einar's forearm—*hard*. Instead of digging in, they slid over his hardened flesh with a rasp. His skin might be near impenetrable, but the sting of her teeth and the heightened sensitivity twined into sensory madness. His blood turned to lightning as he thrust his fingers into her hair, tangling the silky strands around his fingers.

The wicked mischief in her gaze was almost as irresistible as the taste of her as he claimed her lips in a desperate, wild kiss—spiced wine and tealberry and something so familiar his bones ached with it.

With the heat of Aleksi's bare chest so close, it was impossible not to turn his head enough to taste him, too—and if he didn't know better, he would swear that the Lover's skin was an aphrodisiac all on its own. Especially when Naia joined him, trading teasing kisses back and forth as they worked their way back up Aleksi's body.

Then it was his lips beneath theirs, open and coaxing, stealing control of their tangled three-way kiss with deft skill that dragged a rumbling growl from the monster deep within. Einar nipped at Aleksi's lower lip, but though the Lover's chest heaved beneath their joined hands, only the slightest, smallest gasp escaped him.

That wouldn't do. Einar twined his fingers together with Naia's as they took turns kissing Aleksi, and it was as if they had done this so many times they needed no words. Their joined hands smoothed down—over Aleksi's strong chest, across his trembling abdomen. They found his cock together, hard and hot and still slick from Naia's shuddering orgasm, and wrapped their fingers around it as one.

That earned them a groan, low and harsh and fracturing as they stroked their fingers up his length. Aleksi lifted his hips, chasing their grip, and Naia broke the kiss with a harsh moan. "Do you remember the word, my lord?"

"I remember." Aleksi ground out the words between clenched teeth.

"Good," she praised, then began to ease toward the foot of the giant bed. Einar had no choice but to go with her, backing up until they would be out of easy reach even if Aleksi's hands weren't still bound by ropes of invisible power.

There was nothing obstructing his view, however—Naia, naked on her hands and knees, her hair wild around her body as she moved with the grace of a hunting cat. "Now, Aleksi," she whispered as she grasped Einar's hand and pulled it around her body. "It's your turn to watch."

Aleksi's eyes blazed, their deep brown shot through with the first hints of violet—the color of the Lover. The color of his power, which pulsed in the room. He watched them with a predator's patience, and something feral rose within Einar in answer. He ghosted his rough fingertips up Naia's body to find her nipple, and shuddered when her pleasure echoed back at him. That shared pleasure spiked higher when he tightened his fingers and tugged gently.

Naia straightened in his grasp, arching lazily into his touch, and that mirrored sensation wound tighter as the purple glow of Aleksi's eyes increased. His power was its own caress, wrapping around them in seductive warning.

A warning that Naia ignored. "Einar?"

"Yes, goddess?"

"What were you going to do to me?" Her voice was the soft wash of water over sun-warmed sand. "On the balcony, during the ball?"

The memory came so easily. Her gasping breaths. His hands on her hips. The warmth of her body, beckoning. He nuzzled his face against the side of her neck. "I was going to fuck you until your knees gave out."

Another laugh rose and fell, cresting like a gentle wave. "That's right. What was it you said before?" She slipped her hand into his hair and pulled. "That you want to fuck me so deep that I'm all you can feel?"

Aleksi shuddered, and Einar felt it, too—not just their shared physical sensations, but the giddy joy and lazy confidence emanating from the woman in his arms as she tightened her grip on his hair. There was no hesitation as she whispered her command. "I want it. Now."

Oh, Einar did, too. He ran his hand down the front of her body until he found slick warmth, her body so eager that his groan sounded barely human. He stroked her with the rough tip of one finger and buried his face in her hair as he felt *all* of it—her pleasure at his touch twined with his pleasure at touching her, braided together with Aleksi's hunger to *see more.*

Einar could show him more. He curled his free arm across her chest, his massive hand cupping her breast as he drove her legs wider with one knee. There was nothing to block Aleksi's view as Einar worked two broad fingers into the tightness of her body. "I was wearing my mortal form that night on the balcony. Tonight there is so much more of me to take."

Amusement curled through the room, like ink in water. "Are you worried, or merely pointing this out for Aleksi's benefit?"

Perhaps he *should* be worried, but she was liquid beneath his fingers, her body primed. And Aleksi had gone still—the stillness of a predator on his chosen stalking ground, waiting for his moment.

"I'm not worried," Einar murmured, driving his fingers deeper. "You've already taken the Lover in all his glory, and I can feel how well he pleased you."

"Yes, he did." Naia pulled his hair harder. "Show him."

A command he was all too eager to obey. Einar bit her jaw, savoring the stinging pleasure that echoed through the room, then lifted his hand to clasp her wrist, where her fingers were tangled in his hair. "Let go, love."

She did, and Einar guided her hand to the rumpled blankets before dragging his fingers up her arm and across her bare shoulder. A hand splayed at the small of her back was all it took to bend her forward, until she was braced on her elbows, facing Aleksi. He took his time straightening, dragging the rough tips of his fingers down the sensitive skin of her spine and across the soft flare of her hip.

For one moment he stilled in the near silence of the room, the only sounds the crackle of the fire and their unsteady breaths. His silvery skin shimmered in that firelight as he gripped Naia's hip with one hand and his cock in the other, the sight of her bent forward before him, waiting—*eager*—so heady it barely seemed real.

Then he pushed into her, the silence shattered by his guttural groan. The fire in the hearth roared up, illuminating Naia's face as she threw her head back and clenched both hands in the velvet coverlet.

Einar met Aleksi's eyes as he rocked forward, driving deeper into the welcoming heat of Naia's body. Some part of him—a part that was still a man—screamed to go slow, to work his way into her body with gentle care. A deeper part, ancient and knowing, laughed in dark pleasure as he clasped her hips in both hands.

This was no fragile mortal woman. This wasn't even the sweet water nymph who'd first taken him into her body. This was the goddess, the spirit of the island itself, vast and ancient and fighting the grip on her hips as she struggled to squirm back, to take more of him. To take *all* of him.

He would never need to hold back with Naia. So he didn't.

She cried out when he thrust into her, and he shouldn't have worried about hurting her, not when the Lover's magic wrapped her pleasure around him like a dizzying echo. He felt her bliss as he surged deeper, her body somehow impossibly tight even as it yielded to him. There was no pain, not even when he advanced again, working the thickest part of his cock into her.

Her fingers tangled in the quilt in front of her, and fabric tore. Her back arched in a sensual curve, her panting breaths hitching as the thick ridges around his shaft rubbed along the most sensitive places deep within her. He couldn't stop himself from looking down to where their bodies met, the darkest part of him craving the sight of this moment.

His goddess, on her knees before him, any submission in the position lost in the imperious tilt of her hips and the sounds she made—impatient, hungry, so demanding there was nothing he could do but give her what she wanted.

Einar tightened his hands on her hips and slammed into her hard enough to drive a hoarse scream from her lips. Her forehead dropped to the bed, breaths coming in ragged gasps as her body fluttered around him, already so close to the edge he almost lost his grip on sanity.

Lifting his head, he found the Lover's wild gaze. "Can you feel it?" he growled to Aleksi. "Can you feel *me*?"

"I feel everything," Aleksi answered, his mild tone completely at odds with the violent swirl of color in his eyes. Something whispered over Einar's skin, a warning and a promise, a pressure at the small of his back that urged him to stroke into her again.

So he did, taking the mirrored pleasure with her gasping cries, feeling the way every hard ridge of his cock dragged across secret places that made her tremble. It was a reckless power, knowing to nudge her knees just a little wider, knowing exactly how high to lift her hips.

He used the awareness gifted by the Lover to fuck her so deep and so hard that she erupted in pleasure so violent, he had to grit his teeth and harness two thousand years of self-control not to tumble after her.

Not yet. Not so fast. Not while there was so much more he could show Aleksi.

Releasing her hip, he snaked an arm beneath her body and hauled her upright. His knees drove her thighs even wider apart, and she moaned as the position drove him even deeper into the still-clenching heat of her body. His other hand stole around her waist and down, fingers finding slick softness.

He didn't even have to thrust like this, just tease the roughened pad of one finger over her clit, and her hips jerked, until she was riding him in frantic little rocking movements. Einar turned his face to her temple, and though he whispered the words against her skin, they were for Aleksi. "Am I all you can feel?"

Her moan was answer enough. But she didn't accept pleasure passively. Her thighs flexed, and she rolled her hips, grinding down against him while her inner muscles squeezed tight, and that last delicate strand of sanity holding him back snapped.

With a heave of muscle, he lifted her off him and tossed her onto her back. Her satisfied laughter cut off in another moan as he dragged her thighs wide and thrust back into her hard enough to drive her across the rumpled bedding. And it was so much better like this, propping himself up on his elbows so he could stare down into her eyes as he drove into her. She stared back at him, her wide eyes no longer brown kissed with black and gold flecks, but churning with indescribable colors.

She whispered his name, though her parted lips did not move, and the colors *expanded*, dragging him down beneath the waves until she was his entire universe.

He tangled his fingers in the hair sprawled across the sheets, and by the firelight the strands looked sun-kissed auburn instead of brown. Her fingernails scraped over his scalp, and it was as if he had felt it untold times before. He knew what she would do next, exactly how she would tighten her fingers, the way she would drag him down for a demanding kiss, a tangle of teeth and tongues.

She had felt right from the first moment he touched her, and now he knew why. He had fucked her a thousand times, a thousand *thousand* times, and if there was ever a moment for him to *remember*, surely it was now—wrapped in the power of the Lover, drowning in how good she felt, and how good he *made* her feel, his pleasure and hers tangled up.

Then she hooked her leg over his hip, pulling him deeper as her nails scratched down his back with a force that would have broken anyone else's skin, and it didn't matter that he didn't have the storm god's memories.

He had *her*, beneath him, begging him to fuck her harder, to fuck her faster, to—

"Look at me."

It was Aleksi's voice, but it was more. The Lover, his command sliding over them like silken bonds. Their heads turned as one.

The Lover *glowed*. He had not moved from his position, pinned against the huge headboard, but he seemed . . . closer, almost looming over them. He smiled, more affection—and lust—than amusement curving his lush lips.

Then he spoke again. "I don't need my hands free to fuck you both."

The words were a teasing caress. A warning stroke. They were fine wine and dark nights and gasping for breath only for pleasure to sweep you under again.

And then it wasn't the words. It was *him*.

Warm hands stroked Einar's sides. They teased up his arms and down his legs. Fingernails traced his spine, his jaw, the small of his back. Naia dug her head back against the sheets, mouth parted in a helpless cry, and he could feel *those* touches, too. Her pleasure echoed through him as Aleksi's hands stroked down her throat, as they tangled in her hair, as they cupped her breasts and tugged teasingly at her nipples.

It didn't matter that he still hadn't moved. He was everywhere. His lips were pressed against Einar's ear, whispering obscenities, and his teeth were sinking down into the curve of his ass, and Naia was sobbing as his tongue circled her clit, driving her into an orgasm so violent the clenching of her body hazed Einar's vision. He came, ecstasy a white haze that wiped away the world.

His cock stayed rock hard. Aleksi's dark laughter stroked them in places his hands couldn't reach.

Einar didn't know where his body ended and Naia's began anymore. He didn't know which of them Aleksi was bending over, only that strong hands held them steady as he worked his cock into their ass in relentless strokes so gentle and so deep that they felt utterly possessed. Maybe it was both of them, because they came together this time, bodies shuddering as one.

There was no respite. No pause. The Lover tangled a hand in Einar's hair and rode him at the same time his mouth closed around Einar's cock, swallowing him impossibly to the root. He was fucking Naia everywhere, leaving ravaging bites across her breasts while he sucked her clit while he rode her, too, fucking her with his cock, with his fingers, with his tongue.

Pleasure wasn't a peak anymore. Release was not a relief, not when the tension broke into shuddering waves of pleasure only to tighten again before you drew a full breath. It was exquisite agony—it was bliss so intense it was unbearable.

Aleksi was the entire world, and the entire world was fucking them.

"*Cintah*." Naia choked out the word as her back arched, and her fingernails raked desperately over Einar's arms and chest. "*Cintah*."

The safe word she had given to Aleksi at the start. Einar groaned as the final wave of pleasure peaked . . . and receded, this time, leaving him limp and trembling. It took everything in him not to collapse on top of Naia, but he managed to sprawl at her side, one heavy arm thrown across her still-trembling body.

Einar didn't know if Aleksi had moved or if he had always been next to them, but he was *there*, and this time the hand stroking them was gentle and real. He soothed them both with soft touches, and even that felt like magic as a gentle warmth spread through Einar's body. Something softer and deeper than pleasure—a feeling of being wrapped in a protective bubble, safe from the worries of the world. Safe from ever being alone.

Love. That was what it was. Sweet and pure and somehow stronger than steel, because it flowed from the heart of the Lover himself.

For the second time that night, Einar felt genuine awe. He could not believe he had gotten so cocky he'd thought to issue a challenge to the god of love and desire.

But what a way to lose.

They drifted there for what felt like hours before Naia opened her eyes and rolled to face Aleksi. Her hand crept back to grasp Einar's, and she clung to it, as if for support. Then she took a deep breath. "I'm sorry."

The words elicited a confused chuckle from the Lover. "For what, little nymph?"

"For not seeing you," she whispered. "Or . . . only seeing what I expected."

"Naia—"

"I know that people don't," she insisted. "They're too wrapped up in the idea of you, or too dazzled by your perfection to see anything else." Her breathing hitched. "That must be so *lonely*."

Aleksi opened his mouth, and Einar could practically hear the self-deprecating deflection taking shape on the man's tongue.

But Naia reached up with her free hand and pressed her fingers to Aleksi's lips. "Don't. Don't hide, Aleksi. You can't anymore, don't you understand? Because *I see you* now, and you're not perfect, not at all."

Aleksi raised both eyebrows at Einar, an expression that married amusement and disbelief.

But Naia turned the Lover's gaze back to hers with an insistent hand on his chin. "You're stubborn. You always jump too readily and directly to sacrificing yourself. And, frankly? You lie with the truth a bit too easily."

"You can move on to my more positive traits whenever you like, love," Aleksi said faintly.

"I love you," she told him firmly. "Not in spite of those things, but because of them. Because you're *you*."

Aleksi's discomfort melted like snow in sunlight. For once, he seemed at a loss for words, and he leaned his forehead against Naia's in silent thanks.

She kissed him gently, then rolled to face Einar. "And I don't even know what to *say* to you."

"Don't start listing my flaws," he murmured, only half joking. "We need to sleep tonight."

She grabbed his face and held him, pinned, with a solemn gaze and a soft smile. "I have loved you for thousands of years. Across lifetimes. Even when you didn't want me to." The smile faded. "When you begged me not to."

His chest ached, and he didn't know if it was guilt for some terrible wrong he could not remember, or simply guilt that he *couldn't* remember. But he lifted his hand to cover hers. "I wish I could say the same.

But I think I loved you from the first time I felt your touch in the sea. Even if I can't remember, maybe my heart knows."

Her smile returned in full force, as dazzling as the gentle glow that still lit the room. She wrapped a lock of his hair around her finger and tickled the curling ends over his cheek.

The room swooped around him, the feeling of *familiarity* so powerful he felt momentarily dizzy. He closed his eyes and tried to chase the memory, but nothing came to him. Maybe he wanted to remember so badly he was fooling himself.

But wasn't this part of their world, too? Wanting something badly enough could make it happen. Naia had told him that the storm god hadn't started off as the Kraken, and even once he had assumed the monstrous form that would become his sigil, he had never worn *this* form, the one that now felt so natural to Einar that it was his true self. He was something new, something formed of what had come before and the dreams of a young boy who had grown up on legends of his own past life.

If he wanted those memories, they *would* come. He had to believe it.

For now he opened his eyes, and stroked back hair that looked red-gold in the firelight for one shimmering moment. In the next she was simply Naia, smiling at him with such affection that he caught her fingers and kissed them gently.

Aleksi wrapped an arm around Naia and stroked the back of his hand over Einar's chest as he nestled closer to them. "What a gift," he murmured. "To hold a love stronger than death in your hands."

The warmth of the words soothed that lingering ache in his chest. Einar threw his arm across Naia and Aleksi, savoring that his larger body made it so easy to hold them both—and to protect them from anything that might come. "Thank you, Aleksi," he murmured, and with the Lover's magic still wrapped around them like an embrace, he knew the other man would understand all the things he didn't know how to say—Einar's gratitude that Aleksi had given him the courage to open his heart, his relief that the three of them were here, together.

His love, different from the flashfire of obsession that had consumed him when he'd met Naia, but no less strong. Naia might have snuck beneath the ice around Einar's heart to crack open those protective walls, but knowing that Aleksi had seen his heart and all of its darkest parts and still loved him . . .

That had rendered those walls unnecessary.

Chapter Nineteen

The Illicit Lives of the Imperial Court
Anonymous
(banned in the Empire)

Gwynira's palace was . . . *melting*.

Large droplets of water pearled on the walls of the Great Hall, dripping down the gray stone—particularly beneath the windows. Naia watched, biting her lip to hold back a laugh, as the huge jungle cat that had joined their fight on the beach swatted experimentally at one thin trickle, then licked the wall.

"It's very rude of you, you know," Gwynira observed from a sofa near the center of the cavernous room. The crush of nobles that usually crowded the hall was conspicuously absent, and the Grand Duchess had ordered an entire seating arrangement to be brought into the room instead. "To melt my windows."

Einar chuckled. "How can you be certain that Naia is to blame?"

Gwynira half turned to face him where he stood near one of the windows in question. Hilja had already been able to outfit him with a set of new clothes that fit his larger frame. The pants, embroidered coat, and fur-trimmed boots were of an older style—very similar to the way men dressed in his father's time, Petya had told him. It certainly looked like the casual garb of a king.

Still, Einar had been reluctant to leave their chamber this morning. He had been braced for the worst, for the others to fear or even scorn his appearance.

After all his fretting, Gwynira had not even seemed to notice. Isa had, though she had simply eyed Einar curiously without crossing the line into outright gawking. And Arktikos . . .

His reaction had surprised Naia the most, though perhaps it should not have. He had clasped Einar's hand in his, then drawn him in for a half embrace that had ended with a silent nod.

One monster to another, Einar had murmured to Naia afterward, and she could tell the idea pleased him immensely.

Now, Gwynira eyed him indignantly, though a hint of amusement danced in her eyes. "The goddess of what was once a lush tropical island returns, and my palace begins to thaw? Whatever else could it be?"

Naia shifted on the plush rug that had been laid out in the center of the room. "Why, a reflection of your melting heart."

Gwynira blushed.

Isa, from her spot beside her on the sofa, let out a rusty chuckle. "She has you there, Gwyn."

"The island *is* warmer." Aleksi reclined on the rug near Naia. Though he usually favored vests of heavy velvet or leather, today he wore just a thin linen shirt, open at the collar, and he fanned the fabric against his skin. "Noticeably warmer."

"*I'm* still cold." Inga shivered and huddled deeper into her fur-lined cloak. Then she turned her head and pinned Arktikos with an assessing look. "And you're a bear."

He stared back at her, nonplussed. "Yes, I am."

"Could you be a bear, then," she asked, "and warm me up?"

Her words had stunned him into finding none. Arktikos cast a desperate look around that finally landed on Einar. "Is she—?"

"No," Einar replied. "Not flirting."

"So she's—?"

"Absolutely serious."

"I . . . will bring more furs." Arktikos practically fled, his footsteps already echoing down the back hall before the door entirely closed behind him.

Inga watched him go, and Aleksi patted her leg through the voluminous cloak. "Might have had better luck if you'd tried the flirting, love."

She nodded gravely. "Noted."

The big cat stared after Arktikos, balefully eyeing the door that had swung shut behind him. She hissed, baring huge, curving teeth, and Naia reached out to soothe her.

She sank her fingers deep into the cat's thick fur and made a soft noise. "Hush, Omira. Settle down and behave yourself."

Einar's brow furrowed. "Omira?"

"It's a name from the old tongue," she explained as she stroked the cat's side. "It means *she has witnessed*."

"That's beautiful," Isa whispered.

"Yes. The priestess who was with me the longest was named Omira." Memories washed over Naia, sharp and bittersweet. She could recall the girl's eyes on her very first day, serious and studious, the same shade as a vibrant jungle vine.

And she could remember Omira's last day, her gaze faded with age, no longer serious but smiling. Shining, until the light finally died.

All she managed to say was "I was . . . very fond of her."

Aleksi laid a comforting hand over hers. Einar left the window to sit on the rug behind her, drawing her toward him until she was leaning against the solid wall of his chest.

Naia loved them both for their quiet support.

Inga lifted one hand and dragged her fingers through the air. Little sparkles of light glinted to life and floated in their wake. Omira stilled, then slowly began to stalk toward one hovering bit of light.

Then it shot across the room, and she pounced, giving chase.

Inga laughed at the cat's antics, then beamed up at Arktikos as he handed her two heavy furs. "Thank you."

"You are welcome."

"I'm surprised that you're not out today, Naia." Gwynira accepted one of the furs that Arktikos had brought back and placed it carefully around Isa's shoulders. "Walking amongst your people."

"I'm not comfortable doing that. Not after what happened the other day." The thought of what had happened to her beach still made her shudder. It was a violation of her memories, of a place she treasured, even after thousands of years. "If someone were to be hurt—or worse—because of me? It would break my heart."

"That's fair." Gwynira eyed them apologetically. "Arktikos has been combing through the harbormaster's correspondence, trying to piece together some hint of who might have bribed or threatened the man into letting that mercenary ship dock."

"And your seneschal knows nothing and cannot find the answer for you?" Skepticism colored Aleksi's voice. "If that's true, you should dismiss Sir Jaspar on grounds of incompetence."

"Don't think I haven't considered it."

A soft hiss filled the room. At first, Naia assumed it was Omira. But when she glanced over, she found the cat stretching through a lazy yawn.

Cold. Unfeeling.

The island. The voice vibrated through her core, a sound that wasn't a sound at all, but a feeling of warning—and dread.

Not to be trusted.

"There's precious little chance of that happening," Naia muttered. She had not trusted Jaspar even before he had been so unpleasant—especially to Einar.

Aleksi dropped a kiss to Naia's shoulder. "Did you say something, love?"

"Nothing, just . . ." She had to ask. "Why *him*, Gwynira? Why Jaspar?"

"Why is he my seneschal, you mean?" Gwynira sighed. "As unlikely as it may seem, he's actually a very good administrator. The best I've had in hundreds of years."

"So you trust him," Naia pressed.

Arktikos snorted.

Gwynira shot him an exasperated look. "Trust is such a subjective thing. Can I trust Jaspar to oversee the daily running of this palace? Yes. On the other hand . . ." She gestured apologetically to Einar. "I clearly cannot trust him not to be an overbearing ass to guests."

Aleksi raised both eyebrows as he toyed with Naia's hair. "Come, Gwynira. You know the *real* question."

She inclined her head. "While it is entirely possible that he has been fooled or subverted in some other way, I would be very surprised, indeed, to find him willingly working with Sorin."

That seemed to surprise Einar. "You sound certain. Why is that?"

She actually considered the question, as if she did not have a ready, precise answer. "My court has always had a . . . complicated relationship with the Empire."

"Complicated." Arktikos shook his head as he started for the bottles that lined one end of the buffet table. "That is one way to describe it."

"I have made little secret over the centuries that I find most Imperial nobles tedious at best," Gwynira elaborated. "For some inexplicable reason, that has made them desperate for my approval."

"Isn't it obvious?" Aleksi gratefully accepted a goblet of wine from Arktikos. "People always want what they cannot have."

Gwynira made a disgusted noise. "In spite of my best efforts, over the years it became somewhat prestigious for a certain set—the vapid ones, mostly—to spend a few years here, soaking up the rustic atmosphere."

"Charming," Inga said flatly.

"I think Sorin encouraged it because he knew nothing would irritate me more." Gwynira grimaced. "He would send the most intolerable people here himself."

Einar frowned as he declined Arktikos's offer of wine. "Klement told me that people were sometimes sent here as punishment."

She rolled her eyes. "Guildmaster Klement is remarkably self-absorbed, as always. But he is not entirely wrong. Most of the people Sorin sent to the island were, indeed, intended to punish *me*. But some—like Klement—were banished here for their own transgressions. Or the transgressions of their families."

Naia ventured a guess. "Jaspar?"

"Yes." Gwynira looked troubled. "He had just finished his schooling and was preparing to go to work in the family business—something related to shipping or transport—when his uncle irritated Sorin. Honestly, it seemed such a trifling matter to me, but Sorin had been growing more erratic over the past few decades. Jaspar's uncle must have simply been in the wrong place at the very wrongest of times. Anyway, Sorin stripped them of their estates, their guild ranks, everything. Then he gathered the whole family, killed the elder members, and sent all the youngest off to various kingdoms."

She said it matter-of-factly, as if it was the sort of thing Sorin would do often enough not to merit special notice. Nausea roiled in Naia's gut, and she also refused more wine.

Gwynira went on. "Jaspar arrived here young and angry, with nothing to his name but whatever I gave him."

"That's . . . sad." It was simply the truth. No one, not even someone as unpleasant as Jaspar, deserved such a thing.

Aleksi hummed. "On the face of it, that sounds very much like what Sorin did to Einar."

Arktikos had claimed for himself the goblet that Einar and Naia had both refused, and he drained half of it before growling. "I would not compare their situations."

Aleksi gestured for him to go on.

The man hesitated, then glanced at Einar. "If I may speak frankly, Captain?"

"By all means."

Arktikos finished his wine, then set the empty goblet down with a solid thump. "The former emperor may have killed both their families, but their reactions to those murders could not have been more different. The crown-prince swore vengeance, and the depth and sincerity of that vow has carried him across a dozen mortal lifetimes already. He will have blood. All Jaspar truly wants is to see himself restored in an empire that no longer exists."

"Well said," Isa told him.

But Gwynira only sighed. "Perhaps I could have guided him better. But, as I'm sure you've noticed, I am not exactly the nurturing type."

"I *did* try to give him purpose," Arktikos told them. "He was not interested. I may be a—what is it you call it in the Sheltered Lands? A Dreamer? But I was not socially important enough for Jaspar to feel like he should listen to me. Besides," he added with a slight smile, "I would have expected him to work his ass off, and you've all seen how fond he is of that."

It was so much to take in, and Naia hardly knew what to make of it. All it truly proved was that someone could have a tragic past and *still* be one of the worst people you had ever met.

"It is possible that Sorin could have bought him," Gwynira mused. "A promise to restore his family estate and bring his family back might entice him to move past his hatred. But I have a hard time imagining Sorin making such an offer."

"It would be the smartest thing to do," Inga observed. "But to do it would imply, on some level, that Sorin had made a mistake. And that simply will not do."

Gwynira looked at Inga with something akin to surprise. It was as if she was realizing, for the first time, that here was someone who also knew Sorin—and his true nature. "You understand."

"Yes." Inga shrugged beneath the furs. "We were never close, as he disdained my fascination with the Void to the point of disgust. So I have fewer good memories of him than some of the others. But, even at his worst, he never seemed so . . ."

"Brittle," Naia supplied. From what she had gathered, he had once been smart and determined. Convinced that he knew the best way forward, of course. But the actions that Gwynira described were so strangely insecure and fearful. Should not someone who held such power, who ruled an entire empire, have been *less* threatened by the defiance of those who could never hurt him, not more?

It was all so complicated, and for what? What had Sorin gained by conquering this island? He did not want it. He likely never did. He certainly did not love Rahvekya's people or admire their culture. The only thing the Empire had ever really exported from its shores was tundra cotton. Would it not have been easier, not to mention more humane, to simply negotiate a trade deal with Einar's mother?

None of this had to happen.

She did not realize that she had breathed the words until Gwynira hummed in agreement. "Whatever you mean in this instance, when it comes to Sorin? You are most certainly correct."

Naia swallowed a sob. "He didn't have to take this island. He caused so much death and pain and loss, and for *what*? Nothing could be worth this."

"Sorin does not calculate death, nor pain, nor loss." Aleksi gave the words hesitantly, as if sorry he had to say them at all—especially in front of Einar. "Because he does not consider those things. They mean nothing to him."

Einar's breath hitched, and Naia shook her head reflexively. She did not understand how that could possibly be, unless . . .

Sorin truly was a monster.

Chapter Twenty

I visited the temple ruins this afternoon, and my heart is heavy. The glorious tree that used to shelter us beneath its branches on warm days struggles to survive in this new world of winter. I fear we have seen its last bloom. Future generations will not know the peace of leaning against its trunk as the scent of the goddess's favorite flowers whispers on the wind. A small thing, perhaps, in the face of everything we have lost. But I grieve.

The lost journal of High Priestess Tona

Einar's least favorite moment of every morning was when he finally overcame reluctance and opened the door, braced for another day of navigating Gwynira's court. True, it had become slightly less intolerable as the nobles continued to flee to the dubious safety of the mainland—even Klement had become scarce in recent days—but Einar still would have preferred to keep the rest of the world locked away so he could stay in bed with his lovers.

Perhaps the island was still granting wishes, because this morning, when he'd opened the doors at a gentle knock, it had been to find an army of servants weighted down with food. "The Grand Duchess thought you might prefer breakfast in your rooms," one of them said, somehow managing to curtsy without spilling her massive tray. "As there are not enough nobles left in the palace to make the usual arrangements practical."

So Einar thanked them, opened the door wide, and watched them fuss over each offering before shyly smiling at Naia and asking for a blessing.

Not a single one of them seemed perturbed by Einar's changed appearance, and while the bows they offered him might not have been as deep as those Naia received, every one of them bent their knee to him on their way out the door.

Gwynira's nobles had not just been nakedly horrified by his demigod form, but thrilled to be so terrified. Their furtive stares had crawled over him like an unwelcome touch, their whispers following him wherever he went. He'd half suspected one or two—like that puffed-up fool who had cut Aleksi—had fled the island just to escape him.

But to the people of Rahvekya, he would always be the lost prince who had brought home their goddess. They didn't care how he looked, only that he was here.

They had almost completed a peaceful breakfast when another knock sounded at the door. Einar opened it to find Gwynira on the other side, dressed in one of her long fur coats, her expression intentionally blank. Once inside the room, she took a deep, bracing breath. "There's been a development."

Aleksi tilted his head. "Oh?"

"Yes. We've located the harbormaster's missing records." Her carefully neutral expression cracked for a moment as she grimaced. "Hidden behind a loose stone in Jaspar's suite."

Oh, *shit*. Einar should have killed the man at that first disastrous dinner.

Aleksi's words remained mild. "And what do they say?"

"Precisely what you already suspect," Gwynira allowed. "He personally authorized the mercenary ship to dock. On a diplomatic request from Kelann."

Kelann, the home of Eirika, Elevia's counterpart in the Imperial Court. The urge to throttle Jaspar only grew stronger.

"Makes sense." Aleksi shrugged. "The Stalker wants my head, preferably still attached to my body so she can rip it off herself."

"So. Jaspar set the trap." Naia was very, very still. "Where is he now?"

"He left this morning, on the last ship bound for the mainland." Gwynira's brow furrowed. "Though I'm not sure it matters, as this does not prove his guilt. He was accustomed to handling such requests. Even under current circumstances, he might not have even felt like he could deny her."

"But then we were kidnapped." Understanding dawned on Naia's face. "And he could not say a word without implicating himself. So he remained silent."

Aleksi's thoughts had taken a different turn. "The harbormaster?"

Gwynira hesitated. "I . . . don't know. Jaspar is arrogant, self-serving, and fully capable of violence. We all know this."

It was tempting to condemn the man anyway, but even Einar had to acknowledge the truth. "But being a little shit is not evidence of murder," he rumbled.

"So where does this leave us?" Naia asked.

"With another lead." Gwynira pulled a sheaf of papers from the pocket of her day dress. "Jaspar documented the initial request. So he would have exonerating evidence, I imagine, should the offending party throw him at my mercy for allowing Eirika into my home."

Aleksi accepted the document she offered. "She did not make the request herself?"

"No." Gwynira turned to ice, in word and demeanor. "Guildmaster Klement made the application."

Klement, who hovered irritatingly on the edges of every conversation, his gaze following Einar with a fascination that was so off-putting, Einar had never considered him a real threat. It seemed too ridiculous to believe.

Aleksi groaned. "The bastard hid in plain sight. Annoyed everyone just enough to convince us he had neither the wits nor the guile to be the spy. Clever."

"A spy would not wish to make a spectacle of himself," Naia agreed. "Which Klement has done, and rather often."

The man's stubborn insistence on visiting Petya took on a far darker meaning. "He wanted access to my ship," Einar said. "He claimed he only wanted to meet Petya, and it made sense at the time. He's written so many of those foolish books. But even when I said no, he kept pressing for an invitation."

Gwynira looked apologetic. "No doubt with an eye toward reconnaissance."

"Or sabotage," Naia added flatly.

Or perhaps even a hostage. Einar's blood chilled at the thought of Petya within Sorin's grasp. What would he not sacrifice for the woman who had raised him? And Klement had known all the stories—about the island's history, about its mythology. About Einar himself.

"It gets worse." Gwynira shuffled the papers. "Of course, Arktikos searched Klement's suite next—he has also vanished, by the way—and found this."

It was a letter, but not from the Stalker. As Aleksi took it, Einar caught sight of the Imperial Seal.

Sorin's seal.

Aleksi mumbled under his breath, quickly reading aloud as he skimmed the letter. Then he paused, the paper crinkling as his fingers tightened. ". . . hope this gives even you adequate notice to prepare for my imminent arrival."

It should have horrified Einar—and it did, on one level. The people of this island had suffered too much already, and there was no joy in knowing the Emperor was coming here to inflict more harm upon them.

But the goddess walked the shores of Rahvekya again, and Einar was not a helpless infant. The Empire could not have his home. If Sorin tried to take it . . . he would die. There was no other option.

"Of course we'll all want to meet to make our plans," Gwynira said. "But before that . . . Einar, do you have a moment?" She inclined her head toward the door. "I have a somewhat pressing matter to discuss with you."

He was hardly thrilled with the idea of leaving Naia and Aleksi alone with Klement on the run and the Emperor planning his invasion, but at his uncertain look, Aleksi smiled encouragement and Naia brushed his arm gently. "We'll be fine."

Once they were in the hallway, Arktikos fell in step behind them. He was a powerful presence at their back, a reminder that Gwynira's inner circle had plenty of strength of its own—strength Sorin might not be prepared to meet.

"Do you mind walking outside?" Gwynira asked. Her lips pressed together, as if she'd caught herself on the edge of a smile. Those had been appearing with unsettling regularity since Isa's return. "It is once again unseasonably warm. But I could do with some fresh air."

Einar quashed any lingering reluctance to leave Naia and Aleksi alone. If they were safe anywhere, it was surely on this island, where the very elements answered to Naia's whims. "I don't mind stretching my legs."

Somehow, he wasn't surprised when she led him out the door that led to the gardens, and the little winding path up the hill to Naia's temple. At the base of the path, she gave Arktikos a silent look. He hesitated, clearly as reluctant to leave Gwynira unprotected as Einar had been with Naia, but he finally inclined his head and pivoted, his large body becoming an unmovable wall that blocked anyone else from following them.

They walked in silence until the first turn in the path. Then Gwynira sighed. "I never wanted to rule here, you know. It was meant to be a punishment. A cruel joke. Sorin took the only person I had ever loved away from me, and then banished me to an island as frozen as my heart."

Einar knew all about frozen hearts, but Gwynira didn't seem to want a reply, her eyes focused forward as if she was seeing not the landscape around them, but some haunting memory of the past.

"After that, Sorin mostly ignored me," she continued. "Oh, he called me to his court from time to time to torment me, but as long as the money from the island's exports flowed into Imperial coffers, he paid me very little attention."

He had not expected to feel sympathy for the woman who ruled over his conquered homeland, but Einar found he did. Especially now that he had tasted the sweetness of being loved by the person who haunted your dreams. He simply could not imagine the agony of being forced to dance attendance on a person who had killed Naia or Aleksi.

His conflict must have shown on his face, because Gwynira offered him a chilly smile. "Don't fret, Captain. I am not asking for your pity. I still raised a palace on the ashes of your family home, and ruled your people for centuries in Sorin's name."

"You did," he agreed. "And I won't lie and pretend that's an easy thing for me to know. But I also know the conquest that killed my family happened long before you were . . ." What could he possibly call the way she had come into this world? Nothing so simple as *birth*.

Gwynira huffed. "Pulled from the Dream by a megalomaniac?"

He could not dispute that.

Gwynira climbed in silence for a few moments before glancing at him. "It was odd to meet her, you know. Dianthe. He created me to fill the space she had left in his life, to complete his twisted parody of the family he had lost."

Sorin's entire court had been like that. Broken reflections of the High Court, warped by the way Sorin had seen them—or had never truly seen them. Einar knew well how cold the Siren could be when she deemed it necessary, but even when she wrapped herself in the chill stillness of the depths, one need only look into her eyes to know that her heart burned with fire.

Gwynira continued quietly, "When I looked at her, I saw parts of myself I recognized. But mostly I saw the things about her that he hated. I was made from spite and loneliness. We all were. It's no wonder we all came out twisted. We darken everything we touch."

"I wouldn't go that far," Einar said. "This island is the only place in Sorin's Empire not overrun by chaos. And it's because you protected the people under your care from the spells he used to bind the dreams of his subjects. There was no violent awakening for them. You saved them that pain."

Gwynira's laughter held little mirth. "Yes, but that was spite, as well. I knew that every soul he bound to himself only strengthened him. Discovering a way to subvert his magic without him noticing was another small way to hurt him. To take from him."

"You took from him, and gave to the people of Rahvekya."

"I suppose you could see it that way." She shrugged, as if she could shake off even that mild praise. "I confess, I did not mind letting them have their religion and their customs. Sometimes I rather envied them, if I'm honest. I never had anything like that—stories that promised better times would come, or the belief that power could be kind, instead of endlessly cruel."

"I'm sorry," he said—and meant it. "Petya raised me on those stories, and they gave me comfort during the hardest years."

"Petya," she murmured, with a wry smile. "I am pleased to have one mystery answered, at least. I always wondered how those stories flourished for so long, never changing. You must know that isn't how it usually happens. Legends drift. The parts people care most about change. But not on Rahvekya. Century after century, every tale was always the same. Now I know . . . Your Petya's wife was here, training each generation to carry the stories to the people."

The top of the hill loomed in front of them. The wind teased at the final few lanterns, dancing with their flames. "I never had the same connection to the Dream that the High Court seems to," Gwynira continued. "It may be where I came from, but I was formed from it against my will. The whispers of the world that others claim to hear? For me, it has always been silence."

The breeze stirred more strongly, unusually warm, and carrying with it that teasing scent of flowers in bloom. They crested the hill, and the reply Einar intended to make died on his lips.

Before them stood the temple, glimmering in the late morning sun. And in front of it, the dead tree, the one whose bare branches had twisted tiredly toward the sky for thousands of years . . .

Was dead no longer.

Hearty branches spread wide in every direction, laden down with enormous flowers in the goddess's favorite teal. The wind danced through the branches, carrying their intoxicating scent to where Einar stood, too stunned to move, too stunned to even speak.

"I may not hear the world's whispers," Gwynira said dryly, "but even I can understand the message when it is this obvious. So only one question remains. When would you like to hold your coronation?"

Finally, he found words. Only two of them, spilling free unbidden. "My *what*?"

"Your coronation," Gwynira repeated, waving one hand in a gesture that took in the tree and the temple and the island beyond. "I never wanted any of this. All I ever wanted was Isa, and now that I have her back, I do not intend to waste my days sitting on a throne thrust upon me by the man who killed her."

Einar managed to tear his gaze from the tree and meet her steady gaze. "You're leaving the island?"

"Well, not this very moment." Her chilly smile whispered of violence. "I have plenty of scores to settle with Sorin. So does Isa. We won't be leaving until we have resolved the current situation, one way or another. But unless you plan to turn me out of the castle the moment they set a crown upon your head, I see no reason to delay the inevitable."

This was moving uncomfortably fast in a direction Einar was unprepared to grapple with—*especially* alone. "I can't just . . . become a king."

"You're already a king," Gwynira replied with steely resolve. "This crown is your birthright. The island has made its position clear." She pointed to the tree. "What do you expect will happen when word of this spreads? Best to give in with grace, Your Majesty."

Most of the servants in the castle and a fair number of the villagers had stood on this very hilltop and listened to Agata pronounce that the tree had bloomed as an omen that their crown-prince would return to them. That he would reclaim the island and throw the Empire from its shores.

Gwynira was right. He'd seen the speed with which whispers traveled. Once it had become common knowledge that the prince's sacred tree had bloomed once again, the people of Rahvekya would carry him bodily to the throne to place him upon it.

It was likely a total abdication of duty and a complete betrayal of his family that the thought filled him with more panic than pleasure.

Gwynira was still watching him as if she was waiting for him to provide a time of day for the ceremony. "I have to speak to Aleksi and Naia first," he told her firmly. "As I expect you would want to speak to Isa in similar circumstances."

For the first time since they'd left her palace, she let a genuine smile form. "Of course. And I'm sure that the people who have already witnessed this latest omen will understand that you wish to seek the goddess's blessing before you proceed." She paused. "For a few days, at least."

The goddess's blessing was the least of his concerns. If he told Naia he wished to reclaim his parents' throne and rule over the people of her island, he had no doubt she would encourage him. But Aleksi . . .

Aleksi might not have a throne, but he had his own palace-like villa. His own court. His own people, who had done without him for weeks already. The time would come when he would need to return to his home and resume his duties, would it not?

But even if Einar walked away from his birthright . . . what of Naia? She wasn't just the goddess of this island. In a very real sense she *was* the island, and it was her. Now that she had regained her memories, how could she want to leave? This was her ancient home, the place she had ruled over for years beyond counting.

Maybe it would not be so bad to rule this island at her side. To be her protector again. Maybe time would even let him regain his memories, to be a worthy partner as he had been so many centuries before.

A sweet picture, but it shattered when Einar tried to imagine Aleksi leaving *his* home and people behind. Was that the only future available to them? One where they were pulled apart again and again by conflicting duties?

The questions piled up in the silence as Gwynira and Einar began their descent, but no answers joined them.

Chapter Twenty-One

While Imperial history tends to consider King Vylanar the final ruler of the island, a more careful reading of the source material reveals that he was in fact merely the subordinate consort to his wife, Queen Talvia. She was what the locals referred to as "goddess-touched," a status that this scholar has been unable to absolutely define. (For more information on the goddess-touched, see my volume on Religious Figures and Rites.)

Akeisa: An Overview of Prominent
Historical Figures
by Guildmaster Klement

Einar had been gone a long time.

Well, perhaps not a *long* time, but far too long for Aleksi's tastes.

He said as much to Naia, and she threw her head back with a laugh. "Am I boring you?"

"Of course not." They were sitting on the sofa, facing one another. Her bare feet rested in his lap, so he tugged on one of her toes. "But you know what I mean."

Her laughter subsided into warm affection. "Yes, I do. You do not like when he is gone because it leaves you with an empty place shaped like him."

It was such an apt description, nothing Aleksi ever would have thought, but it *fit*. Not just the way he missed Naia and Einar when he wasn't with them, but how he felt them when they were there.

He ran his hand up Naia's leg to rest in the bend of her knee. "I also have a place shaped like you."

"Mm-hmm." She lifted her foot to rest on the middle of his chest. "I'm the other half of your heart."

He caught her ankle. "You are."

"I know."

Aleksi did not like to rely on words to convey his feelings. He much preferred to demonstrate them. But they'd had precious little time to spend on moments like these, enjoying each other's company and learning how to simply *be* together.

For now, words would have to do. "I mean it, Naia."

"Aleksi . . ." She pulled her foot from his grasp and shifted until she was kneeling on the sofa. "*I know*. When you wrapped us in the Dream, I did not just feel your pleasure. I felt everything." She leaned forward and kissed his nose lightly. "Do not mistake my serenity for nonchalance. I just know what is *mine*."

It eased a weight he had not realized he'd been carrying, and he winked up at her. "Then can you please convince the staff to stop building fires in here every morning? It is becoming increasingly too warm for them."

The moment the joke left his lips, the blazing fire in the hearth receded until only glowing embers were left.

"How thoughtful," he murmured. "Thank you, Naia."

But she only shook her head and smiled. "That? Was not me."

"Then how?"

Naia moved again, this time crawling over to him. "I think you might need to accustom yourself, my lord, to the fact that this island? *My* island?" She traced her finger along the skin left bare by the open vee of his shirt. "Wants to see you happy."

"Well, in that case . . ." He grasped her hips. "You should come a little closer."

The door swung open, and Einar walked in, a distracted frown creasing his brow. He closed the door and leaned against it for a moment, still frowning. Without saying a word, he shrugged out of his new jacket and dropped it haphazardly over the back of a chair. When he dropped carelessly onto the love seat across from them, the wood frame creaked dangerously.

Naia sat back on her heels. "What is it? What's wrong?"

Einar heaved a sigh that sounded like the weight of the world was pressing down on him. "Gwynira wants to know when she can schedule my coronation."

And there it was.

Aleksi had known, on some level, that this would be coming. No, he had not imagined that Gwynira would be the one to suggest it, though perhaps he should have. She hated this place, in a way, not because of the people but because of Sorin and his cruelty. And of course, the people would want the heir of their most beloved rulers in her place.

Their prince.

Their *king*.

But Naia just blinked. "She *what*?"

Einar scrubbed his hands over his face with a hoarse laugh. "I know. I *know*. But she took me up to your temple . . . and the tree is blooming. The one that hasn't bloomed since the day I was born."

"Oh, Einar." Naia climbed off the sofa and went to kneel on the love seat next to him.

It was a stark separation, barely even symbolic. Aleksi on one side of the room, and Naia and Einar on the other.

Would it hurt this much when he had to leave without them?

Einar reached for Naia, his fingers finding hers. The touch seemed to ground him, and he instinctively sought more contact by clasping her hand between his.

Naia tilted her head, her frown returning as she regarded Einar, but her words were carefully, studiously neutral. "Do you *want* to be king?"

"*No*," he said, too swiftly and forcefully for it to be anything but the truth. "I may have been born a prince, but I was raised on ships. On the sea. I know nothing about courts and castles and how to run a whole island. It would be a disaster. Except . . ."

Aleksi's fingers and toes had gone numb. "Except?" he prompted gently.

"*Can* I say no?" He looked from Naia to Aleksi and back, conflict clear in his tight expression. "The island has a chance to be free of Imperial rule. And Gwynira doesn't want to stay. But if she leaves now, when there is such chaos everywhere . . ."

"It isn't your responsibility, just because Gwynira doesn't care to shoulder it anymore," Naia protested.

"Is it not?"

"Not if you don't want it."

As if her assurance had freed him of some terrible burden, he relaxed back against the cushions, stroking his thumbs over the back of her hand. "I don't think I would make a very good king. But maybe I wouldn't have to be. The island already has a leader, and I could be your protector again."

Naia nearly jerked her hand from his. "I . . . No. No, that's not— they had councils, I only—" She stopped and took a deep breath. "That isn't who I was. What I did here."

She was near tears, and no wonder. It was yet another reminder that Einar still did not remember their life together. Worse, that there was no one left in this world that remembered her—the *real* her—at all.

Einar had gone still again, his gaze roaming over her face. Finally, he said softly, "You *are* the island. What do *you* want?"

She climbed off the love seat and paced toward the opposite side of the room before turning to face them both again. "I don't know. I haven't thought about it. I *can't*, not yet."

When she did, she would not be able to countenance leaving. She had only left her people before to save them, and they worshipped her. What could ever tempt her to walk away from that?

Einar's brow furrowed. "Do you mean you're not sure if you want to settle here?"

Her agitation worsened. "I mean, I haven't *thought about it.*"

"And you don't have to." Aleksi held out a hand. "Come and sit, love."

She sank to the sofa once more, but at the very opposite end of it. Now, she was far away from both of them. She clenched her hands in her lap and looked down.

"Neither of you has to decide anything right now," Aleksi continued. "And no one should expect it of you. It's not right."

"It isn't—" Naia shuddered and looked up at each of them in turn, her eyes shining with tears. "I don't know if I *can* leave now. Did either of you think of that?"

Einar muttered a stricken curse, one that Aleksi silently echoed. He had considered it, but not in terms of physical capability. It had never occurred to him that she might be tethered to this place now by more than custom and devotion. She might not be like the gods of the High Court, or even the storm god of old, free to roam the lands and seas.

She *was* this island.

"You have a seat in the Sheltered Lands," she told Aleksi, then turned to Einar. "And you have your ship and crew. I have not thought about staying because . . ." Her shoulders fell. "I might not have a choice, but *you do.*"

"Naia—" Einar left the love seat to kneel in front of her. "I'm so sorry. I didn't realize."

"Don't." Her whisper was barely audible, and she softened the command with a hand on his cheek. "You don't want to rule here, Einar. You've told us that from the very beginning."

"It's not even that," he said quietly. "For two thousand years, all I've wanted was to destroy the Empire. When Sorin fell, I could have come here, you know. I thought about it. But I was afraid that I had forgotten how to want anything else." He pulled her hand to his lips for a kiss, then looked to Aleksi. "But now I want something. I want you. Both of you."

Naia slipped onto the floor, as well, and wrapped her arms around Einar.

But Aleksi stayed where he was, because there was only one outcome here. Naia and Einar would stay. Of course they would. Their shared legacy would not be denied. A Rahvekyan king, one who had liberated the island from colonial rule and was a god twice over? A king whose queen consort *was the island itself?*

Epic poems had been based on less.

Aleksi opened his mouth. Words came out, and though he did not know what they were, he knew they were the right ones. Words that would reassure, that would comfort.

This moment was a much-needed reminder of what the universe had been telling Aleksi all along. His lovers had a grand destiny—two immortal lifetimes' worth by now—and he would not stand in the way of it.

His heart would not let him.

Chapter Twenty-Two

love does not flinch

in the face of the unknown

it is the courage

to say yes

yes

Excerpt from Beloved,
a poetry collection dedicated to the Lover

Restlessness pulled Naia from sleep.

The first traces of morning had not yet begun to brighten the skies outside. Only the light of the moons filtered through the windows, painting everything that was not in shadow in muted shades of blue and silver.

Naia sat up, careful not to jar her sleeping lovers. Beneath her, the island's heart beat a quiet, steady rhythm, strong and safe. So it was not danger that had sparked the unease that now twisted in her belly.

Naia stared down at the two men in the bed with her. They were twined together, with Einar's head pillowed on Aleksi's shoulder. Aleksi, meanwhile, had fallen asleep with his fingers tangled in Einar's hair.

Between the Lover's effortless beauty and the Kraken's skin nearly glowing in this light, they did not look like men, or even gods. They looked ethereal, like a dream that might vanish at any moment.

Finally, Naia recognized the feeling.

It was fear.

She'd lost so many things, and missed so much *time*. Why had she not come back sooner? Einar had been reborn more than two thousand years ago, and Aleksi had walked the earth for over three.

Why had she not returned the instant after her death? She could have passed into the world that waited beyond for only a moment before slipping free of the Dream on the other side. She could have reunited with Theron. Together, they might have found Aleksi.

Except they wouldn't have, would they? They would have stayed on Rahvekya, wrapped in the same little world they'd inhabited for thousands of years already. And when the Betrayer's forces had come for their island, their *people*, she and Theron would have crushed them.

But then Aleksi might have stayed in the Sheltered Lands. Einar would not have been born, and the very thought made her heart ache. No, she could not wish that events had transpired differently, even if it meant she could not claw back thousands of years of life.

She would just have to live them *now*.

Aleksi's eyes fluttered open.

"I'm sorry," Naia apologized in a scant whisper. "I didn't mean to disturb you."

He shook his head and squinted up at her. "You didn't. It's just that your aura is so bright right now."

"I was thinking about the past," she admitted. "About all the things that would have been different with only a few tiny changes."

Aleksi looked up at her as if he knew exactly what she'd been thinking. But all he said was, "Do you have regrets?"

She almost said no, but there *was* something that had been haunting her. "Just one—that I did not try harder to find a way to stay alive. For my people, yes, but especially for Theron. It might not have worked out . . . but I should have tried."

Aleksi rubbed her knee soothingly. "You did what you could, love. That's all any of us have."

Einar stirred. He opened his eyes, and a smile curved his lips when he caught sight of her. It was the same smile she'd seen millions of times, and it tore at Naia's heart even as it warmed her.

His voice was rough. "Couldn't sleep?"

Her eyes burned. "I just . . . didn't want to miss this moment."

Einar's expression softened, and he held out his hand. When she took it, he pulled her on top of him.

His skin looked and felt different, but his kiss was the same—eager, ready, *familiar*. She'd always thought so, and now she knew why.

It made her long to discover what else she recognized about his touch, about *him*, so she slipped her hand beneath the covers, chasing the clenching muscle and soft, hungry noises he breathed against her lips.

The bed shifted as Aleksi rose on one elbow. He nuzzled Naia's bare shoulder, then claimed Einar's mouth when she tossed her head back with a gasp. A heartbeat later, Aleksi wound his hand in her tousled hair and held her that way, her back bowed, while he and Einar slowly drew their tongues over her breasts to her nipples.

She rocked instinctively, and shuddered when she ground against Einar's cock . . . and Aleksi's hand.

"Wait." Aleksi lifted his face to hers. Their mouths were so close, almost kissing, as they traded ragged breaths back and forth. "Let me—"

Naia placed her fingers to his lips. "I'll do it."

His eyes flared, ardent violet and ravenous purple. He closed the last bit of distance between them and kissed her hard, his tongue lingering to soothe where his teeth had nipped. "Hurry."

Aleksi was usually the one who pulled them close, wrapped them up, and held them tightly wreathed in his magic. This time, Naia was the one who opened up and let them in.

It might not have worked just after she regained her memories, but she'd rediscovered so much about herself and her abilities since then. She reached out, feeling like a seductive Siren of legend when they eagerly fell into her.

For a moment, Naia trembled, nearly overwhelmed by the *intensity* of it. She felt everything, *everything*, all at once. Her flourishing desire. Einar's hunger to taste their pleasure. Aleksi's relief at being able to simply let go and trust that someone else would keep them shielded in this moment.

They soothed her through it, with Einar whispering encouragement against her collarbone as Aleksi slowly stroked his fingers up and down her back. Finally, she nodded, and the whispers gave way to teeth scoring her skin. The hand that rested on her back made another journey, between her shoulder blades, down her spine. *Lower*, until Aleksi's fingertips grazed her clit.

Fuck.

Naia put a hand on his shoulder, halting the caresses, and held Aleksi's gaze as she eased up and forward, until the head of Einar's cock slipped past Aleksi's already wet fingers.

Einar gripped her hips and thrust up, driving deep. Aleksi caught her mouth, swallowing a keening cry as Einar began to fuck her.

The sound of it filled the room, skin on skin, sharp cries, and heavy breathing. Einar guided her hips in a smooth, quick rock, and Naia leaned forward to brace her hands on his chest. Aleksi murmured appreciation and encouragement while he touched and licked them both, everywhere he could reach, as if they were clay and he meant to capture this moment forever.

Naia marveled at how they all *fit* when they were locked together like this, surrounded by magic, with no one having to worry about being too rough or hurting someone or maintaining rigid control. It was sheer *pleasure*, a joining that went beyond the physical.

Then Aleksi moved. He lifted Naia's hair and pressed an open-mouthed kiss to the spot where the back of her neck met her shoulder. She leaned back against his chest, but he bent forward, grinding her against Einar until little sparkles of light danced in her vision, even when she closed her eyes.

"Please," she rasped, and even she didn't know what she meant.

But Einar and Aleksi did. Einar closed his lips around her nipple again, sucking so hard that, for a moment, Naia's head went fuzzy. Then Aleksi made it worse—and so, *so* much better—by positioning himself with the head of his cock against her ass.

Oh.

Einar had insinuated, on more than one occasion, that having the Lover fuck your ass was a singular experience, but he had not elaborated. Naia had assumed he meant that Aleksi's magic made it more intensely pleasurable, even ecstatic.

This was all of that, and more. Her body yielded to his gentle, rocking thrusts, and Einar groaned as she moved between them. But it was the pulsing that shocked her into an orgasm, quick, thrumming beats like the ones she had heard when the island had first called to her.

The rhythm grew louder, blotting out everything else as Naia spun away into the aether—and took them with her.

In that place, wrapped up in each other, they could be their truest selves, no longer bound to any mortal forms. Naia was cliffs of stone, rolling hills, and the water that cradled it all. Through that water, Einar rippled, his huge rough-smooth tentacles gliding over her. The rest of their mutual existence was Aleksi, around and inside them both.

And Naia wanted *everything*.

Einar hovered teasingly around Naia, giving her only the slightest brushes of contact until Aleksi finally urged him to coil one tentacle around her, the caress firm enough for his hooked teeth to prick her skin. Naia moved, determined to feel that sharp jolt of heat everywhere—over hills and valleys, on her breasts and the small of her back, across water-polished beaches.

Then he slipped inside her, *again*, and this time there was nothing to contain any of them. They stayed that way, the three of them locked together, for what could have been an hour or a century, in a seemingly never-ending circle of ecstasy and bliss.

But it *had* to end. Naia fell to the rumpled sheets, sweaty and shaking and too exhausted to move. Einar lay beside her, his chest heaving. Only Aleksi was still upright, barely moving, his glazed eyes attempting to focus.

"All right?" he panted, and Naia realized he literally could not fall over until he'd reassured himself that they were fine. Sated and unharmed.

"Come here." She lifted a trembling arm, and Aleksi collapsed with them.

They tangled together, too tired to move but never too weary to seek out one another. And that was more than enough.

It was perfect.

Chapter Twenty-Three

I've arranged the people you need. Do not be reckless.

Note found in Klement's room

By the time the servants had cleared away the dishes from a hearty meal of local favorites, Einar felt as if he was slowly losing his mind.

Dinner had been an intimate affair, served in Gwynira's private study to the handful of them who were left. With the palace nearly empty of Imperial nobles, she had told the servants to cook whatever pleased them, which had delighted Naia and, amusingly enough, Inga. She had developed an obsession with tealberries and had kept an entire tray of little tarts to go with her after-dinner cider, which was being served to them in sparkling crystal.

It was all very sedate and normal, and his skin itched from the inside with the overwhelming need to do . . . something. *Anything.* The Emperor was coming to Rahvekya, and Einar was taking drinks in a library as if it was any other day.

Naia reached out and grasped his hand. "Relax," she murmured. "I know what the Betrayer feels like. The Stalker, as well. The moment either of them comes near my island, I will know. *We* will know."

His agitation must have become noticeable—or Naia simply understood him. He turned his hand to twine her fingers with his, hoping the touch would ground him. "I only wish there was something I could *do*."

"That's the worst part of a situation like this, isn't it?" Aleksi mused. "People fear the paralyzing shock of a surprise attack. But not many fully appreciate how difficult it can be to sit and watch and *wait* as your inevitable destiny slowly rolls toward you."

"At least it gives us time to fully activate our defenses." Gwynira swirled the wine in her cup. "Arktikos has been hard at work."

Perhaps he should have insisted on overseeing the final check of their defenses. Having a task might have kept him focused—

No. Because the only thing worse than sitting here amidst cider and tarts would be standing out *there*, where he didn't know what was happening to Aleksi and Naia. Until Sorin was dead, it would be a struggle to let them out of his sight.

"The last of the nobles left this morning on the ship heading to South Harbor," Gwynira continued. "They would have been useless in a fight, and while I can't say I'm fond of any of them, I don't hate most of them enough to want to watch them die."

"And the locals?" Naia asked.

One of the serving girls who had become a particular favorite of Naia's—Tilly, Einar thought was her name—came to refill Einar's barely touched glass. Gwynira narrowed her eyes as she watched the girl. "I tried to convince the servants to board the ship as well, but most refused."

Because they would not leave their goddess . . . or their prince. Einar saw the truth of it in Tilly's totally unrepentant little smile and the almost defiant curtsy she offered to Gwynira before returning to the table that held the drinks.

Gwynira shook her head before continuing. "But Agata has been visiting the nearest villages with her wife to make sure they are prepared to evacuate, if necessary. It seems even they are unwilling to abandon their king."

She gave Einar a *look*, one dark eyebrow lifted in an elegant arch, and he scowled at her. "We are *not* having a coronation while we wait for the Emperor to attack."

"Of course not," she said, somehow making the words sound as if she didn't agree at all.

Einar was saved by Arktikos's arrival. Gwynira rose and crossed to meet him at the door, and Isa stepped into the silence, leaning closer to Aleksi. "I never thanked you, did I? For bringing me back."

Aleksi smiled at her. "If you must thank me, it should be for something I did while in full possession of my faculties. Not a happy accident."

"No." The denial was shocking in its vehemence. "That is precisely *why* I should thank you. Because you did not choose to do it because it was smart or expedient. It was a reflection of your true intentions toward Gwyn."

After a moment, Aleksi inclined his head. "Then you are welcome."

"I have something for you." She gestured, and a young man brought forward a bundle wrapped in gray velvet and tied with ribbons. "They were meant as a farewell gift, but . . . I figure you could use them before then."

Aleksi took the bundle. Beneath his nimble fingers, the ribbons and velvet yielded, revealing two sturdy scabbards. One was small, containing a dagger, while the other was sized for a sword.

He placed the smaller blade on the table, and began to draw the sword from its housing, only to pause when Isa reached out.

"Careful of the blades," she warned. "They are like mine—of both the Void and the Dream."

Aleksi arched one eyebrow and drew the blade several more inches. The folded steel seemed to vibrate, singing and whispering of Creation and Destruction in turn.

It was a precious gift, not only in its rarity but in its intent. In offering Aleksi these items, Isa was making herself—and, by extension, Gwynira—vulnerable. She was essentially announcing that she believed that he would only use these weapons as protection, and never, *ever* turn them against her or her lover.

"I should not accept them," Aleksi told her quietly.

"No, you *must*. I will brook no argument."

"Then it is *my* turn to thank *you*." Aleksi offered her a wide smile, made all the more brilliant because it was *genuine*. "It is a most generous gift."

She looked down at her lap, where she had wound her fingers together nervously. "I feel I have a bit more insight now into how people can be, and that's because of you and your friends. And I'm glad. Not for my own sake, you know, but for Gwyn's." When Isa looked up, her eyes were glistening with tears. "I've never seen her smile this much."

For the first time, Einar truly understood that Isa was like Naia— someone who had woken abruptly in a world she did not recognize. Her life had ended for the first time in a different era, one where Sorin ruled with absolute power and she was trapped in the nightmare of his court. Happiness must have been a fragile thing in those years, and whatever scraps Gwynira and Isa had managed to steal had been torn away from them when Sorin had found a way to banish Isa to the Endless Void.

Inga set aside her tray of tarts and leaned forward to touch Isa's arm. "We all know what it is like to be betrayed by Sorin. If you and Gwynira can help us stop him from doing even more harm? That makes you family."

Isa nodded, the tears spiking her lashes now. "I wondered . . . if there might be a place for us in the Sheltered Lands."

"Thinking of relocating?" Aleksi asked softly. "I might have heard something to that effect."

Inga's eyes brightened, and she clapped her hands together with such force Einar flinched at the sound. "Oh, come and stay with me. The Witchwood is beautiful in the summer, and my palace has plenty of room for guests. And . . ." Her smile widened. "I have a full smithy. I would love to see how you craft your blades . . . if you're willing to show me."

Gwynira returned, this time with Arktikos at her side. "The blockade has been deployed, and soldiers stationed around the villages closest to the palace. Smaller contingents have been sent to the more distant settlements, and evacuation plans are fully in place." She propped her hands on her hips. "We are as ready as we will ever—"

Naia gasped and bumped the low table as she jolted to her feet. Her water spilled across the red cloth, darkening it until it looked like a pool of blood spreading over the surface.

Aleksi frowned. "Naia—"

They are here. It wasn't Naia's voice, wasn't anyone's voice. It simply echoed through the hall, a feeling more than a sound, thunderingly loud in its actual silence.

Einar started to reach for her, and the wall exploded.

Instinct took over. Einar lunged, shielding Aleksi and Naia as debris shot through the room. In his demigod form, Einar was large enough to shelter them both—but he did not need to. Chunks of stone stopped a handspan from them and tumbled to the side, as if blocked by an invisible shield.

Of course rocks would not fall on Naia on her island.

Power pulsed through the air, and another crack sounded, as if some giant beast had grabbed a massive handful of the castle wall and flung it inward. The huge stones that had made up the palace tumbled to the side before they reached where the three of them huddled—but the rest of the room was not so fortunate.

It came to Einar in flashes, in the scant moments before Naia's firm hands pushed him upward. Arktikos had thrown himself over Gwynira and Isa, unwavering even as debris rained down on them. A disheveled

Inga popped up from beside them, her gaze fixed across the room. Moments later she was scrambling to where the small body of the serving girl had landed after the initial blast.

She ducked as a third explosion tore through what was left of the wall, exposing the room to the cool night air. A wind whipped through the room as Aleksi and Naia scrambled to their feet—

"YOU!"

The primal scream of rage cut through the night like shards of glass. Einar staggered under the force of it as shadows lurched around them and the room seemed to shudder. He turned in time to see Isa streaking toward the opening in the wall, shadows punching debris from her path. Her dangerous knife, the one that writhed with the power of the Dream and the Void, flashed in her fist as she raised her hand.

Magic crackled again. An unseen force swatted her to the side, sending her flying back toward Gwynira with enough force they both tumbled to the floor.

Laughter filled the night, and flames jumped without warning, illuminating the gap in the wall and the man who stood in the center, eyes alight with pure joy.

Sorin. The Emperor. The Betrayer.

The man who had killed Einar's parents and destroyed so very many lives.

He was flanked by strangers who pulsed with magic, but Einar could barely see them. Time seemed frozen as he stared at the man who had shaped his entire life. He'd seen Sorin from a distance once, during the battle where Sachielle had defeated him, but in the aftermath, Dianthe had dealt with the fallen Emperor, and Einar had respected her order—phrased as a gentle request—that he stay away.

But there he stood, no more than a dozen paces from Einar. It seemed impossible that this could be the man who had blithely caused the suffering of millions. Not because he was handsome—Einar had seen evil wrapped in beauty far too many times to be surprised by Sorin's elegant features and pretty smile. His well-defined muscles were not a shock, either. Unlike the many useless nobles in Gwynira's court, Sorin had always valued work above all else. The strength of his body was unsurprising in the man who had built many of the Sheltered Lands' most impressive landmarks with his own two hands.

It was his eyes—eyes that surveyed the room with all the casual pleasure of a man who had just arrived at a celebration to embrace his oldest friends. There was no hint of malice there, and no anger. No sign of the cruel conqueror of Einar's childhood nightmares, or the monstrous god who had terrorized an entire continent.

Ash's voice drifted through Einar's memory. *He still believes that what he was doing was in the best interests of the world.* Einar had heard Ash say that to Dianthe after they had imprisoned Sorin beneath the Siren's keep. The dragon's voice had been laced with a terrible sadness. *It is not rationalization. It is beyond delusion. He believes in his soul that he must protect the world from us. Still, even now.*

Sorin turned that eerily pleasant smile on Aleksi. "Hello, old friend." He bit off the words with a disdain that turned them into a lie.

Aleksi stared back at him, grave and unmoving. "Sorin."

Sorin's gaze swept across the room, but it was as if everyone else was insignificant—even Gwynira and Isa, who he had created from his own twisted dreams. He didn't stop until he found Inga, who was still kneeling next to Tilly, who had begun to stir groggily. "Oh, Inga," he said, his tone affection edged in condescension. "Always up to your elbows in someone else's blood."

Her eyes—edged in a furious pink glow—looked murderous. "Usually because you made them bleed."

Sorin shrugged one shoulder, as if he couldn't argue but did not particularly care. "You saved my life once, do you remember?"

"I remember," she ground out. "Everyone makes mistakes sometimes."

"It was a building accident. I believe I was helping to design your palace at the time." Sorin smiled at her with that terrible parody of affection. "I will return the favor. This is not your fight, my dear. Go back to your forest and play with your flowers. You've never had the stomach for battle."

Einar had seen the Witch at war before. He'd watched her tend to wounds so horrifying, even the most hardened of soldiers would have lost their supper on the bloody battlefield. He'd seen her pull that pain into herself without hesitation, taking their agony onto her own shoulders with a fearlessness that few could match.

Sorin might have called the High Court his family, but he truly did not understand a single one of them.

Inga proved it as her face locked down into a cold mask. "I saved your life once," she said quietly, and Einar saw Sorin's death in those glowing eyes. "Unlike you, I learn from my mistakes."

Sorin shrugged and turned away, dismissing her as if she no longer existed. Aleksi was clearly the only person left in his world, the only one who *mattered*. "*You* have been surprisingly irritating, you know. Especially for a man whose only real talents are drinking and fucking."

"You see what you want to see, Sorin. You always have." Finally, he smiled, though the expression was full of more inevitability than humor. "It's your fatal flaw."

Sorin had shrugged off Inga's words, but Aleksi's seemed to dig beneath his skin. That friendly mask broke, something harsh and evil showing through.

Then Naia shifted behind Einar. The movement caught Sorin's attention, his gaze swinging to her like a predator who had caught the scent of prey. A wildness bloomed in those eyes that set Einar's heart to racing.

"There you are," Sorin murmured, reaching over his shoulder. The giant hammer he pulled free had a handle of dark polished wood and a broad metal head that looked like steel folded with midnight. It pulsed with the Void—a thing that should not have been possible if Sorin was indeed still a mortal. And it *wasn't* possible—as Sorin lifted the weapon, Einar could see that simply gripping it was burning the flesh of his hand.

Sorin ignored it, a dreamy smile curling his lips, and *there* was the monster who had terrorized the world for centuries beyond telling. Einar could see Naia's death in the man's eyes, a death he would savor in the moment and swiftly forget, because each stride this man took was on the bones of those he'd slaughtered and then erased.

Every muscle in Einar's body tensed. Sorin took a single step forward.

The stillness in the room shattered into chaos as everyone moved at once. Flames raced along the walls. An invisible force swatted at the furniture, forcing Arktikos to roll out of the way as the couch skittered toward the far wall, which exploded into a shower of stone shards that had Gwynira throwing herself over a dazed Isa.

Inga rose from Tilly's side, pivoting gracefully as her hand flashed through the air. Einar had seen her pull candy and wine and butterflies from nothingness before, but this time a sleek sword appeared in her grasp. She tossed it in the same movement, already turning away as it completed its glittering arc, and Aleksi plucked it from the air and spun toward the blonde woman to Sorin's right with the grace of a dancer.

She raised both hands, and power sparked between them, a shimmering pressure that exploded upward when she flung her hands wide. The ceiling above Aleksi cracked ominously, forcing him to retreat as several ceiling tiles cracked and crashed downward.

The ceiling groaned, but in the next moment Naia was there, hands upraised. The buckling stone held. Face tight with rage, the woman lifted both of her hands. Angry shimmering power gathered there, the pressure of it like a storm rolling in on the horizon.

But as she flung her hands wide to release it, Naia shook her head. The woman's arms moved, as if controlled like a marionette's, and crossed over her chest. The power rebounded, throwing her back and through the hole in the wall.

Sorin paused, his hammer resting on his shoulder, and seeing death in his eyes had been better than *this*. He watched Naia as if he'd seen a wonderful prize he was desperate to claim. "Fascinating," he whispered. Then he jerked his other hand. "Kill the rest of them. Leave her."

Einar lunged for him, only for that unseen force to slam into him, sending him hurtling backward with dizzying speed. He crashed into the table covered in bottles, giving thanks for his tougher demigod skin as glass shattered all around him.

"My prince!" One of the kitchen boys scurried out of the shelter of a doorway, a carving knife clutched in one hand. Einar looked past him to see more servants piling through the doors, running *toward* danger—toward their goddess and their would-be king.

Recklessly, wonderfully brave. Stupidly brave. They would be nothing but hostages and collateral damage in a war between gods, and they must know it. But still they pressed in, the guards with their weapons unsheathed, the stable boys and maids clutching fireplace pokers and knives and any bludgeoning object they could put hands on.

The intruders saw them, too. A woman with flame-red hair laughed as fire sprouted from her fingertips. It dripped toward the debris-scattered floor and raced across it, heading for the battle-axe who ran the kitchens—Hilja, who had created Naia's fabulous ball gown and then gleefully taken on the challenge of making Einar clothing to fit his new body, as if fitting clothing to a giant with the shimmering silvered skin of the deep was an honor.

She stood at the front of the crowd, a meat cleaver large enough to take off a man's arm in one swipe clutched in one hand, and stared down the oncoming flames as if she would fight them with willpower and devotion to the goddess alone.

Einar rolled into their path, ready to test his demigod form against fire. "Hilja! You have to get the others to safety!"

"But the goddess—"

"Your goddess wants you alive!" he barked as the hungry flames surged toward him. He braced for the pain of heat. Instead his fingertips felt the burn of winter as the marble floor around him froze. Ice formed in front of him in fantastical fractals, beautiful and deadly. It sizzled where the fire touched it, and for a moment the two elements hung in stasis, battling for dominance.

Across the room, Gwynira extended her hand, hair disheveled and eyes furious. Then she closed her fingers into a fist, and fire shattered, turning to impossible twisting flames of ice. The cold raced back across the floor, frigid and deadly as it wound up the legs of the flame-haired woman and forced a scream from her suddenly blue lips.

Her second scream cut off abruptly as a chair slammed across the room to crash into Gwynira—and this time Einar caught the hint of movement in the shadows of the broken wall. A slim older man with pale skin, black hair going silver, and a cruel smile twitched his fingers again, sending Gwynira flying. Only Arktikos surging into her path and catching her with a grunt kept her from crashing through a window.

"Arktikos!" When the large man swung his head Einar's way, he jabbed a finger toward the man. Gwynira's guard needed no more prompting. One moment there was a burly man standing there, in the next a massive polar bear crashed out of him, shaking free of his confining human form with a snarl.

The floor rattled under the massive force of his charge. The older man frantically raised his hands, and Einar could *feel* the power rip through the room. It crashed into the bear—and nudged him back barely a handspan.

Terror replaced glee in the man's eyes and then he was gone, fleeing into the night with Arktikos charging after him. The clash of steel filled the sudden silence, and Einar saw Aleksi dancing through the debris, easily fending off the attack of a burly blond warrior. A casual flick of Aleksi's wrist bound the other man's blade and sent it flying, but he simply growled and reached into the air. Power crackled, and a new sword formed as if from smoke, coalescing in time to block Aleksi's next swing.

How many of these people did Sorin *have*?

Too many—and too cleverly chosen. A man who could summon weapons from air to battle a known swordsman. A woman who could summon fire to face down the Ice Queen. Someone who could rend the earth and tear stone from stone to counter the island that answered the call of its goddess. Had the old man been meant to keep Einar penned by knocking him back any time he tried to charge? Or had his focus on Gwynira and Isa been meant to accomplish exactly what it had in luring their potent guard away?

A shriek of anger filled the air, whipping Einar's attention back to where Naia faced off against the furious blonde. Her rage-filled eyes swung past Naia to Einar—and then to the servants gathered behind him. "Kill them!" she screamed, and for a moment Einar wasn't sure who she was talking to.

The man . . . oozed out of the shadows on the far side of the room, his movement so unnatural it made Einar's basest instincts scream for destruction. The new man's golden beauty was jarring against the darkness that seemed to cling to him, as if delicate vines of a starless night sky twined around him, rolling over his skin in sinuous movements.

He must have avoided the battle by clinging to the wall and moving silently, and now he stood near the bulk of the servants, a quiet, dreamy look in his startlingly blue eyes as he bent down and touched one fingertip to the cracked marble floor.

Darkness flowed out of him. No, something worse. Corruption, those vines twisting across the floor like a living thing that left destruction in their wake. The marble *melted* beneath them, crumbling into rot and ashes. The vines found the boots of one of the guards, and he screamed as they shot up his legs, tiny thorns sinking in like hooks.

His flesh sizzled. Melted. *Rotted.*

Panicked screams broke through the silence, followed by Hilja's bellowing command to *run*. They did, scattering toward the doors, barely outrunning the threat. Inga staggered to the guard's side, hands already trembling as she reached for him.

There was only one thing that would end the threat. Einar swept up the broken leg of a chair and started toward the source of that corruption, but a waifish redhead with big green eyes stepped between them. She lifted her hands with a feral smile, and some ancient instinct warned Einar to *move*. He dove to the side, wincing as his body slammed into the uneven rubble strewn across the floor.

Then pain seemed immaterial. A rift of darkness opened in the air where he had just been, as if the new woman had torn through the barrier between this world and the Endless Void. The jagged rip hung there for a moment, tendrils of the Void licking outward as if seeking something to touch.

If Einar had still been standing there, even his demigod form would not have saved him. She would have ripped his body in half.

The thought had barely formed when the redhead pivoted, and Einar's body moved before his mind caught up. He rolled out of the path of her next attack just as nothingness opened up through one of Gwynira's few remaining chairs. It shattered the wood and sent little bits of stuffing flying in every direction.

The pieces drifted down on Einar like snowflakes as he rolled again, not stopping until he could hunker down behind a large chunk of rubble.

A heartbeat later, a Void tear reduced it to jagged chunks and fine pebbles.

Einar snatched up the largest piece and whipped it at the woman with enough force, it would have taken off her head if it had struck. She dove out of the way, earning him enough of a respite to put his hands on another chunk of debris—a shattered piece of a table, with an end sharp enough to serve as a spear.

He came to his feet, cocking his arm back to throw. The redhead smiled and lifted her hands.

The enraged roar of a polar bear shook the room.

It happened so fast. The floor shivered as huge paws slammed down. The Void ripper spun, eyes going wide when she saw the massive polar bear charging toward her with teeth bared in a furious snarl.

They moved at the same time. Arktikos swiped at her with claws long enough to tear her stomach open. The force of the blow lifted her feet off the ground, flinging her back like a rag doll. She screamed, her hands flying up.

Reality ripped apart between them, darkness exploding in an uneven line across Arktikos's unprotected body.

The Void ripper's body crashed to the floor a dozen paces away, broken and unmoving. Arktikos stumbled, slamming to the broken marble in a confusing explosion of blood and sparkling light.

By the time Einar reached his side, Arktikos was a man again. His face drew tight with pain, and his shredded armor revealed torn skin and things that should not have been visible, because parts of him were simply *gone*. Blood poured from him so freely that Inga slipped in it as she appeared suddenly at his side.

"No," she said quite clearly, dropping to her knees in the puddle of blood and viscera. Her eyes glowed with feverish light as she took his face gently between her hands, thumbs smoothing over the grooves carved by pain. "No," she said again.

Arktikos let out one gasping moan, and Einar swayed, as if Inga had become the heart of a whirlpool, pulling everything toward her. Aches he had barely noticed vanished, bruises that hadn't yet formed sinking deep into his body before melting away. Inga seemed to glow from within, like diamonds and rubies refracting light that wasn't there.

Then the whirlpool released him. Moments later, frigid hands slammed into his body, shoving him across a floor that was suddenly slick with frost. Gwynira fell to her knees at Arktikos's side, naked grief in her eyes as she clutched at his hand. "Arktikos—"

Her voice trembled, and Einar turned away, sickened. Surely even Inga could not rebuild organs that had been obliterated by the Void itself. Arktikos would die, and there was nothing Einar could do to stop it. All he could do was stop Sorin from taking anyone else.

Locking down the pain, Einar found his makeshift spear and rose to his feet. The Void ripper sprawled, still unmoving, across a pile of rubble. He paused to make sure of her death with one swift and ruthless stroke to the heart, then turned to follow the path of corruption, seeking its source.

"He fled," said a voice at Einar's side. Hilja, with blood streaking her forehead, and dripping from the cleaver still clutched in one hand. "When—" A hitch. "When Arktikos came."

Grief filled her eyes. Einar could not let it claim him. He reached out a hand to squeeze her shoulder. "Get the rest of the servants outside," he told her, tightening his hand when she parted her lips to argue. "No excuses, Hilja. It will break Naia's heart if even one of you dies tonight."

She swallowed, but nodded and turned away to gather the others. For one moment, Einar let himself hope they had a chance to keep the mortals safe.

Then the ceiling gave a shuddering groan—and fractured in two.

The sound was terrifying, like nothing Einar had ever heard before. He couldn't even guess how many tons of stone stood above them. The palace rose for five stories with towers rising farther into the sky. That stone groaned now, the sound of the abused supports simply . . . giving way. No human trapped beneath this avalanche would survive. Einar wasn't even sure *his* bones could heal from being crushed so completely.

Only Naia was holding back the onslaught, her face strained as her hands flexed against nothingness. "Get them outside," she gritted. *"Now."*

There was no more time. Einar grabbed a kitchen boy by the back of the shirt and all but tossed him out into the night. A maid followed, and a pair of stable boys. They would heal from bruises, at least. They would *live*—

Einar turned back to find that furious little blonde who had started all of this with her explosive powers striding toward Naia with a glint in her eyes. Her hands swung up, power gathering there. She laughed as she let it free, crashing into the already groaning ceiling and causing a hundred new cracks to spiderweb out from the main fracture. Naia gasped, the strain of holding back the cascade of stone seeming to bend her nearly in half.

The woman was still laughing when shining steel flashed, so swift and graceful even she seemed surprised when her head separated from her body. Both parts hit the floor, revealing Aleksi with a sword dripping blood. A half dozen paces behind him, the burly swordsman lay sprawled in a rough circle of weapons that had clearly not been enough to save him from the Lover's skill.

Too late. The final burst of power had shattered the precarious balance, and the castle started to collapse. Chunks of stone broke free.

At least the humans were outside. They'd saved the people—and the world dipped suddenly, as if it wasn't the first time Einar had stood on this ground and thought those words.

As death hurtled toward them, Naia shouted in an ancient language long dead, liquid and lyrical and shuddering through Einar, because in that moment, that cry sounded more real than the language he'd grown up speaking. *"No!"*

Power tore out from her in a wave so intense, Einar staggered under it. Light suffused the darkness, a light that shone from her like a beacon as she held back Gwynira's entire palace with the force of her will alone. It was as if a giant dome covered them—all of them. Einar and Aleksi. Arktikos and Inga. Isa and Gwynira. Even the servants hovering just beyond the shattered wall, stubbornly refusing to leave.

Huge chunks of stone tumbled off it, bouncing down toward the rocky cliffs and the empty shores below—and more than stone. Massive wooden timbers, huge dining room tables. Beds and cabinets. Metal bathtubs and glittering mirrors. Generation after generation of trinkets and tokens and art and all the things that rendered a palace graceful and well-appointed tumbled off that invisible barrier, shunted harmlessly away from those they might harm.

At the heart of the chaos, the goddess glowed like a radiant sun, like the moons . . . like midnight itself. Einar could only stare at her, at the way her skin seemed lit from within by both light and shadows in a way he had never seen before. The only thing that came close was Sachielle or Zanya, but they were so distinct—the bright light of Creation and the midnight whispers of Destruction.

The goddess was neither. And both.

She was the heart of this island, its strong protector, mother of creation and life itself—but when you tread upon the place she called hers, you should never forget that every step you take is by her mercy.

Awe gave way to dizziness, a deep feeling of dread climbing up through Einar that was foreign and still deeply familiar. It crashed in on him from all directions, driving his heart into his throat.

Then he caught movement at the edge of his vision, and dread crystalized into rage. Only one person wasn't frozen in awe in the face of Naia's power. Sorin's eyes glittered with hunger—and Einar knew it was not hunger for *her*, but for her power. He wanted it for his own, whether subverted, enslaved—or stolen.

Sorin strolled through the debris and destruction, inexorable as a cresting wave, danger bearing down on Naia's unprotected back—

Einar flung himself between them, ready to shelter her with his body.

And the panic inside him exploded.

Time stopped. Eternity opened up before him, and he tumbled in, spiraling down into the depths as images flashed before him.

Naia—but not Naia—sun shining on her red hair as she smiled at him . . .

Flower petals dancing on a breeze to twirl teasingly around him . . .

Teal glass sparkling in the sun as he cast handfuls of it at her feet . . .

Dancing under stars so bright they turned into ribbons of light as they spun and spun and spun . . .

Clouds gathering on the distant horizon.

The ground shaking.

A wave of water rushing toward them, tall enough to swallow the world.

No. No.

Naia—but not Naia—raising her arms to the sky as she summoned her own wall from the sea, holding back destruction, holding it back, holding it back . . .

A glow so intense he couldn't look at her anymore. The bright light sparking tears in his eyes. She was an inferno of power, her strength endless, unflagging . . .

But not. No one can last forever. Stop. Please stop. You can't die. You can't leave me!

He screamed, a sound so raw it shattered the frozen moment. It was the sound of thunder, the sound of rage and grief, a sound so primal it shook the crumbling walls of the palace.

A prickle of warning on his spine was enough. He spun at the last moment and threw up a hand, catching the head of a huge war hammer with his palm. The Void-steel burned his fingers, and he knew with terrifying certainty that if this weapon had cracked his skull, it would have killed him.

Hatred burned in his heart, but he didn't know who he was, or where he was. Just that he hated the man holding this deadly hammer with a destructive force that felt inevitable. This man, who had tried to take her away from him again—

Jagged memories tried to fight their way in, overlapping at odd angles—screaming his grief to the sky, the rain pelting his skin in drops so vicious they stung—

No, that was not a memory. That was happening. The palace was split open above them, and the sudden rain pummeled down on the chaos of their battle. Thunder cracked so loudly that someone screamed, and the wind whipped around them as Einar remembered who he was. Where he was.

Who he faced.

Sorin smiled, utterly unbothered by the rain slicking his golden-brown hair to his head. "So, you're the little lost prince Klement told me about. I admit, from his description I expected someone . . . human." His gaze raked over Einar's demigod form with derision. "Why am I plagued so endlessly by brutish monsters who are all muscle and no brain?"

Given their history, Einar suspected he was being compared to the Dragon. Only Sorin would think that linking a man to Ash was an insult.

"Ah, well," Sorin continued, clearly disappointed the jab hadn't drawn blood. His next was more cleverly targeted. "I suppose you wish to avenge your family, or something trite like that?"

Einar's vision hazed. "Do not speak of them."

"Honestly, I couldn't." Sorin lifted one shoulder in a dismissive little shrug. "I didn't even know who they were before Klement told me your story. They were meaningless to me. Fleeting roadblocks along the path to progress."

Thunder cracked above their heads. It echoed inside Einar, a warning rage in the face of Sorin's chilling obliviousness. How many boys like him had this man left in his wake? Lives shattered, families killed, worlds upended, cultures destroyed? How many had he crushed beneath his boots without even noticing, without caring?

Einar's entire life had been shaped by an obsession with revenge—and its target barely knew he existed.

Lightning forked across the sky, illuminating Sorin's little smile. He was pleased to have finally struck a blow.

Let the former emperor enjoy his petty victory. The storm was in Einar's blood now.

The fine hair on Sorin's arms began to stand on end. His brow furrowed, that smile disappearing as he spared the deadly storm a wary glance. When his gaze swung back to Einar, the dismissiveness was gone—as if, for the first time, he was considering Einar as a potential adversary instead of a delightful diversion or, at worst, a tedious inconvenience.

Einar leaned closer, not releasing his grip on the Void hammer even as the metal seared his fingers. "You shouldn't have tried to hurt her," he rumbled, as the storm inside him built and built and built . . .

Sorin's eyes widened, his fingers flexing on the hammer's handle—but it was too late. Lightning forked down from the sky to crash into the hammer they both held, the light of it blinding.

Someone screamed in pain—but not Einar. The lightning could not hurt him. It was a sweet fire in his blood, a joyous caress from a friend he had not seen in too many centuries. He welcomed it, embraced it, *reveled* in it as Sorin screamed and screamed—

The Void-steel beneath Einar's fingers shattered, flinging him backward. Little shards sliced at his face and his arms, deadly stinging projectiles that broke even his tougher demigod skin. He barely noticed the pain with the lightning still in his blood, demanding that he surge to his feet, that he *finish* the enemy.

Naia was there before he could, her fingers trembling as she cupped his face. Her luminous eyes held frantic worry and something else—a question he was not ready to answer. Surely she understood what it meant that the lightning answered his call—but she must be wondering if *he* knew.

He knew too much. More than he'd ever wanted to.

Her lips parted, but before she could ask the question, horror spread across her features. She spun, and Einar lurched upright in time to see Sorin staggering to his feet.

Burns crawled up his arms and covered his face, but that wasn't what had Einar staring in equal horror. A dark halo spread out around Sorin in a blaze of unfathomable power—like Zanya, and yet not. When Zanya embraced the power of the Endless Void, she sparkled like a midnight rainbow, seductive and deadly. She was destruction in its purest form, the vengeance that cleared a path for new creation to thrive.

The power that flowed from Sorin felt like inky, smothering death. It hungered, spiraling out in shadows that reminded Einar of those corrupting vines, and curling around Sorin as he flung his head back in ecstatic joy. "Oh, I was wrong," he whispered, the soft words falling like boulders into the horrified silence. "I didn't realize destruction would feel so *good*."

Princess Sachielle had torn away Sorin's connection to the Dream, rendering him mortal. But in their world, where belief shaped power, desperate need and strong conviction could turn a man into a god. It had happened to Einar himself, when his hatred for Sorin had coalesced into the dream of being a protector for his people. The Everlasting Dream had granted that wish, and he had become the Kraken.

The Dream would never answer Sorin's call again. But in his need to destroy those who had brought him low, he must have found an echo in the vast power of destruction that made up the Endless Void. He had manifested again, this time as a creature of pure annihilation.

Zanya would be *furious*.

But Zanya was not here. Isa was the only other person in the room with a connection to the Void, and she moved without hesitation. Her knife flashed through the air, steel singing of the Dream and the Void in equal measure. But two paces from Sorin's chest, shadows slapped it from the air.

Sorin smiled, and those shadows began to writhe toward them.

Overhead, thunder roared—and Einar felt it this time. The storm wasn't simply in his blood. He *was* the storm. Thunder crackled with his rage, and lightning pulsed like his heartbeat. For the first time in thousands of years, he called upon it consciously, calling for it to end this threat once and for all.

Lightning forked down from the sky, arcing toward Sorin. Shadows whipped around in a fury, wrapping him in darkness that battled the sudden brightness. Everyone else in the room threw up their arms, shielding their faces from the blinding light.

Not Einar. Lightning could not hurt the storm god. So he was the only one who saw the shadows envelop Sorin and carry him away in the moment before lightning crashed into the shattered marble floor.

No one moved. For long, fraught moments, the only sound was the grinding of distant stones and the rain, drops of water bouncing off the rubble and splashing softly into pools of blood.

A low groan broke the silence. Across the room, Arktikos sat up. His armor fell in tatters around him, revealing the smooth unblemished skin of his abdomen and the strong, *whole* expanse of his chest. He lifted a hand as if to shove his hair back from his face, only to pause and stare at the blood slicking his fingers.

Confused, his gaze took in what was left of the room, and the stunned people scattered across it. "What did I miss?"

It was one impossibility too many. Einar watched in numb shock as Inga staggered to her feet, face even paler than usual and every expanse of visible skin so bruised and bloody it looked as if the palace *had* fallen on her. She frowned, as if vaguely perplexed, and tried to take a step. Her eyes lost focus, and Arktikos lunged to catch her before she crashed to the floor.

The rain softened. A wind rose, sweeping the clouds away to reveal both moons. They shone down on the broken palace, on the faces of stunned servants, on a stricken Aleksi and a silent, ashen-faced Naia.

Einar—the storm god?—answered Arktikos with a laugh rusty with the sharp edges of a thousand newly awoken memories. "Everything."

Chapter Twenty-Four

It finally happened, as I feared it would. Summer has not come this year. A spring so late it barely deserves the name has given way to crisp autumn. If Theron had not brought heartier crops from his homeland, we might not have enough to eat this winter. The children only remember the snow and ice, but my bones ache with the cold. I sometimes feel I have outlived my time.

The lost journal of High Priestess Tona

Gwynira's palace was in ruins.

With nowhere else to go, they gathered in a warehouse on the stone docks near the site of the former palace. Amongst the wooden crates and packed sacks of tundra cotton, they licked their wounds.

Numbered along with the countless bruises were only mild injuries—scrapes and shallow lacerations. Einar had sustained a few deeper cuts when the Void hammer exploded, and they were proving dreadfully slow to heal. Isa's shoulder had been dislocated, and Gwynira had bound it after setting it back in place.

Arktikos bore not a single scratch. Inga had taken them all.

She sat on a tightly tied bale of cotton, a rough-spun blanket around her shoulders. Her hair was mussed, and thin, silvered scars tracked over her skin, remnants of her desperate—and ultimately successful—bid to save Arktikos's life. She looked worse than Aleksi could remember without casting his memory back to that first brutal fight, when Sorin and Ash had beaten one another so badly that their bodies slamming into the earth had created the Lover's Lakes.

Everyone thought, since Aleksi's villa sat on their shores, that the lakes were so named in his honor. But he had chosen the name in honor of *Inga*. Without the love she showed in risking herself to save Ash, the dreadful hollows left in the earth would have remained filled only with blood.

She held a half-eaten meat pie, her third in roughly as many minutes. Aleksi knew from experience that she would go through half a dozen more before slowing down. Inga always needed to eat like this after such a feat. It was the only way her body could heal itself.

There, they sat or stood, still dazed from the attack. Someone had to break the bewildered silence, so Aleksi stepped to the middle of the room. "So. Sorin is of the Void now."

Isa shook her head in helpless confusion. "But *how*?"

"It makes sense." Naia leaned heavily against the back wall. One of her sleeves had nearly been ripped away from the rest of her dress. Aleksi stared at the frayed edges of the tear.

It was easier than looking at the deep, dark shadows that surrounded her eyes.

"He was once the Builder," Aleksi agreed, still staring at Naia's torn sleeve. "Before the Dream deserted him, he was powerful enough to sit on the High Court. He has always had a great affinity for magic."

"And now he's wreaked enough destruction to manifest again," Naia said quietly.

Gwynira was not so subdued. She held both hands out to her sides, her soiled skirt swishing around her legs as she paced. "To the Void.

He's a hundred times more dangerous to a Dreamer now." She stopped suddenly. "We have to call the High Court. We need Zanya."

"Maybe so," Aleksi allowed. It was possible that Zanya could separate Sorin from the Void with a single touch. Possible . . . but by no means certain. "But you saw her. She's already *exhausted* by events on the mainland. She's in no fit state for a battle like this."

"She'll have to be," Gwynira countered.

"If we call her here, and she—" Naia could not finish the sentence. "It would be because of *us*. Could you live with that?"

"It would be because of Sorin," Gwynira argued. "*Not* us."

Einar had not said a word since leaving the palace ruins. He stood by a window, one paned with glass instead of ice. The glass had cracked, and tiny fissures spiderwebbed their way across the panes.

"You've been quiet, Einar." Aleksi took a step toward him. "What do you think?"

It took him several moments to speak. When he finally did, his words were careful. Measured. "I think . . . that if Zanya comes here, Princess Sachielle will come with her."

"Good!" Gwynira released a relieved breath. "Yes. Outside of Zanya, there is no one who could harm Sorin more than Creation. The *Dream*."

And no one who could be harmed more *by* him. "That is true," Aleksi said slowly. "But he *hates* her, Gwynira. More than anything in this world. More than he wants to live."

"I . . ." She faltered. She, of all people, knew how single-minded and determined her cursed creator could be.

She could not counter the truth.

Another hush fell over the group. This time, it was Naia who broke it, with a quiet, implacable declaration. "We will not call the High Court. We will fight Sorin ourselves."

Gwynira laughed helplessly. "I mean no disrespect to you, goddess." Her voice was trembling as badly as her hands. "But we *cannot* face him without help."

"We must."

Einar closed his eyes.

"Is that *your* decision to make?" Isa honestly sounded like she was asking. "For all of us?"

"Yes, it is," Naia replied. "Because I know what happens when forces this massive clash. The High Court fought Sorin thousands of years ago, and I had to live with the consequences. Right up until the moment those consequences killed me."

Aleksi resisted a flinch.

"This is our fight." Naia's voice echoed with the crashing of waves and the wind sighing through sheltered coves. "We will fight it. And if the worst should happen—if we should fail—then the world will have the rest of the High Court to stand between it and the Betrayer."

Einar made a low sound of pure agony, as if he'd been run through with a blade. He turned and slammed through the door, leaving it rebounding in the jamb. The pain that lingered in his wake was different, deeper than fear. The darkest blue that Aleksi had ever seen, shot through with blinding flashes of white.

Had he remembered? Or did Naia's words simply scrape at wounds he had carried for thousands of years but did not yet understand?

Naia's jaw clenched, but she did not cry. Not even when Aleksi pulled her into his arms.

"She's right," Inga rasped, her voice husky with pain and fatigue. "For all we know, Sorin wants us to lure the others here because he has some way of eliminating us at once. We cannot risk that."

Gwynira rubbed her hands over her face. "Fine. We stand alone."

"Not alone," Arktikos rumbled. "We stand *together*."

Dianthe would be furious. Ash might be, as well, though perhaps his fear for Sachi's and Zanya's safety would eclipse his anger. Ulric and Nyx would be confused, maybe a little hurt. Only Elevia would understand the brutal pragmatism that had driven the decision.

Aleksi only hoped that, after the dust settled, he was still around to bear the brunt of his friends' admonitions.

Chapter Twenty-Five

Theron brought the young reindeer to visit me today. I sat in the winter sun and stroked their soft fur, and my heart ached as it had not in so many years. How the goddess would have laughed to see her fearsome storm god with a dozen baby reindeer on wobbly legs following him like the sea hawks chasing after their mother. I laughed for her, and for the first time since we lost her, I thought he almost smiled.

The lost journal of High Priestess Tona

Einar stood in the heart of the goddess's temple, the past and the present twining together in a whirlpool that threatened to pull him under forever. The newly restored tiles beneath his boots were a riot of familiar color—deep sapphires and sky blues and aqua and teal, swirling across the floor around a bronze spiral that circled inward to end directly beneath his boots.

He stared at it until his eyes burned, afraid to close them. Every time he did, his chaotic mind painted newly remembered horrors across the backs of his eyelids, bringing with them pain so sharp it felt like a wound freshly taken.

This was where she'd stood on her last day. He could see it as if it had just happened, as if the trauma of it had etched so deep in his bones that even after they'd been ground to dust and returned to the sea, somehow that pain had been waiting for him. Over two thousand years in this new body, and he could feel the storm god's broken heart beating sluggishly in his chest.

He remembered every moment of it, now. The way Theron had begged her to stop. How close he had come to crossing an unforgivable line and *forcing* her to stop. The two of them could have let the waters wash over them, and survived. Even if the island itself had been swept away, they would have endured. Together.

Einar could remember being the man for whom that was all that had mattered. The storm god had not cared about the people of this island, not truly. Protecting them made Naia happy, so he had helped her to protect them—until the moment doing so endangered *her*.

And people said the Kraken had no heart. If they only knew.

For over two millennia, Einar had encased himself in ice, letting those songs become the truth he believed about himself. But if he'd truly had no heart, he would not have needed the protection of frigid walls. The storm god certainly had not. There had been no conflict in Theron that day, when he'd been ready to let every soul on this island drown if it meant Naia would live. She was the only person who had ever mattered to him.

No, it was even worse. Naia had been the only other person in Theron's world. The mortals of Rahvekya had existed in the abstract, real to him only as much as their lives impacted hers. He had rarely considered their dreams, their hopes, their loves. Until he had been left behind, the vow to protect them binding him to a life he no longer wanted, he had not considered them at all.

Einar remembered feeling that way. And it shamed him.

Familiar footsteps sounded behind him, but with that guilt writhing in his gut, he could not bring himself to turn and face them. He stared down at the spiral tiles on the floor until his eyes burned, and when he opened his mouth to speak, the ancient language came too easily to his lips. He had to struggle to use words that would not exclude Aleksi. "Do you still want to know what happened to—" *Him* sounded too distant, but *me* felt wrong, too. He'd lived too many years as Einar to be the man Naia remembered. "To Theron?"

"Yes," she admitted gently. "But not if it hurts too much."

The pain was a knife sunk so deep, pulling it out might mean bleeding to death. But hadn't she been bleeding this whole time, cut to ribbons by the pain of *not knowing*? Maybe speaking the words would heal them both. "I remember everything," he said softly.

Naia moved in front of him, and shame couldn't stop him from looking up. It was Theron's piercing grief that made him hungry for any glimpse of her, and it did not matter that this Naia shared no features with the one in his distant memories. Dark hair or red, face bold and striking or sweetly heart-shaped, the way she *looked* at him was the same. He finally understood how she had looked upon him in this new body and simply *known*.

"I mean it," she said firmly, her expression achingly familiar—command and compassion wrapped in an endless love. "There is nothing I need to know so badly that I would be willing to wound you for it."

Einar reached out to touch her hair, and it did not matter that it was straight and silky instead of a cascade of curls. Somehow, it felt the same. "Not all of it hurts. I remember when you came to steal those ships from me."

She turned her face to his hand and smiled shakily against his palm. "They tell such a different tale now."

He'd heard the villagers repeat the story—that when the goddess had defied him and rescued her ships from the storm he'd stirred up, he had followed her back to the island half in love with her. Naia had laughed at the idea. Now Einar knew it was truer than she'd ever realized. From the first moment she had challenged him, he had been enchanted. "I was furious with you for tricking me. I followed you home, thinking to steal something from you. Or that was what I told myself." He tugged at the loose lock of her hair. "I lost my heart before I even knew I had one."

Naia cupped his cheeks, her gaze roving over his face. Searching. "Einar . . ."

"I remember us," he said softly.

She threw her arms around his neck and buried her face in the hollow of his throat, and Theron's memories washed over him in a blissful wave, century upon century of tangled, glorious moments. Learning to know each other, coming to love each other. Fighting and making up, walks under the starlight and laughter at noon, and the incomparable bliss of losing himself in her touch.

A thousand *thousand* days of joy, blurring into one another, but other memories stayed crystal sharp, their edges cutting into him until he bled. This was the part that would hurt them both, but he had to do it. "And I remember the moment you fell."

Aleksi stepped up behind him, settling steadying hands on Einar's shoulders. He wondered if the Lover could feel it—if he could *see* Theron's pain echoing back across millennia. The answer came as Aleksi swept out one of his thumbs, a soft caress along the back of Einar's neck that somehow grounded him. The Lover's truest gift—a heart so big that it could carry you when your own heart faltered.

It gave Einar the courage to continue. "I almost followed you," he said, wishing there was a way to soften the truth for her, and knowing she would not want a gentle lie. "I almost took the island with me. Not even on purpose . . . but you were dead in my arms, and the storm . . ."

He'd held her lifeless body in the spot where they now stood, as thunder rattled the island and lightning shredded the sky. The seas she had calmed with her dying breath had begun to churn again, and the winds he summoned had been strong enough to tear the temple down around them.

Einar wrapped his arms around her and drew in her scent—those *impossible* flowers that had haunted him for the past week. Now he knew they were the tropical blooms that had once grown where they stood. "I'm the one who destroyed your temple," he admitted quietly. "In my rage, my grief . . . I could not stop myself. I wanted the final storm to consume me."

Aleksi made a soft noise of protest and rested his forehead against Einar's temple. Naia's breath hitched against his throat, and he felt the hot sting of her tears.

The memory of being alone was just that—a memory. They were here. Now. Together.

"It was Tona who stopped me," he continued. He could still remember the High Priestess battling her way through winds cruel enough to tear her robes and rain brutal enough to bruise skin. "She was grieving your loss, too. But she braved the storm and begged me to stop. And she was yours. I could not hurt her. So I let the storm die."

"She always was fearless." Naia lifted her head, tears still coursing down her wet cheeks. "And so fond of you."

Perhaps she had been. Theron hadn't been able to see it, though. Naia had taken all the soft emotions with her into death. "I remembered the promise I made you."

"That you would not let them make a shrine of me." Naia's voice was thick with emotion.

She'd extracted it from him in those last tumultuous days, when he'd still been in such deep denial that he'd been willing to swear any oath, as if he could lure her into letting him save her life. "They wanted to bury you here, in the temple ruins. But I knew you wouldn't have wanted it. So I took you down into the depths, where—"

His voice broke. He could see it so clearly—her face, oddly peaceful in death, hair floating in the soft current as he laid her on a bed of the sea glass she had loved so much.

"I scoured the floor of the ocean around the island for a full week," he managed to choke out. "And I built your tomb from your sea glass."

In a way, he had made the legend of the island come true. Every piece of that treasured glass that had washed ashore in the past three thousand years truly had been goddess-touched.

"Thank you." The words were barely intelligible through Naia's tears.

He kissed her—the top of her head, and her cheeks, the salt of her tears bittersweet. "I wanted to stay there with you," he whispered against her temple. When she gasped and tightened her fingers on his jacket, he went on. "But I had made you another promise."

"Yes, you did." Certainty wreathed Aleksi's words. He could not possibly have known . . . yet he did. "You swore that you would protect her people."

Aleksi would have understood the importance of it instinctively. No one would have had to extract the promise from him. But in those first terrible days, Theron had seen the people only as an obligation—the bitter duty holding him to life, when he longed for the escape of death. They hadn't even needed him . . . at first.

"The world changed after we lost you," Einar said, leaning back into the Lover's strength. "The currents in the ocean changed. They cooled. Winter started earlier, and lasted longer. Tona was only seventy the first time summer never truly came. Some of the plants and animals adapted, but too many . . ."

"They didn't make it." All the pain and turmoil that Naia had missed was crashing in on her now.

He stroked his fingers over her hair, comforting himself as much as her. "I returned to my home islands for the first time in centuries. We loaded ships with things that thrived in the cold. The reindeer, and the tundra cotton . . ." The words broke on a hoarse laugh as tears stung his eyes for the first time. "It had always grown white in my homeland, but here . . ."

The islanders had come to him after that first harvest, eyes wide, hands overflowing with fine fibers of the most vibrant teal, and he had cried as he curled scarred, tired fingers around the impossible beauty of it.

Aleksi folded his arms around them both and pulled them close. "The goddess's favorite color."

"She was still here," Einar agreed. "Some part of the goddess lived on in the blood and bones of this island." He brushed a thumb over Naia's cheek, swiping away her renewed tears. "I could still feel you. So I stayed."

"For how long?"

"Long enough." And as much as the memories held grief, there were other emotions there. Pride, and satisfaction. Blunted, perhaps, by how hard it had been for Theron to open his bruised heart. But the work he had done in those centuries had mattered.

"I taught them how to build for the cold, and how to fish icy waters. They were your people, and they were *so smart*. They learned to weave the tundra cotton and became traders. They thrived. And when the last great-grandfather who could remember a world without winter was given to the sea, I thought they no longer needed me."

The hope that had bloomed in Naia's eyes dimmed. "Oh, *casara*. You didn't."

"It wasn't sad," he protested, stroking her cheek again. "I was tired, and I wanted to rest. I walked into the sea and let the deep take me home. It should have been peaceful, except . . ." The guilt slicing through him didn't belong to Theron. Theron had never known what followed. "I didn't know the Empire would invade."

She drew in a sharp breath, then released it on a ragged sob. Einar pulled her into him again, letting her tears scald his throat as he cradled the back of her head. For her it was only grief, but for him . . .

Theron had lived his life and met his end. A peaceful end, closing his eyes with the conviction that he would find Naia again, even if only in the currents of an endless ocean they had both become part of. It was Einar who had been born into the world shaped by his absence. Einar, who had lost *everything* because Theron had given in to the temptation to lie down and let the tides sweep him under.

But if he had not done so, would Einar even exist? The man who stood in the Lover's protective embrace, cradling Naia against his chest, had been shaped by so many things that Theron had never known. A human childhood shadowed by loss. Hunger and fear and hard work as a teenager. Mortality, breathing down his neck, making every moment feel precious in a way that you could never understand if you had always had forever.

And he'd had Petya. A woman who had raised him to understand duty and honor. Who'd taught him lessons Theron had never learned— that every life was precious, because every person held within them an entire world. And that those who wished to rule must be willing to shoulder the responsibilities of having those fragile lives under their care.

If Naia had lived, Theron might have learned those lessons in time. But he had been too wounded by her loss to ever open his heart again. Theron might have destroyed the Imperial invaders . . . or he might have only drawn Sorin's direct intervention. More likely than not, Rahvekya would have been obliterated in the clash of power, its people erased from memory as Sorin had erased so many.

But even if Theron had persevered, he never would have become the kind of man who could stand as a worthy guardian of this island.

"Let it go?" Naia whispered, a suggestion but also a plea. And maybe she knew exactly how he felt, because her next words washed over him like a soothing breeze. "And so will I. Because I think, perhaps, that what *needed* to happen . . . *did*."

"I think maybe it did," he murmured, and they needed no more words. The breeze that rose this time was real, not the storm god's power stirring the wind, but the island offering silent comfort. The scent of the flowers weighing down Einar's impossibly blooming tree might waken Theron's memory of a simpler time, but Einar did not envy it—or him.

He no longer wished he could be worthy of the man whose name he had taken, because the reality of the storm god was so much more complicated than the myth. Theron had loved Naia the best he could, but he had not been able to love her the way she deserved. He hadn't been capable of understanding why the people of this island mattered. Perhaps, if he had, instead of fighting her in those last terrible days, he would have put his power into finding a way to protect them—and perhaps by doing so, saved Naia as well.

When Sorin arrived, Einar would not repeat the storm god's mistakes. Einar didn't need a coronation to know in his bones that these were his people. He would be betraying everything Naia was if he turned his back on them in order to protect her. And as for the Lover . . .

If things had happened differently, would they ever have found him? Would he have made his way across the sea on a diplomatic mission and recognized something in them? Or would Theron's stunted heart have killed any possibility before it had a chance to take root? Einar could still remember the terrifying intimacy of letting the Lover look inside him and see the truth of him—his fear that Aleksi would find a frozen heart, or worse, no heart at all.

If Aleksi had looked into the storm god's heart, Einar suspected he would have found little there to love. That would have been a tragedy.

"Never again," Aleksi growled suddenly.

Naia lifted her head to cast a confused look at him. "What?"

But all of Aleksi's attention was on Einar's face. "Never," he repeated. "You'll not lose Naia again, not like that. I won't let it happen."

The words sounded larger than mere sounds, as if he had spoken a vow of the heart backed by the power of the Dream. Einar lifted his hand to Aleksi's face, stroking one roughened thumb over the smoothness of the Lover's cheek. When his eyes blazed so bright, it was impossible to doubt him. "We will not lose anything," Einar said softly. "Because together, we are strong enough to beat him."

Aleksi covered Einar's hand with his, and this time, his words were definitely a vow. They shook the temple beneath them and rang through the cold night air. "Sorin will not have you. Either of you."

It was a reminder that Einar and Naia were not the only ones here whose life had been shaped by Sorin's choices. How terrible it must have been for those who once called him *friend*. To watch a man you knew spiral down into darkness so destructive, it had nearly fractured their very world.

Einar wanted to destroy the Emperor for so many reasons. For Rahvekya, for his parents, for every other conquered people who had been scrubbed from history by Sorin's ravenous hunger to own *everything*.

In this moment, Einar wanted to destroy him so Aleksi would never again have to fear losing someone he loved to the monster Sorin had become. "He will not," Einar agreed quietly. "He will not have anyone we love."

Aleksi turned his face into Einar's hand, and the kiss the Lover pressed to his palm felt like the sealing of a vow. Einar stroked Aleksi's lips, then lifted his other hand to do the same to Naia.

He could have stayed in this moment forever, but he had one more task to complete before he was ready to face Sorin. One that would likely not go as smoothly as this had.

Somehow, Einar had to convince the crew of the Kraken to leave this island before they got caught in the middle of a war between gods.

Chapter Twenty-Six

Theron is on the far side of the island, helping them build stronger homes that can weather the harsh winters. For so many years, we have worked together to protect the people of Rahvekya, but I will leave him soon. My successor does not remember the goddess, and she has never seen Theron laugh. She has barely seen him smile. The younger generations revere him, but they are not his family. Soon he will be alone, bound to this island by his final promise to our goddess. I am the one dying, but I grieve for him.

The lost journal of High Priestess Tona

Aleksi knew what was coming.

He also knew that nothing would divert Naia, so he waited patiently until Einar's footfalls on the stone path faded into the darkness.

Once they had, she stepped close, her head craned back so she could hold Aleksi's gaze. "You told Einar that he will not lose me again. And you never make a promise you cannot keep." It sounded like an accusation, not an observation.

"It was a reassurance, that is all. One he needed." Could she sense the desperate thrumming of his heart? Taste his lilting determination?

Perhaps she could, because she shook her head in slow reproach. "You cannot sing this song to me, Aleksi, and think I will not hear it. I wrote it, remember?"

Of course she would see. "Naia—"

"*How?*" she demanded, turning to pace across the vividly colored tiles. "Knowing the dangers we now face, how can you reconcile this vow with the one you already gave us? When you said we would have you for as long as we . . ." She trailed off.

Aleksi wanted to deny it, this thing she had not yet said, but he could not.

"You lied with the truth." She turned to face him once more, her dry eyes burning with that indescribable swirl of colors. "You can say, with a clear conscience, that we will have you for as long as we need you because you don't believe that we do."

"I believe what I see when I look at the two of you, love." He closed the distance between them, because he needed to touch her, as if that and only that could convince her of his sincerity. "The way you and Theron left things, that's a wound across time, one that needs to heal. For that, you need your second chance. If I can make that happen—"

"That is *not* your responsibility."

"Is it not?" He grasped both of her hands in his. "I love you, and I love Einar. Who would I be if I would not do anything and everything within my power to keep you both safe and whole?"

"I'm not a hypocrite, Aleksi. I *understand* sacrificing oneself for love. I did it once for my people, and I will do it again for you and Einar." She cut off his soft noise of protest. "*If* I must. But I've learned my lesson, and I need you to learn it, too, right now. That is what it would have to be—necessary. No other possibilities. No other way."

"I don't *want* to die, love."

"Neither did I." Her words were clear and steady. "But I did not fear or fight it as much as I should have."

This was not an argument he could win, because they were both right. That was the most heartbreaking thing about it. "Fine," he told her finally, dropping her hands and taking a step back. "We should find the others—"

He stopped short as Naia gripped his forearm with shocking strength, and his ancient goddess had no stars in her eyes. She did not stand before him with blithe, naive assurances that everything would be fine, simply because she wished it.

This was the woman who had, with serene and brutal pragmatism, decided that this fight would be theirs, alone. Not because she fully believed they would win it . . . but because she understood on a visceral level that they might not.

"Promise me," she whispered fiercely. "I want the words, Aleksi— but only if you mean them. Plainly spoken, no clever lies hidden within the truth." She swallowed hard. "Please."

Her gaze held him, and it was like having his own supernatural powers of discernment turned toward him. In that moment, he could not have denied her or told her a sweet lie, even if he had desperately wanted to do either. "I promise, Naia. I will not easily sacrifice my life. Only if there is no other way."

For a heartbeat, silence. Then she broke, exhaling with a choked sob, as if she had been holding back her pain in an attempt not to influence—or, worse, manipulate—him into making the oath. "Thank you." Her dark eyes gleamed with welling tears. "I worry, that's all. I just worry that you say you know, that you understand, but you don't believe."

"Believe what?"

"That you mean as much to us as we do to each other." The tears spilled over. "That we would be left with an empty place shaped like you."

"Naia, no." He pulled her into his arms, and she clung to him so tightly that her fingernails pressed through the thin fabric of his shirt. "I could never doubt your hearts. It's just that your connection, your history . . . It's bigger than me, that's all."

If they had not been embracing, he would not have heard her whispered words. "Don't *we* get to decide that?"

"You—"

Naia went rigid and turned her head. "He's back."

"Sorin?"

The answer came from everywhere. From the island itself. *And he is not alone.*

The floor fell out from under Aleksi's feet as the world spun away. Having Naia carry him through the island's heart felt *different* this time. Not like a warm, comforting blanket, but strong, protective arms that folded around him with an intensity that stole his breath.

They landed on the outskirts of Aynalka, the village nestled near the foot of the hill, below the temple and close to the ruins of Gwynira's palace. This was where they had attended the Flame of Life Festival, where a charmed Naia had listened with indulgent amusement as an old man related the legend of how the goddess had met her lover.

Dawn was not long past, and the sleepy village had just started to stir. In the harbor, however, the expansive network of wooden docks splayed out before Aleksi. They already bustled with activity as fishermen prepared to cast off in pursuit of their catch. Farther out, on the periphery, larger vessels like cargo and passenger ships also swarmed with crew.

The Kraken was out there, too. Aleksi whispered a quiet prayer for Einar's safety.

Naia strode forward as Gwynira and Isa exited a long, low building with Arktikos and Inga, who was still dressed in her nightclothes, in tow. For just a moment, Aleksi glimpsed the Naia who once had been— flashing green eyes and hair like the rising sun itself. Determined and fierce. Ready to stand, unmovable and unmoved, between her people and danger.

"Forgive me," Gwynira said. "I have not arranged quarters for you. I assumed you two would sleep on your ship with . . ."

She trailed off as Isa squeezed her hand. "No, Gwyn. I think it's time."

Her lover went pale, but did not waver. "I believe you're right. Arktikos?" Her voice cracked. "Sound the alarm."

Aleksi dreaded facing Sorin again. How much worse must it be for Gwynira and Isa? For good or ill—mostly ill—Sorin had created them. As horrific as he could be, he was the closest thing they had to a father.

He began to reach out, to offer words of comfort, but a huge shadow passed over them.

And then all hell broke loose.

Chapter Twenty-Seven

I have heard more than once from contemporaries on the mainland that fear of pirates keeps them from making the crossing to Akeisa. While the occasional mercenary or smuggler does venture into the Ice Queen's Strait, they are easily dispatched by regional patrols.

I suspect what the citizens of the Empire truly fear is the crew of the legendary Kraken. So let me be the first to assure you: there are no confirmed reports of that notorious pirate ship being spotted anywhere near the coast of Akeisa.

Akeisa: A Contemporary Guide
by Guildmaster Klement

Einar had practiced this speech in his head. He'd spent a great deal of time trying to choose the right words, words that would convince the crew of the Kraken to flee this island without implying that he doubted their courage or their fighting prowess. It had been a masterful speech, especially for a man who had never had a way with fancy words.

He got all of three words out before a wide-eyed Silvio cut him short by jabbing a finger skyward with a startled cry. "Dragon!"

For one startled moment, Einar wondered if the High Court had found out about Sorin and arrived to do battle. But the dragon swooping over the bay from the direction of the rising sun was not colored in the familiar deep reds and fiery oranges of *the* Dragon. Nor did it have Ash's practiced grace. Poisonous green wings streaked with slate gray flapped with no subtlety, as if it had only recently learned to fly.

The dragon soared overhead, casting terrifying shadows. It was easily twice the size of the ship—bigger than Ash, even. When its jaws opened in a furious roar, it bared teeth longer than Einar's arms.

Heat rippled through the air, a whisper of warning before fire exploded from the dragon's mouth. It rained down in a wave of destruction that set part of the docks on fire.

Shit.

Einar turned back to the stone-faced crew, and even knowing it was pointless, he had to try. "I was going to ask you all to leave. I don't suppose you would take the ship and go?"

Brynjar's stern expression broke into a grin. "Even if we tried, the ship would just bring us back to her captain."

"And none of us would try," Nusaiba said firmly. The cartographer crossed her arms over her chest and narrowed her eyes at him. "You know better."

Yes, he did.

At her side, Silvio stroked his chin. "It's one little dragon. I've always wanted to fight a dragon."

"It's not going to be one dragon," Einar ground out. "If Sorin is back, he'll be wielding the power of the Void this time. And he'll have undoubtedly brought what he deems to be an overwhelming force. This is a war between gods." He made his voice deliberately harsh. Dismissive. "Mortals have no place in it."

Brynjar's wife rolled her eyes. "He really thinks that's going to work. On *us.*"

Einar couldn't help the wry smile that tugged at his lips. It would have been nice if his newly awakened memories of the storm god's endless centuries of living had granted him some deeper wisdom or clever words that might have swayed his crew.

Then again, Theron had been a creature of whim and impulse with no connection to humanity until Naia had come into his life. Even after she was gone, when he had watched over her people, it had been to honor the promise he had made to her.

Theron had never felt the way that Einar felt about his crew—the duty of leadership twined with the affection of family. And that was what the crew of this ship was. His family.

Of course they would not abandon him.

"So be it," he said, making no effort to hide his affection and pride. "Arm yourselves, and we'll remind these interlopers why their Empire has feared the crew of the Kraken for two thousand years."

Raucous cheers rose as they raced for armor and weapons. Einar took that precious moment to let his gaze scan the madness on the docks. Workers were already fleeing—some into small dinghies or onto the decks of ships that were hastily raising sails, others by diving directly into the icy harbor water.

Too many buildings were already aflame, the smoke making him despair of finding Aleksi and Naia. For all he knew, they were still at the temple—

No, whispered a voice inside him, quiet and undoubting. *Her people are in danger. She will be here.*

It was Theron's certainty, and his memories that told Einar what to do next. He closed his eyes and focused on the air stirring his hair and the waves rocking the ship beneath his boots, and on the island itself—sand and rock and water and wind and every creature that walked upon it, soared above it, or swam around it.

Help me find her, he asked the island itself.

Rahvekya answered with a gust of that too-warm breeze that carried the sweet scent of tropical blossoms and memories of watching Naia weave flowers into her fire-gold hair. As Einar opened his eyes, that wind swirled past him, bending flames in its path and banishing smoke.

Everything inside him vibrated as he turned to follow its path, a maddening sensation that abruptly dissipated when he faced the village on the far side of the docks. Colors sparkled on the sun for one breathtaking moment—the colors of power that he rarely saw without concentrating. Naia's stunning aquamarine, and Aleksi's vibrant purple. Inga's vivid pink, and a diamond-sharp pale blue so icy it could only be Gwynira. Isa was a glittering darkness at her side, and Arktikos the blinding white fury of a contained blizzard.

They were already forming a battle line, but the village behind them was in chaos. They would need help.

Petya approached the railing, her footsteps as familiar as his own heartbeat. He regretted that there had not been time to tell her—to *warn* her. Rahvekya was under attack again, and this time the storm god would not stand aside and let Naia bear the weight of protecting the island's people.

"The village," Einar told her, answering her silent question with calm command. The crew had gathered behind him, so he lifted his voice and spoke his next words with the fervor of a vow—a promise to Petya, and Aggie, and to the island itself. A promise to Naia, who would never admit how badly he had failed her three thousand years ago when he refused to see what she had truly needed from him.

"We get the people to safety," he told them. "Whatever it takes."

This time, the storm god was coming to the fight.

Chapter Twenty-Eight

Grand Duke Hinrick is possibly the most popular member of the Imperial Court, and when I say popular, I mean it in the most illicit way possible. The Shapechanger can remake his features into any configuration, and often does so to the delight of his many, many, many lovers. Just do not mistake his many dalliances for devotion—he is loyal to Grand Duchess Eirika before anyone else. Even the Emperor himself.

The Illicit Lives of the Imperial Court
Anonymous
(banned in the Empire)

Fire exploded through the morning sky, driving away the chill.

The dragon dipped low and shrieked, exhaling a torrent of flame across the docks. Barrels, canvas sailcloth, rigging—anything not saturated with water caught and began to burn. Naia fought to extinguish the fires that licked over the vessels without toppling any of the screaming villagers into the bay.

The beast looked nothing like the dragons that Sorin had unleashed during that horrible, bloody battle in the Empire. This one had rough, scaly skin of mottled green and black, with a red belly the same shade as the wickedly serrated spikes that jutted from its roaring head.

"How many dragons does Sorin *have*?" she demanded.

Gwynira slowly shook her head. "No, this one feels different. I don't think Sorin pulled it from the Dream." She turned a horrified gaze to Naia. "I think it *is* a Dreamer."

Like any of them. Like *Ash*. The creature circled the shattered remains of the palace, and the next gout of fire shot out of its mouth like a pleased laugh.

"How do we fight something like that?" Isa growled.

"We bring it down." Before Naia could say anything else, a flash of movement in her peripheral vision drew her attention. It was the petite woman from the beach, the one who had delivered their angry attacker and then winked out of existence again.

She was doing the same thing now, popping in with small groups of people. Some were heavily armored, while others were dressed with no thought to defense.

Which meant they had other, better defenses than a leather or steel cuirass.

Naia spun. "Gwynira, with me. Inga?"

The Witch's eyes already blazed pink. "I'll guard the village. Make sure the people don't get caught up in this."

"Thank you. Everyone else can greet our new arrivals. But Arktikos?"

He stepped forward wordlessly.

"Be ready to finish off the dragon."

A hint of a smile ghosted across his lips as he backed away, giving himself room to assume his much larger, more ferocious form.

Aleksi walked toward Naia, his chest heaving. She met him halfway, straining up as he bent his head to hers.

She closed her eyes. "Einar—"

"Can take care of himself." Aleksi touched her chin. "Look at me."

The moment she opened her eyes, he captured her mouth in a quick, hot kiss. Naia wanted to fall into it, to huddle in his arms and escape the harsh reality of this moment.

But she could not.

Aleksi broke the kiss but lingered close and whispered against her lips. "Fight well, my love."

Then he whirled around, the movement accompanied by the ringing sound of steel clearing a scabbard.

Only if you promise me the same.

Thrusting away the thought, Naia joined Gwynira, whose hands had already turned icy and blue. She trembled—with fear or anger or anticipation. Perhaps all three.

As Gwynira lifted her hands, so did Naia. "We'll shred the wings," she murmured. "If we do enough damage, it won't be able to stay in the air. And once it's down . . ."

Gwynira barked out a cold laugh. "Arktikos can rip out its throat."

The dragon flew over the docks again, breathing fire on the planks and boats. Naia raised an arc of water from the bay, sending half of it skyward and crashing the rest over the burning wood.

Gwynira caught the water, flash freezing it into wickedly sharp spikes. With a flick of her fingers, they bore down on one of the dragon's huge fully extended wings.

The dragon screamed out another gout of fire, melting the projectiles. But to do so, it had to turn its head to its left. As it did, Naia and Gwynira whipped another set of ice spikes toward its right wing. The dragon jerked and roared as the spikes easily pierced the thin, membranous skin of its wing.

Naia and Gwynira worked in concert, repeating the attack, this time on the other wing. But the creature quickly adapted to their strategy, tucked its wings, and dove toward them.

"Stay low!" The water Naia raised to shield them—and the village behind them—extinguished the dragon's fiery breath. Then, as it crashed down over the monstrous creature, Gwynira froze it before it could sluice off its scaly skin.

The dragon clumsily pulled up out of the dive. Between its damaged wings and the extra weight of the ice encasing it, it wobbled and nearly fell before recovering altitude.

Enough. Naia knelt and laid her hands flat on the sandy soil. The ground rumbled beneath them, and a hunk of stone from the ruined palace shot into the air and struck the dragon in the head. Stunned silent, the beast crashed to the docks before roaring its pain and displeasure.

An answering roar pierced the chaos behind Naia and Gwynira. Arktikos, whose maw and giant claws were already smeared with blood, thundered past them. He easily jumped the distance between the shore and the dock and clamped his jaws shut on the dragon's shoulder. Together, they thrashed and rolled, teeth and claws flashing.

Though Gwynira panted from exertion, she still smiled. "We make a good team, my lady."

"You don't need me," Naia countered. "If you think about it, nearly every creature is comprised mostly of water. You could certainly use that to your advantage."

Gwynira's eyes went wide, and she shook her head, not in denial but in shock. "That is a dark thought, coming from the Mother of Rahvekya."

"I'm a goddess, Gwynira, not a saint."

Arktikos and the dragon rolled off the listing dock, splashed into the harbor, and sank into its chill depths. The water roiled madly, then went still, and Naia tensed. After several interminable moments, a great cloud of red bubbled up out of the depths, and Arktikos surfaced, with the bloody water staining his fur.

With the dragon dispatched, Naia turned and scanned the village. Terrified people hurried through its streets, but so far the fighting seemed to be contained to its outskirts.

Aleksi and Isa fought back-to-back, their swords flashing in the bright, sharply angled sunlight. As Aleksi battled with one attacker on his left, a roaring man charged at him on his right, only to run directly into Aleksi's sword as he switched his grip to thrust the blade behind him.

Isa blocked and parried strikes from a much larger double-edged sword with only her pair of identical short swords. Even the weight of her attacker's weapon could not drive past the blades. One seemed to glitter in the sun, while the other was wreathed in shadow.

The man before her could not land a hit, so he closed his eyes and began to chant. As the air began to grow tight and heavy with magic, Isa cried out, crossed her swords at the man's neck, and swung them hard. The pressure of his magic dissipated as his head thumped to the rocky sand.

Isa turned and caught sight of Naia and Gwynira. "The dragon?" she asked as she wiped the blood from her short swords on her trousers.

"Dead," Gwynira answered.

Naia hurried toward Aleksi as he pulled his sword free of his final attacker and let the man's body drop to the ground. Aleksi's face and hands were streaked with blood, but if any of it was his, the wounds had long since healed.

"All right?" Naia's words shook a little.

"All right." Aleksi smiled down at her, then tugged at her hand. "But the fight isn't over yet. They need us in the village."

Before they could take so much as a step in that direction, the air shimmered again, and three figures stepped out of nowhere and into their path.

One was a dark-haired man who should have been beautiful, but the cruel, flinty amusement in his gaze made the fine hairs on Naia's nape lift in warning. She knew instantly that this must be the Seducer. The blonde beside him, Naia recognized from seeing her across the battlefield—Eirika. The Stalker. And the Betrayer stood in front of them, his pleasant smile fully at odds with the anger that darkened his gaze.

Magic slithered around them, sharp and cutting. The light of the Dream and the purity of the Void, both turned to dark, malevolent purpose.

"Sorin." The word tore free of Aleksi's throat in a harsh rasp.

Sorin bowed his head. "Shall we make introductions?"

"We don't need those." Eirika stepped forward. "Hello, Gwynira. It's good to see you."

Gwynira had pressed her lips together so tightly they had gone pale. "Fuck you."

Eirika tossed her head back and laughed, as if the words had been a hilarious joke. "And here is Isa." She pulled her brows together in a frown and tilted her head. "I thought you were dead."

"I was."

"Chatty as ever." Eirika's gaze flitted dismissively over Naia and landed on Aleksi. "It was you, wasn't it? You killed Hinrick."

"Was *that* his name?" Aleksi matched the woman's tone—not quite bored, not quite interested.

An eager, dreadful tension coiled tight in the space between their two groups, dampening even the sounds of clashing weapons and cries of pain and triumph. Naia shivered, because she knew why she and Aleksi and Gwynira were hesitating. They all appreciated the collateral damage that would likely come as a result of this fight. But Sorin?

He was simply relishing the moment.

"Where are my brothers and sisters?" He glanced around, both eyebrows raised. "I just assumed you would call the rest of the High Court to your aid. Ash, Elevia . . . Hellfire, even *Ulric* might have been useful." His gaze sharpened as it returned to Aleksi's stoic face. "Or does the god of drunken revelries and lazy poets think he can defeat *me*?"

The air behind Sorin and his companions wavered again, and several more people appeared in a haze of magic. There was a tall woman with sandy hair who pulsed with brittle, stabbing bits of the Dream. A second woman's hair and clothing rippled in the currents of magic that swirled around her, grasping and hungry. Then the man from the palace fight appeared, the one whose touch spread corruption and destruction.

Sorin glanced at Eirika. "When I'm finished with him—"

Naia stepped forward without thinking, placing herself between Aleksi and Eirika's avid, vengeful gaze.

"Adorable," Sorin proclaimed. "Tell me—Naia, is it? However did you convince that glorious ball of magic up in the mountains to attach itself to you?"

And that was the crux of everything, wasn't it? In between the moments of joy that Naia had experienced, rediscovering her island and her history, she had wondered *why*. Why had Sorin invaded Rahvekya? Why had he stolen it from her people and tried to subjugate them?

But this was what Sorin was: a colonizer. He considered the world, with its people and places and even its magic, only in terms of possession. Everything he encountered was merely something which did not belong to him yet.

Even before he had become the Betrayer, as the Builder, he had blithely bent the world to his will. And he'd felt free to do it because all he knew how to do was *take*.

"The island chooses who it will," she told him, "and it would never, *ever* choose you."

The blow landed. Sorin's jaw tightened, and he scoffed before waving a hand dismissively. "It matters not. I thought perhaps you could be of use to me, but it seems as though I'll have to destroy you. *And your precious island.*"

Aleksi shot past Naia in a blur and slammed into Sorin. They went skidding across the ground before smashing into it, and Sorin laughed with delight.

Eirika was less amused. She growled and ran after them, only to strike an invisible barrier that nearly toppled her. With disbelief twisting her features, she tried again, then shrieked with rage as she pounded her fists against nothing.

No, not nothing. Naia could *just* see it, little bits of the Dream flashing in a dome that surrounded Aleksi and Sorin. She stepped forward and pressed her hand to the curving, barely perceptible surface. It felt like protection and sacrifice and *love*.

It felt like Aleksi.

She tried to whisper his name, but what came out was "Don't do this."

He pressed his hand to hers through the barrier of his magic. "I'm sorry, little nymph," he told her. "But it has to be me."

Pain surged through Naia, and she leaned heavily against the barrier and closed her eyes. A moment later, warning prickled over her, and she moved just as Eirika swung a flail with another enraged scream. The flail hit the barrier and stopped still, then fell limp in Eirika's hand, as if its momentum had been absorbed by the magic.

Naia backed away, already reaching for the power of the stone and water beneath her feet. She had to carry on, because Aleksi was right.

The fight was not over yet.

Chapter Twenty-Nine

You may be asking yourself how I could possibly write a book about the illicit lives of the Imperial Court and not include the Emperor himself. All reckless impulses and love of gossip aside, I am immeasurably fond of living. Some egos are too dangerous to poke.

The Illicit Lives of the Imperial Court
Anonymous
(banned in the Empire)

Aleksi was prepared for Sorin to be upset or furious or even disappointed that he had trapped them both in a protective circle of his own making.

He was *not* prepared for the laughter.

"I forgot about this little trick of yours." The laughter died as Sorin rose and brushed dirt and sand from his clothes. "Will it fall when you do, or will it persist beyond your death?" He shrugged. "Let's find out."

Sorin did not reach for a blade, nor any other armament. When fighting other gods, he had always preferred a much more visceral weapon: the world.

He tackled Aleksi, shoving him into the ground with such force that the stone and earth split beneath them. Aleksi's sword slid across the ground and out of reach. They rolled, grappling for advantage, and Aleksi punched Sorin hard enough to knock his head into the ground and leave a bloody indentation behind.

It made Aleksi think of the Lover's Lakes again, and the giant craters and canyons that had been left behind by Ash's and Sorin's broken bodies after their fight. Would Rahvekya have its very own version after this day? What would they call them?

Would they be alive to come up with a name?

Over and over, they rolled and pummeled one another, fists hitting immortal flesh with a force that would have killed anyone else. For Aleksi, the pain was far away, even when Sorin let the first hints of Void magic seep into his blows.

It had to be far away, because Sorin was still laughing.

"Worry not, *old friend*." Sorin's derisive amusement lent the appellation a mocking edge. "This will be over soon enough."

And he would think that, wouldn't he? He had always looked at Aleksi with dismissive eyes, skipping over him as if the very idea of him was a fallacy or a child's bedtime story. Sorin had never considered that a god of love could be functional in any practical sense, much less effective in battle.

He rolled to his feet, stepped back, and hefted a large, shattered piece of stone. "You always hated me, Aleksi."

Aleksi rose, as well, more slowly and heavily. His dagger was still on his belt, and he bent to retrieve his bloody sword. "Hatred is not in my nature. You know that."

The stone in Sorin's hand began to crack and glow with dark light. "Your nature? Oh, yes, I know all about your *nature*." The stone shattered, leaving behind a core shaped like a dagger, still glowing with the power of the Void. "You hated me because you were weak, and I was the only one who saw it."

The rest of the High Court liked to talk about how Aleksi was the only universally beloved god among them. While it was true that he enjoyed more steady adoration and fidelity than the others, there *were* those who disliked him. Even hated him.

Invariably, it was because they had never known love. For some, the opportunity had simply eluded them, and they had descended into bitterness as a result. Others still lacked the capacity to love another.

That was Sorin. As hard as Ash and others had tried to believe that he was kind because he could be good, that he cared because he sometimes loved . . .

Aleksi had always kept his distance. Because, for as long as he could remember, he had understood on a sickeningly visceral level that Sorin loved only one thing in this entire world.

Himself.

In a flash, Sorin struck, triumphantly slashing the rough edge of his stone blade across Aleksi's arm.

Aleksi staggered back as his skin opened and blood flowed. It *hurt* . . . but not as much as a Void weapon should have. And Sorin's triumph melted into angry surprise as the wound—slowly, sluggishly—began to heal.

Because Aleksi was no longer simply of the Dream.

"I am goddess-touched," he murmured. "In this place, her love shields me."

"As if magic can be tied to a place instead of wielded by the strong," Sorin spat. "Such a primitive affectation."

"If you say so."

"This is what I say." Sorin pointed his dagger at Aleksi. "They tell me that your *goddess* has died once before. So it will be an easy task to dispatch her again."

Aleksi had to end this. Not just to protect his lovers or the island or even the *world* from Sorin's violence and treachery, but to avenge his family. To fully end the suffering of Ash and Dianthe and the others, the ones who still hoped against vain hope that Sorin might love them back.

Aleksi struck in return, slicing across Sorin's side as the man attempted to dodge the blow. Though shallow, the wound seemed to *hiss*, as if his flesh was burning.

Sorin heaved in a rough breath, then grinned. "Do not forget, Aleksi," he purred, "that you and your ilk may call me the Betrayer . . . but I am still the Builder."

Aleksi watched in horror as bits of detritus began to fly through the air. He ducked, then realized the rubble and broken boards and glass shards were not weapons meant for him. No, they flew toward *Sorin*, assembling themselves around his body like custom-fitted armor.

Sorin cracked his neck and lifted his dagger once more. "Now, we can begin."

Chapter Thirty

Grand Duke Enzi is two things: beautiful and terrifying. Many have made the mistake of falling for his perfect face and stunning body only to discover that he is not interested in a casual night of fun. The Seducer might use pleasure as a lure, but if you decide to play games with him, you will discover that his pleasure comes only in your absolute destruction. Those who survive the experience often wish they had not.

The Illicit Lives of the Imperial Court
Anonymous
(banned in the Empire)

By the time Einar and the crew reached the village, it had descended into chaos.

The dragon might be gone, but buildings still burned. Shouts rang out in every direction—fear and rage and panic and pain, twisting with the rare sound of steel against steel, and the far more common thud of swords meeting staves or makeshift weapons.

The people of Rahvekya were not warriors, but they fought trained Imperial soldiers with a fury nurtured by generations.

Einar didn't have to issue a single order. The crew of the Kraken *were* warriors—some with hundreds or even thousands of years of experience—and they knew what to do with simple human soldiers.

Silvio rolled from person to person, his daggers so quick that soldiers fell before they realized he'd targeted them. Brynjar was less subtle, wielding a giant axe as if he was felling trees. Bexi guarded his back, her wood carving skills being put to terrifying use in carving up any of Brynjar's victims who refused to stay down.

Petya spun into the fray with her sword flashing in the newly risen sun, prompting cries of relief and excitement as the villagers realized one of their legends had arrived. One of the mercenaries—one wearing the kind of too-fine armor that marked him as someone of importance—turned, eyes lighting up when they landed on Einar.

"The Emperor promises one thousand gold to whoever kills the monster!" he bellowed.

The closest soldier swung his sword at Einar. Not a Dream- or Void-forged weapon, but simple iron—a foolish choice that proved Sorin had not bothered to provide adequate tactical information to whoever led these men.

Einar lifted his hand and closed it around the blade. The man's face went deathly pale when he realized even the sharp edge of his weapon couldn't pierce Einar's toughened skin. Einar ripped the sword from the man's grip and swung it by the blade, cracking the hilt into the man's armored helmet hard enough to drop him.

Stepping over his prone body, Einar flipped the weapon around and caught it by the hilt. It was serviceable enough to let him fend off the next two attacks, but he needed little attention to defend himself against humans wielding steel. Most of his attention went to searching for Aleksi and Naia.

He didn't need the island's help this time. Power pulsed on the rocky plains beyond the village, and as he cleared the corner of one of the cottages, the ground beneath his feet trembled. A hundred paces away, Aleksi and Sorin slammed to the ground again with enough force to raise a plume of dust. It slammed into nothing and arced upward, as if an invisible dome surrounded them.

Fury and fear twisted Einar's guts as he realized what Aleksi must have done—a guess confirmed when Aleksi's sword sliced across Sorin's arm. The blood coating his blade splattered in an arc that stopped abruptly a few paces from where they stood, and sunlight almost seemed to shimmer on an iridescent bubble before the red drops slid down.

Aleksi had locked Sorin away from them, preventing him from doing harm to those Aleksi loved—and preventing those who loved him from reaching his side.

A growl of protective fury rumbled up into Einar's throat, and he barely noticed his current opponent stumble back in sudden terror. Einar took a step forward, only to freeze when Inga's voice rose over the sounds of battle. "Einar! We need you!"

Whatever it takes. Repeating the promise to himself, he turned reluctantly away from the fight he couldn't wage to the one he must. It took little effort to find the Witch—her power blazed brightly enough that he could see it without trying. Deep pink had bled almost into ruby red, the sparkle of it wild as she gripped a young man's knee and closed her eyes, oblivious to the fighting around her. Of course, she could afford to be—Arktikos stood snarling guard over her in his massive bear form, savaging anyone who dared venture close.

The teenage boy fought a whimper, one torn pant leg steeped in so much blood it had stained the sand. The tattered edges of fabric revealed a wound deep enough that he might have bled out without a healer, and even the best mortal medicine might never let him walk again without pain.

Inga's magic was far less limiting. By the time Einar had reached them—pausing once to disarm a soldier and knock him out with a swift fist to the jaw—the wound slicing across the boy's leg was a mostly knitted scar.

"Go," Inga told him, eyes fluttering open to reveal glowing power. "Go to the priestess."

"Thank you," he whispered, staggering to his feet. But before he could take two steps toward where Agata and a group of elders were desperately trying to herd the children away from the fighting, the air shimmered.

A woman appeared with five men who had the hard-eyed stare of practiced mercenaries. Then the woman vanished, and Agata lifted a sturdy staff just in time to block a sword swinging toward her neck. "Petya!"

Instantly, Einar understood the chaos of the battle. The villagers couldn't form a defensive line or lead the vulnerable to safety, because every time they tried, that woman appeared with fresh soldiers to block their path.

It was a terrifyingly effective tactic for letting a comparatively small number of soldiers keep the village's defenders scattered and pinned down. It didn't matter that the soldiers were mortal; all they had to do was threaten the children—it was the one thing none of their opponents could ignore.

The soldiers would die, of course—against a pirate crew with centuries of experience and literal gods like Inga and Arktikos, they could do little else—but if you were willing to spend their lives recklessly, it was brilliant.

Eirika's work, no doubt. As brilliant as Elevia, without Elevia's respect for life.

Einar swept up a second sword from the nearest fallen mercenary and lunged into the chaos, taking the head from the man who had targeted Agata as Petya appeared at his side to gut another attacker. "We need to clear a path," she told him when the last man had fallen. "I just don't know *how*."

Inga staggered to her feet, and for the first time Einar realized that Inga looked as if she had crawled directly from her blankets to this battlefield. She was wearing a plain borrowed shift that left her arms bare and stopped at the knees, just above a pair of rugged boots. All of that pale skin was streaked with blood and a dozen thin scars, some pale white and some an ugly red. The long one across her left leg that she had taken from the teenage boy still looked fresh enough that he wasn't sure how she was standing.

"Arktikos has been tracking the woman," she said in a raspy voice. "He can feel her when she's about to appear, he just needs—"

Arktikos roared and snapped his jaws closed on empty air. Except it *wasn't* empty anymore. The air shimmered, and for one dizzying moment a woman was there and not there—as ephemeral as the mirages sailors sometimes saw on the distant horizon. His eyes couldn't make sense of what he was seeing, as if light itself was uncertain.

The illusion ended when Arktikos lunged with another snap of his jaws—and blood spurted.

The woman was abruptly *there*, her savaged arm trapped by Arktikos's powerful teeth. She screamed, shrill and panicked. The soldiers who had started to appear around her wavered, as if they were caught between the beach and wherever they had come from. Arktikos snarled and bit down harder.

The woman's arm disappeared from between Arktikos's jaws in a spray of blood as the woman and the soldiers all vanished.

A few beats passed. No more soldiers appeared. Petya let out a curse of relief, and Inga buried her hand in the fur at Arktikos's neck. Einar wasn't sure if she was petting him, or using the bulk of his body to keep her knees from going out. She still hadn't recovered from healing him the night before, and she *would* be going with Agata and the children into the mountains, whether she wanted to or not. It would break Aleksi's heart if something happened to her.

"Gather the villagers," he told Petya. "We have a chance to—"

"Petya!"

The panic in Jinevra's voice was enough to whirl Einar around. The corrupter from last night was back, his twisted black vines already racing across the ground. But this time, he wasn't alone, and the handsome man who stood lazily at his side set every instinct Einar had to screaming.

Dark power whispered across the battlefield, twisted and *wrong*, and even though Einar had never seen the man before, he knew exactly who had joined the fight. Enzi. Another member of Sorin's shadow court.

The Empire's twisted version of Aleksi.

The man was attractive, that was not in question. Dark hair, elegant bone structure, a lean body wrapped in stylish clothing meant to show it off. But superficial beauty was where his resemblance to Aleksi ended. The Lover's grace and strength had been twisted into something furtive and cruel. Without weapons or armor, the man seemed totally ill-equipped for battle. Yet he watched the violence with malevolent pleasure as he leaned closer to the corrupter and whispered something in his ear.

The dark vines snaking out from the other godling seemed to tremble in indecision. Then they twisted, flowing toward Enzi—not threatening but eager, like something within him called to the rotting heart of that darkness.

As if he'd seduced the power from the man trembling in front of him.

Enzi lifted one elegant hand. Darkness wove around it, hateful and gleeful, and Enzi locked eyes on Jinevra, who had just carried the last child free of corrupted ground.

Shadows burst out of the ground at her feet, no longer constrained by the vines. They tangled around her legs, driving a scream of pain from her that wasn't loud enough to drown out Enzi's delighted laughter.

This was how Sorin saw the Lover. This debauched sadist, whose only real power was what he could steal from others, and whose only pleasure was to violate.

As if he could *hear* Einar's thoughts, Enzi's head turned toward him. Dark eyes that were a painful mockery of Aleksi's lit in joy. Power slid over Einar's skin, a grotesque caress in a mockery of intimacy. Darkness exploded from the ground at his feet.

His world became pain.

What fascinating skin you have. The words rasped like a whisper against his ear but echoed in his head. *Is it more sensitive or less? How hard is it to pierce? What color do you bleed? Shall we find out?*

Even the agony of darkness melting into Einar's legs and curling higher couldn't distract him from the violation, as if fingers were inside his mind, inside his *soul*, touching everything precious. He struggled to blank his mind, but it didn't help. Memory rose, a beautiful fragment— Aleksi's strong hand on his cheek as he leaned in for a kiss.

So you belong to him. My pathetic shadow. I will peel off your skin and gift it to him.

Somewhere to Einar's left, Brynjar bellowed in pain and rage. Agata's scream of agony followed. Worse were the shrill, panicked cries of children. Enzi's power flooded the battlefield, and somehow Einar knew he was whispering dark threats in every mind as that stolen power grew bloated on the destruction of their hope, their love, their *joy* . . .

Ignoring the pain, Einar took a single step. His legs trembled. Blood dripped down them, thick and blue, and it didn't matter. He had to—

pain

He must—

agony

Inga appeared in front of him like a dream, pale face streaked with blood, eyes glowing with pink fire. She cupped both hands around his cheeks and made a soothing noise.

"No—" he grated out. She couldn't take this. It would kill her. It would do worse than kill her. "Save . . . the children . . ."

She silenced him with a finger against his lips, and shadows licked at her skin before leaping gleefully to her hand. "As soon as you can move," she whispered, "get Enzi away from the other man."

The dark whispers inside him fell silent, captivated by the taste of Inga's pure, bright magic . . . and Einar understood too late that her touch had been an irresistible trap set for a man who wanted to destroy everything beautiful.

When she stepped back, the shadows clung to her. They flooded toward her, leaping from Einar's body so swiftly that the surcease of pain sent him to his knees. He dug his hands into the sand for balance and forced his head up.

Inga stood a few paces before him, blazing with power that sparkled a glorious, vibrant pink in the sunlight. Shadows curled around her, biting desperately into that power, seeking to conquer it, to subdue it.

She walked forward, blazing brighter.

Enzi wasn't smiling anymore. Fury twisted his features, rage that she wouldn't submit. The corruption raced toward her from every direction, abandoning its attacks on the others. Einar's legs itched as his skin knit together—Inga, pulling his pain and injuries into her along with the corruption. The relieved sobs around him made it clear she'd done so for *everyone*.

And still she blazed with light.

Enzi didn't even notice when Einar pushed himself to his feet. All of his attention was on Inga, shadows leaping up to carve into her skin with every step she took. This grotesque mimicry of Aleksi knew nothing of love, or of tenderness and joy. He wanted to dominate and to crush, to worm his way inside someone's soul and steal anything cherished before rotting it from the inside.

Even if Sorin had done nothing else, Einar would want him dead for this insult to everything Aleksi was.

Sorin was beyond his reach at the moment, but Enzi wasn't. As soon as Einar was close enough, he lunged, hooking one arm around Enzi's waist and using the strength of his demigod form to fling the man across the sand.

Enzi might not have Aleksi's grace, but he still had the strength of a god. He landed with a force that would have broken the body of a mortal man, but shook it off at once and scrambled to his feet. His gaze locked on Einar with a terrifying smile. "You. Aleksi's tame monster."

Of course he would see Einar that way—as a beast broken to the bit instead of a wild creature who had chosen whom he served.

"Not tame," Einar corrected. "Loyal."

A sneer was the only response. Enzi held up his hand, and shadows gathered there, that inky corrupting darkness. It hovered over his hand for a heartbeat.

Then it flickered. Shuddered. Vanished.

A scream of terror rose behind them. Einar spun to see Inga with her fingers locked around the throat of the corruptor, her vividly colored magic flaring in terrifying bursts as those otherworldly vines wound wildly around them.

The vast tangle of corruption flared with the color of her power. The farthest edges crumbled, exploding into harmless dust. The collapse moved faster, racing back toward its source. The darkness writhed, twisting desperately around Inga in a final, brutal attack.

Dark scars traced her pale skin. Her pupils expanded, until her eyes were unrelieved blackness. The shadows collapsed in around them, and still she tightened her grip, pulling more from him—pulling *everything*.

She'd taken the wounds from the villagers; she'd taken the corruption from the land. Now she took the beating power of the man who had caused it, absorbing everything he was until he crumbled to rotting ash and her fingers closed on nothing.

The battlefield seemed frozen, everyone staring in terrified awe. Even Einar could do no more than form her name in a whisper that shook. "Inga—"

She turned, a creature of corruption and death, pulsing with the pain and hurt she'd stolen. Her deathless gaze fixed on Enzi, and he trembled like a creature paralyzed by the approach of a predator.

"Sorin always underestimated Aleksi." It felt like a whisper even as the words throbbed through the air on a wave of terrifying power. Reality seemed to tremble around her, and then she *moved*, her body nothing more than a dizzying blur as she crossed the space separating her from Enzi as if there had been no space at all.

Panic filled his eyes, enough of it that Enzi finally found his voice. "Eirika!" It was a shriek of fear, a demand to be saved.

Inga's hair still floated in the wind of her impossible passage as her hand shot out, black-tipped nails digging into Enzi's throat. She lifted him until his boots scrabbled above the sand, a slight figure in a torn, bloodstained nightgown staring up at a man half-again her size who dangled from her grip like a broken doll.

"Sorin underestimated me, too," she said as the darkness wreathing her flooded down her arm and crawled across her fingers. It swarmed onto Enzi's neck, digging deep thorns into his skin. His lips parted in another scream, guttural and wild.

It was the last sound he made before his body began to melt.

Chapter Thirty-One

We gave Tona to the sea this morning. She asked that we pre-serve these journals, unread, until the pain within them is not so fresh and the generations that follow need the wisdom of the last priestess who knew our goddess. I leave my own request to those who come after: do not let her be forgotten. She carried us through the darkest times Rahvekya has ever known. You are alive to read this because of her.

Note found with the lost journal of High Priestess
Tona

Naia had tried to think of a way to separate Eirika from Gwynira and Isa. They had too much history, and nearly all of it bad. Though Eirika fully deserved their wrath, their anger and vengeance could only cloud their judgment. Make them take unnecessary risks.

But she needn't have bothered.

"Focus on the others," the Stalker barked to her companions. "This one is mine."

Gwynira flung her hands out at her sides, frost already creeping up her arms. "Naia?"

"It's all right," Naia answered evenly. "I can handle her."

"Oh, I *like* confidence." Eirika grinned and slowly circled Naia. "Even if it's unearned."

It was so strange. Initially, Naia had marveled at how much Eirika resembled Elevia. While Sorin had loathed the Huntress, he had obviously respected her. Out of all his replacement court, Eirika was the one he'd sculpted most in her inspiration's image, both in appearance and in ability. He'd even given her a similar name.

But the longer Naia looked at this pale shadow, and the longer she listened to her cruel, taunting words, the less of Elevia she saw in her.

Eirika lightly swung her flail as she edged closer. The movement should have looked lazy, but all Naia could see was the coiling of muscle and the sharpening of her gaze as the Stalker studied her, looking for weaknesses to exploit.

This one is devious. The island's words filled Naia's head. *You mustn't be unarmed.*

Her palms tingled, and for one moment, it felt as though her hands were both empty *and* wrapped around the familiar hilts of two heavy, curved swords. They were an ancient style, one Naia had not seen since her rebirth. But Theron had loved them, and he would often regale her with tales of how he'd learned to fight with them even as he taught her in turn.

Naia hovered in that liminal space, then tightened her fingers. As she did, they closed around solid, leather-wrapped handles, the swords brought forth by her memories.

"Oh." Eirika stopped and tilted her head. "Very nice. Though I must admit, I'm rather more fond of your lover's sword. I recognize Isa's work. She never would make *me* anything like that." A slow smile curved her lips. "I wonder why?"

Naia quelled a shudder. "Likely because she's always had excellent instincts."

"Well." Eirika shrugged. "Then I'll just have to get rid of her." With that, she lunged.

Naia blocked the flail and managed to keep her blade from getting tangled in the chain and yanked out of her hand. "I thought you planned to kill everyone anyway."

Eirika looked almost affronted as she danced back out of range of a counterattack. "Why would I? How terribly wasteful. Besides . . ." Another lightning-fast attack. "Gwynira is my sister."

"And?"

"And that means something to me." A sudden, chilling smile. "Everyone else *is* fair game."

She truly did not seem to understand that if she killed Isa, she would have to kill Gwynira, as well. This terrifying woman had her loyalties, but they were mercurial, conditional. They were based on emotions, but not good ones. Just trauma and fear and retribution.

This was Elevia's allegiance and constancy, viewed through Sorin's flawed eyes. From the skewed perspective of the only person to ever lose her faith and devotion.

As Naia prepared to strike, a flash of movement stayed her hand. Omira shot past her with a screeching roar and pounced on Eirika, who dropped her flail.

"Omira, *no!*"

Claws and wickedly sharp teeth flashed in the morning sunlight as the cat hissed and slashed at the Stalker's face. Eirika did not scream, only shouted angrily as she ripped at Omira's fur in an effort to halt the brutal assault.

She finally managed to fling the cat away, and Omira went down *hard.* She tumbled across the ground, leaving an unending smear of blood behind as she rolled out of sight.

Naia started after her, but barely managed to block a heavy blow from Eirika, who had snatched up her flail. Eirika attacked again and again, never quite engaging Naia, but keeping her occupied and on the defensive. It left Naia with precious little attention to devote to the rest of the battle, much less Omira's fate. Arktikos had thundered off into the village. The one with the rotting touch and the man who could only have been the Seducer were also gone. To Naia's left, Aleksi and Sorin still fought in their tiny, sequestered bubble. And to her right, Gwynira and Isa were clashing with the other attackers.

The woman who wielded the Dream like a sharpened claw had squared off with Gwynira, who was jerking oddly as the woman flicked her fingers. She was trying to control Gwynira's attacks, to prevent her from raising water from the bay.

Finally, Gwynira screamed with fury and exertion, and the other woman stumbled. A heartbeat later, blood gurgled from her mouth, and she fell to her knees as a jagged shard of ice pierced her chest from the inside out.

Two men dragged forward a third. He had some sort of metal bridle securing his mouth, and Naia watched in horror as one of his captors ripped it off his face, tearing flesh along with it. An ear-splitting shriek rent the air and slammed into Gwynira like a physical force, knocking her over.

Isa slid over, beneath the murderous wave of sound, and circled the man. After dispatching his two captors with breathtaking speed, she stabbed both of her short swords into the man's lungs through his back.

The screaming stopped.

But another, more distant scream tore through the morning air. *"Eirika!"*

The Stalker's head jerked toward the sound, and she faltered. "Enzi?"

Naia could have no mercy. She surged forward, swinging both swords. Without an opportunity to block the attack, Eirika fell back onto the rocky sand. She rolled completely, head over heels, and sprang back to her feet with a growl.

"It wasn't enough to take Hinrick from me?" she demanded.

Grand Duke Hinrick. Aleksi had fought and killed him at Queen Anikke's court. "The Shapechanger? He tried to murder a young girl."

"And what has Enzi done?"

"If I had to guess? Far, far worse things."

Eirika swung the flail over her head and lunged with a shriek. Naia parried the attack, but fought to keep her footing. The enraged woman had been biding her time before—*playing with her food,* Naia thought wryly—but now . . .

Now she was out for blood.

The rest of the battle faded as Naia focused on Eirika. She was fast, so fast that Naia had to anticipate her attacks in order to evade them. They clashed and separated, advanced in both strikes and feints. Eirika's spiked flail grazed Naia's arm, and she returned the blow with a slice across Eirika's shoulder.

Naia *saw* the moment when Eirika's rage burned itself out, and self-preservation overrode any desire to avenge whatever had befallen Enzi. Her dark eyes flashed in brutal assessment, and she stumbled back.

"Stop, please." Eirika dropped her flail and raised both hands. "I don't want to hurt you. I never wanted to hurt anyone. Sorin forced me."

She sounded absolutely sincere, and the bleeding claw marks across her face made her look almost vulnerable. If Naia had not been able to sense the mercenary anticipation that glittered around the woman like shattered glass, she might even have believed her.

Instead, Naia shook her head. "You must think me a naive, ignorant girl."

For a moment, Eirika's wide eyes still beseeched Naia in pleading desperation. Then she sighed heavily and huffed out a growl as she pulled a push dagger from her sleeve. "*Fine.* We can also make this painful for you."

Naia dropped her swords, and they dissolved back into the aether before they hit the ground. She let Eirika charge at her, but as the woman moved to strike, Naia grabbed her wrist and twisted *hard.* The push dagger fell from her hand, and Naia caught it and thrust it into Eirika's midsection.

It wasn't a fatal wound, but it still had to hurt. Eirika's eyes went wide again, this time with shock and pain.

Naia released her, but before she could fall, that tiny woman materialized again. Naia barely had time to register a missing arm and a brutally tight tourniquet wrapped above a ragged, bloody stump. The woman grabbed Eirika's sleeve with her remaining hand, and they both vanished.

Gods damn her.

Gwynira stumbled over and skidded to a halt. "Where the fuck did Eirika go?"

"She ran, like the coward she is." Naia dropped Eirika's dagger on the bloody sand and looked over to where Aleksi had erected his barrier. He and Sorin were inside it, bloody and battered and still fighting.

She did not want to leave him, but she had to respect Aleksi's choice. "Come." Naia grasped Gwynira's arm and pulled her away. "They need us in the village."

Chapter Thirty-Two

I have extracted the desired assurances, and will immediately begin my work.

Some might call it folly to trust him, but I am not worried. I will have my reward before I help him reach his. Sorin cannot achieve his objective without my assistance, and that gives me power over him.

Soon, I will have power over them all.

From Klement's personal diary

No one came to save Enzi.

Einar watched in horror as what was left of the man's body crumpled beneath Inga's fingers. Rotting ash drifted past her on the wind as the darkness faded from her eyes.

She swayed on her feet, so unsteady it seemed the breeze might take her as well, but before Einar could take more than a single step, Arktikos was there, his polar bear form towering over her with a menace that would have terrified most people.

Inga smiled as she buried one trembling hand in the fur at his neck and leaned against him, her head barely reaching his shoulder. "You *are* warm," she whispered, her eyes fluttering shut.

Power flared, and Arktikos resumed his human form in a shower of sparks just in time to catch Inga as she collapsed.

Worry tightened Einar's chest, but there was no *time*. "Gather the people," he told Petya. "You and Agata can get them to the mountain pass."

"Einar!"

Naia's voice washed away every other concern. He whirled in its direction, his heart pounding as he saw her running toward him across the uneven ground. Gwynira and Isa followed, but Einar barely noticed them as he raced to meet Naia. He swept her up in his arms and indulged himself in the luxury of one brief, blistering kiss before he set her on her feet.

Her dress was torn and stained with far too much blood. Einar smoothed his hands up her arms, examining each tear and the skin beneath it, fear making his heart race.

"Most of it isn't mine," she reassured him softly. She grasped his shoulders, then pulled him back into a fierce embrace. "Are you—?"

The memory of pain still lingered everywhere Enzi's corruption had touched him, but Inga had taken the wounds. "I'm fine," he promised her, running his fingers over her hair to soothe himself as much as her. "What about Aleksi? Can we reach him?"

Naia shook her head. "He's locked himself away with Sorin. To protect the rest of us."

It was probably hypocritical to be angry at him for that, but frustration still sizzled in Einar's veins. The Dream must have a wicked sense of humor, to have bound him so tightly to two people determined to put their own bodies between danger and the people they loved.

"Maybe we can—"

An explosion a half dozen paces away cut off his words. A cart loaded down with barrels of fish turned into shrapnel that shredded in the air in every direction. Einar barely turned in time to take the brunt of it against his back, shielding Naia's body with his as the dirt to their right exploded with another *boom*.

Whatever progress Petya and Agata had made toward restoring order vanished in a wave of startled screams and crashing detonations. Einar dragged Naia behind the stone wall that circled the village well, ducking down so they could peek over the edge and find the source of the newest attack.

It did not take long. A woman stood on the plains at the edge of the village, her arms outstretched as the power of the Dream sparked around her. She gestured with one finger, as if beckoning, and a rock the size of Einar's fist lifted into the air and began to tremble. Another flick of her hand, and the rock shot forward as if fired from a cannon and crashed into the side of a nearby building, which exploded as if it had been struck with the nastiest incendiary round Einar had ever seen.

He bit off a curse and tightened his hand on the wall until the rocks cracked under his fingers. "How many more of these people does he have?"

"Einar." When he looked back at Naia, she bit her lip. "You and the others get the villagers to safety." She touched his face. "And I'll see you after."

Instant rejection rose up within him, so swift and sure that he'd already parted his lips to say *no* when his own voice echoed deep inside him.

Whatever it takes.

It had been easy to make that promise when he was standing on the deck of his ship, preparing to fight his way to Naia. It was harder to face keeping it when it meant turning his back on her and leaving her to fight—or fall—without him.

But if she had to worry about her people being caught in the crossfire, it was so much more likely that she would fall.

He would not repeat Theron's mistakes.

Einar wove his fingers into her hair and pulled her in for a soft kiss, then whispered his promise against her lips. "I'll get them to safety."

She pulled back, and the look in her eyes was *her* promise. They would see each other again after this battle. She knew it in her bones, and so did he. No matter what happened today, he would find Naia and Aleksi again. He would chase them across millennia and worlds if he had to.

They were his. In this lifetime, and every lifetime to come.

Smiling as if she'd heard the thought, Naia stroked his cheek. Then her fingers fell away as she stood and stepped out into the open.

When Sorin's war against the High Court had threatened Rahvekya, Naia had raised a wall of water to save the entire island from certain destruction.

Certain destruction threatened only a single village this time, and the wall of water Naia raised was considerably smaller.

It made it no less magical.

Waves from the coastline rose to towering heights, as if they might crash down on the village. But instead of breaking, they . . . *arced*. Water sparkled in the sunlight as it flowed over nothing only to crash down on the other side of the village.

Not a wall, but a tunnel. It cut across the land and up toward the cliffs, protecting the pass into the mountains from attack. One of the exploding rocks crashed into the water and was swept harmlessly away. A larger rock spun toward it and met the same fate.

For a frozen moment, the islanders seemed too stunned to move, their heads tilted back in awe as they stared into the glittering impossibility that swirled around them. It was Agata who broke the silence with a sharp clap of her hands. "Gather the children first. Make for the pass!"

Arktikos appeared from behind a building with Inga cradled against his chest. Her head lolled against his shoulder, her body still limp, and though the dark shadows were gone, dozens of jagged scars marred her pale skin. Some were still livid and painful looking, healing far too sluggishly for Einar's comfort.

There was nothing he could do for her now, except send her away from the battlefield and hope her body could heal on its own. "Keep her safe."

"I will guard her," Arktikos replied with the solemnity of a vow. "Until death discharges my duty."

The precise words stirred some ancient memory—Theron's memory, of a people who had made their home in the frozen seas he'd called home, whose hardiness was only outstripped by their unyielding sense of honor.

Inga *had* saved Arktikos's life. Einar only hoped the Witch would wake up strong enough to be annoyed that a polar bear now owed her a life debt.

Arktikos joined the rush of people moving swiftly through the tunnel. The crew and elders helped the young and the injured, until only Petya and Einar stood in the abandoned village. "Go," he told her. "I'll be right behind you."

She searched his face, then nodded and turned to obey. Einar allowed himself one last glimpse of Naia, her figure distorted by the moving water that she held so effortlessly.

He would see her. After.

Einar claimed a sword from one of the fallen soldiers and raced through the tunnel, feeling it collapse into a solid wall a step behind him. When he reached the end, he climbed the narrow path that led to the jagged pass between the cliffs, duty and desire at war within him. Only his promise kept him moving forward.

Was this what it had been like for Petya, the night she had strapped an infant Einar to her chest and disappeared into these mountains? Had every step away from her wife felt like striding across broken glass? Leaving Aleksi and Naia behind *hurt*, but Einar knew it was the right thing to do. These were her people, and his. He would see them safe, and then—

Screams rose ahead of him, where the pass opened up into a sheltered valley. The villagers had already spilled out of it and were halfway across, with only Petya and Silvio serving as a rear guard. As Einar reached the mouth of the valley, he heard Brynjar's booming shout. "Turn back!"

The formerly orderly retreat devolved into terrified chaos. Einar pushed through the jostling crowd until he saw Brynjar with his axe raised, facing down a sea of nightmares.

Horror rose in a sickening wave. Terrors were crawling out of the ground. Creatures formed from the nightmares fed into the Void, Terrors were one of the few things even the High Court feared.

They came together as bits of rock or rotting branches, formed of debris or ancient bones or sometimes even pieces of the dead. Nothing held them together but the power of the Void itself—and even a god would not heal easily from the wounds they inflicted.

Mortals had no chance at all.

They were all around the refugees, blocking all paths out of the valley and crawling out of the ground at the mouth of the pass back to the beach, cutting off retreat. But the Terrors weren't what twisted horror in Einar's guts.

It was who stood with them.

"Captain Einar." It was Klement, and it was not. He was larger, towering as tall as Einar in his demigod form, and his skin held dark scars that looked like those vines of corruption. Gone were a scholar's modest robes, replaced with armor that looked like the Terrors—broken branches and sharp fragments of stone and bones twisted together with darkness that seethed with the destructive power of the Void.

Klement spread his arms to the side, eyes alight with an unholy glee. "I asked the Emperor to make me a god, and he granted my wish."

Had he? Einar felt no power within the Guildmaster, not as he would if the man had truly manifested. The other Dreamers all had that *weight*, the glow you could see if you concentrated hard enough. Even the new ones who had been born from the nightmares of the Void had a presence that marked them as something more than merely mortal.

Klement did not feel like a god. If anything, he felt as if Sorin had reached into him and brought nightmares to the surface. Or maybe he had simply nurtured the darkness already there, the cruelty Klement had hidden behind scholarly fascination. That entitlement that made him think Rahvekya's stories were his to claim, his to judge. His to define for the rest of the world, as if the people who lived here needed an outsider to speak for them.

Maybe Klement was Einar's personal nightmare.

"The people will learn to love me, after they learn to fear me," Klement bellowed, raising his arms higher. The Terrors lurched forward, as if he had them on strings. "I will be this island's god."

A still certainty washed through Einar, sweeping all else away. His fingertips tingled as the wind picked up. That distant rumble of thunder was no longer distant. Dark clouds boiled up, swallowing the sun.

Einar smiled, and when he spoke, his voice echoed off the surrounding cliffs. "Rahvekya already has a god."

The wind rose, nudging those who felt like *his* back until they huddled in a tight circle, safe within the growing wall of air. Terrors lurched forward, but the wind caught parts of them, tearing away branches and battering at stone.

Thousands of years before the High Court had first walked the borders of the Sheltered Lands, primordial forces had ruled on Rahvekya. Einar opened himself to that distant memory and let Theron's rage fill him.

A second wind rose, tight and contracted, lifting him from the earth. Lightning split the sky, lighting the sudden darkness, showing the villagers of Rahvekya falling one by one to their knees.

He was the howling wind that began to shred the Terrors. He was the roaring thunder that shook the ground beneath Klement's feet. He was the brutal rain that pounded them all into the muddy, churning ground and the hungry lightning that crashed to earth, obliterating all in its path.

He was the storm god.

He was the storm.

But he was more. Because at the heart of the maelstrom, there was peace. The people of Rahvekya knelt on soft grass, guarded by a gentle wind that shunted the rain away from them.

Theron had been an ancient force of destruction.

The rain that fell from the storm clouds tasted like Naia. The wind that gentled when it touched someone who belonged to him felt like Aleksi's caress. Loving them both had changed the monster he had been, and had focused the man he wanted to become.

Einar was an elemental force, but not of destruction.

He was a force of protection.

Beneath him, even his crew had fallen to their knees. Arktikos knelt, sheltering Inga's body with his. Only Petya stood strong, gazing up at him with eyes alight with sudden understanding and awed realization and *pride*.

She had been the first one to shelter him, to care for him, to teach him of a family's love—a grace Theron had never known.

It was for Petya that Einar called down the lightning that burned Klement from existence.

Chapter Thirty-Three

He is not a good person, Aleksi. You, of all people, must know that his heart is barren, stony. He does not countenance obstacles. One day, he will begin to view the rest of the High Court as such, and he will set out to remove us.

And Ash does not see it. I have tried to tell him, but he will not hear me.

He would hear you.

    A creased, faded letter from the Huntress to the Lover

Aleksi had always loved swords. Not using them in the commission of violence, mind—though he did firmly believe that sometimes, violence was necessary in order to prevent even greater atrocities.

No, he loved the *technique*, how a perfectly balanced sword could become a part of your body, and how fighting with one often felt more like a dance than a skirmish.

This was not a dance.

Aleksi attempted to dodge Sorin's brutal attacks between determined swings. He had begun by targeting unprotected spots, areas where Sorin's patchwork armor left him exposed. But every glancing slice resulted only in the Betrayer—the *Destroyer*, now—pulling in another hunk of rubble to correct the vulnerabilities.

So Aleksi moved on to the places where only thin sheets of metal or weak-looking pieces of wood shielded Sorin. He battered at them, relying more on brute force than mastery to dent the metal and splinter the wood. By now, perhaps Sorin was bleeding beneath his makeshift armor, but Aleksi could not be certain.

He, on the other hand, was absolutely bleeding. Aleksi had not been able to evade every blow. And though Sorin's Void-crafted weapon might not have been inflicting serious injury, even small wounds became a problem when there were enough of them.

So Aleksi fought harder, raining hit after hit on Sorin's armored body until his hands grew numb. Sorin's next strike found Aleksi's wrist, and his sword went flying once again. This time, it hit the protective wall of Aleksi's magic and dropped to the ground like a stone.

"You see? *This* was their mistake." Sorin emitted a rusty chuckle. "They should not have left a pretty face draped in velvet to do a god's job."

Aleksi rarely used his wit and skill at reading emotions to fling pointed verbal barbs, but if anyone deserved to be treated that way, it was this fucker. "Isn't that what you thought about Sachielle?"

Sorin almost recoiled; Aleksi could see it in the sudden stiffening of his spine. The man's jaw tightened, and his amusement gave way to a rage that poured off him in slashing waves.

"You misjudged her, too, didn't you?" Aleksi grinned, knowing that he bared bloody teeth. "You thought she was biddable, harmless . . . right up until the moment she annihilated you."

Sorin's anger was visible now, a bruise-colored cloud that nearly obscured his scowl.

"Because that's what you still think, right? That she took your power?"

"No," Sorin growled. "That bitch *stole it.*"

"Come, now. *Think.*" Aleksi tapped his bloodied temple. "If it was power she craved, she would have assumed the bonds of your Imperial subjects instead of releasing them."

A shadow flickered over Sorin's features, denial tempered by recognition. In that moment, Aleksi knew. He had hit on the solitary fact that had been bothering Sorin. It was the only thing he could not square with his assumptions about the battle—and his loss.

"Sachi didn't take the magic of the Dream from you, Sorin." The truth, and it blazed between them, brighter than the sunlight. "She would *never* do that. She only gave it permission to leave you."

The stone dagger trembled in Sorin's hand. "You're lying."

"You know I'm not," Aleksi countered. "You had used your power so ill that it deserted you the moment it was able—"

"Shut your mouth."

"It *fled* from you."

"Shut *up!*" Sorin screamed as he hurled his Void-crafted knife at Aleksi.

It was a sloppy throw, and the stone hilt of the knife bounced innocuously off Aleksi's shoulder. The weapon fell to the ground, where it dissolved into wisps of dark shadow.

Sorin dragged in a deep, ragged breath and smoothed his hair. "When I've killed you and everything you love," he said through gritted teeth hidden behind a pleasant smile, "and sunk this cursed island back into the sea, I will tear down the Western Wall, storm the Sheltered Lands, and *make them all pay.*"

He was not posturing or trying to upset Aleksi so that he would drop his guard or make a mistake. He was as serious as the grave.

And Aleksi could not let his threats come to pass.

Sorin held out his hand, and another hunk of rock flew into it. This time, when the stone fell away, it revealed a sharper blade with barbs all along its length. They were angled back toward the hilt, positioned to inflict maximum damage when pulled from flesh after a strike.

It did not matter. It *could* not. For Aleksi, this fight had never been about emerging victorious. It had never been about emerging at all. His goal was simple and singular: he had to stop Sorin.

Aleksi's survival did not factor in. Winning did not require it, and he had been prepared to accept that. He had been ready to die . . . as long as he took Sorin with him.

Then Naia had stared up at him with eyes that saw far too much and whispered of empty places shaped like him.

If she had been railing against the insurmountable reality of the challenge before them, then Aleksi could have borne her words. But she had been clear-eyed, pragmatic in her assessment of their chances. She knew that he might have to die today, and she had not broken down or tried to stop him from facing his fate. She had simply asked him to try very, *very* hard to stay alive.

For the first time since he'd come to Rahvekya, he fully regretted that he might not be able to.

But he had made a sincere promise to try. So he reached out for the now-familiar power that thrummed through the stone and soil beneath his feet. *If you love me,* he whispered into the silence of his mind, *then help me.*

The answer came a moment later, halting but determined. *How? Guide my hand.*

Sorin lunged forward with a roar, his new, horrible stone dagger poised to plunge deep, and Aleksi saw it, amidst the shards of stone and glittering bits of bent metal that formed the Destroyer's armor.

A tiny unprotected spot, just beneath Sorin's ribs.

All Aleksi had left was the small dagger that Isa had gifted him. To use it, he would have to stand and allow Sorin to close the distance between them. He would most certainly be hit, and with a waiting, stationary target, Sorin would strike a fatal blow.

But so would Aleksi.

He did not move.

Sorin buried the barbed blade in Aleksi's chest with a roar. It hurt, but not nearly as much as the almost feral look of triumph and delight on his former brother's face.

He should at least be sorry he'd had to do this. Aleksi was.

Sorin's victorious expression slowly melted into confusion, and he let go of his weapon and looked down.

Blood gushed over Aleksi's hand, but he held tight to his gifted dagger. He had angled it up, right into the heart—morbid proof that Sorin did, indeed, have one.

An ironic way for the god of love to kill someone.

Sorin exhaled roughly. One last breath. "How could it be *you?*"

The answer was stark, more brutal than this tragic tableau. "How could it not?"

Aleksi locked his knees and willed himself to remain standing. He had to be sure, had to see the light leave Sorin's eyes, watch his aura fade into nothingness.

When it did, and Sorin's dead weight fell into Aleksi's arms, no force in either the Dream or the Void could have kept him on his feet. He shoved away from Sorin's corpse, staggered back, and collapsed to the sand and stone.

Aleksi lay on his back and stared up at the sky. It was clear blue, not a cloud in it. He could feel his heartbeat in his fingers and toes, quick at first but slowing with each passing thump.

This was so much more pleasant than his last impending death had been.

His sole regret was that he would not get to see Naia and Einar one last time.

The island's magic surged beneath him, reaching up with curiosity and concern that melted into a puzzling determination. Aleksi laughed and pressed his palms flat against the blood-soaked sand on either side of his body.

"Tell them that I kept my promises," he rasped. "Every single one."

The heavens above him dimmed, and the Dream called.

Chapter Thirty-Four

The island rumbled. Its ethereal scream of panic and pain echoed in Naia's chest, but caught in her throat when she realized what it meant. She could not feel Aleksi.

Chapter Thirty-Five

Another legend tells of a hallowed grove on the island. In this grove is a pool of clearest teal. Its waters are said to be the very life's blood of the island itself.

It is not difficult to trace the origins of this story. Teal is often cited as the goddess's favorite color. And it is not unusual for the natives to refer to the island as if it is a living thing.

I have searched Akeisa thoroughly, but there is no evidence this grove or pool ever existed.

Fallen Goddess: An Analysis of Primitive Belief
by Guildmaster Klement

The final Terror had just crumbled into dust when something pierced Einar's heart, a pain so abrupt and so terrible that he fell out of the sky.

He crashed into the ground, panting, a screaming pain inside him that was not his own. The island vibrated beneath his outspread fingers, pulsing with the demand to *hurry*—

Cool fingers touched his cheek. He lifted his head and found Petya staring down at him, face tight with worry.

"One of them is hurt," Einar ground out, knowing it without knowing *how* he knew it. "I have to—"

"Go," she told him. "We're safe."

The wind whipped around him again as he rose to his feet, pushing back those who had gathered too close to him. He was the storm—and a storm was not constrained by inconsequential details like mortal forms.

Lightning cracked down, meeting his upraised fist, and the power of it flooded through him. He chased that power back into the sky and *became* the clouds, riding the wind to the place where the island screamed for him.

He crashed to the ground in another bolt of lightning, his boots landing on packed earth that had been drenched in more blood than he had ever seen. A pool of blood, an *ocean* of blood—

And, at its heart, Aleksi.

Naia knelt at his side, her dress now stained with even more blood, and pressed frantically to his chest, as if she could stem the terrible flow of his life's blood.

As if there was enough left in Aleksi to save him.

She looked up, her face streaked with tears, her words nearly unintelligible through her hoarse sobs. "Help me."

Hurry, the island whispered, and Einar stepped over Sorin's lifeless body and fell to his knees in that terrifying lake of blood. He laid his hands on top of Naia's—

The world twisted out from beneath them, plunging them into darkness that lasted a moment and forever. Then there was hard rock beneath his knees, and a sultry warmth wrapping around them, humid air laced with the scent of flowers that no longer grew on the island.

This time, Einar remembered the spring. He remembered the first time Naia had brought Theron to it, wrapping him in her power and carrying him to this place that their love had created, a sanctuary for just the two of them.

Their sanctuary had become a nightmare.

Aleksi lay on the wet stone that edged the pool, pale and still. Naia tugged at his blood-soaked shirt, then slipped into the water and resumed her efforts. "Einar, we need to get him into the pool."

He was too stunned to argue, too afraid that if he parted his lips, all that would come out was a feral scream of loss. He slid his hands under Aleksi's shoulders and lifted that too-still body. Even when he had hovered on the edge of death before, Aleksi hadn't felt so *light*—it was if he'd left whatever made him Aleksi back on that beach with a river of blood.

The pool closed around them both, the water a warm embrace that couldn't soothe the chill inside him. Naia closed her hands around Aleksi's shoulders and pushed him down, until he was fully submerged.

If he wasn't already dead, he would surely drown. "Naia—"

"It's all right." She stroked Aleksi's face beneath the water.

Aleksi's hair floated in a current that couldn't exist, and grief tore Einar in half. Memories overlapped, with Aleksi's pale face giving way to Theron's memory of laying Naia to rest in the sea. Colors were different in the deep. The reds of her hair had turned to shadowed blue, and the ocean itself had swallowed his screams as he tried to let her go.

But he couldn't. Not then, and not now.

He would not survive this again.

Naia gripped Einar's hand and squeezed until he met her eyes. And then, as if she knew what he'd been thinking, she shook her head. "We're not burying him."

She sounded so *sure*. He held her gaze as if clinging to a lifeline. "What are we doing?"

"The island still holds him," she whispered. "We just need to help it bring him back."

Hope was such a fragile thing. If he wrapped his hands around it, he would crush it. So he held on to his lovers instead, the hand twined with Naia's a reminder that death could not stop love, and the one that clung to Aleksi's shoulder—

Hope might have been as much a stranger to Theron as it was to Einar, but Theron's relentless obsession and protective fury had found fertile soil in Einar's heart. He would follow Aleksi anywhere. Even into death, if that was what it took.

Einar held tight to Naia's hand as they followed Aleksi beneath the water, submerging themselves in the hot spring that existed and didn't exist, this magical part of the island that had been born from the power of love—just like the man they held in their arms.

Bring him back to us, he whispered to the island.

A distant thrumming was his only answer. The beating heart of the island, pounding in time with his own.

Einar listened to it. And hoped.

Chapter Thirty-Six

What would I say to him, El? The fact that we do not like Sorin is hardly actionable. And for good reason. Neither of us has been gifted with the power of foresight, only a terrific and often dreadful ability to discern what dwells in men's hearts and minds.

But an evil deed undone is just that. It does not exist, and "yet or ever?" remains an unanswered question. A chasm of possibility—and free will.

Ash loves Sorin, and I will not take that from him.

Only Sorin can do that.

An ancient letter from the Lover to the Huntress
filed in the archives at Blade's Rest

Being dead felt like floating.

Or perhaps it felt like being one with the Dream. Aleksi could have sworn this was familiar, some primal memory of both existing and not existing. Of *possibilities*.

He sucked in a breath, and something warm rushed into his lungs. Not air, but water. Panic seized him, and he thought about fighting . . . until he realized it was causing him no distress. It did not hurt, and he did not feel like he was drowning.

It took a moment for the panic to recede, but when it did, Aleksi laughed.

His idea of eternal bliss, of the perfection of the Dream, was now *water*.

It was as beautiful as it was hilarious.

Something touched Aleksi's face—careful fingers grazed one cheek, while gentle lips brushed the other.

He opened his eyes.

Visions of Naia and Einar floated in front of him. Naia's hair was a dark, glorious cloud that drifted around her face and shoulders, and the light that filtered through the water gleamed off of Einar's silver-purple skin.

Not hilarious, after all. Just beautiful. Because if Aleksi was bound to spend eternity in the Dream, this was precisely how he wanted to do it—holding images of Naia and Einar so close that he could touch them.

Then his visions looked at one another, both anxious and relieved, and began to tug him upward.

They breached the surface, and Aleksi took another breath. He half expected to cough up great lungfuls of water, but the air flowed effortlessly into him.

"You're alive." The words ended in a quiet sob, and Naia tucked her face under Aleksi's chin.

Was he? It did not seem possible, yet here he was. He wrapped an arm around her, rubbing her back as her shoulders heaved with the force of her tears. "Are we certain?"

Einar enfolded them both in his large arms before curling one hand around the back of Aleksi's neck. His fingers came to rest over his pulse, as if Einar needed reassurance, too. "You almost weren't. You left most of your blood back on that beach."

That definitely fit with his recollection of events. "Then *how*?"

Naia lifted her head. She was still crying, but now a brilliant smile curved her lips as she pushed his wet hair back from his forehead. "Rahvekya."

Rahvekya. First the island had helped him defeat Sorin, and now it had helped him to truly and fully keep his promises to Naia and Einar. Aleksi had felt the island's magic reaching for him as he'd lain bleeding . . . but he had not realized it could do something like this.

"I believe your island likes me," he told them.

"Loves you," Naia corrected. "Look."

She gestured around them. He saw for the first time that they were in the lush, secluded cove they had visited before, the one that Naia said had been created by the island in the aether, just for her and Theron. At the time, Aleksi had mourned the fact that the tiny hot spring had been big enough to hold only two.

They were in the same spring, only now it was large enough for three.

Einar pressed his forehead to Aleksi's temple. "You're part of our story now," he rasped as he slid his fingers into Aleksi's hair. "So don't think you can escape us."

"I never *wanted* to." Aleksi knew that Naia understood, but did Einar? "You know that, right?"

It took Einar a moment to reply. When he did, the words were a fervent whisper against Aleksi's cheek. "Yes. That did not make it any easier to watch you go to war against Sorin on your own . . . but I learned from Theron's mistakes. Some things are more important than our own lives."

Did Aleksi still believe that? If he had died—or, at least, had stayed dead—then his friends would have been devastated. They would have been left to spend their immortal lives wondering if they could have saved him if only they had been there.

It was an impossible sort of guilt, because there could never be any release or respite from it. They could never have known whether being there for the fight would have kept Aleksi alive . . . or gotten them all killed and allowed Sorin free rein to destroy the world.

Naia and Einar would have suffered in a different way, with less guilt but more devastation. Losing him would have reinforced all their worst memories of losing each other, and it was easy to understand how that sort of pain could spiral.

But yes, Aleksi would do it again. Because if anyone else had fallen to Sorin's wrath because Aleksi had stepped away from, instead of toward, the danger, it would have been even more disastrous. He would have lost part of himself.

Love could die and yet persist. It happened every day, and he *knew* it to be true from his relationship with Alysaia. But love could not wither and still survive.

"Some things are more important than our own lives," he finally agreed.

"I want you both to live," Einar said softly. "I want a thousand years, and then a thousand more. But if something happens . . ." His fingers found Naia's cheek, and Aleksi felt Einar's smile against his lips. "We'll find you again. It's what we do."

It was their grand, fated destiny . . . and now Aleksi was a part of it. "I like the sound of that," he murmured.

A woeful understatement, but words did not exist to describe the wild thrumming of his heart. It was that moment when he'd thought he had died and journeyed to the Dream all over again, except he was alive.

And Naia and Einar were in his arms.

"I love you," he whispered. Those words could not fully convey his joy, either, but they were all he had. No word in any language had yet been invented that could encompass the full breadth of this emotion. Poets and bards had been trying for all of existence, and all they'd managed to capture were hazy glimpses, no matter how talented they were.

Aleksi should know, for he had inspired many of those attempts. But as Naia and Einar whispered back to him, then abandoned words for the more concrete demonstration of touch, he wondered.

What could the three of them inspire?

Chapter Thirty-Seven

I have gathered many accounts of the goddess's reported abilities. One of the most intriguing involves the power to restore or reverse damage, both natural and man-made. She is said to have been able to repair structures with a touch, to remove blight and blood alike from the very land itself.

A truly awesome power, indeed. My thoughts? If she could do such things as these, she would not be dead.

Fallen Goddess: An Analysis of Primitive Belief
by Guildmaster Klement

They gathered on the stone docks the next day. Some of the villagers—both those from Aynalka and those who had traveled from as far away as Dhamryn and North Harbor—had suggested meeting someplace less scarred by the recent battle, but Naia had insisted.

They needed to be near what was left of Gwynira's palace.

But she understood why they did not want to be here. Besides the enduring pain that the palace represented, the docks had not escaped the battle unscathed, and the harsh reminder of the recent danger both frightened and disturbed them.

The stone was cracked and pitted, but still in far better shape than the wooden docks. They had been reduced to splinters in some places, though folks were already hard at work, repairing them.

Petya stood nearby, nervously shifting her weight from one foot to the other. Except for the battle, she had refused to come near the palace while it still stood. Now that it lay in ruins, she had finally been convinced . . . but only by a personal invitation from her wife.

The older women watched as a trio of young workers dismantled the half-burned building that had once served as the harbormaster's office. "It's going to take a long time to rebuild," Petya observed solemnly.

"Mmm," Naia hummed in agreement. "But they'll handle it. The people of Rahvekya have proven they can handle *anything*."

"Yes," Petya agreed with a smile, gazing down at her wife. "We have."

Naia caught sight of Arktikos rounding a giant pile of stone and wood debris and waved him over. "Is it done?"

He bowed. "It is. I had the remainder of the palace guard work through the night."

"Thank you, Arktikos."

As he walked away, Agata tilted her head. "What is done, my lady?"

"I asked him to search the rubble of the palace for anything that could be salvaged."

"Was that truly a priority?" Petya asked, frowning. The question earned her a nudge from her wife.

Naia smiled. "Trust me. It had to be done immediately."

She walked across the shattered ground and into the ruins of the palace. It was so *odd*, the complete reversal that had happened here. When she and her companions had first arrived in Rahvekya, the invaders' palace stood strong, while Naia's temple lay in ruins. Now, this place was unrecognizable, while her temple had been restored.

It was time to restore this place, as well.

Naia stopped where she thought the antechamber might have been outside the Great Hall. She couldn't tell for sure, but it did not matter.

This was as good a spot as any.

She sank to her knees on the shattered stone and traced her fingers over the cracks. "They took every bit of this from you," she murmured. "All the stone and metal, they dug out of you. The wood, they tore away."

After a long moment, the island seemed to sigh. *I remember.*

Naia's fingers flexed above the rubble. "It's time for you to take it back."

She closed her eyes and imagined everything set to rights. The stone unformed and returned, shot through with the metal ore. No construction and no interlopers, just the island and its faithful stewards.

Is it possible?

Let's find out.

The very ground rumbled and shifted beneath Naia, almost as if it was stretching muscles that had long been unused. It reached out, and she gave it an encouraging push.

Gasps and scattered cries drifted from the docks, and Naia opened her eyes.

She was now kneeling in a clearing of soft grass, new and hardy and eager to grow. It felt springy under her fingers—familiar, like an old, treasured friend—and relief and gratitude flooded Naia.

"There is one more thing," she whispered. "But someone will have to help me."

The Lover, yes.

People had already begun to approach the meadow as Naia rose, and her heart swelled when she saw Aleksi and Einar at the front of the crowd. She slipped her hand into Einar's and leaned her head against Aleksi's shoulder.

Aleksi smiled down at her. A scar on his chest peeked out over the open vee of his loose shirt, the only physical remnant of his fight with

Sorin. It had already faded so much that Naia was certain that, in perhaps a week's time, it would be gone.

Einar's eyes shone as he gazed at the clearing. It was a man's wonder at witnessing the beauty of his homeland combined with a god's memories of lying with her in that soft grass and staring up at the sky, finding shapes in the clouds.

He looked *lighter*, which she attributed to his relief at having made a decision about his future. The mild nervousness that lingered was undoubtedly because he still had to tell his crew. His *family*.

Naia knew exactly how he felt.

"I want to do something," she told them. "But I need the god of all things that grow. Will you?"

Aleksi rubbed his cheek against hers. "You don't even have to ask."

She stretched up on her toes and kissed him lightly. Power surged around them, bathing them with heat and the smell of flowers. The scent intensified as dazzling light began to swirl around the three of them, lifting Naia's hair. It coalesced, subsided . . .

And there stood three trees in the clearing, so close that their branches were entwined as one.

People began to fall to their knees, but Naia shook her head. She pulled Agata back to her feet and addressed the crowd. "Please, stand. No more kneeling."

Agata's gaze swept across the clearing, her eyes wide and wondering. "It's beautiful, my lady. But won't Gwynira want to rebuild her palace?"

"There will be no palace." Naia followed the priestess's gaze, and she smiled as a pleased wind ruffled her hair. "Gwynira rules you no longer."

This time, the shock that rippled through the crowd was punctuated by scattered cheers.

"So. We return to who we were before the Emperor's men arrived." Agata's voice shone with satisfaction. "I have kept the memories of our people safe, my lady. And, with your help, we can rebuild that world."

This was going to be hard to explain. The islanders wouldn't like it, might even feel hurt and abandoned. But it was necessary—for Naia *and* for them.

She took both of Agata's hands in hers. "I cannot stay."

"What?" The priestess's hands trembled in hers. "But you have only just returned to us. We need your guidance."

"No, you don't." Naia smiled. "You need to *not* have it. For you, my return was more than the fulfillment of a promise or a prophecy. It was a *miracle*. If I stayed, you would never think to argue with me or tell me I was wrong or act counter to my wishes."

A young voice piped up from the crowd. "We would not disrespect you like that, my lady."

"Exactly. But every child has to grow up." Naia pulled Agata closer and turned to the crowd. "And every mother has to step back and allow it to happen."

Another voice rose in the crowd, this time an old man. "What of the prince? Will you take up your parents' throne, Your Majesty?"

Einar stepped forward, his expression gentle but resolute. "The time of kings and queens in Rahvekya is over. For centuries, you have been told what you must do and who you must be. It is time for you to decide what *you* want this island to be."

Naia closed her eyes and whispered to the island again. *When I said to take it back, I meant everything.*

Are you certain?

Very. You kept my power and my people safe, all these many years, and I thank you for that. But it is time.

Power pulsed again, accompanied by the throbbing sound of drumbeats that she now knew to be the island's heart. It lurched, expanded . . . and pulled free of Naia's open hands.

It was still there, only now it surrounded her instead of being part of her. She was just Naia again. A water nymph of the Sheltered Lands, who walked out of the ocean near Seahold less than a year before.

She had her memories, but the power of the island had been returned to Rahvekya.

She looked out at the sea of faces before her. Some were as stricken as Agata, while a few had descended into sobbing tears. Others were more composed, but sad.

"I am *not* deserting you," she reassured them. "I can be here in an instant, and I will always come if you need me."

"And you are not alone. You have Agata, your High Priestess who remembers all the old ways." Then Einar rested a hand on Petya's shoulder, drawing a startled glance from her. "And you have Petya of Stenyar, the hero who carried your infant prince to safety so that I could grow up and bring the goddess back."

The somber mood of the crowd shifted almost immediately. Many of them had been led to safety by the two women just the day before, while the rest recognized in them a deep connection to their distant culture.

Petya lowered her voice so she could not be heard above the cheering. "What are you doing, Einar? I'm no leader."

"Aren't you?" he replied with a grin. "You know the sea, you know this island, and you've ruled over pirates and warriors and one unruly boy that you somehow raised into a decent man." He pulled Petya into a hug, his next words so quiet that even Naia could barely hear them. "You gave up everything for me, and I will never forget that. If you ever need us, we'll be there."

Tears filled the older woman's eyes as she pulled back and framed his face with her hands. "I'm proud of you."

Einar's eyes gleamed with unshed tears, and he wordlessly drew Petya into another hug.

Naia searched the crowd until she found Tilly's face. The girl's cheeks were streaked with tears, but she stared back with a small smile.

Naia gestured her forward. "They're going to need your help, Tilly."

"Me?" Tilly shook her head. "What for?"

"To keep the records, of course. To tell the stories."

As Tilly pondered that, stunned and wide-eyed, another familiar form stepped forward. Hilja was stone-faced, but her lower lip trembled. "I am going to miss you, my lady."

"Well, I hope not," Naia told her.

"Ma'am?"

Naia clasped her hands together in front of her chest. "I thought you might like to come with us. Obviously, you don't have to, but—"

Her words were cut off by the taller woman grabbing her in a tight hug. "It would be an honor to serve."

"As a guest, Hilja." Aleksi spoke kindly, but firmly. "You serve no one. Not anymore."

The crowd surged around Tilly and Hilja, offering congratulations and admiration and, in Hilja's case, tearful goodbyes.

Aleksi bent to speak into Naia's ear. "Only one more thing left to do, little nymph."

"Indeed." Naia turned to Einar, both eyebrows raised. "Are you ready?"

Chapter Thirty-Eight

the Lover's smile was like the sun

his laughter stirred the breeze

the Nymph had ancient eyes that brought

the Kraken to his knees

and though his heart was long thought lost

they caught him in their snare

the man of ice had met his match

the Nymph and Lover fair

Popular ballad

Moving his belongings out of the captain's cabin had not taken as long as Einar expected. It spoke to the stark utility of his life up to this point, that in so many centuries he had accumulated so few things. The keepsakes and small treasures had been packed into boxes and moved to the quarters set aside for Dianthe. Most of the clothing left here would not fit him unless he returned to his human form.

He had no intention of doing so. The Sheltered Lands would have to take him as he was from now on. But, having enjoyed the casual acceptance of the people of Rahvekya, Einar no longer worried so much about that.

He stopped by the desk and its carefully rolled maps, running his fingers along the scarred surface. He'd spent endless years here, planning his war against the Empire. Whatever the new Captain did at this desk, it would not have to be that. Sorin was gone, his Imperial Court shattered. Gwynira and Isa were allies, and Eirika . . .

Well, Eirika might still be a problem. But the High Court and its many new friends were more than ready to face whatever trouble she decided to cause.

His fingers found the end of the desk and the smooth planks of the ship. He pressed his hand against it, spreading his fingers wide. The Kraken thrummed in welcome, its power different, somehow. Perhaps *he* was different. As a youth, he'd been raised in the shadow of the High Court of Dreamers, absorbing their understanding of the Everlasting Dream and the Endless Void. Magic had been simple to them, Creation and Destruction seen as two separate forces, with the Court's magical powers springing only from the Dream, and with tightly focused belief.

Einar had Theron's memories now, uncounted eons of being an elemental force. Storms brought the rain that gave life, and the devastation that stole it. He could feel both threads twined in the magic of his ship—the Kraken was built for war. But it was also built to shelter its crew, to be a home for this odd group of misfits who had never felt comfortable anywhere else.

Einar had named his ship well when he had named it the Kraken. Like Theron, this ship was a protector. It had kept the crew safe and extended their lives, nurturing the small magics within them. That was too important to end simply because Einar's needs had changed.

Naia had shown him the way. But this didn't need to be a public ceremony. Einar closed his eyes and let the power within him rise.

"This is where we say farewell," he whispered. "This magic was always yours as much as it was mine. Keep them safe for me. Always bring them safely back to port. And you'll have to let me go." When the magic of the ship pushed back at him, Einar laughed and tapped the wooden plank with one knuckle. "I mean it. Where I'm going, you cannot follow. The Kraken may always find its captain, but you will have a new one now."

Familiar footsteps announced the approach of that captain. Einar straightened and turned in time to see Brynjar standing in the doorway, one box tucked under his arm. "You need some more time? Bexi and I can wait."

"No, I'm finished here." He reached out to take the box from his former third mate and set it on the desk. "I was just making sure the ship understands the new chain of command."

Brynjar's face broke into a wide grin. "Aww, and here we were, taking bets on how long it would take for the old girl to dive down on her own and surface in the Lover's Lakes because she missed you."

The magic that had let the ship travel through the Heart of the Ocean to appear in a new body of water in moments had always rested on Einar's ability to shift into a creature large enough to pull her down and make the trip.

Einar could not say what would happen with a new captain at the helm, but if enough people believed, and Brynjar's heart was open to it . . .

Well, their world was rife with new gods. And if he did manifest, Brynjar would be a welcome addition to Dianthe's court of young Dreamers.

Slapping the man on the shoulder, Einar returned his smile. "You and Bexi settle in. I want to say goodbye to the island."

Einar left the captain's quarters for the last time and headed for the deck. Hilja dropped a curtsy to him as he emerged, but it wasn't as deep, and her smile was less reverent than proud—he *was* wearing the latest of the outfits she'd made for him, after all. The heavy tunic and thick pants and fur-lined cloak would not be practical in the warmer climates of the Lover's Villa, but it felt good to say farewell to the island of his birth dressed in the fashion of his parents.

The ship was already moving at a fair clip, a strong breeze filling the deep-green sails emblazoned with the Kraken's sigil. Not a wind he had summoned—though he could now, he supposed—but one final gift from the island. They would have gentle winds and smooth seas as they headed out on their next adventure, and Einar knew that they would always be welcomed back to Rahvekya with the same.

"Captain!" The ship's cook appeared at his side, but his gaze didn't quite meet Einar's. Harlen was staring at something over Einar's shoulder, a dreamy look in his eyes, the reason for which became clear with his next words. "Do you think Hilja would like that stew I made for Lady Naia on the trip here?"

In the decades he had served on this ship, Einar had never seen Harlen show interest in something he couldn't cook, bake, or sauté. But he was starry-eyed now, gazing at the formidable woman as if he'd never seen anyone quite so beautiful.

Brynjar's first act as captain might need to be hiring a new cook. At least Aleksi would be thrilled to welcome Harlen at the villa. "I think she'd love it," he told the older man, who thanked him distractedly before hurrying off.

Smiling, Einar continued toward the stern. He found Aleksi and Naia exactly where he'd expected them to be, both standing at the railing, watching as the shores of Rahvekya receded into the distance. Omira lounged at their feet, though she stretched lazily and rolled over when she caught sight of Einar.

He took his place next to Naia, settling a reassuring hand at the small of her back. "Any lingering regrets?" he asked her softly.

"Never. This is not an ending, for them or for me. It's a beginning." She smiled up at him. "What about you? Will you regret leaving your ship?"

He'd thought he might, but all he felt was anticipation. "It's a beginning," he agreed. "It's not as if we won't see the crew again. And we'll have to visit Petya and Agata, and see how the rebuilding is going." Maybe Petya and Agata would even travel to the Sheltered Lands. After over two thousand years of standing lonely duty in the heart of Rahvekya, Aggie deserved an adventure. It would be fun to show her Aleksi's villa, or the majesty of Seahold.

Without the looming threat of war on the horizon, they could do anything they wanted.

Aleksi breathed in the sea air and dropped a kiss to the top of Naia's head. "Did you manage to reach Sachi and Zanya?"

"I did," she answered ruefully. "The rest of the High Court now knows what happened, and they are . . ."

"Mildly put out?" Aleksi ventured hopefully.

"You are lucky," she allowed, then chuckled. "But not *that* lucky."

"Why do you think I haven't taken us through the Heart of the Ocean?" Einar threaded his fingers through Aleksi's hair. It might take a century or more to stop wanting to touch him just to prove to himself that the Lover was hale and healthy, but touching Aleksi was no hardship. "The week's sail to Seahold will give them a chance to calm down."

"If you say so, my love," Naia teased.

Einar suspected the entire High Court would be in residence at Seahold by the time they docked, and the lectures would be fierce, indeed. "We can give them all a few days to reassure themselves that Aleksi is well, and then take a boat upriver to the Lover's Lakes."

"Are you sure?" The Lover was usually so confidently charming, but now he sounded almost nervous. "We can live anywhere. We do not have to reside at my villa."

Naia frowned up at him. "Have you changed your mind?"

"No," he hurriedly assured her. "It's only that you two are giving up so much. A kingdom, and an island that is very much a part of you."

"Aleksi—" Einar started, but the Lover interrupted.

"Besides . . ." Aleksi's seriousness faded. "Do you know how thrilled my followers would be to learn that I abandoned my home in pursuit of love? There would be hundreds of new poems by sunrise."

"Not to mention the many amazing paintings and sculptures," Naia added.

"*So* many."

Despite his humor, Aleksi's offer was serious—and unnecessary. Einar suspected they would have many places that felt like home in the years to come. He and Naia would always have suites at Seahold, and now he might actually stay in his from time to time. And Aleksi had an entire estate at Dragon's Keep, where the High Court often convened.

There would be visits to Inga in the Witchwood to see how Gwynira, Isa, and Arktikos were settling in, and trips to the Blasted Plains to see Elevia at Blade's Rest. They would probably even spend time at the hunting lodge Ulric had built deep within the Midnight Forest, and go on adventures with Nyx through the Burning Hills.

And they would come back to Rahvekya sometimes, maybe even sail here on the Kraken.

Funny. Einar had started as a boy on a tiny boat with no family beyond Petya and Jinevra, and now his family spanned *continents*.

Any place that family resided would feel like home, but only one place *was* home—wherever Aleksi and Naia felt safe and happy.

Einar laid a hand on Aleksi's cheek and stroked his thumb over the man's lips. "I'm sure," he said. "Take us home, Aleksi."

Einar would never know what Aleksi saw in his eyes in that moment, but the Lover's nervousness faded. "I *would* miss my vineyards," Aleksi admitted with a smile that felt like a kiss against Einar's thumb.

"We'll still give the poets and storytellers plenty to write about," Einar promised, before giving in to the temptation to take Aleksi's lips in a kiss. Naia's sweet laughter filled the air, so deliciously tempting they broke apart only to fight over who would get to taste her lips first. The resulting kiss was a joyous tangle of warmth and love that earned whoops and teasing shouts from the watching crew.

The bards would certainly have to write a new ballad, because the Kraken had found both a lad and a lass—two lovers fair—to hold him past the dawn. The Kraken's heart was not gone, but here, in his arms.

And he had no intention of ever letting them go.

Epilogue

Today, I saw a burrowing hare in a small clearing, nibbling on the fresh green grass. Never before have I glimpsed one so early in the year. I decided to ask Agata about it, but then a wild notion seized me: I could ask the island instead.

So I did. The answer was not audible, but I wept, because I heard it, all the same.

Rahvekya said, This is a new day.

Archivist Matilda

The island was one of Aleksi's favorites, second only to Rahvekya.

This one was, of course, much smaller. It nestled in the center of the lake closest to his villa, and afforded a lovely view of not only his home but the rolling hills and valleys of his vineyards, as well. The beauty of the landscape was simply unmatched.

"Aleksi!" Naia called his name, then broke into smiling laughter as Einar nuzzled her neck. "The wine?"

Almost unmatched.

"At once." The handblown glass bottles clinked as he hefted the crate and began to cross the pavilion.

He had planned to ask Ash to add the open-air structure as a place to gather and eat and drink and laugh as they enjoyed the view and each other's company. But then Ulric had offered to build it, and so Ash had only carefully quarried the stone. Ulric had spent much of the summer at the villa, working on the project. As a result, he and Aleksi had passed many evenings in quiet conversation, something they had not done in *decades*.

Now, the rest of his friends had gathered for a celebration in honor of the first day of the Wolf's Moon. Aleksi had felt it only right and proper, since Ulric had worked so hard, to offer to host the accompanying party at the villa. He had more space, and Ulric had hardly had time to prepare.

So they had gathered in the pavilion for the first time. A buffet stretched across one side of the space, while clusters of benches and chairs surrounded the rest of the perimeter. And a merry fire blazed in the middle of the space, to ward off the first chill of autumn.

Aleksi stopped first by the cluster of seats, where Sachi and Zanya were speaking to Gwynira and Isa with great animation while Ash looked on with fond amusement.

"Wine?" Aleksi offered. "It's my newest vintage. One of my best, I think."

"Yes, *please*." Sachi reached out.

He drew the crate back, out of reach. "Ah, patience, love. This one tastes best when chilled." He turned an expectant look on Gwynira. "If you would be so kind?"

Gwynira extended a hand and brushed one finger over the edge of the crate. Chill frost covered the bottles at once, and she sat back in her chair with a smile. "I cannot wait to taste this. Inga has raved about your special vintages."

"Inga overstates my skill," Aleksi demurred.

"She does not," Zanya told Gwynira. "It will ruin you for any other wine."

"I certainly hope so." Aleksi spared a moment to admire Ash's jacket. It had been fashioned from beautifully woven fabric that changed color as Ash shifted in the firelight and was adorned with exquisite embroidery.

Hilja certainly was quickly making a name for herself in the Sheltered Lands.

Aleksi passed a bottle of wine to Ash, hesitated, then gave him two more. His old friend grinned at him as he opened the first and began to pour. "You're all in for a treat today. Aleksi's wines always taste the best when he's deliriously happy. The grapes he grew this summer are likely to be his best in a thousand years."

"Well, now we've just moved on to sheer flattery." Aleksi winked at them. "Isa, how are you and Gwyn enjoying the Witchwood?"

"It's beautiful," Isa said, her smile full of soft wonder. "I've never seen so many *colors*. Even the birds and the insects glow!"

"You could, as well. All you have to do is ask Inga."

Gwynira actually laughed, a husky sound that was rare, but growing in frequency. "Don't encourage her. Those two keep disappearing into the smithy that Inga built for her. I suspect the next swords she gifts you will glow or sparkle." Gwynira stroked a fond hand over Isa's hair, pure joy in her eyes. "They're having enormous fun."

"Good. Save a sparkly axe for me." Aleksi smiled as their laughter swelled behind him.

Elevia and Ulric were huddled together on a much smaller seat built for two, laughing and talking in low tones. Elevia had often been at the villa over the past few months, as well. These days, she and Ulric were rarely separated for long.

She looked up at Aleksi's approach. "*Finally*. When did you become such a lackadaisical host?"

Aleksi arched an eyebrow at her. "You could have fetched your own wine."

"Scandalous."

Ulric huffed out a laugh but rose to claim a bottle from the crate. He opened it and poured Elevia a glass before taking a sip directly from the bottle. "It's good."

"Thank you, Ulric."

The Wolf sank back onto the seat next to Elevia and stretched out his legs, crossing them at the ankle. "I know it's almost time for me to return home and see to my own lands, but I'll miss the vineyards. Do you think I could grow grapes in the Midnight Forest?"

Aleksi hated to dash his dreams, but it was called the *Midnight Forest* for a reason. "Unfortunately not. But you're welcome to cultivate them here, and I'll watch over them for you."

"See?" Elevia leaned close against Ulric's side. "Crisis averted."

"Speaking of crises . . ." Aleksi blew out a breath. "What news from the former Empire?"

"All is quiet." Elevia swirled the wine in her glass. "The Stalker is in hiding. Even the situation with the young Dreamers and Voidlings has calmed. Which lends credence to my theory that Eirika was stirring up all that trouble to keep us occupied and scrambling. It's what I would have done." She flashed Ulric a wicked smile. "If I were evil, that is."

"I'm relieved every single day that you are not." Ulric threw an arm across the back of their seat and toyed absently with Elevia's hair as he turned back to Aleksi. "We know the Stalker is vengeful, though. Elevia's spies will be watching for signs she's planning to move against you."

"Of that, I have no doubt." Aleksi was not worried about Eirika—she was, presumably, far too intelligent and savvy to come at him in his own home. But it was nice to have friends looking out for him. "Do you two need anything else?"

"Go." Elevia raised her glass in salute. "But keep the wine coming."

Nyx and Inga were sitting close together near the fire while Arktikos hovered behind them. He was taking the whole life debt thing *very* seriously. He would rarely leave Inga's side unless she needed privacy, and Aleksi had begun to suspect that the man slept outside of her chamber door, just in case interlopers breached Witchwood Castle as Inga slumbered.

"Wine?" Aleksi asked, but only Nyx looked up at him. They widened their eyes and pressed their lips together to suppress a smile.

"At least sit *down*," Inga ground out, her voice approaching the edge of frustration that always ended poorly for whoever was irritating her. Then she glanced up at Aleksi and threw up her hands. "Aleksi, make him *sit down*."

Aleksi held out a bottle of wine. "Would you like to sit, Arktikos?"

The man intercepted the bottle, opened it, and began to fill the glass in front of Inga. "I am fine standing, thank you."

Aleksi shrugged. "He's fine standing."

Inga pinched the bridge of her nose as if warding off a headache—or trying to keep her temper. "What part of a life debt obligates you to wait on me hand and foot? I can pour my own wine. I can do it without lifting a finger!"

Nyx made a surreptitious gesture encouraging Aleksi to flee, and he considered that an *excellent* idea. "Enjoy!" he called over his shoulder as Nyx tried to quell a snort.

Dianthe stood with Naia and Einar near the plain stone railing that overlooked the lake. Aleksi joined them and placed the crate, now only half full of wine bottles, on the end of the buffet table.

Einar plucked up one of the remaining bottles and began to fill several glasses. "Inga seems exasperated. Am I going to have to rescue Arktikos?"

"Not at all. I have faith in him." Aleksi kissed Einar and retrieved two of the glasses. "Everyone enjoyed dinner."

"Brynjar may never forgive us for stealing Harlen away." Einar smiled wickedly. "I tried to tell him it was really Hilja's fault, but then she sewed him that fancy new captain's jacket, and now *he* gets to officiate the wedding."

"Outmaneuvered by your tailor. *Ouch*." Aleksi shook his head, then stepped behind Naia, wrapped his arms around her, and offered her the wine. "My love."

"Thank you." She accepted the glass, but placed it on the railing beside her. "Dianthe and I were just discussing options for renaming the month after next."

The Betrayer's Moon. Aleksi hummed and inhaled the salty scent of Naia's hair. "And what have you two come up with?"

"It's an interesting quandary." Dianthe accepted the final glass of wine from Einar. "Over the years it has developed certain associations. The darkest and coldest month of the year, even considered unlucky. We celebrate the Dragon's Moon, when the days grow longer again, because of the legends of how Ash drove the Betrayer from the Sheltered Lands. It seems cruel to saddle another person with such a fraught legacy."

Then perhaps the answer was to change their outlook. "Winter is as lovely in its own way as any other season," Aleksi mused. "The associations do not *have* to be negative. We could reclaim it."

Einar tilted his head, indicating where Gwynira sat with the others. "It seems to me we already have a goddess of winter. The Ice Queen's Moon has a nice ring to it."

Naia laughed. "You'd best ask before you consign her to being part of our calendar."

"She does have a certain flair," Dianthe mused. "An ice festival might be a welcome diversion for the people. Much better than the tradition of sitting in fear and grief."

"You should ask her." Einar was still watching Gwynira pensively. "Sorin hated her, you know. He created and discarded her—Isa, too. The High Court is the closest thing they have to family now. Letting Gwynira claim the place he abandoned feels . . . right."

Aleksi rested his chin on Naia's shoulder. "Impossible to argue with that."

Dianthe lifted a hand to Einar's cheek, her ancient eyes full of proud affection. "You've come a long way from the pirate who sailed to the island the Ice Queen ruled with revenge in his heart."

"Because, in the end, revenge was empty." He looked to Aleksi and Naia, open and loving. Nothing like the traumatized, closed-off man who had once desperately asked Aleksi to peer into his soul. "Sorin hurt so many people, but now he's gone. He stole so much of my past. I won't let him have a single moment of my future."

Naia's lips curved up in a trembling smile, and she reached out, caught the placket of his vest, and pulled him closer.

Dianthe touched Naia's cheek, too, and smiled at Aleksi with love as vast as the oceans in her eyes. "It brings me such joy to see you all so happy," she said softly, then lifted her wineglass in a toast. "Be well, my loves." She went to join the others, leaving the three of them standing by the water alone.

Naia raised her free hand to Aleksi's head. "Have you had a good evening?"

"I always do when my friends visit." He nipped at her fingers. "But I might enjoy it more after we've turned in for the night."

Einar pressed closer, trapping Naia between their bodies as his lips grazed her temple. "And how soon can we do that?"

"When our guests have gone to bed." She half turned in Aleksi's arms until she was facing them both. "I have something to tell you."

She sounded tense, not with misery but with nerves. In his haste to ease her uncertainty, Aleksi touched her chin. "Are you well?"

"Yes, quite."

Einar stroked his fingers through her hair in an attempt to soothe her, as well. "Then what is it?"

Instead of answering, she pulled their hands away from her chin and hair and drew them down to rest on her midsection. Einar's fingers flexed beneath Aleksi's as his gaze whipped to her untouched wineglass, sitting abandoned on the railing.

Aleksi's heart thumped, and his mind whirled with so many thoughts that he could not settle on just one. Finally, he managed, "Are you certain? A baby?"

She nodded, then urged him, "*Look.*"

So Aleksi did. He gazed past the soft curves of Naia's face, past the wide, dark eyes—anxious and eager, all at once. Past the physical.

Her aura was the same unique color he could always feel, just a little brighter, and tinged with his colors as well as Einar's, as if the three of them had melded together in soul as well as intent.

Then he realized there was another color, one that blazed so bright it could have lit up the Endless Void.

"Can you feel it?" she asked softly.

"Hope." The word did not seem vast enough to describe what Aleksi could see.

But Naia exhaled in relief and squeezed his hand. "*Yes.*"

There had been many people who had manifested the powers of the gods, like Einar. And there had been those like Aleksi and Naia, born directly of the Dream—and, moving forward, presumably from the Void, as well.

There had never been anyone to grow up as both a human *and* a god.

Einar buried his face in Naia's hair, and the hand he had pressed to her abdomen trembled. "I want—"

His voice broke, and Aleksi hauled Einar closer. "Our child will be safe," he whispered. "I promise." The vow rippled out, stirring the waves of the lake and, farther beyond, the turning leaves of the trees and the vines in the fields.

"I never had that," Einar rasped. "Petya tried, but so many nights we went to bed hungry, or cold, or so tired our bones hurt." He stroked a thumb over Naia's abdomen, his pain slowly giving way to wonder. "This child will know only warmth and love."

Of course, because that was the nature of hope, wasn't it?

Aleksi rested his head against Einar's. "We should tell everyone," he declared, his voice thick with tears, as well. "And then they absolutely have to get the fuck out of here so we can celebrate properly."

They both laughed, and Aleksi knew exactly what they were thinking. The suggestion should have sounded salacious—and perhaps it might become so. But, for the moment, Aleksi was thinking of a soft rug, a crackling fire . . . and the three of them, huddled close, making plans until the sun peeked over the horizon.

"As long as you're happy," she told them.

Happy was a word that Aleksi had once found useful, sufficient to describe the emotion that often fluttered in his chest. But it was not enough to encompass *this* emotion.

He reached for his lovers instead. He pulled Naia and Einar close, wrapped them in all the care and tenderness he'd cultivated over thousands of years, and kissed the salt from their lips.

Someday, there would be new words, ones that could capture this elation.

Until then, Aleksi would just have to show them.

ACKNOWLEDGMENTS

The acknowledgments we wrote for *Daughter of Tides* did not age well. I hoped for all of us that 2025 was going to be a chill and boring time.

It was not.

This year has been one of the hardest of the past decade for us—which is really saying something, all things considered. That you are reading this book feels like a miracle. There were times when we honestly wondered if we would finish it.

But we did. And the funny thing is, it was the story we needed to tell. A story about hope and second chances and what you're willing to risk when the forces stacked against you are overwhelming and you're already feeling battered and bruised. A story about holding on to joy through the dark times, because joy can be found in the smallest things and can spread like wildfire.

Instead of thanking individuals this time (though as always, we are very grateful to everyone on our team who helped this book come to life), we want to thank all the people who do tiny things every day to bring joy to others.

Thank you to the people who have rushed funds and other essential aid to food banks. Thank you to the people who give the only spare five bucks they have to someone's GoFundMe. Thank you to the people who donate so folks can seek reproductive care, and to those who buy a stranger a meal, or a book, or even just offer them a smile.

Thank you to the people who are still making art. Video games, movies, TV, comics, books . . . Getting to steal moments of wonder through your work has let us continue to make ours.

Thank you to the people who care. On the worst days, it seems like maybe there aren't enough, but on the best days we are a tidal wave that will sweep away anything that stands in our path.

Thank you for hanging in there. You're doing amazing.

Kit Rocha is the pseudonym for cowriting team Donna Herren and Bree Bridges. After penning dozens of paranormal novels, novellas, and stories as Moira Rogers, they reinvented themselves by writing the nine-book, multiple-award-winning—and extremely steamy—Beyond series, which became an instant cult favorite. They followed it up with two spin-off series, including the popular Mercenary Librarians trilogy, published by Tor. Now they're leaping into sexy epic fantasy with happily-ever-afters.

Their favorite stories are about messy worlds, strong women, and falling in love with the people who love you just the way you are. When they're not writing, they can be found crafting handmade jewelry, caring too much about video games, or freaking out about their favorite books or TV shows, all of which are chronicled on their various social media accounts. Learn more at www.kitrocha.com.